THE
MEMORY
HOUSE

Don't miss any of *New York Times* bestselling author
Linda Goodnight's books!

Facebook.com/LindaGoodnightAuthor

Twitter.com/LindaGoodnight

You can also find news about Linda's books and life on her blog:
lindagoodnight.blogspot.com

And be sure to check out her Pinterest page for covers,
photos of her characters and favorite recipes:
pinterest.com/lgoodnight2/

THE MEMORY HOUSE

A HONEY RIDGE NOVEL

LINDA GOODNIGHT

HQN™

HQN™

Recycling programs
for this product may
not exist in your area.

ISBN-13: 978-0-373-77964-2

The Memory House

This edition published by arrangement with Harlequin Books S.A.

For questions and comments about the quality of this book, please contact us
at CustomerService@Harlequin.com.

® and TM are trademarks of Harlequin Enterprises Limited or its corporate affiliates.
Trademarks indicated with ® are registered in the United States Patent and
Trademark Office, the Canadian Intellectual Property Office and in other countries.

www.HQNBooks.com

Printed in U.S.A.

I had no way of knowing when I first imagined this book with its theme of grief that I would become intimately acquainted with that excruciating emotion during the writing. With a shattered heart and endless love, I dedicate this book to the memory of Travis Goodnight, the finest son any mother could ever have.

1

"The Child is father of the Man…"

—William Wordsworth

Nashville, Tennessee
Present Day

Freedom was its own kind of prison.

These were the thoughts of Eli Donovan as he scraped drywall mud from his elbow and watched a familiar bronze Buick pull to the curb outside the remodel. With a tug in his gut, Eli tossed the trowel to the ground and straightened. What had he done now?

A man stepped out of the Buick and adjusted his blue tie before squinting toward the house. Their eyes met, held for a fraction of a second until Eli looked down. Once upon a time he would have challenged anyone in a staring contest. Hard time and maturity had changed him. He didn't want to fight anyone anymore. Certainly not his parole officer.

Saying nothing, Eli started across the greening lawn, past the scattered remains of lumber and construction junk. He was no longer arrogant and proud, but the jitter in his belly shamed him just the same.

"Eli." Mr. Clifford spoke first, broke the impasse. "How's it going?"

"Fine." He stopped two feet from the fortysomething officer of the court, taking in the slight sheen of sweat on the other man's balding head. Anxious, afraid of tripping himself up, he waited for Clifford to speak his business.

"I had a phone call this morning."

Still Eli waited, not knowing what to ask or say. If he misspoke, Clifford would get the wrong idea or ask questions Eli couldn't answer. There were always questions.

The parole officer pulled a paper from his pocket and pushed it toward him. "A woman name of Opal Kimble tracked you down through the warden. She wants to talk to you. Says she has something urgent to discuss. Mentioned the name Mindy."

Eli stared at the yellow Post-it note, the dread deepening. He licked dry lips, tasted drywall mud. "Mindy?"

"Is there anything I need to know? If you're into something—"

Eli interrupted. "I'm not. Mindy is an old friend. Did Opal say anything else?"

"No, she just left that number and insisted I contact you. I thought it might be important."

"Doubtful." Mindy was a sweet soul. She probably felt sorry for him and wanted to be sure he was all right. He refused to consider the other issue, certain she was better off not hearing from him.

"You could use a friend."

The comment took Eli aback. In the six months he'd known Pete Clifford, the man had shown him nothing but suspicion, as if he couldn't wait for the ex-con to step out of line so he could send him back to that stinking rat hole.

"I'm all right."

"Do you have a phone yet?"

"No."

Clifford extracted his from a belt holster. "Call her."

Eli considered only a moment before accepting the offer. No point in riling the man. He could make a call to an old woman he'd never met. Find out what she wanted and then get back to work. He needed the payday.

He took a moment to study the fancy cell phone. A lot had changed since he'd been gone. Technology marched on, as they said, and left the caged behind.

As he tapped in the numbers Eli was gratified when Clifford turned toward his vehicle. "I'll give you a minute."

"Thanks." The word was gravel on Eli's tongue but he was grateful. He didn't take acts of kindness lightly.

A woman's voice, stronger than he'd expected from the aunt Mindy had described as ancient, answered the call.

"Miss Kimble? Eli Donovan."

"About time you called, boy."

Her tone stiffened his spine but he remained silent. He focused elsewhere, as he'd learned to do in the difficult moments inside the big house, letting her talk while he only half listened. A pair of courting bluebirds caught Eli's eye as they dipped and flirted. He smiled a little, though the action felt stiff and unfamiliar. Since his release, he'd been mesmerized by nature. The rising sun, a fluttering butterfly, a dog sniffing tires. Nature brought a peace, a rightness to his tumultuous soul. In his despair and self-pity, he'd forgotten those simple gifts he'd once taken for granted.

In his ear, Opal said something that captured his attention. He tuned back in. "What did you say?"

"I said, Mindy left some things for you and I want you to come get them."

He frowned toward the horizon where a single gray cloud hovered like a promise of trouble. "Left things? Isn't she there?"

A beat of silence pulsed in his ear, tightened the knot in his chest.

When Opal spoke again, her tone softened. "I thought you knew. Mindy's gone."

"Gone where?" Not that he'd follow or make contact, but the woman was confusing him.

"Gone for good, Eli." Opal's voice cracked. "Mindy died."

2

She'd kissed him goodbye that last morning. Julia was sure she had. Wasn't she? The action had been so ingrained in routine. Grab the backpack, stick the lunch box in his hand and kiss him, quick and sweet, before he galloped to the bus stop. She'd watched him get on the bus. She always did, though afterward she'd second-guessed a thousand times. If she'd driven him to school, or if she'd kept him home, because hadn't he been a sleepyhead that last wonderful, terrible morning?

Six years had passed and yet the horror and grief never left. It was the not knowing that drove Julia Presley quietly mad. In those moments of solitude, especially right before sleep and like now, upon waking, the thoughts would come in rapid-fire succession before she had a chance to block them. She'd become adept at blocking.

Most days she survived and some days she even thrived. But days like today were the worst. Michael's birthday. He was still alive. She had to believe that. Yet, wondering who had him and what was happening or had happened was too hard to bear. But bear it she did, for what choice did she have? Someday, somewhere, someone would spot him in a crowd or he would simply walk free of his captors and come home. Such miracles still happened, and those children once lost but now found gave Julia hope.

He would be fourteen today, no longer the wide-eyed little boy who hated baths and adored mud puddles. Was he tall and loose limbed like his father, and wouldn't he be heartbroken to know his mom and dad had unraveled within a year without him? That he was the glue holding their ragged marriage together and that in his absence, they'd been unable to comfort each other? They'd laid blame where none was due, such a stupid reaction to a heinous crime. The only person at fault was the evil being who'd snatched a happy little boy from a peaceful town where nothing bad ever happened. And yet, she felt responsible. Mikey was, after all, her child to guard and guide and she'd failed in that essential role of motherhood.

Dragging herself from beneath the ice-blue duvet, Julia reached first for the iPad on the nightstand. With a poke of a finger, she tapped open the Facebook page where Mikey's bright eight-year-old face smiled out at her next to a computer-aged photo. Would he really look like this today?

She trolled the comments, saw the handful of birthday wishes and closed the program with a sigh. No news. No sightings. Just like every day since she'd started the page with the help of a support group. Other mothers who waited for their children to come home. Most days she didn't visit the forums for idle conversation. They depressed her, and Lord knew she couldn't go back down that dark tunnel again.

With a breathed plea for strength to get through another day, Julia dressed and dabbed makeup on the shadowy half-moons beneath her eyes. Though dawn had yet to break, she had to get up and get moving. She had guests to attend, breakfast to cook and a myriad other tasks to address. Keeping busy was important, soothing therapy. Culinary therapy, she termed her cooking obsession. If she worked herself into exhaustion, she could sleep without the oppressive dreams.

She was thankful every day for the rather inexplicable purchase four years ago of Peach Orchard Inn, this big, old oddity of a Southern mansion, now a guesthouse. There was something benevolent about the two-story structure that had survived a Civil War and the century and a half since. The day Valery had dragged her out here "just to look," the house had wrapped itself around her like a warm hug. Though cobwebs and dust had covered everything, her heart had leaped. For the first time in months—years—she'd felt something other than despair. This wonderful old bed-and-breakfast had, quite literally, saved her sanity. She'd yet to understand why. It simply had.

She'd clung to her former home on Sage Street—Mikey's home—too long, fearing her son would return and find her gone, but she was dying there. Depressed, barely able to get out of bed each morning, and some days she didn't get up at all. Since a dead mother was not what she wanted her son to come home to, at her family's urging Julia had sold the modern brick home and moved into a piece of history sorely in need of restoration. In that way, she and the house were the same.

Everyone in Honey Ridge knew about Mikey's disappearance, but most were Southern enough to speak of the loss only among themselves and never to her. She was left alone and they, along with her family, pretended that she was a normal person, an ordinary divorced businesswoman running a guest inn and clinging to history—her own and that of this antebellum house.

She was stuck in the past, both in the distant and the near. Stuck. In freeze-frame for six years, waiting, unable to move forward, unwilling to give up that gossamer thread of hope that one day she'd awaken and Mikey's disappearance would only have been a nightmare.

Bingo, the aging Australian shepherd, rose from his rug at the foot of her bed. When Julia paused to give his blue-merle head a rub, she spotted an object on the floor where he'd slept. At first she thought it was a rock and bent to pick it up, puzzling to discover another smooth, round child's marble. Not an ordinary, modern marble. This one was reddish in color, made of clay, a handmade antique like the others she'd discovered in the house.

"Did you bring this in here, Bingo?" He was forever bringing her little gifts. "Better than the dead snake you brought last time."

She rolled the child's toy in her palm, wondering. She and Valery had found a number of interesting and historic items during the ongoing remodel, each one adding another layer of mystery and history to the old inn. But the marbles were different. They showed up randomly, usually in a place she'd recently cleaned and always on a bad day. They spoke to her, comforted her, and wouldn't Mama have a fit to hear that her unbalanced daughter was now communing with marbles.

"She'd say I've lost my marbles." Maybe she had.

Grasping comfort where she could, Julia slipped the little clay ball into her pocket and started toward the kitchen.

Bingo trotted by her side past the wide stairs that led from floor to floor. Though not as grand as the one in *Gone with the Wind*, the staircase had captivated Julia on sight. She imagined a nineteenth-century bride sweeping down these now burgundy carpeted stairs, one gloved hand on the gleaming oak banister as her heart canted toward her true love waiting next to the enormous marble fireplace in the parlor below.

Fantasy, yes, like the comforting marbles, but a house like

this allowed a certain imaginative license. Part of a Southern upbringing is to believe history lingers in walls and whispers from ancient oaks, and though she believed in so little these days, she believed that. This house was a living entity and Julia had carefully listened as she and Valery worked to create an inn worthy of a special trip to a small town in rural Tennessee. An inn where others might find peace even if the owner couldn't.

Sometimes, when she sat on the enormous wraparound porch, Julia thought she heard the rattle of carriages and horse hooves between the double row of old magnolias. She was careful to tell no one about the incidents. Nor of the time she'd felt a cool, soothing hand on her forehead after a screaming nightmare about Mikey; nor of the little boy's laughter she sometimes imagined in the upper hallway. A woman with a slender hold on sanity had to be careful about her wild imagination, for that is all it was. Julia didn't believe in ghosts or spirits or even much in God anymore.

She'd once made the mistake of sharing one of the episodes with Valery, a confession that had driven her sister to the liquor cabinet. *That* was a move Julia did not want to repeat. Valery and liquor were a troubling pair, especially since her sister's latest battles with Jed the jerk, the worst boyfriend in history.

Though she and Valery were close, Julia had learned to keep her thoughts and grief to herself. No one understood. They expected her to move on and forget she'd had a son, a husband, a family. To forget she'd had a happy, almost perfect life until that horrible October morning.

Rounding into the kitchen, a late addition to the house, Julia flipped on lights and went straight for the coffee and oven dials. She might never win any chef awards but she loved to feed people.

Though her specialty was peach tea made from scratch, her coffee was good, too, a unique blend she ground herself and served French press. Guests were known to linger for hours over coffee, so she started there. The breakfast menu varied but always included a peach dish, mostly with fruit from her orchard. People expected peaches from an inn with a name like Peach Orchard.

In minutes, the ham-and-egg strata was ready for the oven, the peach-muffin batter spread among the tins, and the coffee sang its aromatic siren song. Taking a cup, Julia went out onto the front porch for her favorite time of day. With only the dog for company, she sat in one of four white wicker chairs to watch the sun break over the lawn and come sneaking through the waxy-leaved magnolias and fuchsia rhododendron. Last night's rain glistened like tiny crystals on the verdant grass while Old Glory hung limply from the white-board porch rail.

Julia made a frustrated sound in the back of her throat. Valery had forgotten to bring in the flag again last night, a clear breach of etiquette that would have the townspeople on the phone if anyone had driven past. Hopefully, no one had. Backed by woods, Peach Orchard Inn was off the main thoroughfare on the edge of town. Mikey would have loved this place. Room to run and explore and be a little boy in safety.

But safe was a relative term.

The house was shielded from the road by a thick stand of leafy trees, including the showy pink blooms of the peach orchard that ran to the right of the front lawn and down the north side. Sometimes she heard a car go by but mostly not. The small-town peace and quiet was one of the draws of her little guesthouse.

Julia propped her heels on a neighboring chair, gazed out toward the orchard and sipped her coffee.

"Happy birthday, baby," she whispered, and the hollow heat of grief seized up in her chest. Eyes closed, she heard his small voice, smelled his little-boy and toothpaste scent and felt the warmth of his sturdy body as she'd hugged him that final time. Her throat thickened and tears welled. She'd grieve for these few minutes alone, as she had for six years, and then she'd dust off her hostess smile and get on with her day.

Bingo padded to her knees and whined, nudging. The Aussie didn't want anyone to be unhappy, though he had endured his share of her tears. He, too, had grieved, wandering forlorn for weeks in search of the adored boy who never came home.

Leaning forward, Julia wrapped her arms around the dog, pressed her face to his fur and wept.

"Ma'am. Are you all right?"

Julia jerked upright and dropped her feet to the porch with a thud. Her heart beat in her throat as she stared at a man standing at the bottom of the steps. She glanced behind him, saw no car and wondered where he had come from. He hadn't been there a moment ago. Her errant thoughts of rattling carriages, talking marbles and touches in the night had her wondering if she'd imagined him, conjured him up. Was she hallucinating? He was handsome enough to be a dream but hard looking, too, as if he'd seen too much and done even more. A dark-eyed pirate in a tattered jean jacket with a day's growth of beard, shaggy black hair and a rumpled white T-shirt.

"Who are you?" The words were breathy, harsh and out of character for a Southern hostess.

A frown formed a vee between the man's Faustian black eyebrows. "I didn't mean to scare you. You were crying."

She realized then that her face was still wet. "I'm fine." She swiped both hands across her cheeks in one quick motion. "Where did you come from?"

He jerked a thumb over his shoulder. "The road. My car broke down. You wouldn't have any jumper cables, would you?"

"Sorry, no."

He glanced toward the section of the peach orchard that ran parallel to the house. His shoulders lifted in a hopeless sigh.

"Could I use your phone?" He asked as if expecting a denial.

"Don't you have a cell?"

His jaw flexed, hardened even more. His eyes cut to hers and just as quickly cut away. "No."

Everyone had a cell phone these days. Where had this guy been? The moon?

She heard a slight noise from inside the kitchen and knew her guests had begun to stir.

"The phone is in the kitchen. Come in." She turned, felt his eyes at her back as she reached for the screen door. With a silent move that could have been unsettling, he joined her, took hold of the door and held it open as she entered.

She wasn't afraid of him. But even if he'd been an ax murderer, she'd not have been afraid. A person who was dead on the inside had no fear.

One of her frequent guests, a bespectacled sixtysomething Bob Oliver, stood at the counter helping himself to coffee. He and his wife had been here so often in the past two years, she let them have the run of the place and was glad they felt relaxed. That was the point of Peach Orchard Inn.

"Good morning, Bob," she said. "You're up with the birds."

"I smelled your coffee."

She managed a smile. "I'll fix a carafe for Mattie too."

"Later, maybe. Seven is too early for Mattie. When she retired from teaching she said she was never setting another alarm. And she hasn't."

"Can't blame her for that," Julia offered before turning toward the man who stood uncertainly beside the back door.

Before she could point the stranger toward the landline, Bob said in his usual candid manner, "Didn't know you had a hired man now."

Julia slanted the stranger a glance, wondering if he'd been insulted. His hard face remained impassive.

"Unfortunately, help, other than Valery, is still a pipe dream for Peach Orchard Inn. His car broke down up on the road."

"Probably the battery," the newcomer said, and then as if he'd been reprimanded for speaking too loudly, he looked down at his feet.

"Is that so? Maybe I can help." The older man offered a hand. "Name's Bob Oliver."

The stranger looked at the outstretched hand for an extra beat—long enough to draw attention to the hesitation—before he reciprocated. "Eli Donovan. I'll take you up on that, Mr. Oliver."

"Call me Bob. Mr. Oliver sounds like a professor of physics— which I was for thirty years. Now, I'm just plain old Bob." He chuckled and reached for the silver carafe, giving the plunger a push with the flat of one hand. "Julia here makes fine coffee."

The stranger flicked a glance at her but said nothing. She should offer. Offering coffee was the hospitable thing to do. "Would you care for a cup?"

He swallowed, seemed troubled by the simple question. "If you wouldn't mind."

She poured another cup and handed him the aromatic brew. His fingers trembled the slightest bit, but he quickly wrapped them around the mug while Julia pretended not to notice.

What she did notice was the fatigue around his eyes, the sheer weariness of the man. She noticed, too, that he was fit and muscled, his hands clean but rough, as if he labored for a living. He wore no jewelry, not even a wedding ring, though why she would notice bothered her a little. Good-looking men were not necessarily decent human beings, and even if he was the nicest guy on the planet, she was too empty to be interested.

"The telephone is over there if you still want to make a call."

She motioned to the landline on the brown granite counter and moved to check the casserole.

Mr. Oliver waved her off. "No need. I have jumper cables in my trunk. Never make a road trip without them."

The stranger's quick eyes moved from her to Mr. Oliver as if assessing both and wondering what to make of their friendliness. He was like a caged panther, dark and wary and dangerous.

"We'll drive my car up there," Bob said. "Give you a jump and have you on the road in a jiffy."

"Thanks." Eli Donovan took a brief sip of coffee and moved to set the still-full mug on the counter.

"Take the coffee with you." Julia gestured between the two men. "Both of you."

Eli hesitated. "Your cup..."

"Is returnable."

"Oh. Thanks." The word was rusty in his throat, as if he didn't say it often. In fact, all his words were rusty, careful.

Bob clapped him on the shoulder. Julia couldn't help noticing the way Eli tensed. "Today's your lucky day, Eli. Good coffee from a pretty lady and a man who never leaves home without tools. My car's parked around back. Ready when you are."

"I'm ready."

From the corner of her eye, Julia watched the two men exit her kitchen, their feet thudding against the board veranda. Eli carefully balanced his coffee, sipping as he walked, and Julia could hear Mr. Oliver, in his perky professor voice, chattering away while the other man remained silent.

Bingo trotted around the gravel walkway behind the pair, happy to have a purpose, abandoning his mistress to the quiet smells of her kitchen.

Julia wiped her hands on a peach-imprinted dish towel and

went to the door, watching as Bob Oliver and Eli Donovan disappeared around the corner of the porch.

What a strange morning. Another marble from nowhere, and now a disturbing stranger. Both on Mikey's birthday.

She reached into her pocket, withdrew the marble and rolled an index finger over the smooth clay. Somewhere in her distant memory, a little boy laughed.

3

"What's past is prologue…"

—William Shakespeare

Peach Orchard Farm
Summer, 1864

The sound of advancing hoofbeats should have shaken the ground. Yet, they moved quietly, reverently it seemed, a cavalcade of Union soldiers bearing their wounded.

Charlotte Reed Portland's first inkling that her Tennessee home was about to be invaded intruded as she taught a delicate embroidery stitch to her two sisters-in-law. Seated in the parlor, butter-yellow sunlight streaming in through the windows on a hot and windless day, Charlotte heard the excited voice of a servant, heard the hurried footfalls a moment before her nine-year-old son burst through the French doors, cowlick standing on end.

"Mama, the Yankees are coming!"

At Benjamin's breathless announcement, Charlotte stiffened, her fingers tight on the embroidery hoop.

She had known they would come, an army of men at war with her adopted state, in need of horses and food to fortify the Union. What they didn't understand, or perhaps didn't care, was that the Confederacy had need of the same supplies. Even now, the small, out-of-the-way town of Honey Ridge was strained beneath the burden.

So, of course, the Federals would come here, to Peach Orchard Farm, home to three generations of Portlands, including her husband, Edgar, and their son. Though hardly a plantation, they were self-sufficient in corn and wheat, fruit and livestock, and a handful of slaves.

Please, Almighty God, do not allow them to take everything.

Her two younger sisters-in-law regarded her above their needlework with wide, hazel eyes, mouths dropped. Their milk-bathed complexions had gone chalky. As mistress of the house and an ancient twenty-seven, the responsibility for their well-being and that of the house and servants rested upon Charlotte's shoulders.

"Miz Charlotte, you want I should go to the mill for Mr. Portland?" This from Pierce, the yardman, the whites of his eyes startling in his dark, sweat-gleamed face. A good man, a trustworthy and loyal servant.

Afraid the quiver in her throat would burst free and betray her angst, Charlotte nodded, breathing in for composure.

"Please do, Pierce," she managed, her British accent stronger when she was nervous, an accent her husband had once found charming. "I'll go out to greet them."

With deliberate poise, she put aside the embroidery hoop and rose, smoothing damp palms over her green day gown. Fear vibrated in her stomach.

Edgar would not be pleased at an interruption, whether from

her or the hated Yankees, but they'd heard the gunfire in the near distance early this morning. A battle, or perhaps only a skirmish; it did not matter which. Men would die. She'd prayed the war would not touch her household.

But now it had.

Charlotte could hide most feelings beneath a false serenity, a gift she'd found essential here in the American South, where differences were suspect, human beings were sold and traded and her husband ruled with a cold look.

"Josie. Patience," she said to the younger women. "Lock yourselves in your rooms. Take Benjamin with you. Neither come outside nor look out the windows. Do not show yourselves in any way."

With rigid posture and a sweep of full skirts, she moved out onto the long, pillared veranda, gripped the whitewashed railing and waited. Normally, she loved the scene from the porch, the double row of magnolias along the curving driveway, the expanse of peach orchard to the north. Yet, today her knees trembled and she saw only the advancing army—a straight military line of blue and gold and rows of men astride their mounts. The Union flag, stars and stripes aloft on the front steed, rippled slightly.

She'd heard the horror stories. The armies of the north came to pillage and destroy, but God help her, with her last breath she would defend her family and this home. From the moment Edgar had brought her here, a nervous bride of sixteen, she'd fallen in love with the house in a way she'd never been able to love the man. The house and her son were enough.

Sweat trickled beneath her collar and yet she waited, outwardly composed, searching for a sign of humanity among the enemy.

As the army moved closer, down the winding lane from road to house beneath the magnolia shade, Charlotte saw the lines of weariness on young soldiers' faces, the blood on uniforms, the litters and foot soldiers bearing the wounded. It was a small company, not a great army as she'd first thought. In the haunted faces of barely men, the war came, bringing with it a sense that nothing would ever be the same again at Peach Orchard Farm.

With a heavy heart, made heavier by the knowledge that whether by choice or by chance she was their enemy, Charlotte stepped from the porch onto the grass and made her way forward as the horses and men drew to a stop. Dust swirled up from the hooves into her nose. There was a shimmery stillness in the air, as though the house, too, held its breath.

The apparent leader of the troops, a man of erect bearing with an air of authority, touched his heels to a sweaty gray. Charlotte stood unflinching as he approached. He was young, as they all seemed to be. Perhaps her age. And whether friend or foe, he looked dashing in his blue waistcoat with the gold bars on the shoulders and the matching gold stripe down the Union blue trousers. Dashing and handsome, though dusty and strained from God only knew what, with brown hair, a strong jaw dusted with tidy brown whiskers and a lean build.

"Ma'am." He removed his hat, a navy blue with gold-crossed cannons above the bill. "I'm Captain William Gadsden of the United States Army. Is your husband in residence?"

A simple question, made necessary by the fact that most males in Tennessee had long since donned uniform of one color or another and gone off to fight. She knew Edgar's deferment shamed him, made him bitter.

"A servant was sent to fetch him. What is the purpose of your visit? We are a simple farm of women and children and a handful of servants." She refused to call them slaves. Many were as close as family and some, she suspected, might actually be.

Old Hub, whose only job these days was care of the chickens, hobbled around the house to stand beside her, a devoted if bent and feeble guard. His loyalty and courage buoyed her own.

The captain motioned toward the soldiers. "We have wounded."

"I see that, sir. I'm sorry for your losses." And truly she was. This American war was futile and cruel.

The captain twisted in the saddle with a slight creak of leather and raised a hand toward his troops. "Company, dismount."

In poorly synchronized fashion, the battle-ragged soldiers slid from their saddles while a handful of ground troops broke rank and surged toward the veranda.

"Wait!" Charlotte held out a trembling hand as though she possessed the power to stop an armed military. "What is it you want? Food? Bandages?"

Before Captain Gadsden could answer, a commotion ensued on the line. Charlotte watched with growing horror as a soldier tumbled to the hoof-packed earth and lay still.

"George!" Sword tapping at his side, Captain Will Gadsden hurried toward the fallen. Another soldier knelt on one knee in the lane of Peach Orchard Farm and held an open palm above the fallen comrade's mouth before he pressed an ear to the unmoving chest. He, hardly a man at all, looked up into the face of the waiting officer, his expression stricken. "George is dead, sir."

The captain dropped his head. His chest lifted in a hard sigh. He placed a hand on the soldier's shoulder and paid a quiet moment of respect. The company fell silent, the quiet broken only by the jingle of harness and the puff of equine nostrils.

The reaction touched Charlotte. The captain had a good and caring heart.

But the thought had barely formed when William Gadsden whirled on his boot heels in a decisive about-face. With a voice of authority, he stared straight ahead and said, "With apologies, ma'am, it is my duty to inform you that your residence is hereby commandeered for the good of the Union." He lifted a gloved hand. "Men, move in!"

Will watched the color drain from the woman's delicate features. She was pretty with her fair hair and precise British clip, for he was sure it was England and not Massachusetts he heard on her tongue. His heart squeezed with regret. Genteel and lovely, a woman of grace should not be affected by the evils of war, a woman like his sisters and mother. How he missed home on days like today when nothing but carnage lay in his wake.

He dismounted and approached the woman, removed his hat. "Ma'am, we require your home as a temporary hospital for our wounded. We'll also need supplies, food and rest, but my men have strict orders to bring no harm to your home or family. We will take only what we need."

Her chin lifted higher. "And how much do you need? We, too, have people to feed. I cannot allow you to rob my family."

She was in no position to argue or even to barter, but like a slender oak, she stood her ground, not in anger but with fierce determination. Admiration stirred inside Will. "I will see that you have enough. You have my word."

A man's word was often all he had left in this savage war. His word and his honor. Will was determined to return home to Ohio with both unsullied.

Already his men swarmed the elegant home and he felt duty-bound to set a watch on their behavior. Though most were good soldiers, they'd long been away from the social graces of home. He wanted no trouble, would stand for none. Some companies, he knew, took the spoils of war, but he struggled enough with the decision to commandeer homes and take needed food and horses.

The woman's expression softened, though her posture remained rigid and watchful. She gave a short nod. "Thank you."

The old slave who'd crept around the side of the house and stood bent and twisted at her side spoke up. His furrowed black face shone with sweat and worry and age. "Miss Charlotte, Mr. Portland is comin'."

Her head jerked toward the line of magnolias and then back to Will. It was the closest she'd come to showing disquiet, as if the husband's presence made things worse instead of better.

She quickly regained her poise, a trait he both admired and respected. Then, as if inviting a neighbor to tea, she motioned toward the porch. "May I impose upon you to meet with my husband in the parlor? It is far cooler inside. Hub will show you the way."

Before Will could respond, the surgeon called his name and motioned from the doorway leading into the house. Doc had wasted no time setting up, a necessary deed considering the nature and number of injuries from this morning's skirmish.

"Stokes is asking for you, sir."

Stokes. A good man, grievously wounded. Only God, not a surgeon, could get him through the night.

"I must see to my men first," Will said to the woman.

"Very well. I will inform my husband." Green skirt in her small, delicate hands, Mrs. Portland hurried up the lane.

Will watched her for only a moment before striding to the house and his duty, but the image of brave and pretty Charlotte Portland burned in his mind for a long time after.

4

Honey Ridge, Tennessee
Present Day

Eli climbed inside Bob Oliver's blue Accord, a newer model that probably never broke down. Not like the $500 clunker he drove.

His lucky day, the man had said. Given the circumstances and his destination, Eli wasn't taking any bets. But running into a friendly man *was* an unexpected stroke of luck. The phone request had been an act of desperation. Even if he'd found a mechanic to come out, he couldn't have paid him, at least not the full amount. His only hope had been to exchange work for the bill.

"My car is back down the road about a half mile." He pointed south where the clunker had died on him last night around midnight. Sleeping in the car hadn't bothered him. He liked being in the open where he could see the stars and feel the fresh air.

"You from around here?" Bob angled his face toward the

passenger seat. Morning sun reflected off his black-framed glasses.

"No."

"Me, either. The wife and I are looking to move this direction, but we hail from Memphis."

Eli's stomach dropped into his still-stiff boots. He'd spent seven miserable years in Memphis. Even after six months of freedom, the memory was too sharp for comfort.

Struggling for polite conversation to turn the topic from his least favorite place, Eli blurted the first thing that came to him. "Seems like a nice inn."

"Peach Orchard? The best. The wife and I drive down here to Julia's whenever we get a chance. Unless you're a Civil War buff, nothing much to do but sit around on the porch or walk in the gardens and orchard, maybe fish a little, but that's why we come. Peace and quiet. Beautiful scenery. And great coffee." He laughed and drained the remainder of his cup.

Eli continued to relish the best coffee he'd tasted in more than seven years. His mother had made coffee like this, in one of those fancy presses. He wondered if she ever thought about him. He tried not to think about her or of his father or the life he could have had if he'd been a better son. Remembering hurt too much, carried too much shame and remorse.

He sipped at the cup, glad for something in his empty stomach and grateful to the woman at the inn.

Julia. Pretty name for a pretty woman with her honey-blond hair smoothed back into a tail at the nape of her neck and sad blue eyes. He wondered why she'd been crying. But he shouldn't be thinking about her. Shouldn't be wondering what it would be like to sit down in that sparkling clean kitchen and enjoy breakfast with a woman like her. He didn't let himself think about women of any kind these days, certainly not a decent one.

"Sweet lady," Bob was saying as they turned south and approached Eli's stalled vehicle. "At the end of every visit, she gives us a jar of peach preserves she makes from the orchard. Mighty tasty."

Eli salivated at the thought of toast and jelly, a reminder that he'd not eaten since yesterday morning long before he'd finished the drywall job, collected his meager pay and left Nashville. To fill his empty belly, he took another mouthful of Julia's coffee. Bob was right. Great stuff. Smooth and bold, the way Eli used to be.

He stared out the passenger-side window at the rolling landscape, green and flowery with spring. In the near distance he spotted buildings, a surprise. He hadn't known he was that close to town but now that he thought about it, why would an inn be stuck out in the middle of nowhere?

"Is that your car right up there?" Bob nudged his chin toward a mistreated old Dodge parked at an angle on the side of the road.

He could imagine how a successful man like Bob Oliver must view a rattletrap with rusted fenders and a missing bumper. To the man's credit, he didn't react. A kind man. And good. The type of man Eli hadn't encountered in a long time.

They exited the car and walked to the Accord's trunk, where Bob removed a set of jumper cables. "Might as well grab the toolbox, too, in case we need it."

Eli reached for the red metal container and started toward the front of his Dodge.

"How was she acting when she quit?"

"Just quit. The engine's been sputtering for a hundred miles. I thought the fuel filter might be plugged up."

"You checked that, I guess."

"First thing this morning. Blew it out as good as I could. Still nothing."

"Did she overheat?"

"No, sir. Just quit. The battery is old. It's probably bad."

"Let's have a look."

Eli stashed his remaining coffee on the floorboard of the Dodge. Then he lifted the hood and braced it open with a stick, amused and interested that a physics teacher had offered to do mechanic work. "Where did you learn about cars?"

"Hobby. When I was a kid, we didn't have diddly. The only way I could own a vehicle was to rebuild one I'd bought myself. So I did."

Eli huffed softly. "Sounds familiar." Though he'd once had the finest vehicles, a beautiful home, a good family. And he'd thrown them all away on stupid choices.

He reached into the toolbox for an end wrench and tapped at the battery terminals. "Corroded," he said with disgust. Like his life. He stuck the wrench in his shirt pocket while he wrestled the cable heads loose.

Bob leaned in for a look. "I think you've found your problem. They need a good cleaning, but a wipe down and a jump should get you back on the road."

Eli scrubbed away at the terminals, using a T-shirt from his duffel bag. "Best I can do out here."

Bob hooked up the jumper cables while Eli slipped into the driver's seat and turned the key. After a few feeble grinds, the engine caught and started. Black smoke curled out the tailpipe as Bob slammed the hood and came around to the driver-side window.

"You have that checked first chance you get."

"Sure." When money grows on trees. "What do I owe you?"

"Not a thin dime. Pay it forward. That's all I ask."

Eli gave a solemn nod. "Thank you, sir."

"If you get back this direction, stop in and say hello. If you see this Accord in the lot, we're here."

"Will do." Not likely.

Then, with the morning breeze blowing in his face, Eli aimed the Dodge toward town, Opal Kimble and a piece of the past he'd never intended to resurrect.

The town of Honey Ridge was waking up as the old Dodge wheezed and rattled down the double row of buildings that composed the main street and led to a central square. The concrete was darkened from last night's rain.

A woman washing the display window of Hallie's Gifts and Cards paused, paper towel in hand to watch him pass. Her stare gave Eli a crawly feeling. He didn't want to attract attention, here or anywhere.

A man outside the post office hoisted the flag though not a breath of air stirred. Many of the buildings were from another time but neat and well kept, one of them marked with the date 1884 and painted in colorful murals of the past.

As he passed a doughnut shop, the scent floated through his open window. His belly growled.

Eli fished in his jacket pocket for the scrap of paper and the directions Opal had given. Two blocks east of the stoplight he turned down Rosemary Lane, crawling along until he spotted a blue-frame house with peeling paint, an overgrown lawn and two green metal chairs on the front porch. Opal's house.

The Dodge rattled to a stop at the end of a cracked driveway where a child's plastic motorcycle lay on its side next to the garage. Eli's empty belly cramped. His palms grew wet against the steering wheel.

What was he doing here? Every cell in his body urged him to turn tail and run, but for once in his life he didn't. Couldn't. He'd done very few responsible things in his thirty-six years, but this was different. He still couldn't believe the horrible news. Sweet, giggly Mindy who'd fancied herself in love with him was dead—and she'd left behind a child.

With nerves gnawing a hole in his gut, he got out of the car, crossed the yard and stepped quietly onto the porch. It was early. If the car hadn't broken down he'd have arrived last night. He didn't see a light. Was Opal still asleep? Maybe he should come back later.

Coward, a voice inside his head whispered.

He released a gust of breath, wiped his sweaty hands down his jeans and reached for the knocker. His shaky hand wouldn't quite take hold of the tarnished brass. He hovered there, as if the ordinary knocker had the power to change his life. Maybe he should forget this and head back to Nashville, keep trying to find permanent work. The boy never needed to know him. The boy. His son.

He pivoted to leave but stopped in a half-turn, wrestling with his conscience.

Before he could conquer the demons fighting inside his head, the scarred wooden door scraped open, catching on the threshold as if the wood had swollen with recent rain. An old woman with curly white hair and a wrinkled, pinched face leaned on a cane as she peered out at him.

Eli swallowed. "Opal Kimble?"

"Are you Eli?"

"Yes, ma'am."

She pushed the storm door open. "About time."

He entered the house where the scent of food battled with the musty smell of age. Everything about the room was old. Old furniture. A big, boxy television on a roller cart cluttered with papers. Faded photos on the wall of people from another era. He thought of the inn he'd recently left and couldn't help comparing the two houses. Both were old, filled with history, and yet Julia's home was bright and inviting.

"Sit."

Accustomed to taking orders, he complied.

"You want coffee?"

"Don't trouble yourself."

The old woman ignored his statement and left the room, returning with two mugs and a plate of raisin bread. "I figure you haven't had breakfast this early."

"No, ma'am."

"Help yourself."

"Thank you." He required significant restraint to keep from wolfing down the bread like a wild animal. Careful to sip the scalding coffee between bites, he managed to eat without humiliating himself. The coffee was bitter compared to Julia's. He didn't care. He'd learned the hard way not to complain.

"Go on and eat all that bread," the old woman said. "The boy doesn't like raisins, and I've had my fill."

The boy. The reason he'd come. She'd want money—he was certain of that after seeing her living conditions.

He could feel her watching him so he ate one more slice and stopped, though he could have eaten the entire loaf and still had room for breakfast.

When he'd finished, he sat back in the faded chair and waited, feeling a little better now that he'd had nourishment. She'd summoned him, demanded he come. Let her carry the conversation.

Opal, now seated across from him in a green lift-recliner, leaned forward, her fingers curled around the cane like bird claws. "You knew about the boy?"

"Mindy wrote to me."

"You didn't write back."

"I thought it was for the best." He lifted his palms in a helpless gesture. "Under the circumstances."

"She said he's your son."

"He could be." The news of Mindy's pregnancy, received in a letter not long after his incarceration, had hit him like a ton of bricks. He'd felt like the lowlife he'd become. He and Mindy had only been together one long, hot summer before the trial that changed everything, and he'd always been cautious about relationships. But nothing was foolproof.

"Mindy wouldn't lie. She was dying."

Eli closed his eyes for a second. How could lively Mindy be dead? "I didn't know until yesterday. She was too young."

"Cancer knows no age, young man." Opal raised her coffee and sipped, watching him with hawk eyes. After a few uncomfortable seconds, she went on. "When she knew the end was coming, she brought him to me, her only living relative. I love the child as I loved his mama. I want what's best for him."

Eli breathed a sigh of relief. She loved the boy. She'd take good care of him. "I'll send money when I can."

"Money?" Her tone sharpened.

"Child support."

She tilted closer until he thought she'd tumble from her chair. "Child support?"

Was the woman hard of hearing? "I'm…not working much yet—" A painful admission though he'd long ago lost his pride. "When I do, I'll send all I can."

"I'm not asking for your money, Eli Donovan."

"Isn't that why you wanted to see me? Child support?"

With a shove of her cane, Opal pushed to a stand and tottered toward him, a dangerous expression on her wrinkled face. "Look at me. I'm eighty-four years old. I have congestive heart failure and diabetes. I can barely toddle around with this stupid cane."

Dread started at the bottom of Eli's feet and worked up through his chest and into his brain. Like a wild stallion, his flight instinct kicked in. He knew what was coming. Knew and couldn't stop her.

"Mindy wanted you to take the boy. You're his father." Opal stuck a bony finger in his face. "She expected *you* to raise him."

Eli bolted from the chair. "Are you nuts? Do you know where I've been all of his life?"

She pointed the cane at his chest. "You're out now. And you have a son to care for."

"I don't belong around kids. I'm not even sure it's legal."

"Don't be stupid. He's your blood."

"You don't understand. I can't take care of a child."

A flash of Jessica's face, bloated and white, floated through his head. Floated the way she had, facedown in the water, while he'd rocked to Michael Jackson through his Sony Walkman headphones.

"I don't have a home or a steady job and no one wants to hire an ex-con. I'm at the beck and call of a parole officer who doesn't like me much." He rammed splayed fingers through his hair, panicked. "I can't even take a leak without checking in first!"

"Stop raising your voice in my house. Do you want him to hear?"

His heart pounded as if he'd been the one under water too long. "Look, Opal, let's be reasonable. What you're asking is impossible. You don't know me. I'm an ex-con. I am not father material. I wouldn't know what to do with a kid."

"Do you think any parent knows anything when their child is born? You'll learn like everybody else."

"Impossible." He couldn't take responsibility for anyone, especially a child. Dear God, she didn't know what she was asking!

"Do you know what will become of the boy when I die?"

He shook his head. "Another relative, I suppose."

"You got family that will take him? Love him?"

The ball of ice in Eli's chest became an iceberg. "No."

"All right, then. *You're* his only other relative. He'll go into foster care, into the system." She spit the last word like profanity.

"Anywhere is better than with me. There are plenty of good foster parents who care for kids."

"Mindy never wanted that for her baby."

"I'm sorry, Opal. I can't do this." He stalked to the door, torn asunder but certain he was not a fit man to father a child. Ever. "I'll send money as soon as I can."

"Mindy defended you. She said you were a good man." Opal's thin lips curled. "She was wrong."

"Yes. She was." Tormented by the truth, Eli stormed out of the house, across the overgrown yard and into the safe confines of his car. Breathless, his chest aching, he cranked the Dodge, and was out on the streets of Honey Ridge in seconds.

At the corner, Eli stopped at the stop sign and leaned his head on the steering wheel. He was shaking worse than he had on his first day in prison.

He was the worst possible parent for a little boy, a man who had nothing to offer, a man with no future and an ugly past.

Responsibility tightened around his neck like a noose. He had a son. A son who needed him.

And he didn't even know his name.

5

Peach Orchard Farm
1864

"Lizzy, help me." The stench of blood and gunpowder strong in her nostrils, Charlotte called to her maid above the unholy clamor echoing through the farmhouse.

The groans and cries of distressed men tore at her compassion and frightened the children into hiding, a mercy, Charlotte thought, to spare them this horror.

Chaos reigned over Peach Orchard Farm while Captain Gadsden shouted orders and men dragged themselves and each other into her house.

With the wounded sprawled on the bare floors of her parlor and dining room, Charlotte pulled sheets from storage and ripped them into long strips. She'd been dismayed at the lack of medical supplies carried by a warring army. Indeed, the bulk of bandages and medicine came from the Portlands' belongings, not the military.

Lizzy, her dark, deft fingers quick and strong, took up a sheet. "You tend that one. I'll make the bandages."

Grateful for her maid's able assistance, Charlotte poured a basin half-full of water Cook had heated on the stove and knelt beside one of the many men lying on the dining room floor. He wasn't the first she'd tended during the long wait to see the single, harried surgeon.

"What's your name?" she said, as she slid scissors under his fragmented shirtsleeve.

Through gritted teeth, the man managed, "Joshua Bates. Will I die?"

Charlotte's hand paused as she gazed down at the ghastly wound laying bare the bone. The wound alone wouldn't kill him, but infection was the enemy, as she well knew from her mother's missions of mercy in the slums of London.

"Only a flesh wound." At the masculine voice, Charlotte gazed up at Captain Gadsden as he dropped to one knee beside his fallen soldier. They exchanged looks and she saw that he no more believed his words than she did. He placed a hand across the man's sweaty brow. "You fought bravely today, Private."

Bates, his face as bleached as new muslin, hissed when Charlotte carefully dabbed at the jagged flesh. A river of blood flowed out. "Would you give him a drink of whiskey, please?"

The captain didn't hesitate. He held the other man's head and slowly poured in the numbing liquor while she pressed a bandage into the bullet hole and wrapped a strip of sheet round and round the arm, tying it off with a knot.

"That should stop the bleeding." She prayed it would, for prayer was the only other help she could give him.

"Have you nursing experience, ma'am?" the captain asked, recapping the bottle of whiskey. Edgar would not be pleased at the loss of his liquor cabinet, the medicine he took for his crippled foot and other ailments.

"My mother cared for the sick. She taught me." Though nothing of this grisly nature.

Satisfied that she'd done all she could for Bates until the surgeon had more time, she rinsed her hands in the basin and moved on to the next soldier. The captain remained for another moment at Bates's side. She heard snippets of their soft conversation and from the corner of her eye saw the officer remove a paper from the soldier's breast pocket, read it and put it back. With another murmured word, he moved to the next man.

From the far side of the room, a man screamed. Charlotte jerked and sloshed water before spinning toward the cry. In three strides Captain Gadsden was there. Together with the help of Lizzy and a soldier with a bloody ear, they pressed the hysterical man back to the floor.

"He ain't bleeding nowhere," Lizzy said.

The man's head thrashed from side to side, his shaggy ginger beard making a swish-swish against his blue shirt. He mumbled disconnected sentences, random words. "Get the bucket. They're coming. Donald! Donald!"

At the last, he began to keen in a high-pitched wail.

"Is he blind?" Captain Gadsden passed a hand over the staring eyes. No reaction.

Charlotte knelt beside the man, full of pity. "Shh. Shh. You're safe."

The young soldier grappled for Charlotte's hand and bore down hard enough to cause pain. She flinched but didn't pull away.

"Sally? Sally?"

Dismayed, Charlotte looked to the captain, kneeling on the opposite side. A dozen men in different degrees of distress watched the painful episode.

"Is Sally his wife?"

"Yes."

"Brain fever, Miss Charlotte," Lizzy said. "His mind is gone."

"Captain!" someone called from the doorway. "Come quickly, sir."

The poor captain appeared torn. So many needs. So many voices calling for him.

There were too many strangers in her house.

"I'll tend to this man, Captain. Lizzy, is there a potion that would soothe him?"

In caution, Lizzy's dark eyes cut between her and the captain and the other listeners in the room. Not everyone approved of the maid's medicines. "I'll see what I got."

She scurried from the room just as Charlotte's husband burst in from outside. He gazed around the scene, bewildered, but quickly settled on Charlotte. In a cold, irate voice, he demanded, "Mrs. Portland!"

Charlotte rose to her knees. "Edgar, please. This man is—"

"In my study. Now!" And he stormed through the parlor with little regard to the sick and injured beneath his feet.

Charlotte jumped as her husband slammed the study door and strode to his desk. Hands on the wood, he leaned toward her. His face was florid, his mouth tight with anger.

"Have you no decency?"

Charlotte waited with her hands in the folds of her dress. She knew better than to argue.

Edgar slammed his fist onto the desk. In spite of her efforts not to, Charlotte jumped again.

"Speak when I speak to you!"

Her chin came up. "There are wounded men in our house, Edgar, whether we want them or not. It seems indecent not to help them."

"I don't want them here."

"Nor do I, but there is little we can do to stop them. Isn't cooperating better than being shot?"

"Cooperating? Is that what you call wallowing on the floor with a Yankee?"

"The soldier was out of his head. He didn't know what he was doing." She took a step toward him, one hand outstretched in a plea. Edgar always responded better when she asked. "Please allow me this ministry. Tending the sick is the Christian thing to do."

His face worked for several tense seconds before he cursed and spun toward the narrow window, showing her his back. "Go on, then. Go coddle your Yankees."

Charlotte waited two beats of time, her knees shaking and her stomach twisted in knots. "Thank you."

Edgar whirled and shouted, "I said go, woman!"

With what dignity she could muster, Charlotte slipped out the door and was shocked to see the young captain in the hallway.

"Are you all right, ma'am?" he asked quietly.

Heat burned her cheeks. Humiliated but grateful for the kindness, Charlotte nodded.

Moving closer, the captain murmured, "We've put you in a difficult situation. I apologize."

Charlotte glanced toward the closed study, fearful that Edgar would exit the room and cause another scene.

Captain Gadsden took her arm and led her a few feet down the hall. "Could I fetch you a glass of water?"

Her cheeks burned hotter. "I'm fine."

With a tilt of his head, he released her and started to walk away.

"Captain."

He turned, holding her with gentle eyes, his head tilted to one side.

"Thank you," she whispered.

The moment stood still while she and the handsome captain stared at each other in the dim hallway. The floor seemed to shift beneath Charlotte's feet. Her ears buzzed and she had the strongest urge to reach out to him, this complete stranger who'd offered her more kindness than her own husband.

She sucked in a quick breath, shocked at her thoughts, and hurried back to the groaning soldiers.

6

Valery was late coming down to work, which could mean two things, neither of them good, both of them probable.

Julia served breakfast by herself, relieved they had only four guests this morning. Mr. Oliver came back from his Good Samaritan trip about the time the first couple was leaving the dining room. He slid into place next to a window overlooking the back lawn. Someday she'd have a garden there, and the old carriage house would be a pretty sight instead of a reminder of all that remained unfinished at Peach Orchard Inn. Unfinished. Incomplete. Like her life.

"Did you get the man's car started?" She delivered Bob's breakfast plate and a fresh carafe of coffee.

"Fixed him right up. Brought back your cup. I'm afraid the other fellow must have forgotten about his."

Julia made a face. That's what she got for noticing the man's good looks instead of remembering he was a stranger. "I wonder where he was headed. He seemed sort of lost."

"Said he was going in to Honey Ridge."

"Really? Does he have family here?"

"I wouldn't know. He was polite enough and grateful as a pup but tight-lipped and watchful, too, as though he couldn't believe I was lending a hand."

"I'll have to ask Mama. She knows everything that happens in Honey Ridge, usually before it happens." She smiled at her own joke. "She and the good old boys at the miniature-golf club."

"You keep telling me about that place. I'm going to have to stop in there sometime." He dipped a fork into his casserole. "My wife made an appearance yet?"

"Not yet."

He shook his head and chuckled. "Save her some of this casserole, will you?"

"Like always, I'll leave a plate in the warmer." She bussed the other couple's table while they talked, all the while casting a worried eye toward the entrance. Where was Valery? "Is there anything else I can get for you?"

"No, no. You go on and do what you need to. I know my way around if I want something."

Julia carried the used dishes into the kitchen and set about putting things in order. Once done, she went back for Bob's plate and found the dining room empty. Still, Valery hadn't made an appearance. With a beleaguered sigh, Julia gathered fresh linens for a vacated room and stopped by Valery's room in the private area of the house.

"Valery." She tapped at the door. "Valery, wake up."

She heard a grumble and the thump of feet hitting the floor before the door cracked open. "What?"

Her sister's brown hair was wild and her eyes bloodshot. Julia's heart sank. "Oh, Val, not again."

Valery shut the door in her face. Julia pecked with a little more force, though not enough to disturb their guests upstairs. "I'll bring coffee. Be out of that bed when I get back."

Without waiting for a reply, she went for the promised coffee, the only way to flush out the booze Valery must have consumed last night. No wonder she'd forgotten to bring in the flag.

When she returned with the carafe, Julia let herself in with the master key. Valery sat on the side of the bed, holding her head.

"You look like something the cat vomited. Did you see Jed last night?"

"Don't be grouchy, Julia. We were celebrating our reunion."

"I thought the two of you were finished."

"He loves me."

"He's not good enough for you."

"You never liked him. Give me that coffee. I'm croaking of thirst."

"I don't like him because he's not a nice man." The creep knew Valery had trouble stopping at a couple of drinks. "Here. Take this. I've got work to do."

She softened a bit when Valery's hands shook, reminding her of the dark stranger—Eli—whose hands had also trembled. Had he been on a binge last night, too? "The guests in the Blueberry Room checked out right after breakfast—which is already over, by the way."

Valery groaned and pushed up from the bedside. "I'll get showered and be right up."

Julia had started toward the door when Valery said, "Julia."
"What?"

"I only had a couple of drinks."

Right. "I'll be in the Blueberry Room."

7

Peach Orchard Farm
1864

Charlotte closed her Bible and looked out at a morning sky as blue as the robin's-egg walls of her bedroom.

The ugly incident with Edgar and the subsequent kindness of Captain Gadsden troubled her greatly. She could get neither off her mind.

From this upper-story room she could see the trembling limbs of the orchard with a few rosy peaches still clinging to the branches. Portlands had planted those trees so very long ago, long before she'd come to Tennessee. Long before bloodied strangers invaded the quiet country life.

Directly below the window a tattered score of soldiers milled about the grounds in the gauzy morning, some limping, some bandaged. Four stood guard with rifles to their shoulders. Others lay on the porch where they'd camped since their arrival four days ago. Campfires burned in spots around the summer-green lawn.

An invasion. One that had relegated the Portland family to the second story while the floor below became a hospital for the wounded and quarters for the officers. Inconvenient, and yet the farm had not been completely stripped of supplies; nor had they been driven from their home. And not one resident of Peach Orchard had been molested, a blessed circumstance she credited to Captain Gadsden. He'd kept his promise. He was, she was quite convinced, a good man, perhaps even a godly man, and his soldiers listened to him with respect. Not that they were in any condition to do much else.

She saw him now straight and lean, striding in his long steps, across the lawn, his red trouser stripe a bright flash. Barely daylight, and yet he was up and about and would spend hours in the makeshift hospital ward encouraging his men. She knew because she and the other women of the farm, both white and black, had been pressed into service for the sick. Theirs was a horrifying, heartbreaking task, but how could they do less for men whose mortal souls hung in the balance?

The smell of blood and ether clung to her hands and clothes. During that first long day and night, she'd witnessed grisly, obscene damage that no human form should endure. A merciful God must surely close his eyes in anguish against the barbaric will of man to maim and butcher one another.

Her father, the gentle vicar with too many daughters and too little money, would scarce believe the savagery to which he'd sent his eldest daughter.

Yet, late into the night and against her husband's wishes, Charlotte made coffee for the surgeon and the sleepless wounded and carried water to groaning souls. During the day, she ripped rags and the few remaining sheets into bandages and wrote letters to wives, mothers and sweethearts in faraway places she'd only seen on Benjamin's schoolroom maps.

The worst of the ugliness was over for now. Thank the Almighty.

From somewhere inside the house, a hoarse scream shattered the morning and gave the lie to her thoughts. Charlotte squeezed her eyes shut. Such suffering as she'd never witnessed, not even in the slums of London, as the surgeon went about the ghastly chore of removing limbs that showed signs of infection. Twice already, a body had been carted to the family cemetery, northern boys laid to rest in foreign soil next to her premature babies. She'd watched Will Gadsden mourn each soldier and later sit at Edgar's desk and write a letter to the family. An honorable man, indeed.

A tap sounded on Charlotte's bedroom door. She turned from her desk with a smile, expecting her only son, the joy of her days. But her eldest sister-in-law charged inside, distraught.

"I can't stand this anymore, Charlotte. We're prisoners in our own home. Prisoners and slaves to that bunch of Yankees."

"Captain Gadsden made it very clear that we are not prisoners of war. We are free to leave." She was pleased, if surprised, that most of the slaves hadn't taken the captain at his word but only two, Edgar's most recent purchases, had disappeared.

"Where would we go? This is our home, not theirs, and I am sick of them infesting every fiber of our lives. Yankees everywhere, groaning and crying. Leaving a mess. Devouring every bite to eat. They're like a plague of locusts."

"They're mere men, Josie, far from home, scared and suffering. There's little we can do but endure."

Josie tossed her head. As fiery red as Charlotte was blonde, the twenty-two-year-old wore her cascade of curls in a tight bun, but ringlets slipped out around her face. She was a comely young woman, though her ways were not always gracious. The Portland girls had grown up motherless with only their father and brother as examples, something Charlotte tried to remember when anger flared.

"I suppose you're going down there again today to play nursemaid like a slave girl." Josie paced the room. "Well, I tell you, I am not. No matter what that captain says, I refuse to help another Yankee. I don't know why Edgar stands for this treatment or allows his wife to commiserate with the enemy!"

Charlotte folded her hands against her skirt, refusing to be baited by Josie's sour mood. She was trying to survive, trying to keep her family together and her home intact in the absence of her husband. Lord above, how could she not show compassion to those damaged souls below?

Edgar, in a helpless fury over the invasion, had departed for the mill on the second day of occupation and had not returned. His anger was directed at her, not unusual but difficult because she had no control over the situation. She wasn't quite sure what to make of his abandonment but consoled the other women with assurances that Edgar was protecting the gristmill that housed their corn and grain supply. She did not know, however, if that was true. She prayed it was. They could ill afford to lose much more.

"I don't like this, either, but these injured men are God's children, too."

"Let them die, I say. They're not ours."

"They're all ours, Josie," she said softly. "What if it was your Tom?"

Josie sucked in a gasp, green eyes filled with worry. "We've heard nothing in so long. Do you suppose—"

Charlotte touched her shoulder in compassion. "Think the best, and pray that if your Tom should be wounded, someone would show him kindness."

"I know what you're saying, but I can't. And how you can gives question to your loyalty. These horrible, smelly men have taken over our home, raided our smokehouse, and still you shower them with compassion—you wash their fevered faces and wrap their bloody wounds. I don't understand you."

Of that, Charlotte was quite aware and full of remorse that she had not become what the Portlands needed. Not Edgar. Not Josie. Only sweet and simple Patience seemed to genuinely care for her. Yet, she would not give up trying. They were her family now.

"Did you not sleep well?" she asked, hoping to mollify her stormy sister-in-law. Josie had suffered insomnia from childhood, a malady that worsened after her fiancé marched away with the Confederacy two years ago.

"I wonder if I'll ever sleep again. I miss him until I think my heart will burst. I want him to come home."

"Soon, this war will be over and Tom will return. Then, we'll have a grand wedding and invite everyone in Honey Ridge."

"Oh, Charlotte, I dream of that day—" Josie clasped a fist to her chest "—when I glide down the staircase in Mama's wedding gown and Tom is waiting in the parlor to marry me."

"We'll get your mother's gown from the attic this very evening and check the fitting." After the work. After the patients were tended, the bandages changed, the bloody floors scrubbed and food put on the table.

"Really? Could we?"

"Of course we can." Though Charlotte was bone weary and would rather collapse on her bed, they needed distractions during these long, trying months of war. No matter how petulant Josie could be. "Tonight, I'll ask Lizzy to prepare a tea for you. You'll sleep like a baby and dream of your wedding day."

Josie made a face. "Her potions taste horrid."

Lizzy was Charlotte's friend more than her maid, though Charlotte had been chastised by Edgar for saying as much.

Slaves, he insisted, were property, not friends. Yet, he did not prevent her from tending their sick or teaching the slave children to read scripture. He was a strange man, her husband, and she despaired of ever fully knowing him.

"We'll add a spoon of honey." She moved to the window and glanced out. Soldiers raided the orchard, though peach season had waned and few fruit remained. She prayed they didn't discover the storage in the cellar or the silver and heirlooms Hob and Lizzy had buried below the carriage house. "Have you seen Benjamin this morning?"

"He's probably off fishing with Tandy somewhere. Or lurking with those horrible men. You really should speak to him, Charlotte."

Another soft tap sounded at her door and Charlotte was grateful for the interruption. Short of locking Ben in his room, keeping him away from the soldiers was impossible. They were everywhere, and both he and Tandy were agog with interest.

When she opened the door, the small love of her life threw his sturdy body against her skirts. With him came the ever-present Tandy, Lizzy's son and Benjamin's playmate. "Mama!"

Charlotte's dress pooled around her feet as she dipped low to embrace him. She thanked God every day that this baby had been spared the fate of the others. Though she longed for more, Edgar had turned away from her bed after the last tiny soul was laid to rest. Because she'd failed in that most fundamental of wifely duties, Ben was likely the only living child she'd ever have. So, she loved him all the more. Desperately, she loved him.

"You smell like horse," she said, relishing the scent because it came from Benjamin. With deep affection, she smoothed his cowlick, a stubborn column of wheat-colored hair poking up from his crown.

"Captain Will let us pet Smokey. That's his horse. He's

named Smokey because he's gray but his mane and tail are black."

Josie drew back like a rattlesnake. "You stay away from that Yankee. Why, your daddy will have your hide."

Ben turned worried eyes to Charlotte. "Will he, Mama?"

"Of course not." Though Edgar was not an affectionate or attentive father, he was not cruel to his son. He was, however, full of hatred toward the Federals. "But you be good boys and don't bother the captain. He is a busy man."

"Captain Will is nice. He said boys are no bother at all." Tandy shared a nod with Ben. "'Cause he used to be one back in Ohio."

Ohio. The good captain was a long way from home. She wondered what he'd done before the war and if a wife or a sweetheart longed for his return.

"I like him," Ben declared, and his innocent goodness stirred both fear and pride in his mother. The captain was kind and had given the boy attention, something he often lacked from Edgar, though she felt disloyal for thinking so. "Mama, he wants to talk to you in the parlor."

A sudden anticipation fluttered in Charlotte's belly as unwelcome and disturbing as the onslaught of Yankees. These daily conversations with Captain Will Gadsden troubled her, for she enjoyed them.

Perhaps too much.

Edgar needed to come home.

8

Eli glanced at the gas gauge as he pulled slowly through Honey Ridge. He was running low and had no idea where he was going. Right now, his head pounded and he couldn't think straight. Remembering a park he'd passed on the way in, he headed there. Parks had been his friends and sometimes his bedrooms since his release. Saving enough money to rent an apartment wasn't easy to do when all a man could find were odd jobs. The minute he filled out application forms and admitted he was a convicted felon, employment offers disappeared.

He pulled into the graveled parking space, got out of the Dodge and walked to a shady concrete table. Birds had been there first, leaving behind their calling cards. Glad to be outside in the fresh air with the deep green leaves hanging overhead, Eli propped his elbows on the hard concrete and watched red birds peck the ground for the remains of someone's Cheetos.

Life was a dilemma. As much as he hated prison, he'd understood it. The boring routine, the men to avoid, the unspoken rules about keeping his mouth shut and his head down. But out here in the real world was different. He wondered if he'd ever adjust.

He had a son. That one fact hammered away at him like the woodpecker in the live oak next to the merry-go-round. He wondered if his son played here. Had Mindy brought him? Had she pushed him on the swings or had she been too sick and weak to play anymore? Opal certainly couldn't. What kind of childhood would his son have with a sick old woman who could barely walk?

He tugged his wallet from his back pocket and counted his money. Thirty-seven dollars. A man couldn't take care of a child on that amount.

When a black-and-white car pulled up next to his Eli tensed, watching a uniformed policeman exit the cruiser and walk around the Dodge. The cop would call in the out-of-town plates. Find them clean. No use getting in a panic.

But Eli's palms sweated.

The officer saw him and stepped over the low cable fence. Eli drew a breath, releasing the air in a slow, calming exhale. He had nothing to hide. A stranger in a small-town park would naturally arouse curiosity. He shouldn't have stopped here.

"'Morning."

"'Morning."

"I'm Trey Riley, Honey Ridge Police Department. Don't think I've seen you around before."

"Eli Donovan. I'm down from Nashville. Visiting family." That much was true. He had a son in Honey Ridge. Poor kid.

"Is that your Dodge?"

Eli offered a wry expression. "Such as it is. I had a little car trouble this morning."

"Yeah?" Officer Riley turned to look at the old clunker. "Anything I can help with?"

"Bad battery. It's running now." He chuffed. "Or it was when I stopped. A man at the inn gave me a jump."

"Peach Orchard Inn?"

"Yes."

"Nice place. Julia and Valery have done a great job restoring it. When I was a kid we thought the house was haunted." Trey Riley chuckled, a nice easy sound as though he laughed often. "Mostly wild stories about Civil War ghosts to keep kids out, I think, but I'm glad to see the place inhabited by the living for a change."

Eli didn't know what to say. His conversation skills had taken a hit in the past seven years. "She makes good coffee."

He remembered then, with guilt, that he still had her cup.

"You should taste her peach tea. Man alive!" Riley drew out the last word with a grin and a head shake. "Great stuff. I've been known to show up on her doorstep in the afternoons— official business, of course—" he laughed again "—to beg an ice-cold glass of pure Southern heaven. Julia puts up with me. My mom buys peaches from her."

Eli couldn't quite take in the fact that he was having a friendly, man-to-man conversation with a police officer who seemed to be a decent guy.

"I noticed the orchard."

"I guess it's blooming."

"Real pretty." Like pink, fluffy clouds.

"Spring's the best in Honey Ridge. Lots of things blooming." Officer Riley tugged at a well-creased pant leg and propped his gleaming black service shoe on the cement bench. "Gorgeous morning to stop here."

"Nice park."

"It is, isn't it? Honey Ridge is a nice town. I lived away for a while but when this job opened up, I was happy to come home again."

"You have family here?" There. That wasn't so hard.

"All of them. Mother, Dad, three sisters."

"Three?"

"Yeah, go ahead. Pity me." Officer Riley laughed again. "They're great. Really. They drive me crazy, too. Always trying to marry me off to one of their girlfriends."

Eli smiled. Family. He wished he could go home to a loving bunch that would drive him crazy and care about his single status. Instead, he was alone. No, not completely. He had a child. A son who needed him. And he had nothing to offer but himself.

The thought depressed him. A kid deserved better. There was no way he could care for a child.

But if he didn't, who would? The boy would be as alone as he was. He knew how that felt. He knew about having no one to turn to. He'd been thirteen when life had begun to unravel. His son was only six, a year older than Jessica had been, and already the boy's life was in shreds.

Before he could operate the smarter side of his brain, Eli said, "You wouldn't know of any job openings around here, would you?"

"Are you looking to stay on in Honey Ridge?"

"I might if I can find work."

Officer Riley squinted up into the leafy oak where the woodpecker was having a heyday. "Let's see. If you're not picky, food places like Jose's Pizza and Miss Molly's Diner are always shorthanded. And you can check with the quick-stops, the horse ranches and Big Wave."

When Eli tilted his head at the last, Riley explained. "Big Wave builds custom boats. They're located west of town. I don't know if they're hiring, but it's worth a shot. Ask for Jan. She's the big boss."

"Okay."

"Oh, and Julia out at Peach Orchard wants to renovate the old carriage house into guest rooms. I don't know if she's ready to start or if she has the money yet, but you could ask."

A little thrill zipped through Eli at the thought of seeing Julia again. He tamped back the emotion, feeling foolish for even thinking about a good woman. Yet, he'd much prefer working on a remodel than being trapped inside a building all day.

"Thanks for the ideas."

"I hope you find something. Honey Ridge is a good place for law-abiding citizens to call home." He dropped his foot to the ground. "If you need any help with that Dodge, give me a shout."

As the man strode back to his cruiser, Eli stared, bemused. His wallet still lay on the table but the officer hadn't asked for identification. Other than the remark about law-abiding citizens, he hadn't even seemed suspicious. Trey Riley was either a poor police officer or a very good guy.

Eli pushed to a stand and pocketed his wallet. He didn't know how or why but, in the past ten minutes, he'd made a decision that would alter his future and that of one little boy.

He was going to find employment in the pleasant, family town of Honey Ridge. And he was going to be a daddy.

9

Julia dialed the police department by memory. After six years of regular calls, she was put straight through to the detective.

"Hello, Julia." Detective Burrows's voice was tired but kind. He was a busy man. She'd get right to the point.

"Today is Mikey's birthday. I just wondered if…" Her voice trailed away.

"Nothing new, Julia."

"Nothing at all?"

"Not since the false sighting two years ago in Huntsville, but Michael's file remains active. I talked with the FBI last week."

She swallowed, disappointed but not surprised. The police did their best. She understood that. For a full year after Mikey disappeared, either Detective Burrows or the FBI unit had called her every day with an update. Slowly, as the case grew colder and more frustrating, the calls dwindled.

"You'll call me immediately if there's anything at all." The desperation and pain she heard in her own voice never lessened. It wouldn't until her son was found.

"Of course. I wish I had better news."

"So do I."

Julia hung up and, heavyhearted, had started up the stairs toward the Blueberry Room when someone knocked at the front door. Deciding to leave the cleaning to Valery, she hurried down to answer, hoping for a drive-up guest. The inn had been slow this month and occasionally someone in town sent a customer her way.

She opened the door to find two older ladies standing on her wraparound veranda. Her mood lifted. No one could be around the twin Sweat sisters without smiling at the two old characters. Dressed in identical pink flowered shirtwaists, shiny pink pumps and jaunty white sunhats with matching gloves, Vida Jean and Willa Dean Sweat were throwbacks to the fifties when Southern ladies dressed and behaved with a certain uniform gentility. The octogenarian Sweat twins, however, were anything but conventional. With their painted-on eyebrows, startling red lipstick and hair dyed a specific shade of lemon yellow, they were entertaining icons of Honey Ridge.

"Ladies, good morning. Come in."

"We can't stay long, Julia darling." This from Vida Jean. Julia knew because she was the twin with the mole on her cheek.

"Of course we can, Vida Jean. Julia, do you have any of your wonderful peach tea made?"

"Just finished. If you'd like to sit in the parlor, I'll bring in a tray."

"You are such a darling girl. I was telling Willa Dean this morning. Wasn't I, sister?"

"Indeed, you were." Hoisting an oversize straw bag, Willa Dean said, "I wouldn't mind some coffee cake if you have it."

"Peach muffins?" Julia offered. "Made fresh this morning."

"Lovely. Thank you, dear."

"Coming right up."

With a smile, Julia left the twins in the pretty old parlor, a polished-wood space with a fireplace, the original chandelier and a toast-colored, camel-backed sofa. Across a persistent dark spot near the fireplace, she'd placed a colorful area rug. She'd heard rumors about the spots but didn't want to think about bloodstains.

She returned with the tray and after serving the twins, joined them. Valery owed her a little break. There was always work to do—wood to polish, fans to dust or flowers to weed, even when business was slow. This was in addition to the restoration and eventual expansion that would probably never end.

The Sweat sisters, pinkies lifted from the condensing tea glass, regaled her with news of the townsfolk, including a new baby for the Perkinses and the news that poor Brother Ramsey had fallen while repairing the church roof and had broken his leg. Julia made a mental note to send the pastor a card, though she hadn't darkened the church door in quite a while.

A clatter sounded overhead. All three women looked up.

"Guests," Julia said. "Or Valery cleaning."

The twins exchanged a glance. "Willa Dean and I have been wondering. Haven't we, sister?"

"Indeed. Wondering. You know what they say about this house, don't you, Julia dear?"

She'd been raised in Honey Ridge. Of course, she knew, but she'd always had an affinity for the old place even as a kid when the house peeled and sagged in exhausted disrepair and weeds choked the front veranda. She'd been a child when the last owners moved to Georgia and left the house to further deteriorate, a sad state of affairs that had fired ghost stories and led to keep-out signs and a locked gate across the entrance.

"They say that about all old houses that have sat empty for a while."

"Have you experienced anything unusual since you moved in?"

"Unusual?" Like finding antique marbles in odd places or hearing children giggle?

"Granddaddy told stories. Wasn't he a fine storyteller, Vida Jean?"

"His daddy fought in the war, you know. Chester Lorenzo Sweat, a corporal with the 1st Confederate Cavalry. Sister and I remember the stories, don't we, Willa Dean?"

Julia didn't have to ask which war. In Honey Ridge, the Civil War was remembered, revered and reenacted. Stories abounded, embellished by time and Southern pride.

"We haven't encountered any ghostly apparitions if that's what you're asking."

"Oh."

"Well." Vida Jean's mole quivered.

Straight and prim, the twins crossed their hands atop their straw handbags at exactly the same time in exactly the same manner, both of them clearly disappointed by her statement.

"Would you care for more tea?" Julia asked.

"None for me, dear. The bladder, you know." Willa Dean reached for another muffin. "These are delicious."

"Thank you."

"From your orchard?"

"The peaches are from the freezer, but yes, they were grown here."

"Lovely."

While Willa Dean fawned over the muffins, Vida Jean added another tidbit of local gossip. Or news, as the Sweat twins would call it. "Did you hear about the new family that bought the Akins farm? They have six boys. Six. Can you imagine six little boys running through the house?"

A cloud passed over Julia's heart. She managed a feeble smile. "How nice for them."

"Oh, dear, I've brought up a difficult subject. Forgive me. But that's why we came, isn't it, sister?"

Willa Dean drew an envelope from her purse. "Indeed. That's why we're here. You didn't think we'd forget Michael's birthday, did you?"

Julia was touched. Her own family wouldn't say a word, but the twins remembered. She took the card. "Thank you. This means a lot."

"Well." Vida Jean wiped her hands on a napkin, fussing a bit as if she didn't know what else to say, a rarity for either of the twins. "I suppose we should run. We have other calls to make, don't we, sister?"

"Yes, calls to make." Willa Dean leaned forward to pat Julia on the hand. "We don't like to push, but you call us if you want to reminisce. We have photos of Mikey we cherish."

A lump formed in Julia's throat. "You ladies are wonderful."

"Oh, go on now." Willa Dean took the remaining two muffins, wrapped them in a napkin and slid them into her purse. "For Binky."

Binky was their parrot.

Then with a flutter, a pair of hugs and two air kisses, the twins were off, leaving Julia standing on the whitewashed veranda wondering who was crazier, she or the twins, as she pressed Mikey's birthday card against her heart.

"What were the Sweat twins doing here this morning?" Valery asked. She had finally dragged herself up to the Blueberry Room, looking better than Julia had expected, though her eyes were bloodshot and glassy.

"They brought a card for Mikey's birthday."

Valery paused in sanitizing the telephone. Her already pale face blanched whiter and took on a pinched look. "Oh."

Julia replaced the last blueberry-patterned pillowcase and

artfully arranged the pillows on the bed. A guest favorite, the Blueberry Room was painted in the original blue with white accents and a four-poster bed covered with a blue print counterpane. The fireplace, flanked by darker blue armchairs, was original to the house, and a lace-curtained window looked out on the circle driveway with a view of the peach orchard. There was something special about the Blueberry Room that people enjoyed. Except for now when Valery's reaction to Mikey's name irked her.

"Did you even remember?"

"Of course I did," Valery snapped. She tossed her cleaning cloth aside, grabbed the vacuum cleaner and flipped the switch, filling the room with noise.

That's the way it always was with her family. Silence. Don't talk about the fact that Michael was alive, that he still had birthdays, that the anniversary of his abduction came around with painful regularity. If they didn't discuss him, fragile Julia wouldn't fly to pieces. She wouldn't fall into another depression and forget to eat or dress or pay her bills.

Julia grabbed the Windex and headed into the bathroom, where she scrubbed the already clean mirror with a vengeance.

Valery stopped the noisy vacuum and came into the bathroom. "I saw Gary Plummer at Pico de Gallo last night."

A change of topic. Naturally. "Okay."

"He asked about you. I think he's interested."

"What? In me? No. Gary and I are friends from grade school. Don't be dumb."

"Dumb? Just because I want my sister to open up to the world and be happy again."

What she really meant was that she wanted Julia to forget she'd had a son and stop waiting for him to come home. "Don't, Valery."

"Why not? Tell me that much. You've shut yourself off from everyone."

"I'm with people every day."

Valery scoffed. "That's business. Guests who come and go. I'm talking about a personal life."

"Like yours?" Julia wanted to suck the words back inside. "I'm sorry. That was uncalled-for."

Valery's lower lip trembled. "I had a couple of drinks last night. Stop making a federal case out of it."

Julia pulled her into a hug. "Hey. Want me to do your toenails later?"

"Would you?" Valery returned the hug with enthusiasm and then huffed a short laugh and pulled away. "I'm such a pushover."

Which was exactly the problem. Valery was too nice. Too Southern-girl-accommodating so that men who couldn't even spell *gentlemen* took advantage of her. Julia had never understood why her sister thought so little of herself or why she chose the kind of men who misused her. They'd been raised by the same parents and as the younger sibling, Valery was the favorite. She should have been confident and strong. Instead, she was a rug for men to walk on, and Jed the jerk was only the latest in a long line of creeps Valery had allowed to make her miserable.

"I found another marble this morning," she said as a peace offering. No point in pushing the topic closest to her heart. No one wanted to listen.

"Really?"

Julia took the stone from her pocket. "Looks similar to the others."

"Where did you find this one?"

"On the rug under Bingo."

They both glanced at the Aussie sprawled like an ink spill on the gleaming heart-pine hallway. His tail thumped. Bingo wasn't allowed in the guest rooms, but that didn't keep him from following his owner from room to room.

"Do you still think he's bringing them inside?"

"He must be digging them up somewhere on the property. What other explanation could there be?"

Valery wiggled her fingers beside her head and grinned. "Ghosts?"

"Now you sound like the Sweat twins. If this old place had ghosts, wouldn't someone have seen one by now or had some sort of supernatural experience?" *Someone besides me, the nut job who hears children laughing.*

"Maybe they have and were afraid to tell us."

She was right about that. "Have you ever seen or heard anything?"

"I've had the creepies a few times as if someone was watching me, especially in the carriage house."

The old carriage house *was* creepy but not because of ghosts. "Because we haven't done a thing to it. The cellar's the same way. Once we clean out the spiderwebs and all that ancient junk and start the remodel into more guest rooms, the creepies will disappear."

"Oh, you're no fun at all. I would love to have a ghost or two to make things interesting around here. Haunted inns attract crowds."

Which is one of the reasons I don't tell you everything. "I like things the way they are. Peaceful and quiet."

"No excitement in your blood. I swear you are not related to me. Give me bright lights and party time. Give me Vegas and fast cars and hot men." Valery spun toward the window and stopped. "Like that one. Holy guacamole! Come here, Julia. Check this out."

"I don't have any more guests on the log for today." But she crossed to the window anyway. "Oh."

"What do you mean, *oh*? Do you know him? He is gor-ge-ous. And a little wild looking. Yummy."

"He had car trouble this morning up on the road. Mr. Oliver gave him a jump."

"I'll give him a jump." Valery pumped her eyebrows.

Julia snorted and swatted her sister's arm. "I thought you and Jed were back together."

"We are. I'm kidding, but I ain't dead like some women I know."

Julia ignored the pointed comment. "I'm going down to see what he wants."

"You're not leaving me behind. I might be taken, but I like to look. And you could use a man in your life." She poked a finger at Julia's chest. "Maybe he fell madly in love the moment he laid eyes on you. Maybe that's why he's back."

Julia hit her sister with the pile of dirty linen. "Hush."

Valery laughed, stopped at the mirror for a quick fluff and then followed Julia down the stairs.

Eli Donovan stood at the back entrance, holding a mug imprinted with the logo of Peach Orchard Inn.

"Ma'am," he said when Julia opened the screen.

Valery swept to her side. "She's Julia Presley. I'm Valery Griffin, her sister. And you are?"

Eli looked as if he wasn't quite sure what to make of the vibrant, gregarious brunette who talked a little too fast. "Eli. I brought back your mug."

Julia took the cup from him. "Thank you."

"The coffee was good."

"Would you like more?" Valery pounced on him like a cat on a grasshopper. She pushed the door wider. "Come on in. Coffee is always fresh and available for our guests' pleasure."

Oh, great. Julia fought not to roll her eyes and groan.

Eli glanced her way, and she could have sworn she saw

amusement in his leaf-green gaze. Seeing the humor, too, she smiled. "Might as well come in, Eli. My sister is a steamroller. She seldom takes no for an answer."

Eli followed the two sisters through the immaculate copper-and-cream kitchen into a breakfast room with cranberry-red walls, white trim and a wall of sparkling windows. Six square tables were set with white linen and napkins in the same deep red as the walls. He noticed the scent again, as he had this morning. Subtle. A waft of fresh bread and clean air. A far cry from the rancid human odors of his past seven years.

He felt out of place, miserably so, but he was here and he was going to do this no matter the result. A man looking to start over had to start somewhere.

"Pretty," he said, surprising himself.

The woman named Valery beamed. She was a looker, long, wavy dark hair and lots of curves, with a vivacious personality that promised a good time. But it was the quieter Julia who drew his interest. Dressed in casual beige slacks and white buttoned blouse, she had a calming way about her. Like this house. Serene. That was the word. He hadn't used *serene* in a long time.

"I thought I'd lost this cup forever," she said.

"I almost forgot about it."

"Have you had breakfast? I know it's closer to noon, but brunch perhaps? There's still some casserole left."

"I'm okay." He wondered if she always tried to feed people or if he simply looked pathetic.

"You'll have something, Eli," Valery said. "Julia is a fabulous cook. Maybe her muffins or some peach tea?"

"I heard about that tea."

"Really? Where?"

"A police officer in town."

Julia's blue eyes rounded. "Don't tell me you got a ticket?"

"No, nothing like that." Man, she was pretty, her voice as smooth and Southern as a praline sundae. Classy and cool. Like his mother's. A dull ache tugged behind his breastbone. He averted his gaze, found the view outside the windows.

"Was it Trey Riley?" Valery asked, coming in from the kitchen with a plate of food that made his mouth water. "He's the cutest thing."

"That was his name. Nice guy."

"Sweet as pie. Here you go. Julia's ham-and-egg strata. Julia, get him some peach tea." She winked. "If you hate it, I'll make fresh coffee."

"Nobody hates my peach tea," Julia called from inside the giant stainless-steel refrigerator.

Feeling like the beggar he was but hungry enough not to care, Eli dredged up the dry bones of his mother's manners. "Would you care to join me?"

"Sure." Valery plopped down across from him and propped her chin on her hand. "Julia, bring me some tea, too, and maybe a muffin."

"Are your legs broken?"

Eli smiled at his fork. Valery laughed but flounced up to serve herself. "Sassy wench."

In seconds, both women were back. Valery had joined him at the table while Julia stood a little apart next to the gleaming windows sipping a glass of peach tea. He wished she'd sit down, too, but instantly retracted the wish. She had no business sitting anywhere near him.

Eli sipped at his drink. Cold, sweet and fruity. Three peach slices floated with the ice cubes. "Terrific. Thank you. The casserole is good, too."

He'd said thank-you more times today than he had in years. He was pretty sure he'd wake up in a minute back in his cell.

"I assume you got your car running again."

"Thanks to Mr. Oliver." He reached into his shirt pocket. "Is he around? He left this wrench."

"He and his wife went into town for a while, but I can give him the tool when he returns."

Eli handed it over. He wasn't a thief and didn't want anyone thinking he was. Didn't need the grief and he sure wasn't going back to prison. Especially now when his boy needed a dad. "Tell him I won't forget his kindness."

"I'll do that."

"Yours, either."

She only smiled, but the soft look was encouragement enough to give him an opening. He'd rehearsed his speech, his arguments and ideas all the way from the park. He'd even stopped at the In and Out Quick Stop to splash water on his face and comb his hair, a shaggy bunch of waves that needed a barber's hand. He knew how he looked, like a homeless street bum, a description, no matter how shaming, that wasn't far from the truth. His idea of home was his Dodge and, when money allowed, a room in a rent-by-the-week roach motel. Haircuts and soft beds would have to wait.

What was he doing here? What made him think he could do this? He was broke and homeless. Just because a little boy had his DNA didn't make him a father.

The familiar, dreaded knot formed in the pit of his stomach. *Loser. Convict. Get up and get out of here. You'll never make this work.*

His hand trembled on the fork. He put it down and reached for the red napkin. The delicious ham and egg felt leaden in his belly. He took another sip of peach tea, swallowed to chase away the negative voices.

This wasn't about him. He knew what he was, but his son didn't.

A boy needed a father. Eli should know. Losing his parents'

love and support had been a chain saw through his soul that had left him with a gaping emptiness he couldn't fill.

For the sake of a child he didn't even know, he had to ask. If Julia rejected his idea, which he fully expected, he'd try the pizza place. And if there was an application, he'd lie. They didn't run background checks, did they?

Nobody in Honey Ridge knew him. He could start fresh, his secret tucked away inside, and build a life his son could respect. He should have used a false name, but it was too late for that now. He'd have to hope no one noticed him enough to check into his past.

He folded the napkin and laid the starched cloth next to his empty plate. The Donovan table always had ironed napkins. "Your peach orchard needs maintenance."

The sentence had come out wrong, blurted and abrupt. He clenched his back teeth. Polite conversation was barely a memory.

Julia tilted her head as if she wasn't quite sure what he was getting at. Caught in the sunlight, a stray blond tendril spun gold along the curve of her jaw.

"We'll get to it eventually."

"I can do it." He rushed on before she could reject the idea, stunned by the vehemence with which he desired her approval. "Officer Riley thought you might be ready to start work on that old carriage house."

She glanced toward the tired old building set half a hundred yards beyond the house. "I'd love to, but money is an issue."

"I understand." He focused on his plate, afraid he'd see rejection in her eyes, afraid he'd give away his desperation. A remodel like this could take months, maybe longer, and time was money in his pocket. "What if I made you a good deal?"

"What kind of deal?"

He flicked a glance at her. She gazed at him with more interest than he had right to hope for.

"I need work. I could help with the orchard and other odd jobs around the place. I have experience in construction." Thanks to the prison system, which he was very careful not to mention. "In exchange for room, board and a small salary, I could do those things and repair the carriage house, as well. Whatever you need done."

Julia brought her tea to the table and sat down. His heart beat a little faster, but he kept his expression bland.

"I don't know. Material costs alone—"

Valery pointed a muffin at her sister. "We won't get another offer like that, Julia. A construction company costs out the wazoo. Even Sam Baker charges more than we can afford right now, and he's the cheapest around."

"We can work something out. I'm flexible." Eli tried to keep his voice calm as if he wasn't desperate, but his chest was tight with hope. He'd not hoped for anything in so long he hurt with the wanting. "Hire me on a temporary basis. For the summer. If things work out, we can continue. If not..." He shrugged. He'd make this work. He had to.

Julia stared in the direction of the weary old building. He could see the wheels turning and hoped they were turning in his favor. "I'd sure love to get the carriage house remodeled. It's a distraction from the rest of the grounds."

"The added revenue from renting out the carriage house will offset the cost of remodeling and pay my salary."

Her focus returned to him. "In the long run."

"That's the way business works. Spend some to make more." He knew about business. Once he'd even had dreams, fueled by his father, and he'd shattered them as he'd shattered everything in his path.

"A healthier orchard will produce more fruit," Valery said. "And more fruit means more sales at harvest."

Julia pressed her lips together and looked off into the distance, thinking. Absently, she stroked slender fingers up and down the moist tea glass. The action sent shivers through Eli. He imagined those fingers touching him.

He jerked his gaze away and stood. "Maybe this isn't such a great idea."

"No, wait." Julia turned her attention back to him. "I'll have to look at the books and play with the numbers, but I think you may be on to something."

"I am," he said with more confidence than he felt.

"Are you honest?"

"Yes."

Valery laughed. "What did you think he'd say, Julia? Admit he's a burglar on a cross-country crime spree?"

Eli remained rigid as rock, unblinking. Julia held him by the eyes, studying him as if she could see inside. He wanted to squirm and look away but understood this was his chance. Maybe the only one he'd have.

"You can trust me."

"Drugs? Alcohol?"

The dark days circled in like buzzards. "Neither."

"I won't allow wild parties or drunks or drugs or anything that could harm this inn's reputation. Screw up and you're history."

"You have my word." It's all he had.

"Do you have anything planned this afternoon?"

Oh, sure. An appointment for tea with the queen. "No, ma'am."

"Good. Stick around and we'll talk this out, walk through the carriage house, discuss the particulars and see if you still think this is something you want to tackle."

He didn't tell her he was down to few choices. He'd take what he could get at this point. Even though the thought scared him more than a shank in the shower, he was staying in Honey Ridge near his son. "And if it is?"

"Then you're hired."

10

Peach Orchard Farm
1864

Will paced the foyer at the bottom of the stairs next to the outer doorway, ready to be about the day's work. At the first sound of voices, he stopped to look up the staircase. Charlotte Portland, tidy and serene, came down the curving steps, brown boots tapping softly against the hard wood with two boys following along like puppies. She was lovely, kind and wise, and seeing her each morning had become a highlight of his long, often discouraging day.

Young Benjamin's excited voice carried to his ears. "Captain Will makes marbles back in Ohio, Mama. And he's the only son like me. And he has two sisters and a best friend named Gilbert who works in the factory. And Captain Will—"

"Benjamin, hush." Mrs. Portland's words were soft admonishment.

A smile stirred in Will's middle. He'd taken a shine to the youngsters. Benjamin, fair like his mother, and Tandy, the light-skinned slave with the persistent grin and keen mind reminded him of his oldest sister's boys, not in looks but in manner. They amused him, took his mind away from the worries of war and reminded him that there was some kind of normalcy still to be found in this state of divided loyalties called Tennessee. He prayed neither boy should ever see any more of the war than he'd brought with him. That was horror enough.

His chest tightened when the mistress of the house turned her gentle eyes on him. In the days of watching her in the sick rooms and observing her quiet, efficient running of the household, he'd come to admire her. She was a fine woman. A disturbing hum of pleasure tingled the back of his neck.

Will straightened his shoulders to attention, and the sword bumped his thigh in a reminder of who he was and why he'd come to Charlotte Portland's farm.

She was another man's wife. A Confederate sympathizer. He'd do well to remember both.

"Captain Will, Captain Will!" Benjamin thundered ahead of his mother down the stairs. The young slave boy was not far behind. They came to a breathless, grinning halt in front of him. Ben executed a clumsy, endearing salute. "Sir, your message has been delivered!"

"Well done, boys. Well done." Will returned the salute but his attention drifted to the woman gliding toward him, neither breathless nor grinning.

"Captain," she said simply, coming to stand before him, those small, usually busy hands resting serenely at her waist. "Good morning."

He doffed his cap and held it in his hands, though his shoulders remained tight. "Ma'am, I'm sorry to trouble you again. If your husband was in residence I would take up my concerns with him."

Indeed, Edgar Portland had shown his bloated, furious face

but twice since the company's arrival. Once to express his indignation at the outrage of being invaded before storming away on his horse, and the other to chastise his wife for aiding the enemy. A man who didn't defend his women held no esteem in Will's opinion.

"My apologies." Charlotte's mouth tightened and those tender hands began to work the cloth of her skirt. "Boys, please ask Lizzy to bring coffee for the captain while the pair of you remain in the kitchen for breakfast."

"Aw, Mama, I want to talk to Captain Will."

Will touched the boy's shoulder. "A soldier obeys orders, son." He winked. "I think I smell ham."

Tandy cut a glance toward the kitchen. "I sure am hungry, Ben."

"Me, too."

As the pair galloped into the kitchen like young ponies released to new pasture, Lizzy appeared in the opening of the double doors. "I'll bring the coffee, Miss Charlotte, and look after the boys. You'll be wanting breakfast, too. There's ham and biscuits."

"Have the patients been fed?"

Mrs. Portland's question deepened the affection he felt and didn't want. For indeed, patients lined her parlor and dining room on rows of pallets, makeshift beds of little more than a blanket or quilt or a bundle of rags. All of them provided by Charlotte Portland.

"No, Miss Charlotte. Cook is working on that now."

"I'll eat later."

Lizzy's proud chin jutted stubbornly and doe eyes glittered with fierce affection. "You can't go working all day again without food."

Will's head snapped toward Charlotte. She'd not eaten yesterday?

Charlotte brushed a hand along the hair above her ear, a smooth strip of blond pulled tightly into a bun. A loosely knit blue chignon covered the knot but couldn't hide the golden shine.

Will felt awkward to notice such a thing as a woman's hair. With Charlotte he was noticing too much.

"Don't worry about me, Lizzy," she said. "I am hale."

The maid didn't argue but simply stood in the doorway, her black gaze fixed on Mrs. Portland. Charlotte took no umbrage at the impudence, and Will wondered at the relaxed relationship between slave and mistress.

"Mrs. Portland." Will touched Charlotte's elbow, surprised at himself for taking the liberty. "She's right. You need your strength."

The slave's sharp gaze cut to him and settled there in speculation. Like a man burned, he drew away. "If you please, ma'am, could we have a word in your husband's study?"

Lizzy gave him one long, final stare before fading back into the kitchen.

Once inside the small study, Will rotated his hat in his hands as he waited for Mrs. Portland to be seated at her husband's writing desk, and then he took the black haircloth chair next to her. She was close enough that her lemony scent drifted to him, a disturbingly pleasant variance from the campfire smoke and coppery blood that clung to this stately home.

Without preamble and in defense against her appeal, he said, "Private Stiffler discovered a rebel hiding in your orchard last night."

She blanched, pressing back against the mahogany desk chair, a hand to her throat. "In the peach orchard?"

Had she known? Was she harboring and aiding the enemy outside while inside the house his men bled and suffered?

Will watched her shocked reaction, studied the clear-as-

June blue eyes. Either she'd missed her calling onstage or she hadn't known. The relief he felt disturbed him as much as the persistent attraction.

"Yes, ma'am. Stealing the last of the peaches. Are you aware of other rebels nearby?"

"Until you came, the only soldiers we've seen were new recruits marching off to war from Honey Ridge."

"When was this?"

"Last fall."

Did he believe her? His first inclination was yes, but he had not become a captain because he was foolish or made rash decisions. He'd invaded her home, taken her belongings and would take more before he and his band of injured moved on. Mrs. Portland had been nothing if not cooperative and caring, but she could not want him or his army on her farm.

He was drawn to this woman who worked tirelessly with an uncommon compassion. In another place and another time... Will stopped the rabbit trail of thoughts.

He had a duty and he would do it. But because of women such as Charlotte Portland, he would not become as base as some, looting and robbing and taking spoils of battle like savages.

He prayed he'd never have to.

"What will become of him?" she asked. "The man you found."

"He's our prisoner. When we move out, we'll take him along."

"Won't he slow you down?"

"No." Prisoners were not allowed to slow the progress of fighting men. But he did not share that bit of bad news with Charlotte. "We suspect he's a deserter."

"You could let him go." Her lips formed a thin, worried line. His gaze was drawn there.

"Impossible."

"Why?" She fiddled with an inkwell situated on the open desk, a reddish-walnut affair bare of papers.

"There is a war going on, Mrs. Portland. I have men to protect."

"Is he so dangerous, then?"

Will huffed a short, unhappy laugh. "The only danger he presents is the amount of fleas and lice covering his body. He's so scrawny his bones rattle."

"The poor soul is starving. You could leave him here."

He wished he could. Just as he wished he could send all his men home. But because he could do neither, he didn't respond.

Lizzy, in her snowy apron and head wrap, brought the coffee. Once again her sharp glance slid between him and Charlotte. She was watchful, protective of her mistress, and he would not be at all surprised if she stood guard outside the door.

"Your maid doesn't trust me," he said, after Lizzy left the room.

"Should she?"

The question bothered him. He wanted to be trusted but, indeed, with the enemy, he could not make that promise. "Have you owned her long?"

Something fierce and dark flashed in Charlotte's expression. "My husband owns slaves. I do not. Nor would I if the choice was mine to make."

Her passion gave him pause. He set the coffee on a side table. "You are loyal to the Union?"

"I am loyal to my home and family. Your war bewilders me."

"As it does all of us, Mrs. Portland. There are times when I—" He stopped, aware he revealed too much.

"Times when you what, Captain? Wished you'd never joined such a ruthless cause? I'm sure those young men lying in our cemetery would wish the same if they could."

He blanched. Yes, she'd pinched a sore spot, for he was haunted by the loss of men, some of them hardly more than boys, who'd marched to war filled with fiery idealism only to face the harsh realities of butchery and death.

"I regret every lost man, whether Union or Confederate."

His revelation, one he'd scarce let himself think much less say, softened her. "I'm afraid I do not understand the politics of war, or the propensity of men to purchase human flesh. Both are obscene to me."

"Would you prefer the Union remained separated?"

"I would prefer, as scripture dictates, to live in peace with all creatures whenever possible." She grimaced and a flush colored her cheeks the shade of fresh peach skin. "Forgive me, please. Sometimes I forget myself. I shouldn't say such things to a man of your position and rank."

"Voicing an opinion is not a cardinal sin."

"No? Some believe a woman has no opinion, Captain."

He wondered if she meant her husband but refrained from asking such a private, personal question. As it was, he shocked himself at the ease with which they conversed. She was bright and knowledgeable, qualities he'd been taught to admire in a woman.

"I beg to differ, considering I have two sisters with sharp minds and sharper tongues and a mother who runs the local temperance league and is an outspoken abolitionist. Father has given up trying to contain them."

At last, she smiled, and Will realized he'd been waiting for that glimpse of sunshine. "My father is a vicar, an ardent student of both philosophy and scripture. Unfortunately, my mother showed no interest in his rather lengthy dissertations on the human condition. I, on the other hand, enjoyed them and was allowed to read widely and speak my mind. Perhaps too much, as I have learned since coming to America."

Ah, that explained a great deal. "How did a British vicar's daughter come to marry a Tennessee farmer?"

He was going too far, asking questions that pushed into her private affairs, and yet for the life of him he could not stop. He wanted to know everything about her. If he told himself his reasons were for the good of his army, there was truth in the lie. Until he knew her well, he could not be assured of his men's safety. But the rest was pure self-interest. He admired Charlotte Portland.

If his question offended her, she gave no indication. Rather, she laughed. "In the usual manner, I'm sure. Tell me, Captain, are you a married man?"

"No woman will have me," he said in jest, and yet the stab of betrayal was anything but amusing. A man who'd loved and lost did not take such things lightly.

"Doubtful, sir."

"And why is that?" he asked, amused, intrigued, interested.

She smiled again, the light merry in her eyes. She was enjoying their little spar, as was he. "Are you fishing for a compliment, Captain?"

"Do you have one for me?"

One pretty eyebrow twitched upward as she tilted her head, moving a smidgen closer, enough that he felt the rise in his pulse.

Voice light and teasing, she said, "Perhaps, I do."

How charming, he thought. Charming, lovely and good.

Will leaned forward, tempted to touch the feminine fingers that draped over the edge of the desk and eager to know what she thought of him as a man. To feel the softness of womanly skin, something he hadn't touched in so long the void was an ache as strong as hunger. Charlotte was all the good things he appreciated in a woman. Edgar Portland was a very fortunate man.

Suddenly, he caught himself.

He had no right sharing such a lively and intimate conversation with a married woman. He had less right to touch her—even if that woman's husband had embarrassed and abandoned her.

Abruptly, he stood. "Begging your pardon, Mrs. Portland. I've overstayed. I must see to my duties."

"Is something wrong?" She stood with him, bewildered by his sudden change in behavior, for she couldn't know the turmoil churning beneath his rib cage. And he certainly couldn't tell her that he was attracted to her, man to woman, and would like nothing better than to take the weight of worry off her shoulders. Indeed, to wrap those slender shoulders in his arms and draw her close to his heart with a promise that all would be well.

"Thank you for the coffee." He refrained from taking her hand though he wanted to badly. A touch might prove too dangerous. "I've enjoyed our discussion."

"I hope I didn't offend you with my outspoken opinions."

"You couldn't. I treasure them." Again he fought the urge to touch her, only this time he longed to touch her cheek. Just to trace his fingertips over her dewy skin. "Charlotte—"

"Captain?"

"Will," he said, though he shouldn't have.

The tension left her shoulders. "Will."

Heart thudding in his throat, Will strode to the door and turned the knob. He looked over one shoulder and said, "Eat breakfast before Lizzy has my head."

Buoyed by her merry laugh, he made his exit. Standing in the dim hallway was the red-haired woman they called Josie. She glared at him.

"Good morning, Miss Portland."

Arms crossed tight over her chest, she tossed her head with a sniff.

Will gave a nod, but he felt the pinpricks of her animosity stab him in the back as he strode away.

11

Peach Orchard Inn
Present Day

A honeybee orchestra serenaded the rhododendron as Julia led Eli Donovan out the back way across the plank-board porch and down the steps toward the carriage house. Bingo ambled around the corner of the inn to sniff the newcomer's pant leg. A shadow of his former self, the old dog had once been as hyper as a kindergarten class on red Kool-Aid. Oh, the wonderful times he and Mikey had enjoyed. She wondered if Mikey remembered the dog who adored him, who had looked for him and refused to eat when Mikey didn't come home.

"That's Bingo," she said simply. "He's friendly."

Eli scratched Bingo's floppy ear and ruffled the neck fur, all the while looking toward the ramshackle carriage house. Julia winced, seeing it from a stranger's perspective.

"The previous owner, maybe even the one before that, didn't do anything with it, either. The rooms are piled with old junk."

The tired two-story building with the sagging upper balcony

sported a boarded-up bottom where carriages and later cars had been parked. At one end, near a tangled mass of wild roses Julia hadn't had the heart or time to cut down, was an entrance door with a dirty upper window. The top floor would have been the living quarters for the driver and his family, though now the dormer windows were obscured by cardboard boxes and other stored items.

"What's in there?" Eli asked.

"Odds and ends. Junk. A few ragged antiques. A bit of everything, I think. When Valery and I bought the house, we added to the collection. Anything we didn't immediately toss was stuffed in here or down in the cellar." And both had already been packed.

He paused a few feet out from the building and looked up. He had a quiet about him, a deep reserve. She couldn't decide if he was thoughtful or hiding something. The latter troubled her slightly. She knew nothing about this man who was willing to work for little beyond a roof over his head. What kind of man did that?

A desperate man. A man down on his luck. A man with nowhere else to turn.

But why? He seemed intelligent, well-spoken with the soft drawl of a well-bred Southerner. He was sad, an emotion that circled him like an aura. That alone had kept Julia from rejecting his strange offer outright. She understood bone-deep, unshakable sorrow.

"A lot of work," he said.

"Too much?" She watched him in profile as he perused the derelict building.

He was taller than her by several inches, with broad shoulders and well-muscled arms that had seen work. But he was too thin and the bones of his face were too prominent, as if he didn't eat enough. Neither detracted from his dark and rugged good looks, though noticing men was Valery's pastime, not hers. Yet, there was mystery about Eli, perhaps due to his tendency toward silence. Not that silence was a bad thing.

"No."

Terse, to the point and a little uncertain, as though he expected her to send him down the road in that jalopy of a car he drove. He intrigued her, and she wasn't sure how she felt about that.

Thanks a lot, Val.

She'd never hired anyone for help around the inn other than Dylan Winfeld, a teenager who cut the grass when she or Valery grew overwhelmed. But she'd known Dylan forever. His family lived next door to her on Sage Street. Eli Donovan was a stranger.

They'd reached the weathered entrance into the carriage house.

"Where are you from, Eli?"

The question seemed to catch him off guard. His hand paused on the doorknob and his body went still. He focused on the closed door. "Knoxville. Is this locked?"

She reached into her pocket and handed him the key. The door screeched open and he stepped aside to let her enter. A gentleman's action and one she duly noted just as she'd noted the way he held a fork and used a napkin and the way he'd remained standing until Valery was seated.

"You have family waiting there?"

Her back was to him as they entered the small space, but when he didn't reply, she paused to look over her shoulder.

"No," he said, and something in those mysterious eyes flickered. Family was not an easy topic for Eli Donovan.

"I'm sorry. I don't know what I'd do without mine. When—" She caught herself before it was too late. She'd almost said, *When Mikey disappeared.*

Talking about Mikey today seemed to be emotional quick-sand and she did not want to suffocate in front of a perfect stranger.

"You have other sisters? Brothers?" He asked the question quickly as if he somehow knew about her son and couldn't bear to hear the story again.

"Only Mom, Dad, Valery and me, but a pretty big extended family." She didn't add that her parents had been divorced for years but lived in the same town without killing each other.

"You're not married." Again, that terse comment as though conversation was a struggle. Was he naturally shy?

"Divorced." A wound that didn't throb anymore. David's marriage to Cindy Bishop had ended that. Not that she hadn't wept bitterly when he'd produced another son within a year. He'd forgotten Mikey the way he'd forgotten her. Clean sweep, put the past behind him and moved on as if they'd never lived together in the pleasant three-bedroom brick house on Sage Street. "You?"

Theirs was a casual conversation, nothing personal, a potential employer getting to know a potential employee.

"Never." He gave a short, self-deprecating huff that made her wonder.

When she tilted her head in question, his gaze shifted from the rising stairs to the door leading into the carriage bay. "Up first or through the lower floor?"

"Let's go up."

"You should lead. I don't know the way."

She stepped around him, aware of his size and close enough to catch the earthy, outdoors scent of him. Her elbow brushed his jean jacket and the rough texture prickled the skin on her arms.

Disconcerted, she gripped the railing and started up. His movement behind her was quiet, but she could feel him there, a polite distance though still too close for comfort. She felt self-conscious, as if her hips were too wide and their sway meant something other than advancing up a set of narrow, rickety stairs.

At the top, a musty, dusty odor greeted them. Julia stepped into the open space. "We could make two bedrooms and baths up here, I think. Or perhaps a family suite."

He regarded the crowded space with interest. "A lot of stuff up here."

"I warned you. Valery poked around in some of it. Old trunks of clothes, discarded furniture, tools, anything and everything. It appears everyone who ever lived here left things behind."

"What are you going to do with it?"

"Considering we've had no immediate plans to rehab the space, I hadn't really thought about doing anything, but you're right. To transform this into guest rooms, we'll have to get rid of everything."

"Or store it somewhere else."

"Maybe I could have a sale."

He hitched one shoulder. "Maybe."

"First, we'll have to sort through, I guess."

"I can do that for you." He gestured toward a battered vanity. "How old is this place?"

"Pre—Civil War, though I doubt any of the furniture is that old."

She shoved a box out of the way to make a path to the dormers. A spider darted across her foot. She let out a squeak and jumped back.

A shiny boot, its relative newness out of sync with the rest of the man, obliterated the hairy creature.

Julia gave an embarrassed laugh. "I hate spiders. A neighbor boy used to torment me with them." She didn't know why she'd felt compelled to add that last bit.

"Probably plenty of them in here."

"A joyous thought," she said wryly. "And another reason I have avoided the carriage house."

The corners of his mouth quivered like the stirring of a single leaf by a breath of air. His eyes lit and, every bit as quickly, dimmed.

Had he smiled once today? Did he ever? What weight could a man possibly carry that he rarely smiled? Even she had found her smile again.

"Mind if I look around?"

"Go ahead. That's why we came, but if it's all the same to you, I'll stay right here."

"Spiderwebs everywhere." As if to prove the point, he waved his hand into a thick web strung between a stack of boxes and the wall and wiped the cottony mess down the sides of his jeans.

"Exactly." She remained beside a stack of boxes piled on top of a bureau in need of repair. The bulky piece of mahogany had been here when she'd first arrived and, like so many other things, had simply been too much to deal with at the time.

The wooden floor creaked beneath Eli's weight as he approached the windows. Thick, dusty cobwebs crisscrossed panes so dirty the sun barely penetrated the glass with a hazy, translucent light.

"Can they be saved?" she asked.

"The spiderwebs? Or the windows?"

A joke. The man had made a joke. Julia smiled. "Saving the planet does not include spiders."

The hard face softened. "The windows won't live, either."

"Darn." She stuck a finger between her teeth and gnawed a cuticle. "So much for authenticity."

"We'll save what we can and reconstruct the rest." He traversed the remainder of the second story, testing floorboards and running wide, competent hands over the decayed and peeling wallpaper. Julia had a moment of panic at the thought of her strained budget and the amount of money this project could take.

"Valery and I did most of the work on the inn ourselves. I'm not sure if I can afford to pay someone to do all this."

He turned, gave her another of his long, silent looks before his eyes slid away. There was something about his eyes— a hunger, a plea and, worst of all, a hopelessness that felt too much like kinship.

With a silent nod, he dropped his head and started toward the stairs.

Surprised, Julia put out a hand. "Wait."

He paused to look over one shoulder, holding to the rickety rail. His shaggy hair curled around his ears, a boyish contrast to the hard masculinity.

"Where are you going?"

A muscle twitched along his cheekbone. He met her gaze before glancing away. "To find a job."

He looked as defeated as any man could, a stray dog kicked one too many times.

Something basic and hurting called out to her. And because she understood desperation, she softly said, "We'll figure something out."

Dark eyes flicked up to hers, though there was no real hope in him. "You sure?"

Not in the least, especially not now with this strange awareness humming across the crowded storage area stronger than the smell of dust and age. "Do you really have the skills to undertake a renovation like this?"

"Yes." No waffling, no false modesty, but then she had a feeling Eli Donovan hadn't the energy for either.

"Okay." She released a small breath, puzzled that she wanted him to take the job. The bone-deep, abiding sadness that seemed to emanate from his every pore touched a chord in her, plucked a broken string that needed repair as badly as the carriage house. As badly as he did. "Ready to see the rest?"

Without a word, he descended the stairs. This time she was the follower, looking down on the top of his dark hair, at the growth swirl at the crown and at the broad shoulders that seemed burdened with the weight of the world.

Or perhaps she was merely being fanciful, conjuring images of a wounded soul in need of healing and hope. It wouldn't be the first time her mind had imagined things that didn't exist.

They reached the bottom, another area crammed with the flotsam and jetsam of Peach Orchard Inn's past lives.

"This area's not as packed. Thank goodness. I think the last owners parked a car here and kept the space reasonably shoveled out. There's an office of sorts through that door," Julia said, pointing to the south wall. "Anyway, I take it for an office. It might have been anything. But there's a bathroom, not a great one but with functional plumbing so I'm hopeful this area can become another guest room."

"Plumbing? Must have been added long after the original building."

"The carriage house could be newer than the inn. I just don't know. The old photos we used in restoring the house didn't show the backyard."

"Maybe we can find others."

"I'd like that. The inn's history interests me, but I haven't had much time to research."

They stepped around a bicycle with one wheel, a bedstead, wooden crates and an old telephone before pushing through the door into the other room. Dust and dirt layered everything.

Eli stuck his head into the adjoining bathroom, a three-quarter affair with a brick-bottomed shower. "Good enough."

Julia frowned at his back. If he thought this was good enough for her guests, they might have a problem getting on the same page. "Guests expect nicer."

He withdrew his head and leveled a look in her direction. "For me. I can bunk here."

"Here? No, Eli, room and board means one of the rooms in the house. You can't live out in this."

"Why?"

"Well—" She gestured at the sad, filthy room. "Look."

"You have cleaning supplies?"

"Yes, but—"

"You need your rooms for paying guests. This will do for me."

"There's no furniture."

He nudged his chin upward. "I'll find what I need upstairs."

He was the strangest man and Julia didn't quite know what to think of him.

While she pondered, he crossed to the single window and shoved upward, propping it open with a discarded brick. A whisper breeze of spring freshness wafted inside, bringing along a shaft of sunlight.

"No."

"My requirements are basic at present."

There it was again. The kind of word choice that said Eli Donovan was not an uneducated laborer, though he appeared to be. Who was the man hiding behind the silence?

The question jolted her. *Was* he hiding something? And if he was, did she dare hire him to live on the same property with her guests and two women alone?

12

"Well." Valery leaned against a porch column and watched Eli's battle-scarred car disappear around the curving driveway. "That will make the landscape more pleasant."

"Why do I get the feeling you aren't talking about the work he'll be doing?" Julia asked wryly.

Valery gave her arm a shove and tossed her hair, laughing. "Come on. Admit it. You think he's pretty hot."

"He has a certain rough appeal but don't go starting a romance, Valery. Eli Donovan is an employee. A temporary one at that."

"I don't know how he'll tolerate living in that carriage house. It's awful."

"He's living here in the inn until the carriage house is cleaned and repaired, although he says he's accustomed to roughing it."

Valery shuddered. "That's worse than roughing it. The place is practically falling in. And all that junk piled everywhere. Does the plumbing even work?"

"Barely. That's one of the jobs he'll have to tackle."

"Sounds too good to be true, if you ask me. What if he can't do any of this work and only wants free meals and a roof? Maybe he's a bum looking for a place to land. A con artist."

Julia studied her sister. Hadn't she thought the same things? "A minute ago you were trying to hook us up."

"Yeah, well… A sexy con artist. Not hard to look at."

Julia wouldn't argue that, but there was also another quality about him that touched her. Maybe the closed, watchful expression or the way he seemed out of place in his own skin. Or worse, the sadness.

"If he doesn't appear to be doing anything useful after a few days, I'll fire him." The wind swept a hair across her face. She brushed it away. "We've done enough renovations to know if he's worth his pay."

"That's true. And in the meantime we can enjoy the view." They started inside the house. Valery paused with a hand on the screen door and scowled toward the line of magnolias. "Do you think he'll work with his shirt off?"

Eli thought about the job he'd taken as he drove the wheezing Dodge through Honey Ridge, past the elementary school where small children played outside in the spring sunshine while a pair of sweater-clad teachers looked on. He slowed, careful to observe the twenty-mile-per-hour speed limit. One run-in with the local police, even a friendly one, was all he could take in one day.

With his window down, the children's shouts and laughter drifted into the car. Near the chain-link fence, a pair of small boys scrambled over a domed climbing apparatus.

Did his son attend school here? Was he one of the boys on the dome or perhaps the little guy in the red shirt dangling by one arm from the monkey bars? Or was that him up high, poking his head out the window of a wooden fort?

A tight fist clenched behind Eli's sternum. He knew nothing about children except he'd been a terrible one, spoiled and wild. A pretty little girl skipped past the fence, her dark hair bouncing, and thoughts of Jessica drifted in, quickly extinguished.

Curiously interested, though he'd never been before, Eli watched the children play, car engine idling roughly for a long moment until one of the teachers left her post and started in his direction, her focus on the ragtag car loitering too long and too close to her charges.

Eli lifted his foot from the brake and moved on, hoping the sharp-eyed teacher wouldn't peg him for a predator and call the cops. A crawly, worried feeling had him glancing in the rearview mirror.

He suffered the familiar sweat of fear and wondered if this would be his life forever, always looking over his shoulder, afraid his past would catch up and suck him under again.

Honey Ridge. Could he live here? At least until he figured out what to do about the son he didn't know?

After a stop at a dollar store, he drove on to Opal's house, where the old woman greeted him with a sour "I thought you'd decided to run like a yellow dog."

He deserved the verbal slap, so he took it as he'd taken many other slaps, both verbal and physical, during the past seven years. What was one more?

"I needed time to think." He jammed his palms in his back pockets.

Opal gave him no quarter. "And?"

"I found a job. I thought—maybe—" He was at a loss. So much conversation and too many decisions in one day. He, a man accustomed to having his decisions made for him, floundered.

Opal's stiff stance eased a slight amount, though not completely. She didn't trust him or like him much. Leaning heavily on the cane, she unlocked the storm door. "Come in."

After a reflexive glance behind and around, he left the sunshine and entered the dark, dreary house where his son was being raised. He waited for the hawkish old woman to sit and then retook the same chair from that morning.

"Where's the job?" Opal asked.

"Peach Orchard Inn."

Her thin eyebrows raised above her glasses. "Doing what?"

He told her.

"Is there a place for the boy?"

The boy. His boy. "What's his name?"

Opal pinned him with a long, cool stare. What kind of man didn't know his own son's name?

"Alex." She leaned forward, steadying herself on the cane. Like lady justice, she weighed him and found him wanting. "Alex Donovan Wise. They wouldn't let her give him your surname since you never married the poor girl, so she put it in the middle."

Heat and shame burned in his gut. "I didn't intend—I never meant—"

She cut him off. "Don't matter now, Eli Donovan. She's gone and you're not. The boy needs a parent."

"He doesn't know me."

"You'll get acquainted."

"I can't take him. There's no place yet." And he hadn't exactly told his employer that he had a son.

Opal leaned back in the chair, lips pursed as if she'd bitten into a green persimmon. "Then why are you here?"

He shifted, tugged at the neckline of his T-shirt, the sweat of uncertainty prickling his skin. "He'll have to stay here with you. That's for the best, don't you think?"

"The best for who?"

She wouldn't make it easy, but he could tell she was angry with him because of Mindy. He was angry with himself.

"Him. He doesn't know me. You're his family."

She snorted. "A sorry situation that is, too, but you're right, much as it pains me to admit. He'll need time to adjust to having a father."

The knife in Eli's gut stopped turning. He had no idea what he'd do or how he'd provide for a child. He didn't even know how to talk to a six-year-old. But he'd done so few good things in his life, if he was going to start over, he might as well start here where he'd unwittingly left the seeds of his future.

The front door burst open and a small boy entered the house, toting a camouflage backpack. When he spotted Eli, he stopped in his tracks and lowered the bag from his shoulders.

Eli started to sweat all over again. A gulf of emotion swarmed him like bees, full of both sweet honey and sharp venom.

Alex was a handsome boy, with Mindy's open expression and wide brown eyes, but Eli saw himself in the black Donovan hair, high cheekbones and cleft chin.

Oh, my God. I have a son. Oh, my God.

His breath fled as if he'd been sucker punched. Some primal response swirled up in his chest and throat, a feeling so full and rich as to be painful. This innocent little boy was a part of him, and he prayed to a God he'd nearly forgotten that this child would be a better man than his father.

"Where's my hug?" Opal asked to break the stunned, silent tension quivering in the stale air.

A quicksilver grin flashed as the child threw his arms around the brittle old lady.

"How was school?"

"Maddie ate my red crayon."

"That bad girl. Did it stain her teeth?"

Solemnly, the little guy nodded. "Teacher gave me another one."

"Good. Good." Opal patted the small, sturdy shoulder and turned him toward Eli. "Remember when your mama told you about Eli?"

Eli's heart went into wild palpitations. What was he supposed to say? To do?

Mindy's brown eyes studied him with childlike openness. What exactly had she told their son about him?

Eli swallowed a lump the size of a peach and, through lips drier than the Mojave, said, "Hi, Alex."

The boy hung back against his great-great aunt, wide-eyed and wary.

Eli rubbed his palms over his thighs. What did he do now?

The old-food smells in the house closed in on him, mingling with the smell of his own anxious sweat.

"The two of you need to get acquainted." Gently, Opal nudged the little boy. "Show Eli your dinosaur."

Eli detected a spark of interest and grabbed hold. "You like dinosaurs?"

Alex stared at him for several long, painful seconds and then grabbed his backpack from the floor and left the room.

Opal smacked her lips. "Bless his heart. He's been different since Mindy died."

"Different? How?"

"Moody. Sad. Gets mad real easy."

"Does he know I'm his father?"

"He knows. Can't say he understands."

"Does he know where I've been?"

"Some things are better left unsaid. He's only a child."

Exactly. Eli opened and closed his fists, opened them again and wiped his palms on the top of his thighs. "I'd rather we keep it that way if you don't mind. From everyone."

"Rattling skeletons is not my place. I'll keep your secret, Eli Donovan, but not for you. For Alex."

Eli breathed a little easier. If no one knew, he had a shot at making this work. He'd heard of people who'd moved to small towns to disappear and lived freely for years and years before anyone discovered their pasts.

"Understood."

"What's in the bag?"

In the emotion of meeting Alex, Eli had forgotten about the yellow dollar-store sack. "I thought he might like a Nerf football. A toy to break the ice." He shrugged. "I don't know."

He couldn't remember being six, but he remembered throwing around a football with his dad at some point, though it must have happened before Jessica died. They'd rarely spoken after that except to scream at each other over some idiotic stunt Eli had pulled.

"Take it on in there to him. A toy is a start."

With considerable misgiving, Eli took the plastic sack and followed her directions to Alex's room. The door was open.

"Alex." He stood in the doorway gripping the plastic bag like a lifeline, uncertain about encroaching on the child's space. Uncertain, too, about how to win a child's approval.

Alex sat on the faded brown linoleum playing with a small, plastic dinosaur. He'd kicked off his shoes and tossed the backpack onto a sloppily made twin bed. He glanced up briefly before returning to the toy.

"Do you know what kind of dinosaur that is?"

"Stegosaurus." The voice was soft and small and almost imperceptible, but the fact that he'd responded sent a shot of hope through Eli.

"I brought you something." Eli held out the sack. Alex didn't look up and, after a bit, Eli lowered the bag and stood there like a fool, feeling awkward. "Mind if I hang with you for a while?"

Alex's shoulder twitched ever so slightly and, emboldened by that small sign, Eli slid to the floor in front of him.

An hour later, his legs were asleep and Alex still had not said a word or acknowledged him. Opal appeared in the doorway, leaning heavily on her cane.

"Alex, supper's ready."

The boy pushed his toys aside and scrambled to his feet, ducking around her.

"You can stay if you'd like. I've got plenty of macaroni and cheese."

Eli found his legs and rose. Electric needlelike sensations made him grimace. After the miserable, silent hour, he would like nothing better than to escape.

The voice in his head that called him a coward was back. Running away wouldn't resolve the problem. He owed Mindy, and though the knowledge shook him, he hungered to know this child who carried his DNA.

"Thanks," he ground out, and hobbled along behind her to the dim kitchen.

From the table next to a window bearing faded red checkered café curtains, Eli spotted a small backyard littered with a handful of plastic toys, most of them bleached white in spots from exposure. He held Opal's chair, waited while Alex clambered onto his and then seated himself. Dinner was spare. Macaroni and cheese, carrot sticks and applesauce. He took tiny portions of each, unwilling to take food from his son and an old lady, no matter how hungry he might be.

They were a pitiful trio, full of silences. Eli appreciated quiet, but so much needed to be said that the air practically pulsed. He had no idea where to begin so he picked at his macaroni and watched his little boy eat.

By the end of the meal, Eli felt as hopeless as he had the day he understood his parents would no longer come to his rescue.

Later, back at the inn in a room too nice for a convict, he lay awake a long time and wondered what he was going to do to make things better.

13

After a month, the farm had settled into a rhythm. Healing soldiers meandered the lawn and woods while others camped in the parlor, too injured to do anything other than survive. Edgar had returned home but spent most of the evening locked in his study, refusing to come out except for meals and leaving the bulk of running the farm to Charlotte. Even the meals disturbed him for the officers ate in the dining room with the family. Her husband was, she noticed, indulging in his whiskey more and more. Frequently, he rode into Honey Ridge and didn't return until the morning. She refused to consider where he went.

He didn't even notice the attention a certain captain of the Union Army paid to his son and, yes, to his wife. Benjamin longed for a father, and Edgar's distance broke Charlotte's heart afresh. She couldn't help but wonder if he ignored Ben because of her, though she didn't know what she'd done to deserve her husband's coldness.

This morning, a hot August calm had fallen on the farm. Flies stirred in the thick air, sticky and insistent.

The captain regularly sought her out and, if the conversations about the soldiers and the war turned to tales from their childhoods and laughter over something Ben or Tandy had done, Charlotte figured they needed the moments of light to escape the dark reality all around them.

He was indeed a good man. He taught Ben and Tandy to catch a fish with their hands, showed them the mysteries of crawdad holes and gave them rides on Smokey. He and some of the healthier soldiers snared rabbits and ducks for the supper table, a blessing with so many mouths to feed and supplies rapidly dwindling with no replacement in sight.

After the routine chores, Charlotte left Patience at the piano, playing a lilting, happy Mozart, a daily pleasure that encouraged the healing soldiers. Though as simple as summer rain, Patience was also as sweet as sugared peaches. Josie had gone into Honey Ridge to a ladies' quilting bee while Lizzy and Charlotte searched for wild herbs and edible plants along the wood-lined river.

Ben and Tandy frolicked along in front of them, exploring every knothole and crawling creature. They were easy to keep an eye on. Even in the dabbled sunlight, Ben's cotton-blond cowlick stood out in sharp contrast to Tandy's tight black curls.

"Two peas in a pod," Charlotte mused, shifting her basket from her arm to the ground beneath a sweet gum tree. "I'm thankful they have each other. Ben would be such a lonely child without Tandy."

Lizzy was silent as, on her knees, she pulled a chicory root from the dark soil and added it to her basket. There was no need for words, for they both understood the unusual relationship Charlotte allowed between their sons, and neither knew what the future held for any of them, but particularly for the slave children.

Lizzy, too, understood as no one else did, that there would likely be no more children for Charlotte, which made Ben and Tandy all the more precious. The maid was a shrewd observer and missed little of what went on at Peach Orchard Farm. If Charlotte sometimes longed to ask where Edgar spent his nights, she refrained. Lizzy would know, but some things were better left unknown.

"Mama, the captain is coming."

At Ben's excited call, Charlotte followed the line of his pointed finger through the dappled trees of the woods. Her heart leaped with pleasure at the sight. Will and one of his soldiers came at them, carrying something.

"Would you looky there, Miss Charlotte? He's got a honeycomb." Lizzy started toward them.

With boyish smiles, the men approached with their treasure. "Spotted this yesterday when the boys and I were checking rabbit traps," Will said.

Charlotte brushed the dirt from her skirt and stood, delighted both at the honey and the company. "You robbed a beehive?"

Sugar was a scarce commodity and had been for a long time, so honey was especially welcome.

"With Joseph's smoke screen," Will said, bringing a smile to the other man's craggy face.

"Do it all the time back home," Joseph said. Charlotte noted the scent of smoke emanating from his worn gray shirt. "Pays to be a country boy."

Ben and Tandy buzzed around Will's legs, excited by the find. "We like honey, don't we, Tandy?"

"Sure enough."

Will handed the stick and bucket off to Tandy. "Take this up to the house to Cook." He winked. "Ask her to make biscuits."

"All right!" Carefully toting their treasure, the two boys headed off through the woods and, at a nod from Will, Joseph followed them. His protective gesture pleased her, elevated her already vaunted opinion of the captain.

She offered her gratitude with a quiet look.

When Lizzy walked deeper into the woods in search of herbs and roots, Will restrained Charlotte with a hand on her arm. In a worried undertone he said, "I was surprised to see you out here, Charlotte. What are you doing this far from the house?"

She would have thought her purpose was obvious, considering both she and her maid carried a basket. She hoisted it slightly. "Gathering greens and herbs. Why?"

"It isn't safe. You should stay closer to the house. Soldiers are camped only a few miles from here."

"Captain," she said gently. "Soldiers are camped in my front yard."

"There is a war going on."

She understood his concern, was even touched by the fact that a Union officer cared more for her safety than her husband, but the war had taken away enough. "All the more reason to wake up each morning and embrace the sun."

"I am responsible for your safety."

"Are you, Captain?" She gazed up into his dear face, for indeed, he'd become dear to her. The admission both shamed and delighted her, for Captain Will was a man most worthy. "You take on too much. The soldiers, the wounded and all of us at the farm? Such a burden is too heavy for one man, even a man of your character and strength."

She hadn't intended to add the last, but when his face lit with pleasure at the compliment she did not regret the slip of tongue.

"I promised to keep you safe, Charlotte, and I shall."

"You've done so. Nobly so, and I am filled with gratitude. However, I refuse to be afraid to walk in my own woods to gather much needed greens and berries."

"Then allow me to be afraid for you." He stepped closer, gaze intense enough to set her pulse clattering strangely, foolishly in her throat. "Please, Charlotte. Allow me or one of my men to accompany you on these excursions. I don't want anything to happen to you."

She saw, then, the depth of emotion of which Will Gadsden was capable. Though she'd known little of romance, less of love, the thick swirl of feeling and deep well of yearning was both stunning and beautiful. She must be careful, very careful, not to fall in love with William Gadsden.

"Captain," she said in a breathless whisper, afraid not of soldiers and war but of losing her heart, perhaps even her soul, to this man. She, a married woman, had much to lose. Clutching the basket to her side as if it were her virtue, she began to walk, worried that Lizzy or the boys would notice the intense exchange.

Emotions battled inside as heat prickled the back of her neck and her skin tingled with the knowledge that Will was mere inches away. Had she ever been this aware of Edgar?

Will walked beside her, silent, the crunch of boots on twigs fallen from the trees like the many human twigs who'd fallen to war, mere youth who would never grow to oaks. Even the dying leaves reminded her that the winds of war had blown him here, and those same winds would take him away.

"I don't want anything to happen to you, Charlotte," he said again, and then as if to cover the tenderness reserved for her alone, added, "To any of you."

But she knew and understood this man better than she'd ever understood her husband. He, too, felt the pull that neither of them could acknowledge. She prayed nothing would happen to him, either. He was in far more danger than she, but she dared not admit that she feared for him, cared for him.

Her gaze flicked to his and then back to the pungent sprig of purple sweetshrub.

"My father said something to me when I left England." The folds of her skirt swished, snagged on underbrush only to be released by a quick tug and onward movement. For this was Charlotte's way, as it had been when her father had betrothed her to an American stranger. With an eternal hope, she pressed onward against the snags and tears and clasping fingers of life.

"He said America would change me, but I should not allow it to define me." She flashed a look at his face. "I didn't understand his meaning at the time."

"And now?" he urged gently.

"I understand, and I am committed here." The words were reminders to herself of who she was and to whom she belonged. She let the purple blossom flutter to the forest bed to join its fallen comrades. "War is the same, Will. It will change us. Has changed us already in many ways. But we must never allow hate and brutality to define us. For then, we are eternally lost."

"I have despaired at times," he admitted, eyes downcast and face so very serious.

Though Charlotte's reserve ran deep, her caring ran deeper. She placed a hand in the crook of his elbow. "Because you are a noble man, Will Gadsden. A man of character and decency."

He put his hand over hers, trapping their fingers together inside the bend of his elbow. In gratitude, she thought, for the compliment she'd finally given. Perhaps she should have resisted his touch, but the gesture had been offered in friendship, and theirs was a bond of war and worry as well as understanding and solace neither could find elsewhere. Together, the Yankee captain and the British vicar's daughter walked and talked in the quiet solitude of their leafy seclusion and for a little while were safe from suspicious eyes.

14

Eli awoke with a start. Had someone touched him? He lay as still as death itself, listening, though his heart hammered so loud he could hear little else.

He took a few seconds to orient, to remember he wasn't in a six-by-nine cell where he'd ever been alert even in sleep.

Darkness throbbed around him. The cool night breeze flowed in through the window he'd flung open the moment he'd entered the small room on the inn's second floor. Julia simply would not allow him to sleep in the filthy carriage house or in his car when she had a perfectly nice room available.

He'd relented, more to please her than himself.

He breathed in slowly through his nostrils to calm his pumping pulse. Maybe he'd been dreaming. He often did. Usually of prison or, if his mind was kind, he dreamed of home and his family before they'd cut him off without hope. Those were the times he woke with damp cheeks and a pulsing abscess in his soul.

When no hulking inmate materialized out of the shadows, he sat up and dropped his feet to the side of the bed, scrubbed at his face with both hands and flipped on the lamp at bedside.

Dawn was not far away, so he rose and luxuriated in his second private shower in twenty-four hours.

He halfway expected Julia to change her mind about the job. She'd taken pity on him. He'd seen it in the way she'd looked at him in that moment in the carriage house. Seen the pity and allowed it. Begged for it. That's how far a proud man could fall.

He dressed and, carrying his shoes so as not to disturb the house, tiptoed down the staircase and turned right toward the back entrance. As he rounded into the kitchen a sudden bright light blinded him.

He shrank back, instinctively throwing an arm over his face. Somewhere in his memory he heard a guard laugh. "What's wrong, rich boy, did I scare you?"

"Eli?" The voice was Julia's. "What are you doing?"

Eli blanched, guilty though he'd done nothing. He hadn't considered what she'd think if she found him sneaking around her house in the dark.

He lowered his arm and blinked as his eyes adjusted to the overhead lighting. "Couldn't sleep."

She frowned. "Is there something wrong with the room?"

"No." He wanted to laugh. If she had any idea where he'd been, she wouldn't have to ask. "The room's perfect. Do you always get up this early?"

"I don't sleep too well, either." She went to the counter and began dragging out coffee preparations as he pondered her admission. "So I might as well as get up and get to work."

"I thought the same thing."

"I wanted to talk to you about that."

Here it comes, he thought. She's changed her mind.

While he stood there in his sock feet waiting for the proverbial other shoe to drop, she scooped coffee beans into a mill and pushed Grind. The intense, earthy aroma filled his nostrils.

"Valery and I had a long talk last night over our accounts. We came up with a plan of attack and I'd like to ask your opinion."

Eli did a quick paradigm shift. He wasn't being fired—he was being consulted. "All right."

"The peach orchard is our seasonal cash cow and harvest is only a few months away. Perhaps you can split your time between prepping the orchard and cleaning out the carriage house. What do think about that?"

What did he think? Was she serious? "You're the boss."

She sloshed water onto the counter. He whipped a paper towel from the holder and stopped the oncoming drip. She blinked her thanks, watching him with a quiet regard that made his nerves jump.

"Yes, but you have an opinion."

"I'll keep that in mind."

"In the meantime, you'll keep the room here inside the inn."

He was already shaking his head. "No."

"No?" One fine eyebrow winged upward. He'd overstepped.

"If I'm living in a room, you can't rent it to paying guests."

Casting him a thoughtful look, she pushed down the coffee press's silver plunger and then filled two cups. "Drink your coffee and we'll talk about it."

Grateful, he did as she asked, propping a hip against the counter while she flitted around the sparkling kitchen preparing for the day ahead. She didn't understand his desperate need for privacy, for independence, and the need to sleep with the windows thrown wide open. He didn't expect her to.

As he watched her, this pretty Southern lady, attraction stirred, troubling him, but there it was. If he was going to work for her, he'd have to hold himself in check. He'd been alone for such a long time. As a matter of survival and to maintain his humanity, he'd learned to control his body and his thoughts. Not every man in prison did.

Julia, however, stirred his blood and reminded him that he was male. It had been a long, long time since he'd touched a woman. In his shoes, with his secrets, intimacy could be dangerous.

She'd boot him if she knew about the prison record, and with a child to consider, he could take no chances. An opportunity for redemption didn't come around every day.

He should tell her about Alex.

He circled the coffee mug with both hands, gripping tight while he found the right words. "I may eventually need more space than a room in the inn. That's another plus for living in the carriage house. We wouldn't disturb you."

Julia's cup paused en route to her pretty mouth. Eli glanced away from that tempting spot.

"I'm not sure what you mean. Who is we?"

His throat tightened around the unfamiliar words. "I have a son."

Julia heard the tick of the oven as the pilot kicked off, signaling readiness for the morning coffee cake. Her ears hummed with a peculiar out-of-body sound. Surely, she had not heard him correctly.

"You have a son?" She slowly set her coffee on the counter.

"Yes, ma'am." He fidgeted, his thumb tapping the edge of the cup.

"You said you weren't married."

He glanced up and right back down. "I'm not. Never have been."

She could see the subject pained him, but this was the last

thing she'd expected. A child? A little boy? Pictures of Mikey flashed through her head with lightning speed and squeezed the breath from her lungs.

"You should have mentioned this yesterday."

"I'm sorry." He'd gone back to that rusty, uncertain voice. "This won't affect my work."

"Do you expect to bring him here? What about his mother?"

Tilting his head back as if to examine the ceiling, Eli inhaled a long breath. As he exhaled, he said, "His mother died recently. I didn't know. That's why I'm here."

A motherless child. A fist of compassion clutched inside her chest. Little boys needed their mamas. *Oh, Mikey, where are you?*

"I'm so sorry. Poor little child." And Eli had been an absentee father. He hadn't known, he said. Did that mean he hadn't known about the child or about the mother's death?

His fingers lifted from the coffee mug in a shrug. "So, you see…"

She saw everything and nothing. A man she didn't know, who fascinated her, who was going to work for her, had a son he hadn't told her about. Should he have? Or was she overreacting because of Michael?

She'd second-guessed herself so much these past few years, wondering at her mental competence, wondering at her decisions.

"Where is he now?" she asked softly.

"Staying with his mother's great-aunt in Honey Ridge. She's his only other relative."

"Will he remain there?"

"For the time being while we get to know each other. I just thought you should know because eventually… He's my son. We'll be together."

"Who is his aunt?"

"Opal Kimble. Do you know her?"

"A little. At least by name." Though somehow in the mania of years since Mikey's disappearance, she'd lived in a cocoon of grief and depression and missed too many social events in Honey Ridge.

"She's in poor health. And Alex is…" He faded off again as if at a loss.

"Alex is what?"

"Sad."

Pity flared. "Of course he is. He's lost his mother."

"Exactly, and he doesn't know me at all. I wasn't…around."

Every dormant maternal instinct ached for the child. "How old is Alex?"

"Six. I hope this isn't a deal breaker."

She struggled, battled against the fear and grief rising like a tiger to consume her and the deep compassion for a motherless child. "No."

He flinched. "No?"

His haunted green eyes seemed to plead for understanding while expecting none. It killed her, this propensity he had for making her feel things.

"The inn has a no-child policy."

A tick of time passed and then two before he sighed, dejected. "Right. I understand."

The trouble was, Julia didn't, and she was left feeling guilty, as if she'd extinguished a lost man's only candle.

One afternoon, when the weather was especially warm and sweat beaded on Julia's face and under the neck of her camp shirt, she and Eli were in the upper level of the carriage house in search of usable items. Eli thought, and rightly so, that any found vintage items were not only cost effective but desirable to guests looking for a historic bed-and-breakfast.

After a week, his words remained few and cautious, but his

ideas for the restoration of both the orchard and carriage house were intelligent and insightful so that she'd stopped second-guessing the decision to hire him. He took his meals in the dining room almost apologetically and though Valery, when she wasn't out somewhere with Jed, talked a blue streak, she'd yet to crack the code that was Eli Donovan. And every evening after dinner, he drove the coughing old Dodge into Honey Ridge to see his son.

She felt guilty about the child, especially after Eli told her that Alex was having problems accepting him. They needed time together, but she couldn't give it to them. Having a child on the property was too much to ask. Still, there was something heart twisting in Eli's dogged efforts to be a good dad, and the fact that he'd not argued about the no-child policy.

She'd seen him walking the orchard in the moonlight, a restless soul like her who fought for sleep. She'd seen and wondered what haunted him. Was it the problems with Alex? Or the woman who'd died and left him a son?

"I can handle this," he said, motioning to the piles of junk and boxes they were sorting. "You have guests."

"The main work's caught up and Valery is around to take care of any needs that arise. This is kind of an adventure." She flipped the lids on a cardboard box. The truth was she found the restoration work with Eli more interesting than cleaning rooms and washing sheets. They'd discovered some fascinating antiques, including an old photo of a couple standing in front of the carriage house.

"Look out for the spiders," he murmured.

Julia instinctively jerked back and then caught Eli's smirk and laughed. He'd been joking. She found his levity endearing considering how bottled up he was most of the time.

"Better watch out, Donovan. I have a mean side."

His mouth twitched as he shouldered a headboard to one side and lifted a dusty tarp. In his quiet way, he said, "Eureka."

With considerable reservation, Julia eyed the claw-foot tub filled with more junk. Anything that went into her guest rooms needed to be of good quality. "It doesn't appear to be in very good shape."

"Don't let the dirt and old paint fool you."

"I'll have to take your word on that."

They'd found a number of unusual old items, many of which she didn't recognize, and she lived with curiosity about what she'd find next. Buttonhooks, quilting frame, an antique hair crimper she'd had to look up on the internet to identify, and even a set of porch corbels Eli planned to use as decorative shelf supports. He was a genius at ideas for repurposing items she'd likely have junked and admitted having watched more than his share of HGTV. She hoped he was right about the claw-foot tub. They were popular if in good condition.

"How are things going with Alex?"

"He doesn't say much."

"Neither does his dad."

Amusement flared his nostrils. "Believe it or not I used to be a mouthy kid."

"What happened?"

The humor faded. He bent to dig through the tub. "Life."

"I know what you mean. Life has a way of changing us all." Since that was a direction she didn't want to go, she said, "Maybe you should take Alex somewhere for fun. Boys like places they can run and be active."

"I thought about the park on the edge of Honey Ridge."

"Perfect." Mikey had loved the park, especially the monkey bars where he'd hang upside down by his knees and make gorilla sounds. The memory was so clear and sharp, tears spurted beneath her eyelids. She blinked upward to hide the reaction. "Say, I never noticed that before."

Eli followed her gaze. "An attic hatch."

"How can this building have an attic?"

"It may be only a crawl space to get to the electrical works."

"Or filled with more junk."

"One way to find out." He dragged a ladder over and centered it beneath the hatch. Julia steadied the ladder while Eli climbed up for a look.

Fingers splayed, he pushed upward with one muscled arm. The board groaned a warning before it gave and an avalanche of debris showered down.

"Eli!" Julia ducked her head.

"Get back!"

Dust and plaster and rotted boards created a thunderous landslide. Eli thrust both arms over his head and bowed at the waist, trapped on the ladder.

Clinging to the ladder lest Eli fall, Julia slid to her knees in a body curl, coughing and batting her eyes from the onslaught of dust.

The incident took only seconds, but it seemed much longer before the noise ended and they were left in a silent cloud of thick dust.

The ladder rattled and wobbled as Eli jumped to the floor and knelt beside Julia. "Are you okay?"

She coughed, fanning dust.

He grasped her forearm, the first time he'd touched her other than an accidental brush of fingers or arms, and hauled her to her feet. Julia gazed at him through the haze. His black hair was now gray and he was covered head to foot in dust and plaster.

She didn't want to think about the feel of his fingers on her skin or about how close they stood. "I'm fine. You got the worst of it."

Eli did a quick perusal. As he turned one forearm for inspection, blood dripped onto the floor.

Julia reached for his arm. His flesh was warm and firm. "You're bleeding."

"It's nothing."

"You may need stitches."

He recoiled as if she'd shot him. "No."

The reaction tickled her. "Don't tell me you're one of those tough guys who faints at needles."

"Something like that."

"I have a first-aid kit in the house. We'll try Steri-Strips first."

"Thanks." Using both hands, he dusted his T-shirt and jeans. Dust foamed up.

"Here, bend your head down."

He did as she asked and Julia dusted plaster and trash from his head. His too-long hair was soft and springy beneath the dirt and his scalp warm enough that Julia realized the intimacy of the action. She jerked her fingers away.

"You're going gray, Mr. Donovan," she said to circumvent the unwanted feelings Eli Donovan aroused.

"Wait till you look in the mirror." He picked a square of cardboard from her hair.

She turned his arm up and the underside continued to bleed. "Come on. We need to get this cleaned up."

"I'm too dirty to come inside." He glanced down at his filthy clothes. "Give me ten minutes."

"I'm just as dirty."

He jerked one shoulder. "My mother would kill me if I went inside her house looking like this."

Other than the day he'd arrived, this was the first time he'd mentioned his family. "You must miss her."

"Every day."

"How long has she been gone?"

"She's not. I—" He wagged his dust-covered head. Then as if the subject was too difficult, he pivoted toward the stairs. "Meet you in ten minutes."

He left her there, dusty and curious, as he disappeared down the steps. Something about his family hurt him. If not dead, were they estranged?

She debated asking him. Maybe she would at some point, but not to pry, not for cruel curiosity's sake. Only if, like the Sweat twins, she could comfort, for she, better than most, understood the type of callous voyeurism that had driven the memories of Mikey inside. The news media had nearly driven her mad.

Everyone had past sufferings and if Eli kept his tucked away, he had a right.

He didn't reappear for fifteen minutes, which gave Julia time to shower and change. Wet hair yanked into a ponytail, she headed to the laundry with the filthy clothes.

"What happened to you?" Valery met her on the staircase. She was dressed to go out and wearing expensive perfume.

Julia told her. "Where are you going this time of day?"

"Nashville. I put the day on the calendar a few days ago. Do you need Mom to come over and help out?"

"No, I'd forgotten is all." Nashville was a long drive. "Who's going?" They descended the steps together.

"Jed and me."

Julia made a disparaging noise. "Be careful."

"I'm a big girl." Valery grabbed her for an air kiss. When Julia frowned, she added, "Grumpy old thing. You're worse than Mom."

"I worry about you." She might as well save her breath.

Two taps sounded on the back door. Valery flounced to open it. Eli was there, his hair, like hers, wet and slicked back from his forehead. Small worry lines creased from side to side.

"Would you stop with the knocking and just come in. This is a place of business." At Valery's sharp greeting Eli raised his eyebrows.

"Don't mind her," Julia said. "She has a date with a guy who would make anyone crabby."

Eli came inside, left hand pressing a paper towel to his forearm.

"You're hurt! Oh, my gracious. Get in here." Valery, for all her flounce and spirit was a compassionate woman. Another reason Julia didn't understand what she saw in Jed Fletcher.

"It's nothing, but your sister insisted..."

"Trust me, I know." Valery rolled her eyes. "My sister is caregiver to the universe."

Before Valery could go on about things better left unsaid, Julia interrupted. "I think I hear Jed's truck."

A horn sounded, long and irritating. Julia ground her teeth. "Remind him that we have guests."

Valery lifted one shoulder in a helpless gesture. "Sorry." She wouldn't tell him any such thing.

Julia peered out the window and watched her sister climb into Jed's high-rise truck without so much as a gentleman's hand to hold. Jed remained behind the wheel, tapping his fingers in impatience. Her heart grew heavy with the knowledge that he was one more of too many men who didn't respect her warm and beautiful sister.

When she pivoted, Eli's green gaze was on her. He was no fool. She'd already figured that out.

"Some people don't know what's good for them," she said, and then because she didn't expect a reply, she turned their attention to his bleeding arm.

"The first-aid kit's in the utility mudroom." She led Eli through the kitchen toward the end of the house opening north toward the orchard.

The mudroom was her addition to the house, a combo bath and utility room for laundry and storage. She indicated a black countertop surrounded by white beadboard and deep gray walls. Eli dutifully surrendered his arm. A three-inch oval of red adhered the paper towel to the skin.

"The bleeding's stopped, I think. I cleaned out the dirt in the shower."

There was intimacy in the word *shower* with them standing close in the narrow space breathing the same laundry-fresh air. Julia focused her attention on gently peeling away the paper towel.

"Just rip it off."

"Don't try to be tough now. I know your secret fear of needles." She dabbed peroxide on the paper to soften it enough to peel away.

Black hair sprinkled the corded muscles and thick veins of his darkly tanned arm. She hadn't been this close to a man in a long time, and that itchy sprig of interest sprouted up again.

She flicked a gaze upward. Saw him watching her and said the first glib thing that came to mind. "You washed away the gray."

He grunted softly and broke eye contact.

His black hair was still wet and slicked back from his forehead. Drying edges played flyaway around his ears and neck. "This may sting. I'll try to be gentle."

Using her fingertip, Julia stroked antibiotic along the cut. His skin was warm and firm. "You might need a tetanus."

She fished a Steri-Strip from the box.

"Had one." He shifted slightly, readjusted his arm and, as he did so, his body brushed hers. "I'll hold the edges together and you tape."

Awareness sprang up like spring dandelions. With their heads together over the wound, Eli's damp shower-fresh scent filled her nostrils. His soft, warm breath feathered over her fingers as he leaned close to pinch the wound closed.

Voices sounded in the entry, a fitting distraction that reminded her it was time to set out the afternoon refreshments in the parlor.

She added a wide bandage atop the wound. "If that doesn't hold, you should see a doctor."

"It will hold." He removed his arm from the counter and straightened. A bloody smear remained behind.

From the kitchen, the telephone jangled.

"Go ahead." He nudged his chin toward the insistent caller. "I'll clean up."

Julia rushed to the telephone. Reservations were too important to miss a call.

But the call wasn't about a reservation.

Eli tossed the paper towels into a lidded trash can that popped closed with a metallic *thwang*. Nice of Julia to patch him up, but he was eager to get back to work now that he'd discovered the claw-foot tub. With a little TLC, the old tub would be a centerpiece in the downstairs bathroom. Julia would be pleased. She'd smile and say he was right, the way she had when he'd cleaned up the old iron bedstead he'd found for what would hopefully become his living quarters.

Warmth ballooned in his chest. Things were going better than he'd expected, better than he'd dared hoped.

He'd had that moment after the dust cyclone when he'd almost told her about his family. Not everything, of course. He'd never tell her that. She liked him, maybe even trusted him, and a prison sentence could wipe that away so fast, he'd be down the magnolia lane before the peaches ripened.

"Eli!" Julia appeared in the doorway, her eyes wide. "Come to the phone. There's an emergency."

Adrenaline shot up his spine. "Alex?"

"No. No. Alex is okay." She put a hand out, calming him. "It's Opal. She's been admitted to the hospital."

He hurried to the phone, the ramifications of Opal's illness banging around in his head. He listened to the nurse on the other end, made note of the details and hung up. The news was anything but good.

"She's had a stroke," he said grimly. "The prognosis isn't good." The old woman didn't like him but she'd been kind to his child. "Alex will be scared to death."

"Is he still at school?"

Eli shot a glance at the digital clock on the stove. "Not for long."

Her whole body tensed. Her breath came fast and short as if she was in danger of hyperventilation. "You have to go get him right now. You can't leave him alone."

Curiously, her voice had risen, almost in panic.

"I'll call the school and ask them to keep him there until I arrive."

"I'll call. You go get your boy. He's going to need you."

The gesture touched him even while her words scared him. With Opal in the hospital, he had no go-between and Alex had no anchor. They were about to embark on a shaky journey with an uncertain destination.

He was halfway to his car when Julia's voice called out. He turned and saw her hurrying toward him, her pale hair lifting as she moved.

She stopped in front of him, breathless, as she raised a worried, uncertain face to his and put him in mind of that first morning when she'd been crying.

He had the awful, unfathomable urge to crush her to his chest.

"Get Alex," she said, "and bring him here."

His hand stilled on the door handle. He hadn't even had time to ponder what he would do with his son. "Are you sure?"

She pressed her lips together in a thin line, gave one sharp nod and said, "Yes."

The answer cost her something that he didn't understand, but Eli was too grateful to question.

Unfamiliar emotions washed over him until his knees felt watery and weak. His mind worked to express his thanks, but his throat was so full he could only nod as he slid into the driver's seat and headed to Honey Ridge.

15

The afternoon in the woods with Will lingered in Charlotte's mind as she sorted and cleaned herbs, washed roots
and put the greens on to boil. She felt Lizzy's watchful gaze
upon her, certain her guilt showed though she'd done nothing wrong.

Finally, the work complete, Charlotte stole upstairs to the
blue room. She wrote to her mother, read Proverbs 31 three
times as penance for her troubled heart, and she prayed.

Edgar came home that night, and Charlotte took his return
as an answer to her prayers.

"You're tired," she said, following his limping gait into the
study where only this morning she'd met with the captain. She
was careful not to look at the chair where Will had sat that very
morning talking to her as if she was more than the conquered
foe, more than a farm wife who barely knew how to speak to

her husband. And wasn't that what drew her to the handsome captain and loosed her tongue and, God forbid, her heart?

Edgar grunted, expression sour. Since the coming of the Yankees, his jowls sagged more and bags pillowed beneath his eyes. The Federal occupation was taking a toll on this proud Confederate, and Charlotte was thankful for the pity that welled in her breast. Regardless of her prayers for love, pity and duty were all she could give her husband. But give him that, she would.

"Jacobs, that fool of a foreman quit the mill," he grumbled. "I'm left to do all the work myself." Her husband lowered his bulk into the desk chair with a heavy sigh. He looked as worn as old Hub and his foot was every bit as twisted as the arthritic old slave.

"What of Silas and Percy? Aren't they helping you?" She folded her hands in the fabric of her skirt, the smooth, cool softness of cotton a familiar comfort, a means to appear serene when her mind was anything but.

"Bah. Worthless. You and Lincoln have ruined them all. They're getting ideas in their heads."

Though Charlotte refused to apologize for teaching the slaves to read the Bible, Edgar's words raised the hairs on her neck. "They won't leave us, will they?"

"Who can say what slaves will do in these trying times? I should sell the lot of them while I can make a dollar. Worthless fools." He bent to his boots, rubbing at his right calf. "My leg aches all the way up my back. My laces, Charlotte."

Skirt forming a puddle of blue cotton, Charlotte knelt at her husband's feet and began to loosen his boot strings. She'd done the task many times before, but tonight the kindness was more than a wife caring for her husband's deformed and swollen foot. Tonight, the act was penance and a promise to be the wife she'd once vowed to be.

She tugged the slick black boots away, letting them fall to the wooden floor with a clatter that reminded her of the marching feet of soldiers. Soldiers. Captain Will.

Taking Edgar's hot, doughy flesh between her palms, she massaged along the crooked bone, rotated the bent ankle, and dug her thumbs into the ball and sides of his foot until his head tilted back in a pleasured moan.

In childhood, Edgar had suffered the agony of having his bones broken and reset in plaster. Charlotte could not see that the treatment had done a bit of good, though Edgar claimed the foot had once been turned ninety degrees inward. Now, it was only a misshapen lump of bone and flesh. She could imagine how much it pained him to stand and walk. She imagined and let compassion well.

After a bit, she rose and gently touched his shoulder. "Rest, dear. I'll heat water for a soak."

His head snapped up. "My foot pains fiercely. Bring the whiskey."

Her fingers tightened on the door edge as dread tightened around her middle with more grip than a corset. She stared at her husband, not daring to speak against his wishes but admonishing him with a pleading look.

His return stare was belligerent. "Do as I say, Charlotte."

With a dip of her chin, Charlotte exited the room, leaving her husband slumped in the chair, one arm on the writing desk, his bare and damaged foot jutting out across the polished boards. Defeat wreathed him like a laurel. Defeat and anger and disappointment. The latter was because of her, she was certain. She, his British wife with the strange ideas who had never quite been embraced by the Southern women of Honey Ridge, was a disappointment.

Her pulse clattered against her collarbone with the knowledge of how badly she'd failed and how much she desired to please her husband. Especially now when her heart threatened to betray them both.

The house had settled, though the voices of men playing at cards or sharing stories flickered with the lamplight. There was little she could call normal about her dwelling in these days of occupation, but at least the night was quieter than in the beginning.

At a sound from above, she glanced up at the ceiling, thinking of her sisters-in-law and son on the upper floor. Upon her return from town, Josie had been subdued, an unusual if welcome turn of events. Patience—dear and gentle Patience—had taken to her room to nurse a broken-winged bluebird found in the orchard by one of the soldiers who seemed particularly taken with the youngest sister.

Benjamin was tucked safely in the room next to hers with Tandy on a pallet at his side. Safe because of Will's promise of protection. She'd hugged them and listened to their excited re-telling of the beehive and the biscuits they'd dipped in sweet cow's butter and honey. If Will was in every other sentence, Charlotte could do nothing to change it. The captain had given them both something they sorely lacked.

While heating water and measuring the herbs, she listened for groans or calls of distress from the wounded and, relieved to hear none this night, hurried back to the study. Back to the husband to whom she'd pledged her troth.

In the hall outside the parlor, she heard Will's gentle, reassuring laugh. Her heart leaped toward the sound. Her memory flashed to those moments in the wood, moments of innocent conversation that felt stolen and wrong because of the pleasure they'd given her.

Why, dear Lord, did her heart not leap and dance toward her husband?

Edgar hadn't moved from his position at the desk, but now

he was writing in the ledger that housed the finances of the farm. At her entrance, he slapped the ledger shut with a vehemence that made her jump and slosh a few drops of water. Edgar gazed coolly at her from tired gray eyes.

"You have Lizzy to fetch and carry. I don't know why you insist on playing the maid."

He knew so little of the household these days. Did he not understand that they had all been pressed into service to the point of exhaustion?

"I am pleased to tend to my husband's needs." The choice of words thickened in her throat and she dared not glance at his face. For she suspected his most manly needs were met elsewhere.

Gently, she lifted his foot and placed it into the warm bath salts. With careful, intentional strokes she massaged and flexed, aching for a man embittered by a curvature of bone.

"Did you bring my liquor?" His tone was harsh and cutting. He knew she hadn't. Knew she didn't want to. The times when Edgar drank too much whiskey proved unpleasant for them all. Two months ago, he'd raised a horse whip to one of the slaves and his unleashed anger had frightened her more than the Yankee onslaught.

"Is the pain so terrible, Edgar?"

"Yes." The tone was colder than snow and harder than iron.

"I thought…perhaps…" She stroked a light, caressing touch along the muscles of his calf and raised her eyes to his. Holding a steady gaze wasn't easy with his dispassionate response, for her knowledge of seduction was sorely limited. And yet, she must try, both for duty and for honor.

"Perhaps you would join me in my room—" she intentionally lowered her lashes, feeling the fool, her heart thundering with hope and embarrassment "—for…a back rub."

Edgar simply watched her, but he didn't push her away and

she was emboldened. Her hand moved higher to his thigh. "Remember how you enjoyed my back rubs?"

In the early days of their marriage, he'd wanted her hands on him, wanted to touch and kiss and stroke and smooth his fingers through her unfettered hair. She'd almost forgotten how good it felt to be treasured.

When he said nothing, she rose and moved to his side. This was her husband. She'd borne him a son. She reached for his hand, entwining their fingers. She turned his palm up and placed her lips there. His skin smelled of corn grist.

"Wouldn't you like another baby, Edgar? Perhaps a little girl with your dark hair or another boy as smart and strong as Benjamin. Couldn't we try again?"

He reached for her, settled his grip on her waist and...dug in his nails. Charlotte remained perfectly still, absorbing his cruel fingers, throbbing with the brokenness of their relationship.

"I'll bury no more children, Charlotte," he rasped out, his face distorted with sorrow and fury. "Get the whiskey."

16

A child was on the way. A little boy.

Oh, dear God, if only it was Mikey. If only her gap-toothed eight-year-old who wasn't eight or gap-toothed any longer was on his way home from school, but there was no homecoming for Mikey today. Yet another small, hurting boy would be here soon.

During the agonizing wait, Julia served the afternoon refreshments with peach tea, made sure her guests were all provided for and then hurried up the stairs, thinking about the child. Anxiety made her hands shaky.

When she stepped outside the Blueberry Room, she heard a sound like pebbles rolling on tile, but there was no tile at Peach Orchard Inn. In that infinitesimal moment, a gossamer thread spinning out of time, she thought she heard a child's voice. She froze in the hallway, listened with such sweet hope that her chest was near to bursting, and when the sound didn't come again, she shook her head at the fantasy and went on with preparations.

By the time Eli's Dodge wheezed into the parking space at the back of the house, she was as ready as she'd ever be to welcome one small, frightened guest. With the smell of chocolate-chip cookies warming the house, she stepped out onto the veranda and down the steps, where dozens of butterflies colored the flowers in rainbow hues.

Eli and Alex stood beside the pitiful old car on the graveled driveway. Alex was a pretty child, the image of his father. Even from here, Julia could see the resemblance in the dark skin, the deep chin cleft and the glossy black hair.

Eli rested one hand on his son's back, but Alex seemed reluctant to go any farther. Julia could hear Eli's soft encouraging voice, but Alex was crying. Silent silver tears glistened on round, still-babyish cheeks and propelled Julia forward.

"I want to go home," a small voice said.

"Alex. Buddy, we talked about that."

Eli glanced up at her approach, worried and utterly helpless looking.

"Hi, Alex," Julia said gently. "I'm Julia, and I'm so glad to have you come for a visit."

Alex gripped a green plastic dinosaur in one hand. "I want to go home."

Pity clutched at Julia like a tight fist. She desperately wanted to take the child into her arms and comfort him, but he didn't know her and Eli seemed not to know what to do. So she held out a hand as she would have to an upset Mikey and said, "I have cookies fresh out of the oven. Do you like cookies?"

Alex, shoulders drooped and head down, didn't answer. Julia smoothed the top of his hair, and a rush of memories swamped her.

Mikey had this kind of smooth, dark hair, though his was

usually covered by a red baseball cap. Some kids drag a blanket. Mikey never forgot his Cardinals cap—not even then.

Licking dry lips, she said, "I prepared my favorite rooms in the inn especially for you and your daddy."

Eli's head jerked up. "But you said—"

"The policy is mine to keep or break."

She saw him struggle against the favor, but when he murmured "thank you" in deference to his son, she knew she'd made the right choice.

Bingo ambled down the back porch steps, tailless rump swinging in greeting. The Aussie brushed Julia's legs as if to say *I've got this* and nudged his head beneath Alex's limp hand. The boy startled and then fell to his knees, buried his face in the old dog's neck and sobbed.

That night, Eli sat beside his son and watched him sleep. They were both lost and he hoped they could somehow find their way to each other. Julia and the sweet old dog had helped ease the transition, but what could anyone say to comfort a very small boy who'd lost everything familiar in his life? Eli had been comfortless as a man when his world was stripped away. How much more difficult for a child?

Before bedtime, he'd phoned the hospital for an update on Opal, hoping for something positive to share with Alex. Instead, he'd heard the worst. If Opal survived the stroke at all, rehab would take many months. Alex wouldn't be going back to the house in Honey Ridge for a long time. Probably ever.

With a lump in his chest, he brushed the fringe of dark hair from Alex's forehead, a gesture the boy would likely have shrugged away if he'd known. Long, black eyelashes, still moist, lay against tanned cheeks, a painful reminder that Alex had cried too often tonight.

"You don't want me, little man, but I'm all you've got. And, for now, this is home."

★ ★ ★

Saturday morning, Julia found another clay marble in the hallway outside the Blueberry Room. This one, a deep shade of red, felt warm to the touch and the warmth had traveled to her heart. Bingo was nowhere around, but he had trailed Alex up the stairs a number of times in the past three days. Perhaps Alex had found the marble and left it here. Bemused and oddly uplifted, she added the clay ball to the collection dish on the foyer credenza right next to the rack of tourist brochures announcing historic Civil War sites and river outfitters. The old marbles were interesting conversation pieces, though she was beginning to think they were more.

That afternoon, after all chores were finished and her guests happily out and about in the sunshine, Julia put ingredients for peach ice cream into the churn, dried her hands and went to the windows overlooking the backyard. Eli had driven Alex to the hospital to visit Opal this morning and both had returned rather glum. Now, Eli was in the orchard, clearing dead limbs that had fallen during a thunderstorm. Though the weekends were his, he seemed at loose ends without a task. Alex was with him, one hand on Bingo's back.

The picture reminded her so much of similar scenes in her memory bank of Mikey and his dog, young then but every bit as devoted to the child. Watching Bingo with Alex was both pleasure and pain, just as having a child scarf down her spaghetti again both thrilled and stabbed. He was a silent little waif, a ghost of a child who needed cheering, and if the gentle dog could help, she was glad.

Eli seemed as lost as his look-alike son.

"Do you think he'll ever warm up?" Valery asked as she and Connie, their mother, came through with armloads of sheets. Weekends were the busiest at the inn and Connie came to help as well as to spread her special brand of hospitality to Peach Orchard guests. Perfectly groomed and proper, she had a Southern charm that guests seemed to appreciate, and like Valery, Connie could drag conversation from a porch post.

"Eli took him to see Opal this morning. I'm not sure if that was a good idea, but Alex kept saying Opal was dead like his mama."

"Oh, that poor baby." Palm pressed to her throat, Valery turned to her mother. "Mama, you should get the church ladies to do something. Maybe take some flowers or cards to Opal or whatever you all do."

"I will, honey. Some of the other women know her better than I do." Her focus drifted to Julia. "Julia, I hope you don't upset yourself with this. You've finally come out of that awful depression. Are you still taking your medication?"

In other words, was Julia going to go off the deep end again because there was a child on the premises?

"Mom." Valery bumped her mother's side and murmured, "Leave her alone."

"I saw Daddy yesterday," Julia said instead of answering. "He asked about you."

"He can ask until the South wins the war and it will do about as much good."

But the distraction was enough to send her vital sixty-year-old mother in another direction.

Julia left them talking about Daddy and Aunt Sylvia's new husband who "wasn't from around here."

With glasses of cold peach tea and a few leftover slices of banana bread on a tray, she followed her instincts to the orchard. With the inn commanding most of her energy, she'd spent minimal time here among the rows of fruit trees with their arms lifted high to the sun. Now she took the time to appreciate the elemental wholesomeness of nature, the fresh grass scent mingled with the heady sweetness of thousands of pink blossoms. The orchard was quite beautiful.

"You guys need a break."

Eli swiped a forearm over his head. "Sounds good. How about it, Alex? You thirsty?"

Alex shrugged, but Julia noticed how his gaze lingered on the banana bread. Rather than cajole, Julia handed him a thick piece and a glass of tea. He eyed the floating peach slices with considerable suspicion and poked one with a finger before sipping.

"You're getting a lot done. I had no idea we had that many dead limbs."

"There's still a lot of deadwood in the trees that needs to come out."

"Can you do it?"

His eyebrows came together. "I'm not a horticulturist. Pruning has to be done at the right time."

"You can look on the internet."

He swigged the iced tea. "Good idea if I had a computer."

"Use the one in my office or the one in the parlor."

"I've been meaning to ask you about that, anyway."

Julia tilted her head in question. "What about it?"

He flicked an eyebrow toward Alex. The little boy was feeding Bingo a bit of banana bread, which the dog took in a careful, delicate nibble.

Eli turned to the side and in an undertone commented, "I don't know anything about being a parent. I thought I could read up."

Her heart went out to him. He tried hard with Alex. "No one does, Eli."

"That's what they tell me." He sipped at the tea. "He had another nightmare last night."

"That's three this week."

"This time he woke up saying his mother was at home waiting for him and begged me to take him there."

"Oh, Eli." She wanted to touch him. Not in a personal, I-want-your-body way but in comfort and kindness. Concern for Alex had become their touchstone, their point of easy conversation. Though close to the vest about himself, Eli wrestled constantly with the need to help the son he'd known such a short time. "He's dealing with a lot."

And so was Eli.

"Maybe I could find advice on the internet about his particular situation. Losing his mother. Getting to know a strange father."

"That's not a bad idea. He's going through a lot of emotional turmoil."

"With a clueless dad." He downed the rest of his tea in a series of swallows that flexed his masculine throat. His naturally dark skin had darkened even more in the spring sunlight. A tiny pulse beat there, the lifeblood that was Eli Donovan.

Distracted to notice him so much, Julia took the empty glass from his hand and set the tray on the ground. "Don't be hard on yourself. No one knows what to do in situations like this."

"Most times, I feel helpless. Parenting is complicated."

"Yes, parenting is very complicated," she said softly.

His expression said she couldn't possibly know and Julia glanced away, not ready to share Mikey's story with a man who was already struggling enough.

A whisper breeze made the peach blossoms quiver in the glinting sunlight while out on the circle driveway a brown SUV rumbled up, stirring gravel. The Ratcliffs were back from a river float. Bingo, who usually lumbered into the yard to greet guests, didn't appear.

Julia glanced around for the dog and boy. A finger of fear

tapped up her spinal cord. They were gone. Something inside her turned to ice water. "Where's Mikey?"

Eli's eyebrows snapped together in bewilderment. "Who?"

Julia shook herself. Had she really said Mikey's name? "Alex. Where is he?"

Eli looked to where the dog and child had been a few moments before. The glass was on the ground, tipped over with ice scattered onto the greening grass.

"Alex!" He spun in a circle, but the thick blanket of flowering trees obstructed his view. "He can't be far."

Julia clutched at Eli's arm. Panic rose to choke her. As visions of one horrible October morning surfaced, she started to shake. "We have to find him. We have to find him now!"

Eli refused to panic, though Julia clearly was about to. He'd learned long ago that panic made him brainless, and he had the scars to prove it.

"Julia," he said, taking her by the upper arms. "Hey. Calm down. He can't be far, and there is nothing here to hurt him."

With a nod, she licked her lips, though he could see she remained unconvinced. "You're shaking."

"We have to find him. Someone—" She bit her lip, her eyes wide. "Anything could happen!"

Her lips trembled, pretty pink lips, soft and vulnerable.

He jerked his gaze toward the trees.

"Boys explore," he said gruffly. "Stop worrying. He's fine."

To prove the point, he started through the orchard, calling for Alex. Julia ran the opposite direction, also calling out, though her voice was high-pitched and terrified.

He wondered at her fierce reaction. Such a worrywart, as his grandmother would have said. *Grandmother.* He hadn't thought of her in a long time. She'd been strict and dignified, but kindhearted, too, a grandmother who'd spoiled him with gifts and trips to Dollywood and Disney World. Long after he'd become hopeless, Grandmother Deborah kept trying until, like the others, she'd faded out of his life at his father's command. A bad seed had been surgically, radically, completely culled from the family tree.

He wondered what Grandmother would have thought of Alex.

"Alex!" he cried, louder this time. Where was he? And why didn't he answer?

From the other side of the orchard, he heard Julia yell. "Bingo. Come here, boy. Bingo, come."

A rush of admiration swooped through him. She was brilliant. A little overdramatic, but smart.

Something stirred in the brush to his left. Eli whipped around to see the blue merle dog picking his way to the clearing between rows, ears cocked toward Julia. Eli rushed toward the Aussie and found his son huddled not ten feet away amidst a tangle of uncleared brush and weeds.

"I found him!" he yelled in the general direction Julia had gone. Then he went to his haunches in front of Alex, aware that his pulse thudded and he'd been a little more anxious than he'd let on. "Hey, buddy, are you okay? Why didn't you answer me? You scared us."

Alex humped his shoulders, his hands crossed over his stomach. "My belly hurts."

The thunder of footsteps announced Julia's arrival. She was out of breath as she collapsed beside him. "Thank God, thank God!"

She'd been crying, an over-the-top reaction that puzzled him. Her face was white as cotton sheets. "Is he all right? What happened?"

"I'm not sure. He says his stomach hurts."

"Oh, baby. Sweet baby. You're okay. You'll be all right." She put a still-shaking hand to Alex's forehead. "Maybe the banana bread disagreed with him?"

"One piece?" Eli shook his head. He was as concerned about her as he was his son, though her breathing had slowed and she was starting to calm down.

"I have something for an upset stomach in the first-aid cabinet." She rubbed Alex's shoulder in small, comforting circles. "I might have some cartoon DVDs somewhere if you'd like to watch them."

Julia was good with Alex. Better than he was, for sure, even if she was overprotective—probably because she had no children, but still she was motherly and gentle and seemed to know what to say and do for a small boy. Eli wondered if parenting was innate and he'd been left without that genetic disposition. His son wouldn't even call him Dad.

"What do you say, little buddy? Want to lie down awhile and watch some TV?"

Alex looked at him with wide, sad eyes. Two fat tears quivered on his black lashes. "I want to go home."

Sorrow clutched Eli right in the center of his chest.

Worried and heartsick, he scooped up his son and carried him into the house.

17

Eli was walking the orchard again.

Julia had awakened from a gauzy cobwebbed dream, strangely content and rested though the alarm clock glowed 4:00 a.m. After her usual examination of Mikey's inert Facebook page she'd pushed open the drapes to stare out at the starlit night. A three-quarter moon lit the acreage in shadows and shapes, one of them the restless man.

Eli Donovan was trying hard to be a good father and his struggle was both real and endearing. Alex was most certainly a concern. Boys were supposed to run and be rowdy and make noise, but the dark-eyed Alex was withdrawn and mouse quiet. He tugged at her sympathies, pulled at her need to be a mother and tore at her resolve never to love a child again.

Alex needed love and lots of it. The old Aussie seemed to understand that more than anyone. But love could bring such searing, ferocious pain. Her mother was correct. She couldn't live through that again.

What if something terrible happened to Alex while he was here at Peach Orchard? What if he, like Mikey, simply vanished from the face of the earth? She'd been so scared when he'd disappeared that day in the orchard. For those few terrible minutes, she'd relived the stunned instant six years ago when the truth had slowly seeped into her frantic mind. The unthinkable had happened to Mikey.

Fear was a familiar claw with three-inch nails embedded in her chest. Simply having a boy child in the house brought the dragon roaring back. She'd called Detective Burrows three times this week, as if that would somehow keep Alex safe.

She sucked in a slow, relaxing breath exactly as Dr. Smith had instructed. Alex was asleep, she reminded herself, safe and sound upstairs while his father paced the grounds below.

Eli. She put a hand to the cool windowpane. He was a deep and complicated man, nothing like the suspicious pirate she'd first thought him to be. Courteous and smart, she was glad he'd found his way to Peach Orchard. The inn needed a man's attention and he took a load from her and Valery.

She'd already begun to depend on him, a dangerous thing considering he was a temporary employee. With the small amount she paid him, she wouldn't be surprised if he left, especially now that he had a son to support full-time.

In the splash of moonlight, Eli lifted his face toward the house and, even though her room was cloaked in darkness, Julia was convinced he could see her. It was as if a thread of connection ran between them, an understanding that life was painful and dark and the battle to reach the light was never ending.

Without stopping to think, she threw a robe over her pajamas and padded down the stairs and out the back door. The inn was filled tonight and guests had long since returned from their explorations. One light glowed in the Magnolia Room, a young pair of newlyweds who probably had more to do at four in the morning than most. She smiled, envious of young, fresh love, that fleeting fire of romance that had come and gone before she'd had an opportunity to fully appreciate it.

She stepped across the back veranda, held to the railing for a moment while she found Eli again in the moonlight.

A quick glance toward the parking pad troubled her. Valery hadn't come home tonight, at least not yet.

Descending the wide, white-painted steps, she traveled the short distance from house to orchard. The night air was damp and scented with spring.

Eli saw her coming and stilled, a long, dark shadow beneath the white, flat moon and blanket of far-slung stars.

Voice hushed, she said, "Are you all right?"

He seemed surprised by the question. "Me? Sure."

"I've seen you out here pretty often, but not since Alex came."

"I'm afraid to leave him very long, but sometimes I need... Outside clears my thoughts."

"Then I should come out here more often," she said, lips curving. "How is he?"

"Sleeping solid. Bingo stayed with him." He plunged his hands deep in his pockets. "I hope that was okay. With the dog and the plastic dinosaur, he calms down."

The old Aussie, who had been her companion since Mikey disappeared, had found a new soul to comfort. She missed his solid presence at the foot of her bed, but the child needed him more. "No nightmares or tummy aches?"

"No. Not tonight, anyway."

"Any luck on the computer?"

"Some. Plenty of parenting advice and articles on children who've lost a parent."

"Was anything helpful?"

"I'm in the beginning stages, but I saved some articles to

reread. One thing I learned is that children respond to grief differently than adults."

She pushed her hair behind her ears, aware she hadn't even run a brush through the tangles. "I never thought about kids and grief at all."

"Apparently people once assumed kids were too young to understand the significance of loss. Not true, of course. They feel every bit as deeply but can't articulate their feelings well."

Articulate. There he went again, with that educated vocabulary that did not fit his laborer image. Someday she'd ask him.

"He's definitely grieving."

"Agreed. Nightmares, withdrawal, headaches, stomach upsets are signs of grief he can't process."

"How can anyone ever process grief? The agony digs into the bones and sets up residence."

He tilted his chin down toward her. "Voice of experience?"

"We've all lost someone." Saying it that way almost seemed like a denial of Mikey. She wanted to blurt out that mourning a precious, living son you could no longer touch was far worse than grieving a death. Grief over an abducted child was a type of walking, living death that never ceased. The endless frustration of dead ends and false leads and, worst of all, the silence. But her losses wouldn't help Alex or Eli so she kept them to herself.

They were quiet for a few heartbeats, a pleasant, comfortable silence. Far in the distance, a train moaned into the night, and across the road, the security light shone at the old abandoned gristmill, a yellow halo against the darkness.

"Mama and the ladies from the church visited Opal today," she said.

"Nice of them. She has a long road ahead. She could use the friends."

"Trey Riley's mother is in that group. You met Trey."

"The police officer?"

"Yes."

Eli crossed muscled arms over his chest, catching his hands beneath his armpits the way men do. "He has three sisters."

She laughed. "He does. Good family. Nikki is my age. We used to be close a long time ago. Best friends in high school. In tenth grade, we dyed each other's hair the same shade of purple. Mama had a hissy fit."

"Mine would have, too." He chuckled softly, a breath on the air, and Julia liked the deep-throated masculine sound. She was pleased to hear some laughter from so serious a man. "What happened?"

She tilted her head in question. "What happened to what?"

"Your friendship."

"Oh, you know. Life." Hadn't he said something similar to her at one time? An evasive answer for sure, but how did she explain the terrible emptiness when friends had drifted away, unable to deal with her depression. A few had tried, she'd give them credit though they'd been at a loss for words and she'd been unable to accept platitudes anyway. Since the inn opened, some had drifted back for peach tea and to see what she'd done with Honey Ridge's haunted mansion. "Nikki was a bridesmaid at my wedding."

"You hold that against her?"

Julia laughed again, pleasantly surprised at the humor. "No. Though maybe I should. My ex is a lawyer. A good one. He married his intern about five minutes after our divorce. A very young intern."

"Brutal."

"Hmm." She didn't know why she'd told him that. The intimacy of the darkness, she supposed. "I'm not bitter anymore."

"Were you?"

"For a while." A long, ugly time. "They had a baby right away, which bothered me, and Mama said she's pregnant again."

"And the two of you never had any children."

Julia sucked in a tiny hiss. All right. She'd said too much. "You probably need to get back to Alex."

At her abrupt change of subjects, a pause shimmied on the night. "I apologize for being nosy. That's not like me."

No, it wasn't. "No problem. I'm touchy sometimes."

"You've built a great life here at Peach Orchard Inn. You don't need a bast—guy who'd cheat on you with his intern. You're better than that."

The last statement seeped through her like the first warm sun after a harsh winter. She *was* better than that though she still struggled to believe in herself again. "I'm trying."

Julia tilted her head all the way back, looking up and up into the darkness, to that mysterious realm that watched everything here below. The hem of her robe was growing damp in the grass and her bare feet were cold. Eli was standing close, his body heat reaching out to her. A man, it seemed to her, was always warmer than a woman. Long ago, when she was the young, unfrozen Julia, she might have flirted, leaned into the manly chest and absorbed his warmth and perhaps more. Even in her frozen state, the idea held a certain appeal.

"Look at that moon."

"Gorgeous." His voice was a husky mumble.

The magic of moonlight and shadow created intimacy as if they knew each other well, as if they were more than a reticent handyman and a spiritless innkeeper. No wonder love songs had been written and couples had fallen in love beneath the glowing beauty of a night sky.

"Spring is my favorite." She crossed her arms, drawing the soft robe closer against the cool night. "New life sprouting up everywhere. And every day the air holds a delicious new smell."

Hope. That was the scent of spring. How long since she'd noticed?

A vehicle's engine whined from up on the road and a pale wash of car lights pushed like pale yellow fingers through the magnolias.

"Someone's coming up the drive."

"Probably Valery." The most reasonable possibility this time of night.

They stood together in the darkness watching the car pull in. Valery got out of the Honda, dropped her keys and almost tumbled face-first to retrieve them. Then she weaved and wobbled toward the side entrance of the house. Julia's heart sank.

"Oh, Val." The words slipped out in a whisper.

Valery stumbled, and Eli surged forward as if to go to her rescue. Julia put a hand out to stop him. "I'll take care of her." It wouldn't be the first time.

Valery went to her knees in the grass. Even from this distance, Julia could hear her muttering and crying. Her sister could be a maudlin drunk.

Leaving Eli, she hurried toward Valery, despairing that she was drunk again. And she'd been driving. Dear God, what was wrong with her!

When she reached Valery's side, Julia grabbed her by the elbow to get her off the ground. Valery didn't budge.

"Leave me 'lone." She was crying more softly now.

"Come on, honey. Let's get you in the house."

"You're the bes' sister."

"I sure am. Now, get up before you ruin that new fifty-dollar skirt."

Valery tried, but her legs collapsed under her and she went down. The crying started again. "I'm no good for anything. No good."

Eli, quiet as a burglar in his approach, spoke next to Julia's ear. "It'll take both of us. Let me help. I'm not exactly a virgin at this kind of thing."

Frankly, she was grateful. She'd not seen Valery this inebriated in a while. "Thank you. She's not usually this bad."

She didn't want him thinking negative thoughts about her beautiful sister.

"You get the doors and lead the way. I've got her." And before Julia could process his intent, he swept Valery into his arms against his strong chest and started up the steps. One of Valery's turquoise shoes dangled from her heel.

Julia hurried ahead of him, opening doors, flipping on lights and leading him down the hallway to Valery's rooms, which Julia opened with her master key.

Valery was muttering about being no good and Jed and a spate of other gibberish, her face pressed against Eli's shoulder. "Mmm. You smell good."

Julia saw the clench of Eli's jaw, but he gently placed her sister on the bed and tried to back away. Arms around his neck, Valery clung like a tick. "So nice. Don't go, sugar."

Eli peeled Valery's arms from his neck and backed away. Julia blushed, humiliated for her sister's behavior. She pulled off Val's shoes, dropped them with a thump to the floor and left the rest.

After pulling a cover over her fully clothed, rambling sister, she clicked off the light and left the room.

Outside in the hallway, she murmured softly, "She'll hate herself in the morning."

"Hopefully, she won't remember," he said.

"She's not a bad person, Eli. Please don't think…"

He touched the upper arm of her fuzzy robe. "I don't."

They were standing inches apart in the semidarkness and Julia was deeply grateful for his quiet, competent, nonjudgmental handling of an unpleasant situation. She touched her fingertips to his chest, startled at the powerful arc of need that sparked through her. The need to be close to someone again, to be held, to be cared for. Was that what Valery saw in her destructive relationship with Jed?

Eli's green gaze centered on her face. Something smoldered there before he blinked and doused the ember. "I should check on Alex."

"Yes." She stepped back, broke contact.

He hesitated, watching her. "You all right?"

"Worried. I love her, Eli."

"This isn't the first time." It wasn't a question.

"No. But she's been worse since she started dating Jed. This is his fault."

"No, it isn't."

The response shocked her, but even if she wanted to blame someone else, Eli was right. Jed was a bad influence, but the problem was Valery's. She didn't have to share in Jed's partying lifestyle.

"You can't fix her," he said with a weary conviction she didn't understand.

"I know. But I want to." She flicked a glance to the closed door and back to him. "Thank you, Eli."

He nodded. "Good night, Julia."

"Good night."

As she turned to walk the half-dozen steps to her suite at the end of the hall, Julia thought she heard the faint sound of piano music.

18

Peach Orchard Farm
1864

Will heard music as he stepped up on the veranda and opened the front door. Mozart, perhaps. Certainly something he'd heard before. A soothing trickle, like a babbling brook, that sent the mind to happier times. Patience Portland, the simple young woman who soothed with her music. Patience, sister of the austere owner, Edgar Portland. Will couldn't bring himself to like the man and respected him less after he'd heard him, more than once, railing at Charlotte, but the ladies of Peach Orchard Farm were a different matter.

Private Barney Timmons, thin as a whipcord with a beard down to his chest, limped up beside him leaning on a thick stick. "She plays like a dream, don't she, Captain?"

"She does."

"She's pretty, too, and real sweet."

Patience drew attention with her flowing corn silk hair and unaffected manner. "Leave the ladies alone, Private."

"Aw, I didn't mean no harm, Captain. Nice, though, to be around a lady again. Makes a man forget about the war for a while."

Will couldn't argue that. Yet, the women were the biggest problem with camping here at Peach Orchard Farm. They were all pretty in their own way and turned heads. His men were lonely and had they not been mostly injured and sick, he'd have had his work cut out for him. As it was, they were too feeble to do much beyond admiration and talk. He'd sent the handful of healthy ones, other than those needed to care for the wounded, back to the front.

Feeble. Sick. The ghastly wounds had taken a toll on his company. How would the Union ever win a war without healthy soldiers? He'd dispatched a messenger to General Rosecrans for further orders, but a reply could take days. For now, he had little choice but to hold his position. Soon, though, he and the able would return to the front.

He was torn between the desperate need to fulfill his duty to the United States and the longing to spend more time with the most troublesome woman, at least for him, at Peach Orchard Farm.

Since their walk in the woods, he'd thought about Charlotte's wise advice and of the way she helped him believe again. For a while, war had stripped him of hope. Charlotte's quiet strength and faith that good would prevail had given it back again. There *was* good, and he'd found it again here at Peach Orchard Farm.

Though careful to maintain a respectful distance, he was as enchanted by Charlotte Portland as Barney was with Patience's piano music.

Leaving Barney to listen to the lilting Mozart, Will strode through the parlor and into the dining area toward the pallets spread from one side of the long room to the other. The stench of too many poorly washed men and too many wounds filled his nostrils like cannon smoke. Flies stirred the thick, hot air. Would cooler weather never come to southern Tennessee?

Conversations of home and food and pain littered the air. Bushy-bearded Sergeant Paxton held sway in one corner with his humorous poetry readings, and a few others read from Bibles they'd carried from home.

Cries of "Captain" followed his passage, and he paused with words of encouragement or to hear that a letter had arrived.

He found Charlotte on her knees spooning broth between the parched and fevered lips of Private Johnny Atkins whose hands were burned and his eyes wrapped in bandage from a minié ball blast that barely missed taking out his skull. He was lucky, if losing both eyes at age eighteen could be considered fortunate.

"Charlotte." Will approached her from the back and saw the spoon pause. He knew a moment of pleasure in watching her quiet hands, in gazing at her shiny, tidy hair and the bent nape of shapely neck.

She turned and flashed him a smile that lit him from the inside out. "Will."

"Is it the captain, ma'am?" Private Atkins asked, his blind face moving left and right as if to see.

"Yes, Private, Captain Gadsden is here to see you."

"'Morning, Johnny." Will motioned to the broth. "May I?"

"Of course." Charlotte moved aside and offered the bowl and spoon. "Private Atkins was telling me about his sweet Betsy back in Ohio."

Will took her place on the hardwood floor and leaned toward his soldier. "To hear Johnny tell it, Betsy is the prettiest girl in all of Ohio."

"She is, Captain," Johnny insisted. "All the boys wanted Betsy, but for some reason, she picked me."

"Because she is a wise and fortunate young lady," Charlotte said, her voice smiling.

Will spooned soup into the young soldier's mouth, heart heavy. For indeed, no one could say what Betsy would think when she learned of her beau's misshapen face and missing eyesight. The war was over for Johnny, but his battles were yet to begin.

"Didn't mean to take anything away from the present company," Johnny said. "I bet Miss Charlotte's mighty pretty, too, ain't she, Captain?"

Will lifted his eyes to Charlotte's, saw the blush crest her cheekbones.

"You'd win that bet, Johnny," he answered softly, purposely keeping the tone light. Charlotte Portland was more than pretty. "One more bite, Private."

The private opened his lips like a pitiful baby bird and Will spooned in the last of a rich, savory soup.

Johnny awkwardly dabbed his crooked mouth with the back of a bandaged hand. "Thank you, sir. These womenfolk are fine cooks."

"I'll pass along your compliments." Charlotte took the bowl from Will. "Rest now."

Leaving the injured soldier, Will walked with Charlotte through to the summer kitchen, where she added the bowl to a pile of unwashed dishes. The very magnitude of what the Portland women and slaves did for the Union Army humbled him. Some, like Josie, made no bones about their distaste or outright hatred of the Yankee, and he supposed, in their place, he would feel the same.

The kitchen was alive with smells and activity. One slave woman scrubbed dishes while another worked a large bowl of pale brown dough with long fingers. A sturdy black man—

Pierce—came in from outside with an armload of wood to feed the hungry stove.

A clatter of noise at the back door drew Will's attention as Ben and Tandy thundered inside. Fast and energetic was the way of these two, who were as close as brothers though their skin contrasted like sun and moon. Exuberant and full of boyish curiosity, they reminded him of his childhood days in Ohio.

"Just the pair I was searching for," he said.

"Captain, sir!" Benjamin's sturdy shoulders jerked back as his body stiffened to a charming salute. His cowlick vibrated from the motion, a feather in his pale cap of hair.

Slender and taller, Tandy followed suit. "Reporting for orders, sir."

Will returned the salute, aware that Charlotte and the kitchen slaves watched, the former with mild amusement, the latter with wary, shifting gazes. "At ease, men."

"Captain Will, we found a snake. A cobra, I think."

"A cobra, is it?" He fought to keep the smile from his lips.

"Benjamin," Charlotte said, "there are no cobras in Tennessee."

"But it was, Mama. Like the one in my book on the pharaohs. I'm sure it was a cobra." He spread his fingers in an imitation of the snake's head, his young voice insistent. "It puffed up something fierce and tried to strike us."

"I killed it, sir," Tandy said, his bandy chest stuck out. "I saved Ben from a sure death."

Lizzy whipped around the worktable, her white apron flapping with the quick movement. "Snakes be a bad omen. You stay away from them snakes."

"Aw, Mama."

She clutched Tandy by the shoulders. "I mean it, Tandy. Something bad's gonna happen you go messin' with snakes."

The boy dropped his head. "I killed it real good, Mama."

"All right, then. All right. You killed it. That's good. That's right." She clutched the boy to her apron front and patted his back. "Ain't nothing gonna happen. You're a good boy. Go on, now. Go on. Mama's got more work than sense."

Her fingers trembled and Will could see the episode had shaken her, though he did not understand her superstition.

Tandy squirmed away from his mother's embrace and glanced at Ben. Both boys stood quietly now, downcast, their former exuberance crushed.

"I have something for you," Will said, and was pleased when interest flared on both faces. He reached into his greatcoat and withdrew the drawstring leather bag he'd carried for three years. "Remember how I told you that my family owns a marble factory?"

Two heads nodded and Charlotte, who'd been murmuring softly to Lizzy, looked up.

"You boys like to play marbles?"

"Don't know how," Ben said.

"Would you like to learn?"

The boys traded glances and the boyish excitement was back.

"Tell you what, come on outside. I'll show you how it's done."

"Really? Will you really show us, Captain?" Ben's eagerness touched him. Did Edgar Portland not play with his child?

Will led the way out onto the back porch, down the steps and into the side yard, surprised when Charlotte followed. Two amputees lounged against a live oak, playing cards, their walking sticks leaned against the trunk. Otherwise, the browning lawn was empty. From the front porch, he heard conversations, and someone laughed. Standifer, he thought, with his rowdy personality and never ending repertoire of bawdy jokes. From the direction of the slave quarters came the scent of corn bread, and someone sang in a deep, rich voice.

"'There is a balm in Gilead to make the wounded whole...'"

Will wished the words were true, but he'd seen too many wounded like Johnny who would never be whole again.

At the bottom of the porch, he went to his haunches, balancing on his toes, and was amused when the two boys imitated his stance. He opened the leather bag, worn and faded now from use. "I've had these since I was a boy."

"Did you make 'em in your factory?"

"My grandfather made them there." He'd had many bags of marbles over the years, but these he treasured because his grandfather Gadsden had passed to his reward not long after the gift was given. Will dumped the contents into his hand and jiggled the hand-smoothed clay.

"Do you still play with them?" Ben asked in his sweet way. The blue-eyed child was more like Charlotte than his father in both looks and personality, and now Will understood why. Edgar Portland didn't appreciate his blessings.

"They're yours now." Though he treasured them still, these simple clay reminders of home and family, of the family business that would someday be his if he survived this endless war, giving them to Ben seemed the right thing to do. He could give nothing to Charlotte, but he could do this for her son.

On nights before a battle, when the soldiers were skittish and distractions at a premium, a boy's game could remind men of why they continued to fight. They fought so innocent boys could knuckle down in a game of ringer. So children of this great nation, including the Africans, could live in peace and freedom. Marbles soothed the troubled soul, like that balm in Gilead someone was singing about.

He drew a circle in a patch of dirt and explained the simple rules, not a bit surprised when Ben and Tandy caught on quickly and began to play. Charlotte watched, brown skirt brushing the side of her son, who was on his knees, tongue in his teeth, focused on a shot.

Will felt Charlotte's presence, saw her buttoned boots from the corner of his eye. Once the boys had grasped the game, he rose to join her.

"Are you sure you want to part with them?" Charlotte's blue eyes met his. His breath hitched in his throat.

For her and her son, he would. Their pleasure was worth the sacrifice. "The war has stolen enough from them."

That she agreed was obvious in the dip of chin. "Thank you."

"I hope they'll remember me with kindness when I leave rather than recalling the…difficulties." He didn't want them to hate him when they were old enough to look back and understand what the Union Army had done to their home.

"Are you leaving soon?" The words were spoken in a mild tone, but she'd tensed and the corners of her mouth turned down.

"Every dispatch could bring orders. Any day now, I'd think."

"I see." She rested her hands at her waist in a sign he'd come to recognize. When she was agitated most was when she seemed the most serene, and now those hands went quiet at her waist.

"I'll miss you," he said.

She twisted her head toward the empty back porch before surveying the backyard. He'd already looked. There was no one about to hear him but a pair of boys intent on a marble game.

"You mustn't say such things."

She was right. He mustn't. He tipped his chin. "My apologies, then."

"Oh, Will." And in her sigh were the words neither could say.

19

Honey Ridge
Present Day

The old beater wouldn't start again.

Eli had cleaned the battery cables and still his car engine wouldn't turn over. So here he was, taking Julia's clean, smooth SUV to the lumberyard with the agreement that he could stop at the hospital and the school. He felt weird about driving her car. The caramel leather interior smelled like her, a subtle blend of spice and elegance that put him in mind of black-tie galas and warm Southern nights.

He had trouble keeping her out of his head today, the way she'd looked last night in her bare feet with her hair mussed and her voice sleep-drenched and sexy.

Someone should shoot him.

At breakfast, he'd had to fight to keep his attention off Julia and on his apple-smoked bacon and French toast with fresh strawberries and cream, a breakfast that should have kept any man's focus. Not that Julia went out of her way to look enticing.

She was just so darned classy. Both early risers, she'd sat across from him at the table cradling a cup of her magnificent coffee and they'd spoken in hushed tones of Valery, of Alex, who did not want to go to school, and of the supplies she wanted him to pick up in town.

So far this morning, Valery hadn't shown her face. The sister troubled him, though, like Julia, she was none of his business and he would be better served to give both sisters a wide berth. Personal entanglements could tangle more than his emotions.

Entanglements. He had his share of those already. Without a car, he couldn't attend the weekly check-in with his parole officer, and he hoped Pete Clifford didn't decide to drive to Honey Ridge and ruin everything. A phone call would have to do, one he'd better make today while he was away from the house. Somewhere.

Over the next hill, Honey Ridge came into view, a pretty jewel nestled in a hollow below a long mountain ridge. The small town's streets were busy this weekday morning, relatively speaking. He eased off the accelerator as he passed the park where he'd met the cop and later taken Alex to play. That, like most of his ideas concerning his son, had been a bust, though Alex had laughed when he'd spun him on the merry-go-round, the only time he'd shown any pleasure. The sweet sound still played in Eli's memory recording and gave him hope.

That was the trouble with a guy like him. He kept hoping, and the vicious emotion was like a jealous lover, snubbing him one minute and nuzzling him the next, just enough to keep him hanging on.

At the Ace Hardware and Lumber Company on the far west end of town, he parked the SUV in the semi-filled lot and headed inside. Thick gray clouds threatened thunderstorms and fueled zippy winds that sent dust and trash somersaulting across the parking lot. He didn't mind getting wet but wondered if wind would damage the peach trees. He was growing fond of that orchard and wanted a bumper crop this year for Julia's sake, for her trust in him. She'd never know how much she'd bolstered him with this job. He almost felt like a real man.

The cavernous hardware store, a remodeled Walmart, smelled of new wood and axle grease and emitted the quiet hum of relaxed industry. A woman in a red smock helped a customer in the paint department while another pushed a sale basket of odds and ends to the front entrance. A couple of male employees rolled a dolly of prefab cabinets out the door, accompanied by a stout lady with an enormous black purse.

Eli subtly catalogued them all, alert to suspicious glances though he'd been to this store a number of times. Citizens of Honey Ridge were generally accepting or politely ignored him. He preferred the latter.

Because of his prominent parents, his face had once been splashed in the Tennessee newspapers, but his crime was long ago, and other scandals had replaced the sizzling news of the rich boy sentenced to prison. The public quickly forgot, thank God.

He found the aisle with the door hinges and perused the selection in search of something with an antique appearance without the high cost.

"I thought that was you." At the unexpected voice, Eli stilled and then slowly turned his head to see Trey Riley, the police officer. "Eli, right?"

"Right."

In a crisp navy blue uniform, the affable man extended one hand. The other held a new smoke detector. "Good to see you again. How are things going out at Julia's?"

He shook the outstretched hand. "Coming along."

"Already have a war wound?" Trey motioned to the bandage on Eli's arm.

"Ah, just a little cut. Nearly healed up." Though he couldn't forget those moments when Julia had touched him. He'd forgotten what tenderness felt like until then. "Probably the first of many."

"A place like that could keep a man busy forever."

Eli hoped so. "I have you to thank for that."

"I'm glad it worked out. Julia's great." Trey chuckled. "I had a crush on her when I was about thirteen."

Eli's mouth tipped up. "Yeah?"

Couldn't blame the man for that, but Eli wondered if the police officer was still interested in his employer.

"Yeah. I doubt she ever knew that her best pal's snot-nosed brother thought she was hot. Julia is a beautiful woman, and her ex is a jerk." He dragged a hand over his grinning mouth and pointed. "Don't mention I said that. I have to work with the guy in court sometimes."

Eli was starting to like this cop. "Can't say I disagree."

"When I saw her SUV in the lot, I thought she was in here and was going to update her on a couple of things. But I guess you're driving her car?"

Eli pulled a door hinge from the rack, feeling guilty, as if he'd stolen the vehicle. "Mine gave up the ghost."

"Call Timmons' Garage. Billy's a great mechanic. I'm sure he can figure out the problem for you."

"Later, maybe. I'm a little short of cash right now."

"Too bad. Well—say, I'm off duty for the next couple of days. I'm not a mechanic but I tinker a little. Maybe the two of us could put our heads together, watch a few YouTube videos and come up with a solution."

Stunned, Eli blinked at the police officer. "I couldn't ask you to do that."

"You didn't." Trey patted his chest with the flat of his hand.

"I feel a major thirst for some of Julia's tea and some guy time. Think you could wrangle some for me?"

A flow of warmth, small like a candle flame but definitely there, pushed up inside Eli. He'd once been a social animal with tons of what he'd foolishly thought were friends. During the past seven years, he'd stayed to himself out of self-preservation, and some part of him still believed that was the best route. Friends could drag you down an ugly path. An afternoon talking cars with another man, especially if they could get the Dodge up and running again, tempted like a snort of cocaine once had.

But Trey was a cop.

Refusing could look suspicious.

After a few seconds of weighing options, he relented. Having a cop on his side couldn't be a bad thing. How much trouble could he get into with a cop around? "That would be great."

"All right, then. I'll run out tomorrow afternoon and see what we can do." Trey turned the smoke detector over as if reading the back. "Sorry to hear about Miss Kimble. My mom told me she's some relation to you."

Eli didn't correct the misinformation. "I'm headed over to the hospital now."

"Give her my best." With a quick, one-finger salute, the friendly officer sauntered down the aisle and disappeared from sight.

Eli waited a full three minutes before choosing a hinge and heading to the check out. He didn't know whether to be thrilled that he was assimilating into small-town life or terrified of blowing his cover.

Opal was awake when Eli pushed open the door of room 37 at Honey Ridge Hospital. Oxygen mask in place, she rolled her face on the pristine white pillow, recognition glittering in her glassy eyes.

"Opal. How are you?" He felt ridiculously lame for the stupid question and for coming empty-handed. He should have brought flowers.

"Furious." Paralyzed on the right side, Opal's mouth drew down so that speech was a struggle. The word was slurred but clear enough to understand.

Eli's lips curved in a combination of pity and humor at her feistiness. "Anything I can do for you?"

Her eyes fell shut, the right one partway, and, to his horror, a tear seeped from the corner. "Alex?"

She wanted to know how Alex was doing.

How did he answer that honestly without upsetting her? "He's adjusting. He misses you." And his mother. He talked about Mindy as if she had dropped him off for a visit and would return any moment.

"My house." The sibilant *s* hissed and twisted.

"What about your house? Do you need something from there? I'll get it for you."

Agitated, she cut her eyes toward the bedside table. Her helplessness tore at him. "Call her."

Eli, trying to read between the lines, searched the tabletop and found a business card with a note on the back. A social worker. "Meryl Vargas?"

"Yes."

"Okay."

"Now."

The room was equipped with a telephone, something he didn't have, so, not wanting to agitate Opal any further, he dialed the number.

After a ten-minute conversation with the elder-care social worker, he understood Opal's concerns. She was headed to a long-term nursing facility in a few days and her house, a rental, would have to be emptied and closed.

With a heavy heart, he replaced the receiver. Opal's good eye pinned him with a long, moist stare. Her expression questioned him. Since their first meeting she'd disliked him—and for good reason—but all he saw was a kind woman who'd loved his son when he couldn't.

He resisted the urge to put a hand over hers. She wasn't the touchy kind, so instead he said, "I'll take care of everything, Opal. Anything you need."

He didn't know how he could promise that, given his situation, but he'd figure out something.

"Not much," she said, laboring to be understood. "Sell all. For Alex."

A lump thickened in his throat. She didn't have much worth selling. "Okay."

He stayed awhile longer, going over as well as he could her wishes, all the time wondering how he would break the news to Alex that Opal was never going home again. That "home" was actually a rental that didn't even belong to Aunt Opal.

Finally, the old woman, exhausted from the effort, drifted off to sleep. Eli slipped the notes he'd made into his pocket and, when she didn't awaken, he went to the door.

"Eli." Her whisper turned him around. "Mindy…was… right. Good man."

Julia heard Alex's small voice through the back door as he sat in the wicker chairs with Eli. His short legs swung back and forth in a pendulum rhythm as he listened to the bad news about his aunt Opal.

Julia's whole being empathized with both father and son, so she responded in her usual way. She cooked his favorite dinner and put on a batch of peanut-butter cookies.

"We're all going to weigh five hundred pounds," Valery said. She was changing the linens on the breakfast tables, looking as bright and vivacious today as the crisp, white napkins. She'd refused to discuss her drunken state the other night, had acted as if nothing had happened at all and told Julia not to be such a nag.

"Little boys love cookies, especially when they need cheering."

She pulled back the lace curtain and peeked out at the two males. Eli sat with hands clasped between his open knees, earnestly saying something to his son. Alex listened, head up, chin cleft prominent, his dark-eyed expression both afraid and trusting. There was an endearing tenderness about the fragile relationship as they tried to find their way to each other.

Along the porch, pink peonies poked their nosy heads through the railing in a burst of color as if listening to every word between father and son. Julia credited Valery and Mom, both of whom had green thumbs, with the flower beds. Her skills, such as they were, were in the house and kitchen.

"*Eli* likes peanut-butter cookies, too." Head ticked to one side, Valery gave an exaggerated wink.

"Hush."

Her sister laughed and tossed her curls.

"Alex needs more than cookies. He needs something fun to make him feel normal again."

Valery joined her at the window. "He liked that little truck I bought him."

This was the Valery she loved with a fierce protectiveness, the woman who would drive into town solely to buy a hurting child a toy. The woman who had single-handedly dragged Julia out of the bonds of depression and despair by insisting she purchase an exhausted, dying mansion.

"Such a sweet thing to do. I heard him va-rooming that

truck up and down the porch yesterday." Valery had hit on something. Though Eli had brought a few old toys from Opal's house, Alex had outgrown most of them. "Will you keep an eye on the cookies for a few minutes?"

"Sure. Why?"

"I have something in storage he might like."

"What could you possibly have that a boy—" Then, as if the tumblers clicked into place, she uttered a small "Oh, Julia."

Ignoring the clutch in her chest, Julia hurried down the hall to her living quarters and opened the storage closet. The lidded box sat in the back corner where she'd put it the day they'd moved in.

With trembling fingers, she drew out the oversize plastic bin, set the container on the floor and went to her knees. A snap sounded as she released the red lid and looked inside the innocuous storage box that contained her only remaining connection to Mikey. The plastic zip bag of his pajamas, still unwashed, lay on top. She held the bag close to her nose and eyes closed, she sniffed low and slow, breathing in the faintest scent of her little boy. Perhaps the smell lingered only in her mind, but the reminder that Mikey had lived and breathed and worn these very pajamas staved off utter despair.

Trey Riley had called earlier, but only to let her know that Detective Burrows was on medical leave, and he'd be her contact. Not that either had anything to report. Like her, Trey had asked the question a thousand times. How did a second-grader in a red ball cap and matching Nike shoes disappear without a trace?

She lingered there for a long moment, hurting for the child she loved more than life until she thought she felt another presence, like a comforting hand on her shoulder, a sympathetic friend. Silly, she knew, and completely imaginary, but she kept her eyes closed and let the fantasy soothe her.

For a few more minutes, she remained on the decades-old heart pine floor cradling what her son had left behind, aware of the imaginary presence and strangely at peace. If this was crazy, she welcomed it.

Then, satisfied, she breathed in one final draught of the past, put the pajamas back and reached into the bottom of the box. Toys and books, a whole array of young-boy items Mikey had treasured. She selected a beloved bag of Lego he'd played with for hours on end and returned the bin to the closet.

Though she'd fiercely protected this sacred box for years, she'd taught her son to share. How could she do less for another hurting child?

With a tug below her heart, like a rusty hinge forced open, Julia started out of the room and stepped on something. A marble.

She pocketed the clay ball and took the Lego to a small boy who needed them more than she did.

20

Peach Orchard Farm
1864

Charlotte sat at her vanity, brushing her hair one hundred strokes. She'd reached fifty-six when Lizzy came in, carrying a tea tray with slices of shortcake. Charlotte laid aside the brush and, as had become their nightly ritual, joined her maid for the herbal tea. No one slept well at Peach Orchard Farm these days.

"I got some worries, Charlotte." From a flowered teapot, Lizzy poured pale golden tea into two cups. The lemony fragrance perfumed the air.

Charlotte stirred a spoon of Will's honey into her cup and sipped. "There are plenty of those to go around."

"Don't get riled now. I'm talking about you and the captain."

Slowly, Charlotte set her cup aside. "What about the captain and me?"

"There's starting to be talk. You got to be careful."

"The captain is a friend, Lizzy. I am a married woman, and Will is an honorable man."

"This ain't about your marriage papers. I'm talking about the heart, about what I see in your face when you look at him. And he looks at you the same way. Brings you things. Asks your opinion. He cares, Charlotte."

"Oh, Lizzy." Charlotte bit down on her bottom lip.

"Do you love him?"

The fact that a slave could speak frankly to her mistress would have shocked many of the ladies in Charlotte's acquaintance. But she and Lizzy, a young slave she'd reluctantly received as a wedding gift, had long since dispensed with formalities in private. Charlotte had taught Lizzy to read and write. Lizzy had taught her the ways of Southern women. Here in private they could simply be Charlotte and Lizzy without the social constraints between them.

Charlotte's cheeks grew hot. "He's a good man."

"Do you love him?"

Charlotte pushed from the chair and went to the window. Below, in the darkness, campfires glowed beneath the Southern moon. Somewhere Will walked among his soldiers, or perhaps he'd retired for the night. She clutched a fist at her throat, "I fear I do."

And *fear* was the proper word. Fear of displeasing God and of being unfaithful, at least in her heart. Fear for the day Will would ride away and she'd be left with an emptiness she hadn't known existed until he'd come.

The soft rustle of clothes and pat of feet brought Lizzy to stand behind her. A pair of warm, trusted hands stroked down the length of her hair, took up the locks, divided them and began to braid.

"That Captain Will, he's something," Lizzy said softly. "The way he plays with them boys of ours and brings you honey and me fresh fish. He don't have to do that."

"No. No, he doesn't." *Oh, Will. Why couldn't you have been the American to come to England?* "The boys have taken to him, haven't they? If only Edgar was more—" She clamped her lips tight, aghast at her rambling thoughts.

"The Yankees is gonna have to leave soon. You got to brace yourself. Orders is coming."

A cord of tension tightened around Charlotte's heart. "How do you know that? Have you heard something?"

"I hear a lot. Nobody pays any mind to slaves. Except Captain Will."

"I thought you didn't trust him."

Those competent hands stilled on Charlotte's hair. "I don't trust any man. They can break a woman."

"Is that what happened to you, Lizzy? Tandy's father broke your heart?" Her maid had never discussed the man who'd fathered her son, and Charlotte hadn't pried. A woman had a right to keep her intimate life private. But Lizzy had become pregnant and borne a son without a man to celebrate the occasion.

"No man ever broke my heart. I ain't got one."

Charlotte smiled into the cheval mirror, glad she'd diverted the conversation from Will to Lizzy. "Except when it comes to Tandy."

Lizzy's long, elegant face glowed in the lamplight. "True enough, though I know when you're trying to distract me, Charlotte Portland."

"Some things are best left unspoken."

"Don't I know it," the maid said softly. "Don't I know it. But this is one time I got to speak out whether you want to hear it or not. There are those who think you're consorting with the Yankees against your own husband."

Charlotte clamped a hand on Lizzy's wrist. "That's not true."

"Don't matter. If them Rebs in Honey Ridge start pointing fingers and calling you a traitor or, worse, a spy, there'll be trouble."

Fear crawled along Charlotte's spine like spiders down a wall. Tennessee was a hotbed of division, but the Confederacy was strong in Honey Ridge and those with Union sympathies were in danger of retribution. Just last month, the mercantile owner was beaten and his business ransacked because of rumors he'd supplied a Union soldier with a pair of boots.

"Is that what's happening? Is someone calling me a spy?"

"Not yet, but there's plenty of loose talk since the Yankees come to Peach Orchard. Getting worse all the time. Captain Will and his soldiers needs to leave before you get hurt. They's too many eyes in this house."

Lizzy always seemed to know what was happening long before Charlotte did. A slave in one place told a slave in another and word spread.

Indeed, there were eyes everywhere.

Long after Lizzy's departure, an anxious Charlotte knelt on the pine floor beside her bed and prayed.

21

Eli sat cross-legged on the aged wood floor of the den, a private area of the house accessed only by family. He felt a little weird and a lot good to be invited in. He, Alex, Julia and the dog formed a circle in front of the dormant fireplace, a stack of Lego blocks in the center.

The past hour weighed on him, heavy as shackles. During the conversation with Alex, he'd been lost, unsure of how much to tell a six-year-old about his failing relative. His son had taken the information in silence and, when the conversation ended, had hopped down from the chair and, still gripping the beloved dinosaur, had gone inside the inn, leaving Eli to wonder if he'd handled the situation properly.

Opal had been wrong. Parenting did not come naturally. He still couldn't grasp the right way to deal with Alex, especially in a circumstance like this.

Without Julia as a buffer, he'd be doomed.

He was still puzzled about the Lego blocks she'd given Alex. She hadn't been to town today. He'd been driving her vehicle.

Wherever the blocks had come from, they'd sparked Alex's interest.

"What should we build?" Julia asked.

Alex's small fingers fiddled with the colorful blocks as he considered. "A castle."

"Perfect." She plunked down a wide red base and scooted the other blocks to one side. "Your dad's rebuilding my carriage house. I bet he's good at castles."

She pushed a pile of Lego toward Eli. He took the hint. She was more intuitive about this parenting business than he.

"You live in a castle," Alex murmured.

Julia's smile was warm as toasted marshmallows. "My house is a castle?"

"Uh-huh." Alex clicked two yellows and a blue together. "Are you a princess? Mama said princesses live in castles."

"No, I'm just the woman who lives here and makes really good cookies." Pretty crinkles appeared in her cheeks and around her eyes.

"You're a princess." His son was matter-of-fact, no arguments allowed, and Eli had to agree. Julia was pretty special.

"And you," she said, tapping Alex on the nose, "are a superhero. Who's your favorite?"

"Spidey."

"Good choice."

"He saves people so they don't get dead."

Julia and Eli exchanged glances. The haunted, helpless feeling crept up inside Eli's chest. What was he supposed to say to that?

Alex maneuvered his dinosaur through the wall of Lego and into the fort, then let the toy fall on its side. He lay down on his side, too, drew his knees to his chest and closed his eyes.

"Alex?" Eli said, touching his shoulder. "Are you tired, son?"

Alex's lips moved in a soft murmur. "What will happen to my dinosaur when I'm dead?"

The horrible helplessness drained every last ounce of Eli's energy. He looked at Julia, scared and uncertain of what to do. She pressed her fingers to her lips, her expression as troubled as his heart.

The ball was in his court. He was the father. He was elected to fix the problem. What a cruel joke the cosmos had played on this innocent, hurting child.

"Alex, buddy, you're a little boy." He swallowed the thick knot in his throat, searching for the right words. "You aren't going to die for a long, long time."

"Mama died. She went to the hospital and never came back."

That sharp stab came again, deeper and harder this time. He should have been here for them. He should have done... something.

"I know." What was he supposed to say? How did he help his son cope with a loss of this magnitude? "I'm sorry. Your mom was a beautiful lady."

"She read me books."

Julia stroked a hand over Alex's back. "You miss her, don't you, Alex?"

"I want her to come home. Aunt Opal is dead, too. What's the use of making castles if I'm dead?"

"Aunt Opal is not dead, Alex. She's in a rehab center trying to get better."

"She won't. Everybody dies. That's what my friend Ryan said. He said everybody dies all the time."

"That's not true. Little boys live many years."

But Alex covered his ears with both hands and didn't play anymore.

★ ★ ★

Later that night, after Alex fell asleep, Eli sat at the small table in the corner of the spacious Blueberry Room and opened Julia's laptop. He was grateful for the use of the device, considering all the time he spent online researching. Between home-make-over videos and parenting advice, he burned the candle late.

Tonight, his research took a deeper turn as he searched for grief forums. Somebody somewhere must share his experience of being a new, clueless father with a grieving child.

He read through a number of sites before settling on a general forum that caught his attention. Everyone had lost someone. Everyone was hurting, mourning, begging for help to get through the days and nights. Eli's chest tightened and grew hot. A gripping pain clawed at his belly. Jessica's five-year-old face seemed to flash on the screen. He blinked her away as he'd done since he was thirteen. Don't think about it, don't talk it about it, and the pain would go away.

But the pain didn't go away. It never had.

Jessica's death swarmed on him, caught him off guard, a kick in the gut that left him breathless and shaky. Is this how Alex felt?

His forehead dampened. He clicked off the website and went into the bathroom for a drink.

This wasn't about Jessica or him.

He gulped down the cold water and breathed deeply for several seconds, hands propped on the bathroom sink. Blood still thrumming in his neck, he strode to Alex's bedside and watched the child's small chest rise and fall in peaceful slumber. Slowly, his pulse settled and his aching heart beat for his son instead of his own long-ago tragedy. Alex was so small and sweet and brokenhearted, and Eli hoped someday the boy would love him.

The thought surprised him. He hadn't expected this, to want

love from a child he'd never known. Nor had he expected to love Alex so quickly and fiercely, but he did. Oh, he did.

With a kiss to Alex's smooth tanned forehead, he breathed in the soap and clean scent of his son's bath and went back to the computer.

When he took up the laptop again, something rolled off the desk and hit the top of his foot. Curious, he discovered a hard little ball, like a marble but made of reddish clay and not perfectly round. He turned the object over in his hands, recalling the dish in the entryway containing similar items. Antique marbles, Julia had told him, found on the property...but where had this one come from?

Night pulsed through Julia's open window, a mix of tree frogs and cicadas. She'd listened as the last of the guests came in for the night, the usual time when she could finally sleep for a few hours. Attuned to every nuance of the comforting old house, she felt the hum of pipes vibrate as one of the women in the Mulberry Room showered. Spring brought guests for area history, the reenactments and the river and often for the ambience of a Civil War house filled with memories.

This afternoon, a pair of ghost hunters had checked in asking questions she didn't want to answer. If Peach Orchard Inn had ghosts, she welcomed them. They'd been here first and they understood what the living didn't.

There she went again, being crazy.

She rose, checked the iPad and, upon seeing Mikey's precious picture, kissed her fingertips and placed them on the beloved face.

The night wind carried the call of a whippoorwill. She loved that mournful sound and, restless now, tossed on her robe and went out on the back veranda. Bingo followed her, a bit of a surprise given his recent propensity for Alex.

She propped her bare feet on the bottom porch railing and tilted her head back, listening to the bird calling for his true love.

The moon was a half chunk of mozzarella tonight, a fanciful thought that made her smile. A soft Southern wind whispered through the orchard and the magnolias, lifting the flowering fragrances over the acreage.

She heard it then, the sound of many horse hooves, slowly tramping up the driveway. With eyes closed, she listened, or imagined, whichever the case might be. A heavy ache accompanied the sound as if the very air remembered something that had happened here. There was another emotion, too. Something strong and hopeful, the elements that had first attracted her to Peach Orchard, the emotional tug of the house that made her believe she'd find peace in this place.

And in some ways, she had.

All old houses in the South carried memories and, whether those memories lingered in the walls or only in the mind, they existed for a purpose. Learning that purpose was now her task. What did her house have to teach? Something, she was sure, given the marbles and the echoes of the past.

She heard the crunch of boots on gravel, coming closer, so close as to seem real.

"Julia."

Her eyes flew open, surprised to see a real human being. As he had that first morning, Eli came toward her, only this time she wasn't startled. A welcome rose inside her and she smiled.

"Have a seat, fellow seeker." She realized how silly the words sounded, but Eli didn't snicker. He scraped a chair near to hers.

"I heard you come outside," he said.

She rolled her head toward him. "Did I wake you?"

"No."

"Alex?"

"Sleeping. He let me read to him tonight."

"That's a good thing."

"I feel...useless."

"You're doing fine."

"I don't know." He sighed, one strong puff of air that dissipated beyond the shadowy porch, blending with the figments of her imagination. "I've been reading grief forums for the last hour, seeking answers. How much can a six-year-old understand?"

"I don't know." Had Mikey ever had a reason to mourn? If he had, she didn't remember, and that made her a little sad.

"I'm afraid of saying the wrong thing so I say nothing, but is that even worse?" His baritone rumbled quietly as if he spoke more to himself than to her, a man seeking answers that neither of them had. "Should I encourage him to talk about his mother? Or is it better not to stir up memories and upset him more?"

"I'm a woman. We talk." About most things. "But I'm not a psychologist. Have you considered counseling?"

"Thought about it."

Julia heard what he wasn't saying. Counseling cost money he didn't have. Not with the pittance she paid him.

He held something toward her in the palm of his hand. "I found this tonight in my room."

"Oh. The marbles." So far, she was the only one who had ever found one, and only her craziness made her believe that she was special, sought out for the comfort of a tiny clay ball. "You've seen them in the credenza bowl in the foyer."

"I have, but until tonight I hadn't considered them much. Did you know they're pre–Civil War era like the house? I looked online."

"Yes, I know." She curled one foot beneath her and turned to face Eli. "Where exactly did you find this one?"

"On the desk in my room. I don't recall seeing it earlier."

She trailed her fingertips across the dog's head. "I found one tonight, too."

"No kidding?"

"Could I ask you something, Eli, without you thinking I've gone off the deep end?"

"Sure."

"What were you feeling right before you found the marble?"

If he considered her question bizarre, he was too polite to let on. "Lousy. Helpless. Worried about Alex."

"Hmm." She uncurled her legs and went to the porch railing, one hand on a smooth column. "This may seem fanciful but every time I find one, I've been down, in need of cheering. Tonight—" She stopped, caught herself before she told him about Mikey. Another child needed their attention now. "I was troubled about some things, and I'm positive the marble was not on the floor when I went into my room. But when I started to leave, I stepped on it."

"I felt the same about this one. I don't think it was there before, but how could a centuries-old marble have suddenly appeared?"

"Old houses," she said, leaving the rest unsaid.

"I don't believe in ghosts."

"Do you believe in angels sent to comfort?" All right, enough. She was going off the deep end.

"I don't know. But I am curious now about the history of this place. What do you know about it?"

"The house was built before the Civil War and local lore says it was used as a hospital for the war wounded. Slaves once lived in cabins below the knoll not far from the creek, though there is nothing left to prove either of those stories."

"Those are pretty significant facts. You'd think they'd be recorded somewhere."

"They probably are, if they're true."

"Do you think they are?"

"I do. Valery and I found old newspapers in the walls dating from back to 1840. We found some Civil War uniform buttons, too, and a couple of coins. They're in the display cabinet in the parlor next to one of the framed papers. Oh, and the rumors that a woman who lived here consorted with the Yankees and now the place is haunted. They say that about the gristmill across the road, too."

"Southerners put a lot of stock in the past clinging to the future."

"Or vice versa," she said, thinking about Mikey again. "The Sweat twins might know more. They're walking history books."

"Sweat twins?"

"You remember. The ladies who came for tea and scones. The same ones who declared, behind their white gloves, that you looked enough like Colonel Otis Champ to be his twin." She turned her head to gaze at him with amusement. Indeed, the twins had been taken with her new worker when they'd popped in again a few days ago. "And everyone knows Colonel Champ was the handsomest devil in Southern Tennessee." She pressed a hand to her heart in imitation of the dear sisters. "Why, Vida Jean almost married the man in the summer of 1950."

Eli chuckled, exactly the reaction she was going for, so she laughed too. The glorious freedom of laughter had a curious healing effect.

He came to the railing and stepped close enough that her skin prickled but far enough away to be polite. "I liked them."

"The twins are wonderful. They're frank and open, funny and eccentric. Their friendship has meant a lot to me these past few years." Talking to Eli beneath the cover of darkness was natural and easy.

"You have a good family, too."

"I do. The best." Behind them, the old house sighed and seemed to hover, a motherly, protective presence, the very presence that had drawn her here in the first place. If this was a ghost or an angel, she was glad it had chosen her.

She was glad, too, for the presence of this man at her elbow who'd come as a stranger, unwittingly complicating her life while giving her new reasons to get up every day. He was still a puzzle, a mystery as much as the marbles, but he was neither ghost nor angel. The growing hum of awareness assured her of that.

"Tell me about your family, Eli. What happened to them?"

Eli took his time answering as a shooting star rocketed across the Southern sky, a blink of flame older than this house, older perhaps than the earth itself. Julia saw the flash, too, and pointed.

"A falling star."

"I saw."

The night was magical, or perhaps the magic was in Julia and the way she made him feel. Once, long ago when he'd been another man, he would have dropped a casual arm around her shoulders, maybe made a move or two. Tonight, he gripped the porch railing, grounding himself in the present even though the house whispered of the past and Julia asked to know more than he dared tell her.

The leaves in the live oak whispered their secrets to the moon, but he did not have the freedom to do the same. Freedom came with the stringent price of silence.

But there was nostalgia at Peach Orchard and tonight he missed what he could never have again.

"As a boy, I had a tree house in the backyard. In the summer I'd sleep out there and watch the stars. My parents may have indulged me a little." A lot, and he still didn't understand why they hadn't been enough to make him happy. "I had a telescope, too, and was sure I'd discover a new planet every night."

"Maybe you did."

"Maybe." His lips curved. "Mostly, I discovered blinking airplanes and claimed them as the newest comet. My dad would come out sometimes and watch the stars with me." The memory hurt like a jab to the eye.

"He must have been a good man."

"He is."

At the change in verb tense, Julia tilted her pretty face toward him. He could see the shadowy curve of her cheek and wished he had a right to touch the smooth skin. Some crazy part of him wanted to trace a fingertip over her perfect eyebrows. Among other things.

"Is your father still alive?"

"Both parents are, but we're...estranged."

"I'm sorry."

"So am I." Afraid she'd press for more, he freely offered what he could. "I was a wild, reckless teenager. I hurt them a lot."

"That doesn't sound like you."

"Losing everything changes a man." Being in prison had nearly killed him and, though he'd lived, he'd been stripped bare of the person he'd once been. "My parents couldn't take any more, I guess."

"How long since you've tried to talk to them?"

"Years." He recalled the exact day, the last time he'd heard from his father. At the time, he'd blown off the threat of being disinherited and ostracized from his family. Dad was furious the way he had been every time Eli screwed up, but this time he hadn't gotten over the anger in a few days. When the lawyer sent notice that he'd been fired and Eli would be at the mercy of a court-appointed attorney, Eli had been more angry than convinced. When neither Mom nor Dad appeared at his trial, he'd gotten scared. Slowly, the truth had sunk in, just as his prison sentence had. No one on either side of his family contacted him ever again. No one responded to his letters or calls. He'd burned his final bridge home.

"You're different now. Grown-up and mature. Surely, they'll see that and want you back in their lives. Perhaps you should try to mend fences."

He shook his head, but the empty spot in his chest hungered for that very thing. "My father is a strong, confident man. In business, when he makes a decision, the deal is done and he doesn't back down. He loathes me. In his mind, I don't exist, and that's not likely to ever change."

"One thing I can promise you. A mother's love is never ending. I'll wager she misses you." She touched his forearm and the warmth of her skin was a balm. "You should try."

Eli battled the urge again, the need to be close to this soft, lovely woman. He'd been controlled for so long, but Julia untied the ropes that held him bound. She didn't know, couldn't know, what she did to him or that she made him wish he was a better man than he'd ever be. Like his family, the beautiful innkeeper deserved better.

"Someday, maybe." When he had his life together. When he'd done something to prove that he was worthy of the Donovan name again.

At the rate he was going, that could be a long, long time.

Some days Eli wondered if he'd taken on more than he could accomplish. Not that he was complaining. A man who'd had someone looking over his shoulder for years relished the freedom of setting his own pace and being able to travel inside and out without electric, barb-tipped fences to hold him back.

His parole officer was the only one still keeping tabs on him, and he'd kept the man happy with vague answers about odd jobs in construction and the news that he had a son to support. It was the truth, and Mr. Clifford sounded satisfied. But the worry of discovery hung over Eli's head like a noose.

He was in love with this old carriage house, with all of Peach Orchard Inn, to tell the truth, and wanted to stick around. History seeped from the walls and sometimes, when he was alone, he'd sit and ponder the past, who had been here and what kind of lives they'd led. Even the clay marbles had him wondering about the child who'd played with them in this house.

The nerd factor he hadn't known existed had surfaced in prison as he'd been left alone to discover who he really was without the drugs or his parents' money. If any good thing had come from prison, it was that. He'd been forced to find himself, only to discover a man who liked to learn. The business degree completed in prison and useless to a man who had no credit and no stake to start a business was evidence of that. Nevertheless, he was proud of that degree. What else did a convict have to do to keep from going mad?

He smirked at the irony of how interested a man could be in everything when he had nothing.

The antique marble had opened up a whole gamut of interest, and he and Julia had begun to research the house's history in earnest.

He thought about her reference to an angel, but he was a skeptic. Still, the marbles had come from somewhere, whether the walls of the old house or, as she suspected, from somewhere in the woods that Bingo had unearthed.

With dust swirling in the sunbeams, he tossed a broken board onto a wheelbarrow and waited while Alex added a couple of scraps of drywall. Julia didn't approve of Alex's involvement, but the project seemed a way to connect with his son. He was trying everything he'd read in the forums.

"Good job, buddy. You got some muscles."

His son responded with a double-armed flex that made Eli grin. Alex grabbed him by the heart and wouldn't let go.

Julia carted out a five-foot sheet of the same water-damaged drywall to contribute to the pile.

She grabbed him by the heart, as well.

"We got this, Julia."

"I don't mind. Val and Mom are looking after the guests so I'm free to work out here for a while."

"Did the arguing couple leave?"

She rolled her eyes. "Oh, no. That kind stays forever. I think he was jealous of you this morning at breakfast."

"What? Me?"

"Come on, Eli. You had to have noticed Mrs. Barkhimer."

He had. She'd made sure of that. "I don't pay attention to married women."

"Smart man. But she was paying attention to you, and Mr. Barkhimer didn't like it."

"I'll steer clear of the house until they're gone."

"Oh, Eli, I didn't mean that."

"Plenty to do out here, anyway. Even with all the time I've spent in the orchard, the office is coming together. Alex and I can move out here soon."

"Too much dust. Let's wait."

He'd done most of the basics to make the former office space livable, at least for him, as a temporary bed and bath, but the upper compartment was proving to be a challenge. The amount of items stored was overwhelming, and little could be done until they'd been sorted and relocated.

They traipsed back upstairs with Julia hovering over Alex as if she expected him to disappear. Alex didn't seem to mind when she insisted on holding his hand or hoisting him over questionable flooring.

"What should we do with this old box of books?" Eli asked, eyeing the ragged cardboard. "Dump them?"

"Hmm." Julia picked her way through the maze of items. "Let me look."

She plucked a book from the top and flipped it open. "I suppose we should go through and see if any of these are valuable."

"Okay." He opened another and a yellowed piece of paper fluttered to the floor. "What's this?"

Julia picked it up. "Looks like part of a letter." She sucked in a breath. "Oh, my goodness."

"What?" Frowning, Eli moved to her side and peered over her shoulder. She smelled good, like springtime. "What does it say?"

"Look at the date." She touched a fingertip to the top of the page.

"'1864. Dear Will...'" He met her gaze, incredulous. "Do you think it's authentic?"

"I'm no expert but it could be. We've found some really old items. Maybe the content will give clues."

Eli shot a glance at Alex, busily digging in one of the endless boxes, and then read the letter over Julia's shoulder.

Halfway through, both snagged on the same sentence.

"Eli," Julia breathed. "She mentions a bag of marbles this Will person gave her son."

"They couldn't be the same as those on the credenza. Could they?"

"The date matches, and they had to come from somewhere. Wouldn't it be fascinating if they were the same ones? If a child who lived in this house during the Civil War period played with those very marbles?"

"And we could discover who he was?"

"Exactly." Her face lit with excitement. "I can't help thinking there's a reason they keep appearing. If we could discover their original owner, maybe we'd understand—" She stopped in midsentence and shook her head. "I'm getting carried away."

"It's worth checking out." His reply seemed to please her. She looked at him with gratitude.

"Sometimes I imagine things about this house. I don't want you to think I've gone crazy."

"The marbles have been on my mind all day. Both of us finding one last night and now this letter today is…perplexing."

Her lips tipped in a soft smile. "You don't believe in ghosts."

"That letter is not a ghost." He wasn't one for fantasy or the supernatural, but the facts remained. Both of them had found marbles last night. Or maybe the marbles had found them. Then today they'd discovered a letter reference from over a hundred-and-fifty years ago.

"A single mention in a partial letter is not much help. We don't even know who wrote it." Julia gently turned the letter over and found nothing. The paper was brittle and yellowed with age. "The paper is so fragile. I doubt if any others could survive this long."

"Maybe we'll get lucky." The phrase should have been a joke to a man whose luck had run out years ago. For Julia's sake, he hoped it wasn't.

22

Will's orders arrived the next day. Charlotte was in the sewing room off the downstairs parlor, a tiny space with good light not used by soldiers, where she and Edgar's sisters could mend and sew. This cloudy, dreary afternoon that threatened rain, Patience sat next to the silent fireplace, darning socks and humming *Für Elise*, her needle keeping time with the music. Josie was absent as usual. She refused to frequent the downstairs as long as it was "infested with filthy Yankees" and, like Edgar, spent her days as far away from the house as possible.

Her husband's neglect had never bothered Charlotte before, but now it did. Three days ago, she'd walked to the mill with a picnic lunch, seeking to repair whatever she'd broken in her marriage, but the outing had been strained. Other than the farm and the mill, they had little to talk about. Mentions of Benjamin had been met with grunts, whether of approval or disapproval Charlotte despaired of knowing.

She'd wanted to tell him about the honey and the catfish and the pleasure Benjamin had taken in his new marble game, but refrained, afraid. Any discussion that included the Yankees threw him into a red-faced rage. Perhaps, too, she'd been guilt ridden, for most of her conversation would have contained references to Will.

So she'd listened to Edgar's list of complaints against the lazy slaves and Mr. Lincoln, who bore the fault for what had happened to his beloved home.

With a heavy heart, Charlotte stitched a new collar for her husband's shirts and prayed she could mend more than his clothes.

On the pine boards at her feet, Benjamin and Tandy played marbles, a game that had kept them fascinated from the moment Will had offered the small leather pouch.

The house, thankfully, had returned to some semblance of its former self. Most of the sick had recovered sufficiently to camp outside with the other soldiers. Only a handful remained in the parlor, too grievously wounded to go anywhere for some time. They were a sad lot with an uncertain future.

From the window overlooking the veranda, she spotted an unfamiliar rider trotting down the lane of magnolias toward the house.

She wove the needle through the fabric and put the snowy-white collar aside, rising to greet the newcomer. Few from Honey Ridge had darkened the Portlands' door since the Yankee occupation, and she'd lain awake last night wondering what was being said and what she could do to assuage the rumors. Out on the veranda, she paused, recognizing the blue uniform as Union Army, not a visitor from town. A hard knot clutched inside her chest.

She watched as the man dismounted, spoke to Will and handed him a packet.

The knot grew tighter, harder.

Charlotte spun away, crossed the length of the porch and headed north toward the trees. The peaches were long gone, but the arbor of green leafy arms embraced her as she disappeared into the orchard. This was her sanctuary, her solace, the only place where all the watchers couldn't see.

She walked, head down, praying. A wind had picked up, whipping the scent of a dying summer into her nostrils. Dying. She didn't want to think of it, especially if Will was going away, but dying was a major part of war. Dying, not winning some great cause but stealing away everything a man was and everything he could ever be.

Oh, and Will Gadsden could be so much. He already was.

"Charlotte."

Lost in thought, she'd not heard his approach. She whirled, her skirts whispering over the stiff August grass. "Will."

It was enough, this acknowledgment of their Christian names. They stood three feet apart, their eyes clasped in the embrace their bodies were denied. Charlotte gripped the folds of her skirt to keep from reaching for him. She could see the news in his face.

Will removed his cap, held it resolutely, as she did her skirt. "Lizzy told me you were here."

"Lizzy always knows." The words were stiff on her dry lips.

"Orders arrived from General Schofield."

She swallowed. "You're leaving."

She struggled to maintain composure, to present a cool, unflappable British facade, though inside she wept.

Will canted toward her, then seemed to catch himself and stiffened to military posture. "Tomorrow at daylight."

The umbrella of tree limbs shuddered in the breeze. Clouds overhead darkened.

"What about the wounded?"

"Most can travel. The handful too sick or injured will remain. I trust you'll care for them."

"I will do my best." Edgar would be furious but, for Will, she could do this one thing.

Will took a step. "Charlotte."

Oh, his dear and wonderful face. The eyes of kindness. The spirit that had met her as an equal. The man who desired her, who made her feel womanly again. How desperately she wanted to touch him.

"I will miss you, Charlotte."

Every fiber of her being yearned for him. *Don't go. Don't go.*

"Will, I—" She prayed they could both stay strong in these final moments.

"There are things I want to say but mustn't."

"Yes. We mustn't." But how wrong it seemed to send him away, perhaps to his death, without knowing.

He rolled his fingers round the cap brim. Round and round. The thick cloud of silence quivering between them held all the words they could not say for honor's sake. She watched the fine, long hands that had never caressed her because they had no right. Yet the man with rights did not want her.

The conflict confused and wounded. Edgar didn't care. Will did, and the emotion between them was bigger than the sky, bigger than the war, bigger than the differences between north and south.

She looked down at the dying grass, struggling to accept God's will. The handsome captain was not hers. She was not his.

"Will you write to me, Charlotte?"

Her head snapped up. A tiny pulse beat, like winged hope, fluttered madly against her collarbone. "How is that possible?"

"I'll find a way."

"Nothing can come of it, Will. Of this—" She dared not voice the obvious. Would not say *love*.

He held her gaze another long, long moment while a crack splintered through the center of her heart.

Sorrow backlit Will's coffee-dark eyes. His hurt tore at her fading strength.

He retreated a step. "I understand."

Slowly, he replaced his cap, adjusting the fit until he was once again the constrained, professional military man.

Charlotte's throat filled.

"You mean a great deal to me, Charlotte. I wish you well."

"And you, Will Gadsden." She swallowed thickly. "Stay safe. Godspeed."

There was so much more she wanted to say, but silence was more prudent.

He gave a curt nod and pivoted on his boot heel.

Long after the flash of red stripe against Union blue trousers disappeared through the peach trees, Charlotte stood in her Tennessee orchard and tried to breathe.

23

May in Southern Tennessee was a radiant burst of color and sunshine. Eli had missed too many springs not to appreciate them now. Red and yellow tulips and purple Johnny-jump-ups waved from the town's street planters. Citizens strolled from store to store, stopping in the middle of the sidewalk to talk with friends while two white-haired gents occupied a bench outside the sporting goods store.

He stepped up on the sidewalk next to Julia. They'd come into town together on a half dozen errands. First stop was the hardware store, where Julia had chosen paint colors for the carriage house. Then, she'd helped him inventory Opal's house for an upcoming sale, an uncomfortable task that left him feeling empty.

Picking through the remnant of others' lives seemed macabre, especially when one of those people had borne him a son. He hadn't expected to find Mindy's clothes still in the closets.

"Thanks for the help." He didn't know how he would have gotten through it without her. She'd been the one to recognize the importance of preserving a few of Mindy's things for Alex.

"Once gone, they're gone forever," she'd said, her voice sounding strange. "Hold on to memories for him, Eli. He'll thank you someday when he's old enough to understand."

So he had, though the box that was left of Mindy brought his guilt back to slap him in the face. Guilt or not, he'd do whatever his son needed.

"I owe you lunch," he said. "What do you say?"

"After all that work, I'm starved."

He hadn't eaten out since coming to Honey Ridge except to treat Alex to McDonald's fries after school one day. His wallet could manage lunch.

"Lead on. You know the best spots."

She pointed down the street. "Miss Molly's."

His mind, that faithless demon, slid off the path into thoughts of what-if. What if Julia was his? What if he was a respected citizen with a right to a woman like Julia? What if they were a couple going to lunch?

She looked as pretty as the flowers in a silky blue blouse and gray skirt with her shiny hair tied back with a gauzy scarf and her ballet flats tapping on the concrete. Her ex must be an idiot.

Miss Molly's Café, an eatery housed in an old Victorian home between the doughnut shop and the thrift store, buzzed with lunchtime customers and the delicious smells of Southern cuisine. His belly rumbled in anticipation, freeing him from errant thoughts about his boss.

A young waitress offered a smile and a menu as they entered. "Hi, Julia. Eli, right?" When he nodded, surprised, she went on. "Y'all might have to wait a few minutes. I think Boots and Clara are about done, though, and you can have their table."

"No rush, Sarah," Julia answered with her usual graciousness. "We'll decide on our order while we wait."

They retreated to an empty spot inside the door next to the window and had barely opened the menus when a pregnant brunette and a tall, brown-haired man in a black business suit entered the café. The man immediately spotted Julia.

"Jules, hello. How are you?"

Julia's fingers tightened on the edges of the menu. Eli didn't know who the guy was, but Julia was not particularly happy to see him.

"Hello, David." She offered a slight smile to the woman. "Cindy. Congratulations on the new baby."

"Thank you. We're excited for Brandon to have a playmate. I want a girl this time." The pregnant woman looped a possessive arm around her husband's elbow and leaned into him. "David is ecstatic, aren't you, honey?"

"Of course." The man absently patted her hand, but his focus had moved to Eli. "I don't believe I've met your friend."

Julia gave him a long, cool appraisal and said, "Eli Donovan, meet David Presley and his...wife, Cindy."

Presley. Julia's last name. So this was the idiot ex. The lawyer. Eli vacillated between revulsion and fear and settled on a reminder that a lawyer in Southern Tennessee had no reason to recognize an ex-con from Knoxville. Nevertheless, sweat prickled on the back of his neck.

Eli fought the negative reaction and shook the offered hand, assessing the man. Slick, well dressed and good-looking with a firm handclasp and a confident air. The kind of attorney his father would hire. He could see Julia with a man like this.

"Eli, my pleasure," Presley said. "I know most people in Honey Ridge, but I'm not familiar with any Donovans. Are you new in town?"

"I've been here a while." Keeping a low profile. Avoiding

circumstances like this one. Keeping his parole officer at bay. Now he felt vulnerable and conspicuous, as if the word *ex-con* was branded on his forehead.

"Eli and his son are staying at the inn," Julia interrupted.

David remained cool, but his eyes narrowed. "You have a son?"

Julia stiffened. The conversation with her ex disturbed her more than him. He wanted to get her out of here.

"I think our table is ready," Eli said. "If you'll excuse us. Nice meeting you."

Without awaiting a reply, he put a hand to Julia's back and guided her to the open table.

Julia wanted to hug Eli.

"Thank you," she said, when they'd been seated. "That was awkward, and I'm sorry you had to be involved."

"Your ex, I gathered."

"Yes."

One black eyebrow twitched upward. "Still gets under your skin?"

"Not because I pine after him. Trust me on that."

"Bad memories?"

She fidgeted with the edge of the menu. "I never thought he'd do the things he did."

"He hurt you."

"Ripped my heart out at the worst possible time of my life and then pulled every lawyer trick in the book against me."

"It must be tough to live in a small town with your ex and his new wife."

"At first, seeing them was horrible, but now…" She shrugged. "These little run-ins are merely uncomfortable."

He tapped the menu. "What are we ordering?"

The quick change of subject startled then pleased her. "You're right. David and Cindy do not deserve any more of our time." She flipped open the menu and pointed out her favorite. "Grits and shrimp. They're terrific here."

"Make that two, then, and iced tea, though nobody's tea can match yours."

"Why, Mr. Donovan, you say the sweetest things." Her intentional imitation of a Southern belle worked. His face lit in amusement. She liked that, liked the changes in Eli since he'd come to work at the inn, liked believing she had a part in making him happier and easier in his skin.

The waitress came and took their orders and remained long enough for Julia to inquire about her sick mother and offer to take a casserole by on Sunday. David and Cindy breezed past and took a table kitty-corner from theirs. Unfortunately, she could look directly into David's unfaithful face, though David wasn't the one who made her the most uncomfortable. Cindy and her pregnant belly scraped at an open wound.

Making a concerted effort to forget about the couple, she said, "I have some business at the courthouse before we go home. Want to come along or do you have something else to do?"

At least once a month, she paid a visit to the evidence room. Detective Brower was kind enough to let her look through the file, though nothing new had been added in a long time. Still, she lived for the day when some missing piece of the puzzle would jump at her.

Eli frowned. "The courthouse? No, I'll—" He seemed to be searching for an answer. "Maybe I'll go to the library and read up on local Civil War history."

"Brilliant idea. Ask either of the librarians, Tawny Brown or Carrie Riley if they can recommend anything."

"Carrie Riley?"

"Trey's sister. She works at the library."

"Good to know. It would be cool if we could learn something new about the house."

"Or about Will and those marbles."

Before they could continue the conversation, two women breezed up to the table. One woman was a knockout with long, dark auburn hair, stylish clothes and a high-maintenance appearance. The other was pretty but in a simple way and had the studious look of a librarian, which she was.

"Julia!" Nikki, the stylish sister, bent for a quick hug.

"Hey. Speak of the devil. Carrie, I was just telling Eli to ask you for help at the library."

"Oh, sorry. I'm off today, but Tawny's there. She'll help you, or you could drop by tomorrow." Carrie's sweet smile settled on Eli. "Introduce us, Julia."

Still single, the librarian was a quiet woman who'd lived in the shadow of two gorgeous, outgoing sisters and was still searching for Mr. Right. In high school, Julia had felt sorry for her. She wasn't surprised at the brunette's obvious interest in Eli. What did surprise Julia was the sour stir of jealousy in her belly.

"Eli, these are two of Trey Riley's sisters, Carrie and Nikki."

"Oh, do you know our baby brother?" Nikki grew more animated.

"He helped me fix my car a few days ago. Nice guy."

"He's a darling. If only he'd let us run his life." Nikki grinned at her own joke. "Isn't that right, Carrie?"

Carrie snorted. "Nikki tried to fix him up with Madelyn Baker."

"The widow?"

"Yes," Carrie said pointedly, "the widow with five children and a live-in boyfriend."

Nikki widened her brown eyes and said, "Oops."

The sisters cracked up laughing and Julia joined them. She

looked at Eli. He was grinning, too, a rare event that softened him and made him deadly attractive.

"So, what are the fearsome Riley sisters up to today?"

"We're on one of our marathon shopping sprees." Nikki tossed her hair back with a quick flick of her hand. "Carrie absolutely must have a new purse. Look at that ugly thing." She motioned to her sister's handbag.

With a sheepish grin, Carrie lifted the offending bag. "I hate purse shopping, but you know Nikki."

"I do, indeed. She once dragged me all over Chattanooga in search of purple espadrilles."

"Bet you found them, too. Eventually." Carrie laughed.

"You'd win that bet. Nikki always gets her shoes. Or in your case, purse."

Carrie made a cute face as though she didn't care nearly as much about the handbag dilemma as Nikki did.

"Well, hey," Nikki said. "We could talk forever as you well know, but we need to get a table and then get rid of that god-awful purse before the sun sets on another day."

"Good to see you both." And Julia meant it. Having Trey's long legs stretched out on her porch last week had reminded Julia of the people she'd let slide away, people she'd cared about. "Why don't you come out to the inn soon and have tea or something? Bring Bailey, too, if she's free."

Nikki blinked. The sisters exchanged glances. "We'd love to, Julia. Like old times."

"I'd like that very much."

The slightly overwhelming pair headed to their table, leaving behind their exuberance and a good feeling.

"Now, you know why Trey became a police officer."

"To protect himself from three sisters?"

"Exactly."

Heads close, they laughed.

Inadvertently, she glanced up and caught David watching her with a curious expression. Darn if it didn't feel good to be laughing with a good-looking man after all this time alone. Let David think what he liked.

They parted ways at the library, a short walk from the café. The intense interest from Julia's ex worried Eli. He was getting too comfortable in Honey Ridge, and that was dangerous. David was a reminder of why he shouldn't.

People accepted him, probably because of his association with Julia, who was obviously liked and respected. He'd made a friend or two and was settling in like a normal citizen. Julia had introduced him to everyone who had stopped at the table. He'd especially liked Trey's sisters.

He'd noticed Carrie's interest and couldn't deny the ego boost, though he'd be out of his mind to pursue a relationship with any woman. Even the one who interested him most. Julia deserved a good guy like Trey, and if Eli suffered a heavy dose of envy that the cop had every right to Julia while he didn't, he'd have to get used to it.

The tight feeling stretched inside his chest, constraining him. Like handcuffs.

"The courthouse is the building in the middle of the square." Julia interrupted his thoughts to point toward a stately brick building with a flagpole and an enormous lawn clock. "I guess you knew that."

"Yes." He'd driven around town to become familiar with the place. He could find the school and the police station in his sleep. The courthouse, too, the kind of place he had no desire to see the inside of ever again.

He entered the modern brick-and-glass library that smelled of books and floor polish. At the desk, he asked for Tawny Brown, a woman with extremely short hair and huge earrings who directed him to a wall of local history books. As he perused the information, his mind kept drifting to Julia.

Her ex-husband had stared at them throughout their meal, and Eli wondered if the curiosity was because of Julia or him, the stranger who might look too familiar to an officer of the court. He tried to ignore the trickle of fear down his spine and refocused on the research. He was as paranoid about being recognized as Julia was about Alex getting hurt. No one here knew him. His secret was safe, and with time and familiarity, maybe he could stop looking over his shoulder and expecting the worst.

He was bent over a memoir written by a local veteran of the Civil War when he heard whispers and looked up. The Sweat twins stood on the opposite side of the round table waiting for him to notice them. And who wouldn't. Identical from their straw sunhats to their white patent purses and sunflower dresses, the ladies stood out in a crowd.

"We were sure that was you, weren't we, Vida Jean?"

"Yes, we were. I told Willa Dean. That's Eli Donovan right there." She patted a white-gloved hand over her heart. "Makes me almost swoon to think of how much you resemble dear Colonel Champ. God rest his soul. And here you are."

"Ladies." Eli stood in deference to the women.

"Oh, would you look at those manners, Willa Dean?" Vida Jean tittered. "May we join you, sir?"

"I'd be delighted." He pulled out a chair for each of them, enjoying the opportunity to further impress with the etiquette classes he'd attended at an early age. It had been a long time. A very long time. "Julia and I were going to pay you a visit today."

"Really?" Willa Dean sat as straight as one of Julia's porch columns, her hands on the clasp of her pocketbook.

"We're researching the inn and thought you might be of assistance."

"Well, certainly we could." Vida Jean tapped the corner of her bright pink mouth. "Granddaddy Beacon owned the property behind the Peach Orchard, and we girls grew up playing along the creek that runs by the grist mill."

"I remember the house when those foreigners lived there." Willa Dean leaned forward and in a stage whisper said, "Yankees, you know. They were from Ohio, weren't they, sister?"

"Indiana."

"No, no, I have it now. Idaho. Remember, we joked about the potatoes and fully expected them to grow spuds at Peach Orchard."

Vida Jean waved away her sister's comment and said to Eli, "Grandmother Beacon on Mama's side was a cousin to Stephen Cower whose great uncle Bertrand was the original owner of Peach Orchard."

"No, Vida Jean, the Cowers were hired hands. The Portland family built Peach Orchard."

"I do believe you're right, sister. The Portlands owned Peach Orchard."

"Wasn't there was some kind of scandal over a slave and the owner?"

"Oh, yes, indeed. The house wouldn't be haunted if there hadn't been scandals. Mr. Portland had a slave mistress so Mrs. Portland took a Yankee lover, they say, and spied for the North, a terrible scandal if ever there was one. Everyone in those days had a scandal or two to keep life entertaining." Vida Jean leaned toward him in a cloud of Estée Lauder. "Isn't that right, Mr. Donovan?"

"The house is haunted?" Eli asked with interest, thinking of his conversation with Julia about the marbles.

"My dear Mr. Donovan, half the buildings in Honey Ridge are haunted by a Civil War soldier or his sweetheart left behind to mourn him to eternity. Indeed, half the South is haunted if one is a believer in such things. But the inn is special."

"How so?"

"Well—" Willa Dean looked over one shoulder and then the other as if checking for eavesdroppers. And then, as if she feared breathing the word, she whispered, "Yankees. The house was occupied by Federals during the war."

This was not new information, but he didn't let on.

"A lot of Tennessee homes were occupied during that time," he said. "That doesn't make them haunted."

"Yankees died there. Tons of them, I'm sure." Willa straightened with a sniff. "Cousin Tobias once saw an apparition in the upstairs window."

Vida Jean snorted. "Yes, and he also claimed to have been abducted by aliens four times. He painted a green dot in the middle of his belly as proof."

Willa Dean frowned, drawing together a pair of painted-on eyebrows. "He is a bit eccentric, I suppose, the way he quotes *Star Trek* with a Scottish brogue and wears a kilt to the family Christmas party."

"And not a drop of Scots blood in our lineage."

They were making his brain spin.

Eli cleared his throat. In tandem, two heads swiveled toward him.

"We found a letter dated 1864 addressed to someone named Will. Any idea who he was?"

"A letter? Oh, how romantic. Isn't that romantic, Willa?"

"Yes, sister. Terribly romantic." Willa Dean gripped an enormous tote bag to her stomach. "Never heard of him, though. Did you look through the books and the microfiche?"

"And the computer," Vida Jean said. "We find all kinds of things on the web. It's quite exciting."

Eli nodded. "I searched. No luck."

"Well, fiddle." Both ladies looked crestfallen. "We have not helped you one bit."

"You have." He glanced at the wall clock and then stood, collecting the books he wanted to check out. "I have to meet Julia at the courthouse in a few minutes. Thank you, ladies."

"If we think of anything else, we'll pop by for a visit."

"Yes, we will." Willa Dean opened and closed the snap on her purse with a flick of her thumbs. "We try to drop in on Julia weekly to make sure she's all right."

"Bless her heart."

"We think the world of that sweet girl. Why, she practically lived at our house when she was a little tyke. Prettiest little doll."

"Adorable, and these past few years haven't been kind to her. We've had hope, though, that things were improving."

"When she let you bring that precious boy of yours to the inn, I said to Willa Dean, maybe she's beginning to heal. Didn't I, sister?"

"Yes, you did. She's finally started to heal. That's what you said."

"Bless her heart. But having a little boy on the property has to be a reminder."

Baffled, Eli asked, "A reminder of what?"

Identical stares turned on him.

"Why, of Michael, of course."

"Michael?" Were they talking about Julia's ex-husband? But his name was David.

Vida Jean put a finger to her painted, wrinkled lips. "She didn't tell you?"

"Tell me what?" He was prying and shouldn't. He certainly wanted no one prying into his affairs. But everything about Julia interested him. *Everything.*

Willa Dean placed a gloved hand over his. "Julia lost a son. About six or seven years ago, Michael was abducted and has never been seen again."

Eli left the library, reeling from the tragic story told by the Sweat twins. He had to fight against running the dozen blocks to the school to make sure Alex was safe. And once that emotion calmed, he fought not to run to the courthouse and pull Julia close. She'd lived a nightmare. Still lived it.

How could a child vanish and never be found? How could a parent ever come to grips with the terrifying unknowns?

He'd only been a father a short time, but Alex had become his world, his reason for trying to make a better life, his future.

"Julia," he whispered. No wonder she was paranoid about Alex's safety.

He crossed the street, hands balled into fists and chest aching for the woman he'd come to care for. She was too good for this to happen to her. It wasn't fair. It wasn't right.

He wanted to hit something.

Head down, he barely saw the shadow in time to avoid running into Trey Riley. The officer was coming from the direction of the courthouse.

"Eli, great seeing you. How's the car doing?"

"Fine." His mind was not on his vehicle. All he could think of was getting to Julia. He didn't know what he would do, but he had to see her.

"Glad to hear it."

"Thanks again." He started on toward the courthouse and Trey fell in step with him.

"I was going to give you a call."

Eli pulled his thoughts together enough to reply. "That so?"

"Yeah." The affable officer waved a hand at the sky. "Great weather coming up this weekend, so I was thinking about fishing Sunday after church. I promised my seven-year-old nephew, but he'd probably have more fun with Alex along. What do you say?"

"Sure. Sure." Eli rubbed the back of his neck, heart pounding. Julia's son had been abducted. Right here in small-town Tennessee where kids should be safe.

"Are you okay?"

"What?" He tried to focus on his friend. "Sorry. I—I just learned about Julia's son."

"Oh. Yeah. Julia was in my office not ten minutes ago." Trey slowed, shook his head in a kind of denial that such a thing could occur in Honey Ridge. His cheeks puffed out in a gust of air. "I was living away at the time, but the case is still open. Not that there's been any new information."

"Unbelievable." Eli had been sitting in a jail cell, hoping for reprieve while Julia's little boy was being abducted. His nightmare was nothing compared to hers. His had been his own doing.

"We get leads now and then, but nothing ever comes of them."

"How does a parent survive that?"

"Nikki said during the first few days and weeks, Julia and her husband were wild people. They worked the press, made flyers and helped investigators. Julia even got security cameras installed outside the school and on all the buses. But as hope diminished, she fell apart."

"Media must have been intense." He knew a little about that himself.

"For a while. I've heard it was crazy around here. This is a small town and nothing of that sort had ever happened. After a while, Julia couldn't take the pressure and attention anymore. Before she and Val bought the house at Peach Orchard, she had become reclusive and depressed, but who can blame her?"

His thoughts exactly. And her cretin husband had divorced her.

Eli stopped at the bottom of the tall courthouse steps. He hadn't been in a courthouse since his sentencing and didn't particularly want to go in there now.

Trey started up. Eli took in the big redbrick building with the dozen steps leading to the double wooden doors.

What he'd endured was nothing compared to Julia.

Head down, heart pounding, Eli started up.

24

On the short drive back to Peach Orchard Inn, Eli listened to Julia chatter but couldn't have repeated the conversation if his life had depended on it. He brooded.

Should he say something? Or keep his mouth shut? If she'd wanted him to know about her son, wouldn't she have told him?

After they'd parked the car and unloaded the bag of groceries she'd grabbed at Kroger, Julia stopped in the parlor to offer advice, refreshments, and a take-along snack to three guests planning a hike. Her graciousness meant more to him now than before. Julia, with her heart of anguish, nurtured her guests the way she must long to nurture her son.

He was struck then by the things she'd done and said that hinted at her loss, and the foolish things he'd replied, not knowing about her child.

While she conversed with her guests in her warm, charming manner, Eli went ahead of her into the kitchen. He was capable of pouring tea.

He took a tray, as he'd watched her do a dozen times, and

poured glasses for each guest, added emerald-green napkins and a plate of sliced lemon cake.

She came in and her face lit at the simple gesture. Her pleasure made him happy. His chest was full of her.

After she left with the tray, he wandered out onto the porch, past the place where they'd shared confidences and whimsy in the night. Where the temptation to hold her had nearly overwhelmed him.

The air was scented flower sweet and thick with the coming heat. A pair of bluebirds dipped and fluttered in courtship near the birdbath.

Hands jammed into his pockets, Eli started toward the orchard. Today, the hunger to be outdoors outweighed the need for property restoration. Since prison he always reacted this way. When the world pressed in, he wanted out.

He heard the doors open behind him but kept walking. Julia caught up to him. "Don't you want tea?"

"Changed my mind."

"Is something wrong?"

"Yes."

They'd reached the edge of the orchard and he entered the rows of trees, moving down the alleyway he'd cleared almost to the center of the fifteen-acre area. He stopped and turned to face her.

"Your son." He didn't know how to approach a subject so dear and yet so terrible. "The Sweat twins told me."

Her mouth opened but no words came out. She closed it again. A myriad of emotion flickered across her face like a terrible kind of channel surfing. Pain, sorrow, helplessness. "It isn't a secret. Mikey has a Facebook page and is on all the missing-child sites. I even increase the reward every year, but I don't know how to tell people. The words are so hard to say. I'm sorry."

"You don't owe me that," he said harshly. "Me or anyone."

She crossed her arms and pulled inside herself as she must have done so many times for self-protection. "Now you know why I worry about Alex."

"Yes, I'm the one who's sorry. I didn't understand." Somehow his hands were on her upper arms. Through the silky top, her bones felt fragile and small beneath his strong fingers. Crushable. She'd been crushed before, and yet she'd withstood the most heinous thing that could happen to a mother. "You're the bravest woman I've ever met."

Tears gathered on her bottom lashes. She shook her head, denying him. "I'm scared all the time."

"Courage is moving forward even when you're scared to death." The sentiment he'd read somewhere took on real meaning. He wanted her to know, needed her to see how she moved him. "You do that every day. You're strong, Julia. Strong and brave." And beautiful and kind and good. But he didn't say those things. He couldn't. He, the man who knew the danger of words, had already said too much.

The silvery tears slid to her cheeks. Others followed in silent sorrow. They ripped him.

"Don't cry. I didn't mean to make you cry."

Then, because he'd caused her pain, he could do no less than offer comfort. He slid his hands from her arms to her back and stepped into her, engulfed her slender form with his much bigger one. Her arms went around his waist and she leaned in as if she, too, had a void of human comfort. Emboldened, he cradled the back of her head, stroking the silken hair as he gently pressed her to his chest. Her breath was warm and moist against his T-shirt and he breathed in her perfume along with the fruity sweetness of young peaches.

More than seven years had passed since he'd been this close to a woman. Feelings rushed through him like summer rain flooding down Magnolia Creek. A woman's touch was a magical thing. He certainly hadn't forgotten that, and oh, he'd missed it.

Eli held her gently, loosely, but she didn't move away. A hard spot inside him softened.

"He was the most beautiful little boy," she murmured, and Eli's heart broke for her.

"Tell me about him." He rubbed her back in slow circles, the sun warming his hand and the peach trees bending low to listen as if they'd been privy to many shared confidences.

She told him of the second-grader who'd been stolen somewhere between the school bus and the elementary school and never returned. Of a boy who'd loved baseball and frogs and corn on the cob. Who'd always worn his red Cardinals ball cap and carried an Albert Pujols trading card in his backpack. And when she told of that final devastating morning when her world had shattered, his heart shattered, too.

She wept, and he held her, giving what comfort he could, a pitiful offering in the face of so great a loss. He knew then that the Legos given to Alex had belonged to Mikey. A chink crumbled from the wall he'd built around his heart.

He wanted so much to make her world better, and to his great consternation, Eli realized he might be falling in love.

Later, Julia wondered what had come over her in those moments in the peach orchard, for when Eli had asked about Mikey she'd crumbled. Not because of the loss, though that would be a fresh wound until Mikey came home, but because of Eli's concern, because of the tender way he'd pulled her into his arms, a wary man who held himself aloof. He was the brave one, not her, brave enough to listen to recollections that her family found too painful to hear.

After an embarrassing amount of sniffling, she'd stepped

away from his embrace and begun to walk, talking about Mikey. Eli had fallen into step and the fact that he'd held her hand as they walked was a solace she couldn't deny.

For an hour or more they'd roamed through the trees, mostly hidden from the house, while she'd shared her lost son with a man who'd found his. The irony was not wasted on either of them.

Eventually, Valery had texted an SOS demanding to know where she was, and Julia left Eli to his work in the orchard and returned to the inn. As she walked away, she'd felt him watching her and she'd wanted to turn back, to stay in the sanctuary that was Eli Donovan.

Now, as she prepared dinner, she thought about the final embrace. She wasn't sure which of them instigated it. Her, perhaps, in what began as gratitude but ended in something else. He'd held her and she'd wondered if he might kiss her. She'd wanted him to.

"Anything I can do to help?" Valery came into the kitchen with her usual bounce and verve.

Though breakfast was for guests, dinner was a private family affair with only the two of them and now with Eli and Alex.

"Set the table?"

"Can do." Her sister took four plates from the glass-front cabinets. The china place settings had been rummaged from an antique store and though they weren't a perfect match, they were exactly right for the old inn. "What were you and Eli doing out there for such a long time?"

Julia fought a blush. She couldn't hide from her sister. "Talking."

"So that's what they call it these days?" Valery's mouth twisted in a funny face.

"Hush."

"He has a thing for you."

"I said stop it, Valery. Eli is an employee." Right. An employee she'd wanted to kiss. An employee who made her remember what a woman could feel for a man.

The back door opened and male voices, one mature and one childish, penetrated the kitchen. A funny quiver of anticipation came over her.

She frowned a warning at Valery, who tossed her saucy head and took the plates to the dining room.

Father and son appeared beneath the white-trimmed archway. Eli dropped a hand to Alex's shoulder and Julia couldn't help thinking about those hands on her. He'd smoothed her hair, rubbed her back, and his body had touched her chest to thigh. A weakness flooded her limbs to think of him touching her again.

She wanted to blame Valery for planting the thoughts in her head but couldn't.

"My partner here is thirsty," Eli said. The smell of heat and green-peach limbs wafted from him. She liked it. "Mind if we grab something to drink?"

Alex stood shyly in the entry, watching Julia. She wiped her hands on a towel and went to him. "Dinner's almost ready. Will water do?"

"Yes, ma'am, Miss Julia," Alex replied. "Thank you."

Eli's face glowed with amused affection. "We've been practicing."

"Did I do it right?" Alex asked.

"Yes, you did," Julia said. "You're becoming quite the gentleman." She flicked a glance at Eli. A sizzle of awareness, hotter than before, hummed between them. "Like your daddy."

"You okay?" Eli asked softly so that no one else might hear though only Alex was in the room.

"Yes. Thank you."

His gaze held hers. Lingered. "Anytime."

Behind her the smell of lemon chicken rose from the oven and out in the dining room Valery clinked silverware and scooted chairs. Deep inside Julia's withered heart, a slow unfurling began, like rosebuds opening to the warmth of summer.

From the top of the stairs Julia heard the voices. Thinking Eli and Alex were in the foyer, she peered over the banister to say hello. The black-haired child sat alone on the Oriental rug at the base of the staircase playing with the antique marbles. Curious, Julia looked around for Eli and saw him coming out of the Blueberry Room.

"Have you seen Alex?" he asked.

She pointed over the railing and, together, they went downstairs. Alex gazed up at their appearance.

"What are you doing, buddy?" Eli asked, going down on his toes beside his son. "Where did you get those fancy marbles?"

Alex shrugged.

Eli examined the marbles before looking toward the credenza. "So you took them from Julia's bowl?"

"The marbles are still there, Eli," Julia said.

"But where did these come from? Did you find them somewhere, Alex?" Eli asked. "It's okay if you did. Julia and I found some, too. We're finding all kinds of interesting things in the carriage house."

Alex's voice was a murmur as he stared down at the marbles. "Ben gave them to me."

The adults exchanged puzzled looks. Julia shrugged. She'd never heard him mention a boy by that name.

"I don't think I've met Ben. Is he in your class at school?"

"No, Eli," the boy said with weary patience. "He lives here." His small eyebrows came together. "Anyway, I think he does. Sometimes he's here, and we play."

Julia lowered herself to the floor and picked up two of the

marbles. They matched the ones in the bowl. "Tell us about Ben, Alex. Where did you meet him?"

"In the hall by my room. He's real nice."

Oh, okay. Maybe she understood. "Is Ben an imaginary friend for those times when you don't have anyone to play with?"

"No. He was here till you came."

They had no child guests in the inn. She allowed no child guests. Had a stranger somehow gotten into the house when no one was looking?

Fear shimmied down Julia's arms. Was a predator targeting Alex as someone must have targeted Mikey?

Another thought piled in on top of the first. Had Mikey had a secret friend she hadn't known about? A friend who'd abducted him?

Fighting the tremble in her voice, Julia asked, "How old is Ben, Alex?"

The small shoulders jerked. "I don't know. He's bigger than me a little bit. But not as big as Eli."

Eli must have understood the bizarre direction of her thoughts because he said, "He's not a grown-up, is he, Alex?"

"No. He's a boy. His hair sticks up funny." He motioned to the crown of his head. "And I think he's from Heaven because he knows my mommy." Then his face crumpled, and as if the conversation was too much for him, he kicked the marbles away and buried his head in his arms.

25

Peach Orchard Farm
October, 1864

A month passed before the first letter arrived. A month of caring for the handful of wounded soldiers, some with lost limbs or, like Johnny, no sight. A month of missing Will and praying for the feeling to subside. A month of listening to Edgar and Josie smugly malign the Yankees. Charlotte absorbed the discussions with silence and her eyes downcast, though once Josie had remarked about "Charlotte's friend, the captain" and caused an unpleasant encounter with Edgar.

As such, she'd redoubled her efforts to be a wife her husband could esteem.

No one had come to accuse her of spying.

The cooler breezes of fall swept over the farm, blowing away the scent of Union campfires, of the stench of blood and infection.

The slaves toiled the earth for harvest though little was left but yams and pumpkins after the Yankees. Tandy worked the fields alongside the others at Edgar's orders, declaring him too big to be useless. Little Benjamin, already saddened by Will's departure, moped at the loss of his playmate, but school began and Charlotte kept him busy with lessons, chores and his beloved marbles.

So it was, that breezy October evening when, beneath a bruised sky, a bay horse and a Union rider ambled down the magnolia lane. The ever-watchful gander squawked a raucous greeting and roused the household. Edgar, weary from a long day of haggling over corn prices, cursed and tossed his napkin onto the dinner table with a vengeance. Charlotte carefully chewed and swallowed the bite of fried catfish procured from the pond by Tandy's quick hand.

"A dispatch, Edgar," she said calmly, "come to inquire of the wounded."

Edgar's lips tightened. "He can take them all to the devil, for my part, and go with them."

"Shall I greet him? Or perhaps send Hob?"

"Hob's useless. Like all the rest of them." He barked toward the kitchen. "Lizzy, get out there and see to the Yankee."

Lizzy appeared in the archway, drying her hands on her apron. "Should I ask him inside? He'll be hungry."

A vein in Edgar's forehead bulged. His face mottled. "Send him to the study. I won't feed the enemy if I can help it."

Lizzy's gaze cut to Charlotte, who blinked an answer. Peach Orchard Farm would never turn away the hungry as long as they had anything to share.

With a nod, Lizzy left the room but reappeared a short time later. Her dark, expressive eyes found Charlotte's, signaling something Charlotte could not understand, though she prayed for word of Will.

With the patient reserve that kept her sane, Charlotte made small talk with her sisters-in-law and Benjamin. She passed the black-eyed peas and biscuits, all the while refusing to consider that Will might have written. They'd made no promises. Word was all she needed. Word that the good captain was safe and well.

When the interminable meal ended, Edgar stomped toward the study while she and the other women cleared the table. Her gaze kept returning to Lizzy, but the maid refused to look at her. When, finally, she left the company of others and started up the stairs to her bedroom, Lizzy was not far behind.

The maid glanced up and down the hallway before closing the door. Without preamble, she murmured, "Captain Will sent you a letter. Told the man to give it to you or me."

Charlotte sank onto the fainting couch, relief flowing like Magnolia Creek. "He's alive, then. Thank God."

"That man don't have a lick of sense writing to a married woman, a Confederate wife."

"Don't scold, Lizzy." She raised a plea to her maid.

With sympathy in her dark face, Lizzy pulled the single sheet of paper from her apron and said more gently, "The soldier will take a reply if you have one."

Charlotte battled her conscience for less time than it took to open the letter and scan for Will's beloved signature. "He's well. Oh, Lizzy, he's safe."

"Give me the letter when you're done writing. I'll see to it. You got to be careful."

But Charlotte was already lost in Will's words. When she glanced up minutes later, tears in her eyes, Lizzy had quietly slipped out of the room.

September 30, 1864
Dear Charlotte,
Forgive me, but I must write this letter. Your kind and generous hospitality during those trying days last sum-

mer linger in my mind and, yes, in my heart. I think of you often. You gave me hope when I had despaired of ever seeing an end to this war.

Yesterday, we engaged the enemy near Fort Donelson, and two men were lost, Stanfill and Giles. Good Christian boys, honorable and brave, who suffered much for the cause of liberty, have closed their eyes for the last time.

The Confederates are gathering north of us. We hear the cannon fire beyond the hills, though the Rebs we encounter are as threadbare and sorry as we, perhaps more so. We have orders to march onward double quick. A major effort looms, though I cannot tell you more, but I ask that you pray for us.

If you should agree to write, I would be pleased to hear from you and to know that you are well. For let me say that your memory, indeed the memories of Peach Orchard Farm, are dear to me. If we never meet again on this earth, I shall cherish a fond recollection of you and think often of the pleasant hours passed in your company. In fond remembrance,
William Gadsden

PS The dispatcher, Corporal Johnson, is a trustworthy man.

Charlotte clutched the single page to her bodice, fighting her own inward war. Will was marching into a major battle, the great unknown that could be his final march. Though the fighting had moved on to the east and up near Nashville, she'd read the newspaper reports about Chattanooga and not so far away Tullahoma. Scores of men had died, were dying still across the hills of Tennessee. Would Will be one of them?

October 21, 1864

Dear Will,

I am overjoyed to hear that you are safe, though the news of the war is frightening. As promised, I pray for you daily. Indeed, I think of you daily, constantly.

We are all well. Benjamin suffered a fever and cough last week but is hale and hearty now. He delights in the marbles still and speaks of you often. He misses your fatherly kindness, something Edgar seems unable to provide.

I do not want you to think harshly of my husband, though he was less than kind during your time here at Peach Orchard Farm. Edgar is a man of strong opinions but also of deep wounds. His own father was austere and distant and all three of his children were imperfect in his eyes. But which of us, dear Will, is perfect this side of Heaven? Whether in physical damage, in sinful ways, or fault of will, which of us can lay claim to perfection? Certainly not I, for if I was perfect, I would know what to do with this wayward heart of mine that cares for one man while married to another.

I scarce can believe I wrote those words, but I will not blot them out. I assuage my conscience with the knowledge that this may in some way encourage you. Take heart, dear captain. Be bold and brave and always kind, as I know you are. May God bless and protect you.

Sincerely yours,

Charlotte Portland

26

Peach Orchard Inn
Present Day

Eli thought seven years in prison had taught him the meaning of fear, but looking into his son's face and wondering if he'd lost touch with reality was the scariest thing he'd ever encountered.

Alex insisted, adamantly, that Ben was a real person who'd come down from Heaven.

Helpless and inept, he'd gathered Alex onto his lap. The boy had remained curled and stiff, his face hidden.

Later, after he'd carried Alex to bed and waited until he'd settled into a sound sleep, Eli sought out Julia. She was in the kitchen, putting away dishes. He'd joined her.

"Lots of kids have imaginary friends," she'd said.

"Who know their dead mother in Heaven?" he'd asked skeptically.

"No. No. He's hurting and confused, Eli. He needs help."

"Don't you think I know that?" He'd slammed a hand onto

the counter. Dishes rattled. "Don't you think I lie awake at night wondering how to help my son? Wondering if I'm ruining him? Wondering if he'll ever laugh and play and be a normal kid?"

She'd shrunk back, wounded by his harsh tone. He reached for her, crushed her to him in his fear and anguish. "I'm sorry. I'm sorry."

He was worthless scum.

With a soothing palm to his back, Julia forgave him, and her easy acceptance broke him in half, made him more culpable than ever. If she knew who he really was...

"Eli," she'd whispered, and because he was half out of his head, he'd kissed her.

Now, as he sat at the desk in the Blueberry Room using Julia's laptop to search for free counseling, his mind was a jumble of his son and Julia.

He was stunned by his lack of control. He shouldn't have kissed her. Should never have touched her. And he'd told her as much though he couldn't tell her why. She'd reacted with a strained smile that indicated he'd said the wrong thing. He'd apologized at least a dozen times until she'd said, "The important one here is Alex. We're both worried."

Like a coward, he'd grabbed on to that explanation as if the kiss hadn't happened, as if he didn't want to carry her up the staircase like Rhett Butler and show her what she'd come to mean to him. As if he had a right instead of an ugly secret.

He was a fool, a loser and a fool. A man who couldn't even care for his own flesh-and-blood child. Hadn't he told Opal as much? Yet, each time he visited the rehab, the old woman expected a positive report, as if an ex-con could suddenly become father of the year.

Expectations. He was a failure when failure was not an option.

Where had Alex found the leather bag of marbles? Why did he insist they'd come from an invisible boy who knew Mindy?

With a shudder, he jabbed at the keyboard again, opening one of the grief forums in search of answers. He typed in his user name and logged in with the question, "Does anyone know of free counseling for children in Tennessee?"

He was nervous about including the state, but no one could identify him from the fake name. And why would they want to? He was nothing but another dad with a grieving son, not an ex-con afraid of revelation.

In seconds, a post appeared. Then another and another. He scrolled, reading the suggestions and jotting research tips until his gaze snagged on a name. Gloria. His pulse stutter-stepped. Gloria was his mother's name, a mere coincidence. He read her post...about her five-year-old daughter's death.

His face and neck grew hot. His pulse began to beat a heavy bongo in his throat. He scrolled the forum for the woman's full name, finding bits and pieces of information. She posted often, words of consolation and advice, and the overriding element of never-ending regret.

Her words brought him nearly to his knees. A mother posting to encourage others, a woman who'd been there.

Jessica was only five when she drowned. After twenty-three years, the pain has lessened, and that's my message to you, dear Annalee. The days do get easier. The tearing grief will lessen and you will sleep again. The heavy feeling in your chest will gradually lift and you will laugh again. You will find joy again someday, but you will always miss your precious Clare, and you will always wonder what she would be like today.

All the blood drained from Eli's head. His mother. Gloria Webber Donovan. After all this time.

Tears prickled the back of his eyelids. *Mom.*

For a narrow wedge of time, he considered responding to her, revealing his identity, but in the end, reason prevailed. He'd caused his still-grieving mother enough shame and heartache. Her silence of seven years meant she never wanted to hear from him again.

With shaky fingers, he logged out and closed the laptop.

May moved into June, a glorious time in Tennessee when butterflies kissed the saucer magnolias and restless schoolchildren pined for fishing holes and baseball games.

With Alex perched behind him in a booster seat, Eli drove his wheezing car through the streets of Knoxville, where trees and flowers bloomed in profusion. He'd found a free grief clinic here in his childhood city, and though the drive was long and nostalgia made him yearn for the impossible, he came.

Some days, such as this one, the counseling sessions were grueling. Today, when another child had shared about his mother's death, Alex had moved away from the circle into a corner with his back to the group. A counselor had gone to him and talked quietly. Alex had ignored her, choosing instead to play with the bag of clay marbles. He never let them out of his sight, and he never stopped insisting that Ben was real. And that Ben talked to Alex's mother.

Eli left the session feeling defeated and alone.

Then mid-June arrived and with it the beginning of peach harvest. Renovations and research took a backseat to the peach orchard.

Julia enlisted the help of her mother and aunts to begin the massive process of preserving and freezing the abundant fruit while Eli organized and directed the pick-your-own harvest. Business to the inn increased as guests arrived to partake of fresh peaches and take home a special basket of recipes and peach products, some of which they'd processed themselves as a bonus for visiting Peach Orchard Inn at harvest time. Julia credited this genius promotional idea to Eli.

As she carried an emptied bushel basket into the orchard, Eli was there, directing a circus-like atmosphere of peach pickers, eager for the first peaches of Honey Ridge. He met her at the end of a row, a spring in his step. He'd found some element of comfort here at Peach Orchard Inn and his smile came more often. Julia was glad to see the change in him.

Except for worry about her sister's binge drinking, she was happier, too. Maybe it was the arrival of summer after a long winter. Or the quiet presence of a little boy watching TV in the family room with Mikey's aging dog. Or maybe it was Eli himself.

From his long hours in the sun, Eli's skin had baked to a rich olive brown, giving him more of a pirate look than ever. She thought of that one kiss, given in desperation but never repeated, and blushed a little to think how much she'd enjoyed it, how much she wanted more from Eli than he apparently had to give.

She'd tried to put the kiss out of her mind, but the unexpected rush of longing kept returning like flies in summer.

Not that she had any reason to complain. Even though he could be reserved to the point of mystery, Eli had given her so much with his hard work and business acumen. His handling of the harvest, something she'd done haphazardly in the past, was nothing short of astonishing. She might even make some decent money this year.

"Great crowd this morning," she said, handing off the basket she'd emptied in the house. "Business is better than it's ever been."

"Yeah?" That seemed to please him. "I see areas we can improve for next year."

"For instance?" A milieu of chattering townspeople gingerly put peaches into containers as children played tag through the trees. Valery sat at a folding card table where she weighed peaches, directed traffic into the picking areas and received payments. Last night she'd come home early, and though Julia had smelled alcohol on her breath, she hadn't been dog drunk. This time. "Looks perfect to me."

"Next year, we'll prune lower to facilitate easier picking. We'll feed the trees on a regular schedule and pay more attention to thinning. You might create a booklet of your recipes instead of recipe cards, maybe even set up a separate webpage for the orchard."

She stared at him in amazement. "You've given this some serious thought."

"Business requires organization. You do that with the inn. Why not the orchard?"

All she had ever done was open it up for pickers. "I see your point, but it's a lot of work and time that I don't have."

"We'll figure it out."

Would they? Would he still be here next year? He drove so far every week for Alex's counseling, she sometimes wondered why he didn't move closer to Knoxville. With his skills and intellect, he could find a better job than this one. When she'd broached the topic one morning over breakfast, he'd mumbled something about keeping Alex stable and then had closed up tighter than a cling peach. If his reticence stung, she tried not to let on.

"Where's Alex?" she asked, nervous when she realized she couldn't see him.

Eli touched her arm with his fingertips. His silent understanding meant more than he could know. "With your dad. They walked down to the creek to catch tadpoles."

"Dad always wanted a boy." He'd had one in Mikey. She crossed her arms and turned her head toward the creek. "Does Mom know my father is here?"

"I don't know. Is that a problem?"

"Not usually, but I'll warn her. Even though they've been divorced for years, she's funny about Dad. She wants to be sure every hair is in place when he's around."

"Neither of them ever remarried?"

"Nope."

Eli scratched the corner of his eye. "Interesting."

Julia smiled. "Isn't it?"

A navy blue Crown Victoria, vintage 1980s and the size of a tank, pulled into the driveway. The Sweat twins exited the vehicle with a pair of cheery waves as they approached Valery's table. Dressed in lavender pantsuits and massive straw hats tied with purple ribbons, they looked ready for a Sunday picnic instead of a peach harvest.

A pickup truck pulled in behind the Crown Vic, and Jed Fletcher hopped out. Julia stifled a groan. Why couldn't he go away and leave her sister alone? Too many mornings, particularly on weekends, Valery came to breakfast with a hangover and left in a huff if Julia said a word.

Mom, as she'd done with Mikey, swept the issue under the rug. If she didn't talk about the elephant in the room, it didn't exist. Valery did not have drinking problem. She had a boyfriend problem.

"I guess we should get back to work. Mom and my aunts are inside slicing and dicing while I'm out here talking." She tapped the basket he held in one hand. "Want to help me fill this up?"

"Sure." After a quick survey of the ongoing harvest, he led her down the alley of trees, nodding to happy customers.

Friends and townspeople called out greetings, and Julia returned them. In the bright summer morning with the buzz of harvesters and pleasant industry filling the yard and house, contentment settled over Julia. Mikey would have loved this day. He would have toted baskets too big to carry and eaten too many ripe, juicy peaches and fallen asleep under a shady tree with a sticky face and an ornery grin.

A squeeze of longing tightened around her heart. Someday he'd come home. Someday.

Eli walked them far into the orchard, away from the customers crowded near the entrance and began to tug ripe peaches from the trees.

"My son would love today," Julia said. "He loves festivals and people and holidays. To him, this would be a party."

"That's the first time I've heard you mention him since you told me." He glanced at her, serious. "Any news?"

"No."

"Frustrating." His green eyes softened with his tender words. "You okay?"

"Nostalgic, but okay."

"I know what you mean."

She cocked her head. "Yeah?"

"I found my mother's name on a forum a while back. Every time I drive to Knoxville, I get nostalgic."

"You found your mother?" She frowned at the implications of the discovery. "Why was she on a grief forum?"

He turned his back again, plucked a couple of golden peaches. "My sister died when I was thirteen."

"Oh, Eli. I'm sorry. For you. For your family." Her empty mother's heart filled with compassion for the family she didn't know. A family whose child was irrevocably gone. "What happened?"

He slipped a few peaches into the basket, dusted his hands,

stared at them. "She drowned in our swimming pool. She was five. Mom and Dad...never got over it."

Julia hurt for him. For herself. "The worst thing that can happen to a parent is to lose a child."

"You would know."

"But Mikey's out there somewhere."

"Of course he is."

Whether he believed it or not, she was grateful for the affirmation. Hope still burned, but the flame grew smaller with the passage of time and every fruitless phone call.

"Did you make contact with your mother?"

"No."

"Why not?"

He reached high to pull down a golden peach. Sunlight through the leaves dappled him in gold and shadow, laced him in dark and light. "I burned too many bridges."

"Eli," she said softly, wanting so badly to touch his stiff back, to share his sorrow as he'd shared hers. "Don't you want to see her again?"

His hand clenched on a soft piece of fruit, smashing it. Juice dripped between his fingers. "Very much."

Aching, unsure how to encourage him as he'd done her, Julia added fruit to the basket. The smell of ripe peaches filled the air. "What have you got to lose? At least try."

His eyes sought hers. Julia saw the regret and anguish he wore like a suit of armor.

"I don't know."

So she left the subject dangling, wondering how to help him break with his past and wondering even more, why it had become so important to her.

"Here come the tadpole fishermen," she said, as the two of them exited the orchard, Eli carrying another full basket of peaches. Alex and her father came toward them from the direction of Magnolia Creek. In his early sixties, Gary Griffin remained fit, with only a small paunch beneath his maroon golf shirt. Tan lines from outdoor living crinkled around his eyes as he watched Alex hop and skip in boyish abandon.

"Eli, Eli!" Alex shouted. "Come look. Hurry."

Eli shifted the basket onto one hip. "Look at him."

Love for his son throbbed in the sunlight.

"He's getting better, Eli." Julia watched the excited child lope toward them, a Mason jar in hand. "He's attaching, little by little."

"Think he'll ever call me Dad?" The question was poignant, aching.

"I'd bet on it."

Eli's expression was one of cautious hope and painful longing as Alex approached and he inspected the jar of tadpoles. "What are you going to do with them?"

"Mr. Griffin said they turn into frogs. Can I keep them?"

"I don't know, buddy. Maybe you should put them back in the water."

Julia saw the worry on Eli's face. A similar jar of roly polies had lasted only a few days before Alex had discovered them rolled into tight balls, dead. The incident had produced two days of silent depression while the child did little except sit in the hallway upstairs and play marbles.

Alex nodded solemnly. "Yeah. They'll die, anyway." His little shoulders heaved in a deep sigh and he trudged off toward the carriage house, head down.

"I'll catch up with him."

Julia touched her father's wrist. "Thanks, Dad."

As her dark-haired father hurried after the little boy, Eli said, "I was hoping he'd be well enough to stop counseling soon."

"It may be a while."

"That's what worries me."

"The drive is grueling, isn't it?"

"And expensive, but he's worth it. I don't want him going through what I did."

Julia tilted her head, interested in this peek into Eli's early life.

"Because of your sister?"

"I didn't know." His tone was soft and distant as if he spoke to himself. "Until we started counseling in Knoxville, I didn't know."

"You didn't know what?"

"That grief can screw up a kid for a long time." He started walking toward the house. "Forever."

"The sessions have been good for you, too?"

"Something like that, but I wish—" He waved his free hand as if to erase the comment.

"Tell me. What do you wish?" She had wishes, too, giant wishes that had crept in unnoticed. She'd never expected to wish again for anything except Mikey's return.

"Kids in small towns are hit with loss the same as kids in cities, but the grief centers are miles away. All the free ones." They reached the back door. He opened it with one hand and, even with the basket, waited for her to enter into the mudroom. "What if there was a mobile center?"

"You mean counselors that travel to rural areas?"

"Exactly. Traveling psychologists, free of charge to guide kids through the darkness." He set the peaches on the cabinet.

"It's a brilliant concept."

Eli made a wry face. "Which requires resources I don't have. There are great places already available, but most of them charge. Not everyone can pay. Not everyone can drive two or three hours to access services."

"I wish I had the money. It's such a great idea. Maybe there are philanthropic groups or civic organizations that would fund something of that nature."

"It's exactly the kind of thing my family's foundation would underwrite."

Julia blinked. "Your family has a foundation?"

Eli shifted, looked away and then back again. "Yes."

"Then they must be—" The word *rich* got stuck in her throat as the implications settled over her. Not just rich but super rich. Filthy rich.

"They are," he said, as if reading her thoughts. "Not that their money has a thing to do with me. The black sheep, remember?"

No matter what had caused the rift between family and son, no matter how rich or how poor they may be, one thing was clear. Eli hurt with regret.

"Contact them, Eli." She put her fingers on his bare, muscled arm. "Isn't it time?"

He scoffed. "They'd never listen to an idea from me."

"It isn't just about the idea, as good a reason as that is. It's about you. You miss them."

"Some things are too broken to fix. I can't go there." When she started to protest, he held up a hand. "I can't, Julia. They won't allow it. Trust me on that. But I've done some research on other funding avenues—"

Her heart ached for his aloneness, but she followed his lead and moved to easier ground. "Why am I not surprised?"

With a slight smile, Eli hooked an elbow around her neck. "Because you're starting to know me too well."

Julia instinctively leaned in. Eli's grin slipped away. He touched his nose to hers, his breath warm and peach scented. Julia's pulse stuttered. She wasn't an inexperienced adolescent, but she was having adolescent fantasies. Or maybe she'd simply forgotten the joys of being a woman with a man, the rush of blood, the hungry desire, the sweetness of attraction.

She watched emotions shuffle across his face. Wariness. Fear. Longing. His other arm found her waist and pressed her closer.

He smelled of peaches and grass and all things nature. His warm, corded arms were strong and hard from hours of work. His chest was muscled and manly against her feminine softness. Perfect. Absolutely perfect. She sighed into him while deep in her frozen soul, a thawing began.

Though aware of the voices in the next room and the hubbub of activity all around the inn, Julia let them fade away in exchange for Eli Donovan's mouth on hers. Soft, questioning, tender and hot. Entirely different from that first desperate kiss, this one said things to her heart. A flare of desire she'd thought dead leaped into bonfire mode.

A voice broke in. A throat cleared. "Excuse me."

Eli and Julia jerked apart. Julia bumped the cabinet, cheeks hot, to see her mother standing in the archway.

"Mom." She wanted to look anywhere but at her mother.

"We're out of peaches in the kitchen." Mom arched one penciled eyebrow. "If the two of you can find the time."

"Oh, right. Sorry." Julia pressed a hand to her flaming cheeks. "We have them right here."

Eli reclaimed the filled basket and, with a soft, apologetic glance, moved past Connie into the kitchen.

"Julia Yvonne, I'm surprised at you. Here, in a place of business."

"Mom, I'm sorry."

"Sorry you were kissing Eli? Or sorry you got caught?"

"Yes, the last one. I don't know what I was thinking, but I—" Embarrassed but without excuse, Julia shrugged.

Her proper Southern mother studied her for a long moment.

Out in the kitchen one of the aunts said something about simple sugar syrup and pans clattered.

"I'm concerned, Julia. You're sparkling and happy, but what do you really know about this man?"

She knew he worked hard, loved his son and made her feel like a woman. Wasn't that enough? "Mom—"

"Just be careful, honey." Connie Griffin's eyebrows pulled together. "Be very careful."

Eli's neck and shoulders ached, but he continued working late into the evening. The moment in the mudroom had been embarrassing, but he wasn't sorry about the kiss. Maybe he should be.

Guilt pushed in, but he'd pushed back. Julia was special. He'd never hurt her. Not intentionally. As long as she didn't discover the lie he lived, she was safe. They both were.

But the nagging fear of discovery dangled like a noose.

The first morning of harvest had gone well and he was pretty proud of that. Julia seemed impressed.

The harvest had cut into his work on the carriage house and he was eager to get back to it, though his eagerness to move out of the inn had waned.

In cleaning and sorting, he'd found some cool old items amidst the junk, but he was hoping for more letters or a diary or something to clue them into the marbles' owner. He wondered if the old house was trying to send a message, and then he scoffed at the foolishness. Wouldn't the counselors have a field day if he shared those thoughts?

"Eli?" Alex clutched his marble bag in one hand and a peach in the other. His face and hands were orange with sticky juice.

The familiar heart clutch grabbed Eli. Would his boy ever call him *Dad*? "Yeah, buddy?"

"Can I go in the house with Miss Julia?"

"Tired?"

"Uh-huh."

"Sure." He put a hand on his son's back and guided him down the alley of grass to the porch, where he called into the back door. Julia came smiling, eyes weary, as she wiped her hands on a tea towel. The air was heavy with the fruity scent of cooked peaches.

Eli's gaze fell to her mouth, remembering a taste sweeter than any peach. She blushed, though her eyes sparkled.

"I have a tired boy here. Do you mind if he hangs out inside with you?"

"Anytime. Alex knows that. And I bet the two of you could use something cold to drink."

"Later for me. I have work to finish."

He left his son in her care, grateful for her kindness. Alex liked her, clung to her more than he did to his own father, and though the knowledge hurt, Eli was glad his son connected with someone. Julia read to him, colored with him, told him stories and tolerated his messes the way a mother would do. The way she'd probably done for Mikey.

Though they visited Aunt Opal in the nursing facility, Alex was uncomfortable there and restless to leave. True to her word, Julia had helped him clear out Opal's rented home and stage a one-day garage sale, a pitiful project that hadn't taken long. The Sweat twins had come by, friends of Opal, to select items for a keepsake quilt they were making for Alex. It was a sad business, and he marveled anew at Julia's strength. She must have done the same with Mikey's things at some point.

The last of the day's harvest customers pulled out of the driveway. A feeling of contentment settled over him. He offered a wave, feeling proprietary about the orchard in a completely improper manner. This wasn't his farm, any more than Julia was his woman. She might let him kiss her, but she wasn't his. Couldn't be, but he felt good to help her this way. She'd done plenty for him. If not for Julia, he and Alex might be living in his car.

He wasn't sure why he'd told her about Jessica any more than he knew why he'd lost control and kissed her. Maybe because she'd told him about Mikey, and because they'd shared confidences in the months since he'd come here, a broken man looking for a place to land. Honey Ridge was a good place. Peach Orchard Inn, with Julia, was even better.

He was falling in love with her, and on days like today the emotion threatened to overwhelm him. She cared for Alex as she'd probably done for Mikey. She cared for him, too, nurtured him so that he found joy in the mornings and pleasure in the evenings. He wanted the world for Julia, wanted to give her everything, but he had less than nothing to give.

When he spoke by telephone with his parole officer, the past pressed in, rendering him hopeless. He was an ex-con with a guilty conscience, and neither would ever change. Then, on days like this, when he'd had the ability to make someone happy, when he'd kissed and held Julia as if he had a right, when he'd seen her pleasure at the work of his hands, he almost believed in redemption.

The sun eased down in the west, a stunning display of gold and red as bright as a ripe peach. He rubbed a hand over the back of his neck and gathered empty baskets and boxes into stacks. The ladders could remain in place, but he walked along the rows checking for damage to the trees and places to direct customers tomorrow afternoon.

He'd created a business plan for the orchard. After harvest he'd show it to Julia and admit he owned a business degree. Maybe. He hadn't quite figured out how to answer the inevitable questions without lying. And he wouldn't lie to her. Not to Julia.

Voices lifted to his ears and he paused to listen. No one should be left in the orchard but him. He moved toward the sound until he spotted a man and woman—Valery and her boyfriend, Jed. Not wanting to eavesdrop, he had started to turn away when Valery's voice rose. He spun back, saw Jed's fingers dig into Val's upper arm.

This was none of his business. He should back off and leave them to deal with their own issues. Valery was a grown woman, making her own choices.

"Don't screw with me, Valery," the boyfriend said. "You know better."

"I promised to help Julia tomorrow."

Jed's face darkened. "Screw Julia. Screw this whole stinking place. I made some promises, too, and we're keeping them."

"I can't this time." She tugged against his grip. "Let go of me, Jed."

Stay out of it, Eli. Don't be stupid. Don't draw attention to yourself.

"Not until you say yes. You know you want to. Keg parties rock, and you love the river. Just say yes." Jed's fingers tightened. Eli could see the skin on Valery's arm mottle. The war inside his head continued. This was not his business.

"It sounds fun, but I'm not going." Valery tossed her head, though Eli could see she was not as confident as she was trying to pretend. "Sorry."

"Sorry? I'll show you sorry." Jed's face darkened in anger. He yanked the back of Valery's hair, pulling her close.

Okay, that was enough. Eli moved.

Valery cried out, put a hand to her hair. "Jed. Stop it!"

Eli picked up speed, pushing branches aside.

Jed's lips sneered as he mocked Valery's pain. In a high voice, he said, "Jed, please, don't hurt me. Jed, I love you." He pulled her closer. "I'm tired of your crap, Valery. If you love me, you'll do what I say."

"Let go of me now." Valery slapped against his hold. "I'm not going with you. You're mean today."

"Mean? I'm mean?" He slapped her.

Forgetting caution, Eli bolted through the trees, knocking ripe fruit to the ground. Teeth tight, he said, "Hey, man. Back off."

Jed loosened his grip on Valery and spun toward the unexpected interruption. "Get lost."

Eli's fists tightened at his side. "Can't do that."

"This is not your business."

"You want to get rough with someone, try a man. Keep your hands off Valery."

Jed pushed his chest into Eli's. They were equal in size, but Eli knew ways to fight Jed had likely never considered. He hated using prison-learned skills, but he could. He just didn't want to.

The other man took a swing. Eli caught his arm and shoved. Jed stumbled backward. "I wouldn't do that if I were you."

The calm in his voice didn't surprise him. He'd learned to stay cool, stay aloof. Mostly, he'd avoided trouble in prison, but not always.

Something flickered in Jed's expression, a sign Eli had learned to watch for. He'd met men like Jed in prison, cowards and bullies who picked on the weaker but ran like water against a strong opponent.

"You'll regret messing with me," Jed said, though he stood an arm's length away, fists tight at his side and face crimson.

Eli simply stared, body tense and ready, jaw tight, another prison trick. Truth was, he regretted the interference already, but he wouldn't back down.

Jed spun toward Valery, teeth tight. "Bitch," he spit, and then stalked away.

Eli and Valery stood in the orchard, silent until a truck

started and roared out of the driveway. They could hear the gears grind for miles.

Head down, Valery mumbled, "I'm sorry you had to see that."

Eli shifted, the need to say more pounding at the back of his throat. He should keep his mouth shut. Getting involved was dangerous. But Valery was on a path he recognized, and he cared. He didn't want to care, but the alternative was being empty again.

"Look, Valery." He flexed his hands. Blew out a breath. Fought the urge and lost. "Can we talk a minute?"

Her head came up. Wariness was on her face. She didn't want this conversation any more than he did.

"Don't worry. I can handle Jed."

"No, you can't."

She opened her mouth, closed it, an admission that emboldened him.

"The only person you can control is yourself."

"Isn't that the truth?" Valery huffed, her mouth twisted in sarcasm. "And you're saying I'm doing a lousy job of that, right?"

Why couldn't he just stay out of it?

"I'm saying you're better than getting drunk every weekend with a man who pushes you around."

"You sound like my sister."

"She's worried."

"I'm an adult."

"When did that matter to people who love you? Don't you ever worry about her?"

"Of course I do, but—"

"There are places that can help you, Val."

"Couples fight all the time. Having a fight with Jed doesn't mean I need help."

"Getting drunk every other night does."

"I don't—"

"You're a beautiful woman, smart and talented—"

Some of her sauciness returned. She faked a curtsy. "Why, thank you, kind sir."

She was good at avoiding the truth. He recognized that trick, too.

"I've known people who had everything, but they chose the wrong crowd, got into drugs, and ruined their lives. Don't do this to yourself."

She stiffened. "I don't do drugs. A few drinks now and then are not the same as being a druggie. I don't appreciate the insinuation."

Frustrated, Eli rubbed the back of his neck. This wasn't going well. "Look, you're right. This is not my concern. I shouldn't have said anything."

"I'm fine, Eli. Really. Jed and I just had a little argument. He'll probably send me flowers tomorrow."

"He's going to hurt you, Valery."

"You worry too much." With a light laugh, she leaned in to kiss him on the cheek and then stepped back as if to leave.

Disappointed that she could blow him off so easily, he caught her wrist. "When you're ready to get help, I'll be here for you."

27

Julia put away the last of the stainless-steel pots and checked on the roast beef in the oven. Every bone in her body ached with satisfied exhaustion. After weeks of harvest and preserving peaches, business had begun to wane with the diminishing peach crop. Eli made noises about planting different varieties next year to lengthen the harvest season into fall, but Julia wanted to think about it later.

So much work remained to be done on the inn property that taking on anything else seemed onerous. As the peach crop slowly disappeared, Eli had turned more of his attention to the carriage house, a seemingly unending project. Not that she minded. As long as she had work, she had Eli.

The thought brought her up short. She walked into the dining room and stared out the double windows in search of this man who had inadvertently become an integral part of her life, an important part she didn't want to lose. He must be inside in the carriage house, though he'd come to the inn soon. He and Alex had an appointment in Knoxville later today.

Because of the harvest, they'd had limited time for researching the inn's history, something they both found fascinating. Neither had found a marble in a while but Alex was obsessed with his.

They'd had limited opportunity, too, to explore this thing bubbling between them.

Her mother's caution bothered her. But Julia knew enough about Eli. Didn't she?

He exited the front door of the carriage house with Alex at his side. He had something in one hand and bent to speak to the child, his opposite hand gentle on Alex's dark hair. Julia watched, mood soft and wishful, as Alex climbed aboard his father's back for a gallop to the house. His smile was a good sign. So was the father's.

"Why don't you jump his bones and put both of you out of your misery."

Julia jumped. "Valery. I didn't hear you come in."

"Because you're off in la-la with Eli. You probably didn't hear the car drive up, either."

"Who is it?"

Valery made a face. "Your inimitable ex."

"David?" Julia recoiled, unpleasantly surprised. "David is here?"

"He must have heard about the good harvest and wants to sue you for his share."

Julia turned from the window with a wry grin. "Sarcasm becomes you."

"I thought so, especially when it's aimed at Mr. Jack-wad Attorney."

Julia didn't bother to mention the obvious. Both sisters had fallen for the wrong men, though David hadn't been a jerk until Mikey disappeared.

"Want me to run him off?" Valery rubbed both palms together in anticipation.

"You know how persistent David can be. I might as well find out what he wants. Offer Eli and Alex some iced tea, will you?"

"Sure."

Leaving the dining area, Julia went to the front door, where she took a moment to be perfectly composed before facing her ex-husband.

He stood on the porch, immaculate as always in a brown suit and gleaming shoes, his dark hair tidy in a way Eli's never would be.

Julia scratched the thought. There was no comparison between the two men.

"David, this is an unexpected surprise."

"I need to speak with you."

"I'm listening."

"May I come in?"

She hesitated long enough to make him uncomfortable before leading the way into the parlor.

"This looks great," he said, gazing around. "You always had a knack for the domestic."

If his comment was a cut, she ignored it. "I'm happy with what I do."

He made himself comfortable in one of her parlor chairs. "Are you happy with your hired hand?"

The question came out of nowhere, putting her on edge. "Why do you ask?"

"When we met that day at Miss Molly's, something about him bothered me."

"He's none of your business, David."

"Does that mean you're involved?"

"That means exactly what I said. My business is not yours. Neither is Eli's."

He leaned forward, hands gripping the chair arms, earnest in a way that once had swayed her to agree to anything he wanted. A lawyer's ploy, she knew now. "What do you know of Donovan's background?"

"Enough."

David paused, his face pulled down in artificial sympathy. "Julia, don't tell me you didn't do a background check before allowing a strange male to live in your house."

"I am more than satisfied with Eli's work. He's been a model employee."

She fidgeted, anxiety rising. He knew something and, though she wanted to ask, she didn't want to hear it from him.

A sad, sympathetic smile, completely false, lifted his mouth. "A model employee. That's how the warden described him, too. A model prisoner."

Electricity jolted her. "What?"

"Donovan didn't tell you about his prison record? That he spent nearly seven years as a guest of the Tennessee Department of Correction?"

Shock rolled through her in giant, engulfing waves. *Stunned* didn't even begin to describe the feeling.

"No," Eli's voice broke in. "I didn't tell her."

Julia jerked her head toward the arched opening. Eli stood there, face pale and mouth flat, his son at his side. Alex must have felt the adult tension, because he pressed closer to his father and stared up at him. Eli draped an arm along Alex's back.

David rose from the damask armchair. "I'd advise you to leave Honey Ridge. We don't appreciate drug dealers here."

Julia found her tongue. "David, I want you to go."

Her ex-husband, the man she'd once loved with all her heart and soul, reached out a hand and touched her. "If you need me—"

Julia recoiled. "I don't. Please go."

"I realize this is shocking for you, but I was concerned for your safety."

"She's in no danger."

David turned a cold eye on Eli. "An ex-con is always dangerous."

"David," she said firmly. "I'll show you out."

Julia started walking toward the door. Her ex-husband and Eli glared at each other for another few seconds before David exited the house. Julia carefully closed the heavy oak door, her back to Eli, afraid to turn around, afraid of the hurt and disappointment, afraid of the truth.

"Julia?" Eli had come closer but hadn't touched her. She wanted him to deny the allegation, to take her in his strong arms and promise that he was exactly the man she'd come to believe in.

She did a slow inhale and turned to face him. Alex had left the room. "Is it true?"

His face was stone. "Yes."

She crossed her arms. "Why didn't you tell me?"

His eyes met hers and then skittered away. "Would you have hired me?"

Arms at his sides, shoulders slumped, he looked vulnerable and lost the way he had the first day she'd seen him.

"No."

He nodded once. The lines in his forehead—furrows she understood now—were prominent while he waited, as if for execution. "Do you want me to leave?"

"I—" She paused, searching for the answer and finding none. "I don't know. I need some time to think."

"All right." He left the room as quietly as he'd entered.

The sharp arrow of humiliation pushed deeper into Eli as he climbed the stairs to the Blueberry Room. He'd known better than to want something too much. He'd known his record would catch up with him sooner or later.

Alex lay on the bed watching television. "Are we going to counseling?"

"Yes. Better get your shower." Eli sat on the end of the bed, his body heavy as a freight train. Fifteen minutes ago, he'd been eager to get to Julia and show her his latest discovery. Now, the fragile old letters lay on his dresser, their importance lost for the moment.

Alex pointed the remote and clicked off the TV. "Is Julia mad at us?"

"Not at you, buddy. At me. I did something wrong."

"Oh." His son started to the bathroom but turned. "Eli?"

"Yeah?"

"Why is she mad?"

Someday his son would have to know. But not now. Not when Alex still reeled with too much loss. "I made some stupid mistakes a long time ago and she found out about them."

Dark brown eyes considered him for two beats. "That's what erasers are for."

"What?" Eli cocked his head, not understanding.

"My teacher says everyone makes mistakes. That's what erasers are for."

A hot rush of emotion flooded Eli. His detached son was reaching out, offering comfort. The sweet gesture lifted a stone from Eli's shoulders.

Chest full, he said, "Thank you, son."

The bathroom door clicked shut, leaving Eli alone in the Blueberry Room. He rubbed both hands over his face, broken anew.

How he wished life was as simple as a pencil eraser.

Weeks of building trust and, yes, a relationship with Julia had been dashed in seconds. His fault. His responsibility. But it still hurt.

If she fired him, where would he go? What would he do to support Alex? And how would he face each day without Julia?

Heart thudding painfully against his ribs, Eli pushed up from the blue bedspread and dragged himself to the closet. He didn't have much in the way of clothing, but he wouldn't go to counseling looking like a bum.

He flipped on the closet light. There on the floor was a clay marble.

28

Peach Orchard Farm
November, 1864

Dearest Will,
Your letter of October 30 pleased me greatly. You asked
of your men, and I am pleased to report that Henry and
Private Miller are leaving with the dispatcher at dawn,
though how they can rejoin a regiment and fight, I do not
know. Johnny has learned to do much without eyesight,
though he seems fearful of returning to Ohio. I think he
wonders if Betsy will still love a blind man, for she hasn't
written since before you left.

I do hope you can find supplies for your men before
the cold sets in. My heart aches to think of you cold or
hungry. Lizzy spoke with Corporal Johnson, who has
agreed to carry a gift of gloves and socks. Please accept
them with my devotion.

The girls, Ben and I attended church on Sunday and
so much of the talk was about Lincoln's reelection. Fury

abounded though Lizzy says the slaves are secretly delighted. They smell freedom, and though I do not know
how the farm can manage without their help, enslaving a
man is wrong, and I am surprised they have not run away
already. I wish an end to this terrible war, no matter the
outcome, so that good men such as yourself can go home
to your families and peace can come again.

I, too, miss our daily conversations. When I walk into
the study, I see you there. I see you, too, beside the fireplace in the parlor, your hands behind your back and feet
spread in that elegant stance of a proud officer as you listened with your soft smile to some tale spoken by Ben
or Tandy. The house clings to your presence as if you are
just outside and, any moment, you'll come bearing a kind
word or a gift from the woods. Only in these letters can I
share my deepest thoughts. I miss you, dear Will.
Yours,
Charlotte

Fall deepened into late November, and the newspapers were
filled with a miserable and ironic mix of stories—of quilting
bees and gospel meetings, the fighting in Nashville and fallen
sons and husbands. Beneath the threadbare semblance of what
was once normal, black-draped windows in Honey Ridge told
the mounting tale of death and heartbreak. With each bit of
news, Charlotte's heart clutched as she wondered if Will was
part of this battle or that skirmish.

Her concern was temporarily soothed when the occasional
letter arrived, slipped to her by the faithful Lizzy. She hid these
letters beneath her mattress, devouring every single word each
night by candlelight. Afterward, she wrote long, detailed re-
plies and Lizzy found creative ways to get them into the hands
of the courier.

Charlotte suffered for her deceit. She wrote to her mother for advice, studied the scriptures for wisdom and redoubled her efforts to be a dutiful wife. In appreciation for Edgar's long days at the mill, she made sure his favorite foods were prepared, the house sparkled, the remaining Yankees were kept from his sight. Though her own days were long and labor-intensive, she greeted him with a tender word and smile.

She felt like such a hypocrite.

Edgar seemed oblivious, as he was oblivious to the shy way his son begged for his attention. His immunity to these efforts tugged her ever closer to her dear captain, who seemed delighted at every detail of her day. So she wrote to him of her worries and joys, her childhood in England and the peculiarities of life on a Tennessee farm. When their letters gradually edged into topics of the heart and soul, of hate and love, of grace and God, loss and need, Charlotte comforted her conscience with thoughts of giving guidance to another soul. She was, after all, a vicar's daughter.

"What harm can there be," she said to Lizzy, "in writing encouragement to a soldier who spends each breathing moment in mortal danger?"

"None at all," Lizzy said knowingly as she slipped the latest missive into her apron for delivery to the courier before the morning. "As long as Mr. Edgar don't find out."

December 1, 1864. Near Nashville
My dearest Charlotte,
I received your letter with joy and a heavy heart. Heavy because I miss you and I despair of ever seeing you again. Your letters and those from my mother and sisters are the lights that keep me going.

Yesterday, I lost seven men. The Rebels lost many more. The soldiers have bloodlust and plunder the battlefield for spoils. I can do nothing to stop them, and, truly, I don't know if I should. A dead man no longer needs his boots or tobacco, his bayonet or gun. Only the living have such needs, though the desecration of the dead seems unconscionable. The army is worn and has seen too much of blood and savagery. Sickness runs through the camps, and the rain keeps us in wet, cold misery. The unearthly screams of battle echo in my head tonight, a haunting I can't escape. I will not write details of today's events, but I see them yet in my mind, and I fear we shall all become unholy barbarians. Indeed, I despair of losing my very soul to this endless enterprise.

Pray for me, my dearest love.

With everlasting devotion,

William Gadsden

The door to the blue bedroom slammed open, reverberating against the wall. A sampler crashed to the floor.

Charlotte, dressing her hair for the day, leaped from the vanity with a gasp. "Edgar. You frightened me. What's happened?"

Edgar, who rarely stepped foot in her bedroom, stomped toward her, his eyes ablaze, his face florid. He thrust an envelope at her, the very envelope she'd sealed last night and given to Lizzy for delivery this morning.

A chill ran through her, colder than January.

"Did you think I wouldn't find out my wife was carrying on behind my back?" He leaned close. His breath reeked of whiskey-laced coffee. "With a filthy Yankee!"

"Edgar! That isn't true." But her heart thudded painfully in her breast, her culpability looming large as she tried to keep from looking at the letter. Oh, the things she'd written, sharing her heart and soul.

"Were you laughing behind my back? You and your Yankee. Laughing at the pitiful cripple while you ate my food and carried on your shameless affair under my roof?"

Charlotte forced a calm she didn't feel. Though shaking inside, she rested her hands in the folds of her skirt and said, "Captain Gadsden was kind to me and to Benjamin during the difficult time of occupation. I saw no harm in repaying that kindness with a letter."

She'd hardly made the admission when Edgar raised his hand and struck her. Charlotte stumbled back, stunned, hand to her flaming cheek as he came at her again. "Liar. Traitor. My own wife. I can't believe how stupidly I believed your pretense of devotion."

"I *am* devoted to you." She held a hand to her burning cheek, fighting for control though her voice shook. "Can't we speak of this reasonably?"

"Reasonable? You're asking me to be reasonable about my wife bedding a Yankee?" He jabbed a finger into the air. "Did it happen here in this room? In that bed?"

"Edgar, no. Nothing happened!" She reached out with a shaky, pleading hand. "Please. I have never been unfaithful to you. I would not—"

The next blow knocked her into the edge of the vanity, bruised her thigh and caused her to stumble against the window. She grabbed the sill to avoid pitching face-first to the floor.

Edgar lurched forward and loomed over her in rage.

"I don't believe you." He crushed the letter in one fist and shook it in her face. "I read it, Charlotte, and Lizzy confessed there are others."

Charlotte cringed, afraid for Lizzy, afraid of another blow. He'd read her reply to Will's letter. He knew of her feelings for Will.

"No matter what you think right now," she managed, "I am devoted to my family. To you. You are my husband."

His face contorted in disgust. "More's the pity for me. I can no longer stomach the thought of you. You are no wife to me. I will never touch you again."

The months and years of humiliation and suspicion coalesced more quickly than Charlotte could control. Hurt and fury spewed out.

"And when did you ever?" Like a fishwife, her voice rose. "I've asked you to my room, to my bed, but you prefer a mistress in the cabins. Don't think you've kept your sin a secret, Edgar. I know about her."

Aghast to reveal the terrible secret she'd harbored for years, Charlotte clapped a hand over her mouth.

Edgar had gone rigid with shock. Rigid and so frighteningly silent that Charlotte knew she'd said the wrong thing. Fearing another blow, she huddled against the wall and whispered, "I'm sorry."

In a menacing voice, deathly quiet, he said, "Would you like to escape me, Charlotte? Is that it?" A sly look crossed his florid features. "Perhaps you long for England?"

She said nothing, afraid of saying too much again. It wasn't England she longed for and Edgar knew it.

Edgar watched her, a cat watching a cornered mouse, and laughed, though the sound was anything but joyous. "I think that's what I shall do. I'll send you back to your pathetic, penniless family in England. Far, far away from your Yankee lover." He tapped a thick finger against his malicious smile. "Would you like that? Would you?" When she didn't answer, he nodded. "All right, then, my dear unfaithful wife. You will go, but my son remains here with me."

Terror burned through Charlotte faster than acid. "No! I beg of you, Edgar. Don't separate me from Benjamin."

"Why shouldn't I? Give me one reason why my son should remain with a Yankee's whore?"

She fell to her knees in front of him, no longer driven by pride or anger or even the hurt of his infidelity with a slave. She'd do anything, endure anything for her son. "Forgive me, Edgar. Forgive me. Let me stay. I do not want to leave. This is my home. You are my husband. I belong here."

He glared down at her, nostrils flared and expression smug. He had the upper hand. He'd always held the upper hand.

She gripped his trouser leg and bowed her face to his poor, crippled foot. Once, she'd had compassion for his infirmity. Now, all she felt for her husband was fear and loathing.

Her body shook, not from the blows, but from the threat of losing the most precious gift in her life—Benjamin.

"I will do anything, Edgar." Her voice fell to a weeping whisper. "I'm begging you. Beat me. Punish me, but do not separate me from our son."

He jerked his boot away, grazing her already wounded cheek. She remained crumpled on the floor, afraid to look at him.

His boots moved toward the door. She heard the knob rattle and looked up, pleading with tear-filled eyes.

"I will think about this, Charlotte. In the meantime, you are to remain in this room until I decide the best course of action. No one comes inside. No one." He felt above the door for the room key and, giving her one final, smug glance, slammed the door hard enough to rattle the walls.

She heard the key turn in the lock.

29

Long after Eli's beat-up Dodge puttered past the double row of blossom-heavy magnolias, Julia worked and worried about David's revelation. She checked in a new guest and checked out two others, then hurried upstairs to clean the vacated rooms. Valery came in to help.

"David told me."

Julia snapped a sheet from the bed with an air pop. "David should keep his ambulance-chasing mouth shut."

"Ouch. She bites." Valery whipped off a pillowcase. "But I have to agree. Forget David. Eli's one of the good guys."

Julia paused, hoping, *needing* to be convinced. "You think?"

"I know."

"I thought so, too, but now…"

"Trust your gut. He is. Don't run him off, Julia." Valery took up the disinfectant cleaner and began wiping down the desk and television. "You've changed since he came. You're almost you again."

"He's an ex-convict."

"*Ex* being the operative term. He paid his debt. He was paroled for good behavior. He even earned a business degree in the pen."

"A degree?" Another revelation of a man who'd said she knew him too well. Apparently, she didn't know him at all. "How did you learn all this?"

"I followed David to the car and asked more questions than you did. I'm nosy and persistent."

"I wanted him gone."

"David or Eli?"

"David—" She caught herself and stopped, mulling the truth that popped out so easily. She didn't want to lose Eli. Regardless of his past, she trusted him. Except for hiding the prison record, he'd earned the right to be trusted. His work ethic, his scrupulous attention to detail on her behalf and his care of Alex indicated his integrity, at least to her.

"I wish he'd told me."

Valery looked at her in the mirror. "Are you sure?"

If he'd told her about his record, she wouldn't have hired him. And she'd also never have begun to feel again, to live again and, yes, to love again. Eli had done more than bring in a peach harvest and work on her remodel. He'd reached inside her broken soul and touched some long-silent chord. She'd lived too long in a state of suspension to go back there.

"You're right. I'm glad he didn't."

Valery tugged her ponytail. "You're in love with an ex-con."

Julia plopped down in the chair and put a hand to her forehead. "As unbelievable as it sounds, I think I am."

The trip to Knoxville seemed a hundred times longer today and, to make the day worse, the counseling session had dug deep, probing at too many buried memories. Counseling was primarily for Alex, but the psychologist didn't seem to remember today as he'd asked too many questions of both father and son.

The scene with Julia grieved him. The memories of Mindy and the wrong he'd done her and their little boy grieved him. His fault, of course. No one to blame but himself.

After the grueling session, as he drove through the city, he passed his father's office building. Another grief of his own making.

All he'd ever done was screw up.

What insanity had possessed him to think he could start fresh and create a new life? He knew the answer, though. Alex had. Julia had. Julia, with her belief in him and her pride in his work. Julia, who knew deep sorrow and suffering, had opened her home and her heart to a man like him.

A deep, empty chasm yawned inside him.

Before he'd considered too long, he aimed the vehicle toward Sequoyah Hills, the affluent older neighborhood in West Knoxville where he'd grown up. The place where he'd first begun to fall apart. The counselor today had unleashed the gnawing dog called home and family.

Alex leaned forward from the backseat. "Where are we going, Eli?"

"Just driving around." Wishing and dreaming like a fool.

He drove past the park. In the distance, the Tennessee River flowed and a pair of Jet Skis skipped along the mirrored water.

Memories flashed through Eli's head. He'd played on that river, run in the park and tossed a Frisbee to the family dog, Winston, the Springer spaniel. Jessica had come here, too. With Mother. With him.

"Can we stop and play?"

"Not today." Not any day.

Nostalgia engulfed him. He drove away from the park, knowing where he was headed though he didn't want to admit how much he wanted to see his childhood home.

He slowed the car on the street in front of the house.

"Is this a mansion?"

"Yes, I guess it is." To the boy who'd grown up there, the estate hadn't been anything special. He'd been privileged but he hadn't known. Spoiled and angry, he'd destroyed everything in his path, including himself.

"Who lives here?"

His mouth went dry. "My mother and father." *Your grand-parents.*

Mother and Dad didn't even know they had a grandson. Would they want to?

A small frown appeared in Alex's brow as he stared out the window at the stately home surrounded by elegant gardens and verdant trees. After Jessica's death, Eli's parents had thrown themselves into work. His mother had hidden her grief in activity at the foundation, clubs and manic rose gardening. Dad had disappeared into his office. A heartbroken thirteen-year-old boy hadn't understood. He'd thought they blamed him, hated him. He'd certainly hated himself, though at the time he hadn't understood that, either.

In the years since, Mother's roses had flourished and now bloomed in a profusion of colors. Eli could practically smell them from here.

At one corner of the house, a swimming pool sparkled aquamarine in the sunlight. He tried not to look, tried not to remember. Jessica had died there. On a sunny day like today, his baby sister had died.

He saw her then, inside his head. At five years old, her little belly pooched over her swimsuit bottoms and her black hair swung down her back. Indulged and adored, she was cute and knew it. She was also full of energy, forever nagging big brother to play.

God, how he wished he'd listened when she'd asked him that day to swim with her. But he hadn't and she'd broken the rules and gone in alone.

A cold sweat broke out on his forehead. His stomach rolled. Nausea filled his throat with a nasty taste.

He pulled into a wide, grassy spot outside the gates.

Memory rolled in, a violent tidal wave. His mother's screams. The sirens. The terror of watching a paramedic pump on his sister's lifeless chest. The awful noise that had slowly, terribly dwindled away to silence.

Eli gripped his hands around the steering wheel. His belly quaked. He shook with memories he'd blocked for twenty-three years. He took deep breaths and tried to clear his mind. Tears burned at the back of his nose. He laid his head on the steering wheel.

He was a man. He didn't cry. He raged and kicked against the Fates, but he didn't cry. He hadn't since Jessica's death and, even then, no one had heard him. He'd hidden in his room with headphones pumping loud music in his ears so no one knew how scared and confused and angry he was.

A tear seeped onto his cheek. He fought against the volcanic thrust of bottled emotion.

"Eli?" Alex's small voice asked, worried.

Eli couldn't answer. His throat was full. He didn't want Alex to see him this way.

His body shook, as cold as he'd been that day by the pool. Blood pounded in his temples. Pain rattled his chest, pushing to get out.

He heard the snap of a seat belt. A small hand touched his shoulder. "Eli."

That's when he lost it. Twenty-three years of regret poured out in rasping sobs.

Shame kept his head against the steering wheel. Alex shouldn't have to see this. The seat gave as his son joined him in the front.

A small hand patted his back exactly as he patted Alex when he cried for his mother.

"It's okay, Daddy," Alex murmured. "Everything will be okay."

"Eli's running late tonight." Valery rose from the dinner table with her plate in hand. "He never misses your cooking, especially your Shrimp Scampi and pasta."

"Maybe he's not coming back." Julia contemplated the left-overs.

"Maybe his pitiful car broke down, Julia. It wouldn't be the first time. Don't start thinking the worst."

The sisters carried the dishes into the kitchen to begin the task of companionable cleanup.

"But I sent him away."

"Did you?"

"I told him I need time to think."

"That's not the same as sending him away. Did he take his stuff with him?"

"No." From the breakfast room window, she'd watched him leave, and every part of her had wanted to run to him. "Am I a fool for wanting an ex-convict to live in my house?"

"I don't think that's all you want." Valery laughed.

"No, it isn't. He makes me happy, Val. I like coming down the stairs in the morning to find Eli in my kitchen, leaning his cute behind against the cabinet while he sips a cup of coffee and talks to me about his plans for the day. I like the way his brain works."

"I bet that body can do some work, too."

Julia bumped her sister with her hip. "Shut up."

"Don't tell me you don't think about it."

"That's the funny thing. I hadn't thought about *it* in years."

"Because you've been a zombie."

"Then Eli comes along and my hormones light up like sparklers on the Fourth of July. And Alex is a bonus. I love watching him bloom. It's so good to see a little boy playing with Bingo again. It's almost as if—"

"Julia, don't." Valery dropped a plate into the dishwasher with a loud rattle, stopping the mention of Mikey. Facing unpleasant facts was not Valery's strongest suit.

Julia caught her bottom lip between her teeth. "Sometimes I get scared thinking of what could happen."

"Alex is safe here. Eli takes good care of him."

"He does, doesn't he?" But she and David had taken good care of Mikey, too.

"I hear a car coming up the drive."

Julia cocked an ear. "Eli."

"Why don't I take Alex on in a game of…something and give you and Eli some alone time?"

"You really think I should let something of this magnitude go? He was in prison!"

"You're a fool if you don't."

"This coming from a woman with absolutely no sense about men."

"Eli's an improvement over David."

"Can't argue that." David had been close to perfect at one time, at least in her view. She couldn't afford another mistake.

Eli felt strangely calm as he parked in the gravel lot and guided his son across the green lawn, beautifully manicured by his own hands. He'd taken pride in his work for Julia and if she chose to fire him, he'd go, knowing he'd given her everything he had.

The knowledge, however, would not make the next few minutes any easier. He'd faced rejection before and survived. He could do it again, probably would do it many times in the future because a prison sentence never went away. His biggest concern was his son. A boy should not be punished for his father's sins.

"Dad?" Alex slid his tiny hand into Eli's. "I won't tell Miss Julia you cried, okay?"

Tenderness welled inside Eli. "Did I scare you?"

"No." Alex tilted his head with a frown. "But don't do it again. It makes me sad."

"We all get sad sometimes, buddy."

"Yeah, like when Mama went to heaven. I was real sad. I cried."

"I know you did, Alex. I'm still so sorry about your mama. I wish I could have been here to make things better for you."

"It's okay. I'm not mad." Alex looked down at his tennis shoes. "Daddy?"

"Yes?" Hearing his son call him Dad was worth the humiliating tears.

"Is it hard being a dad?"

"At first it was, before we knew each other, but I'm glad I'm your dad. You're the best thing that ever happened to me."

Alex walked a few more steps, still contemplating the ground and his shoes before saying, "I'm glad, too."

So full of love for one little person, he could hardly breathe, Eli swung his son up against his chest. Alex looped an arm around his neck and pressed his babyish cheek against Eli's whiskery one.

This new connection with his son was worth the wrenching moment at the Donovan estate. The journey wasn't over, but they'd finally begun.

"Daddy, can we go see Aunt Opal? I made her a picture."

Counseling was a combo of talk, art and play, and Alex loved drawing pictures. Julia had one on her refrigerator. "Good idea. We'll go tomorrow."

They reached the porch of the benevolent old mansion, feet clomping on the wooden steps. Eli gripped the railing, found it loose and made a mental note to make repairs.

If he was here.

David Presley knew his secret and had made it clear he wanted Eli gone from his ex-wife's home. The lawyer wasn't the kind to keep silent. Word would get around Honey Ridge.

Inside the mudroom, he let Alex slide to his feet and stood awkwardly, as he had that first morning months ago, afraid to hope too much. Only this time, more was at stake.

Kitchen scents greeted them, mingled with the constant peach potpourri fragrance of Peach Orchard Inn.

The house was quiet, unusual this time of evening.

"You hungry, Alex?"

"Yes." He patted his stomach. "My belly's growling."

Coward that he was, Eli would have delayed the inevitable confrontation with Julia and skipped dinner.

"Let's see what Julia left in the microwave." She might not feed him, but she was too maternal to forget about Alex.

When he found two plates inside the microwave, the knot in his shoulders lessened.

He heard the soft pad of footsteps as Julia entered the gleaming kitchen.

"You must be starved. Go sit down and I'll get your drinks."

Like a thief caught red-handed, he stood gripping a plate in each hand. "You don't have to do that."

She looked at him mildly. "I know. Now sit."

All during his meal in the dining room, Julia remained in the kitchen, only a few feet away, but she said nothing to him. The heaviness bore down. She'd feed him and send him packing. He could hear the rattle of dishes and the drawers open and close. Preparations for tomorrow's breakfast, he guessed.

Valery came into the dining room and chatted with him and Alex. He looked at her eyes, bothered to be suspicious of the bloodshot whites. Her drinking hadn't eased up. She was just hiding it better.

Eli knew a little about that, too, just as he knew that a time would come when Valery couldn't hide the truth. Until then, no one could help her.

When Alex finished his shrimp and pasta, Valery turned her bright smile his direction. "How about taking a walk with me and Bingo? Or we could color or play a game."

Alex patted his mouth with a cloth napkin. "Marbles?"

"You'll have to teach me."

"Okay. It's easy. Ben showed me."

Valery's gaze flicked to Eli. He shrugged. No amount of dissuasion had erased Alex's connection with his imaginary friend. The counselors were working on it but for the time being advised him not to press the matter.

Valery held out a hand. "Ready?"

Alex put his tiny hand in hers. "Can my daddy come, too?"

Julia appeared in the archway between the rooms.

"We'll play later, son. I think Miss Julia wants to talk to me." Get it over with.

Alex contemplated the adults with a solemn expression. "Okay," he said, and followed Valery out of the room.

Julia took Alex's spot across the linen-covered table. Eli wanted to touch her so badly he ached.

"He called you Daddy. Did something happen today?"

"Yeah." He put his fork aside. The pasta stuck in his throat. He took a swallow of cold peach tea. It didn't help.

"Are you going to tell me or is this another of your secrets?"

He'd hurt her with his silence. Inwardly, he cursed himself. "I'm sorry. I wish there had been a better way."

"So do I. What happened, Eli? David claims you were a drug dealer."

Eli blew out a nervous breath. The damage had already been done. He owed her the truth. So he told her of the wild playboy parties, the expensive cars and high-maintenance women, the drugs and booze and debauchery. He'd lived high and hard, thinking he was in charge, that he had the world in his palm. Money talked and he had plenty of it...until his final arrest.

When he'd finished, drained dry of his ugly past, the room pulsated like an abscessed wound, putrid and poisonous. Julia had fallen silent, fiddling with the saltshaker, her eyes down as if she couldn't bear to look at him.

Here it comes, he thought. The ax would fall. He was history.

He tried to tell himself he'd been through worse moments in his life—and he had—but saying goodbye to Julia would hurt for a long time.

He licked his dry, dry lips and tried to swallow, but his throat was like cotton.

Julia carefully set the saltshaker to one side and raised wounded blue eyes to his. The knot in his shoulders tightened. How had he screwed this up so badly?

"Thank you for the truth."

The statement was an indictment of his silence, but he'd known no other way. Mercy was all he could hope for. "I know it's not a pretty story. I'm sorry."

"Now I understand why you didn't know Alex until now."

"Mindy and I...we only dated one summer." If you could call it dating. He'd been too busy paving the path to prison to do much but sleep with her. He'd been such a user and she'd been young and innocent and in love with him. "She wrote me in prison about the pregnancy, but I'd gone in for years. I thought it best if she find someone else and give her baby a decent dad."

"But she didn't."

"No. Opal said her illness started when Alex was about three. She fought it for a long time. She didn't write to me about that."

"Would it have mattered?"

"I like to think I'd have found a way to help her." Though how, he couldn't say. Friends had vanished. His parents had wiped him from their lives.

"I think you would have."

He jerked his head up. "What?"

"I've done some serious soul-searching while you were gone."

"If you fire me, I'll understand." He'd hate it, but he could expect nothing else.

"I'm not going to."

He blinked. "You're not?"

"I may be crazy—I probably am—but I think you're a good man. Whatever happened before, you've changed. I want you to continue working here. You've earned that right."

Relief and tingly shock raced through him, hot enough to burn his eyes. He closed them for a moment, tried to get himself under control. "I won't let you down."

"I'm counting on that. From now on, no matter what it is, tell me the truth. Just *tell me*, Eli."

"I will. I promise."

He desperately wanted to ask about them, about their budding relationship that had led to wishes he had no right to make. But now that she knew who he was, he was stupid for thinking there could be anything between him and the lovely innkeeper.

He decided not to press his lousy luck. She hadn't fired him. He'd have to be satisfied with that.

"I don't know what to say, except thank you." He lifted his hands. They seemed too big for the delicate china plates.

"I'm not sure—" she started to say then waved the words away. "Never mind. We can't change the past, so tell me what happened with Alex, instead. He called you Daddy."

"Yeah."

"Was there a breakthrough in counseling?"

"Not there." She was turning his guts inside out tonight with all his failures and this one small success. He pushed his plate aside and propped his fists on the table edge. "We drove by my family's home."

Julia sat back, mouth open in a small gasp. "Did you go inside? Did you see your parents?"

"No." The breakdown had been bad enough in the car. Inside the house, in front of either of his parents, would have been the end of him.

"How does this relate to Alex?"

"I was…upset. Alex has a tender heart." The sweet boy had taken after his mother.

"He's a sensitive soul."

"He tried to comfort me. Can you imagine? A six-year-old comforting a grown man?"

"Apparently he succeeded."

Eli huffed softly. "Just that one word—Dad—melted me. I felt…worthwhile, as if all the rotten things I've ever done didn't matter as long as that little boy loves me."

"I know." Her voice was soft and aching. "Michael was my crowning achievement in life. As long as I had him I could do anything. Then, when he disappeared, I didn't care anymore. Nothing mattered. I felt so…unnecessary."

He couldn't imagine. He knew the terror of his sister's death, but Julia's pain was on a different plane.

"You're an amazing woman, Julia. Necessary on many levels. To this inn. To your family and friends. To Alex…and me."

Emotions kaleidoscoped across her face. "I hope you still think that after you hear what I did."

He tilted his head, thinking that nothing she did could upset him tonight. Not after she'd given him a reprieve.

"Remember when you found your mother online and showed me the forum?" She leaned back in the chair, distancing herself. "I sent her an email."

A nerve ticked beneath his eye. "She won't respond."

"She already did."

30

Inside the Blueberry Room, Julia stood behind Eli, her hands on the back of his chair as he sat at the desk gathering the emotional energy to read the email from his mother. She longed to touch him, to put her hands on his shoulders, lean in close and promise everything would be all right. There must be something fundamentally wrong with her.

He was a convicted drug dealer. Her mother would have a fit when she found out, inevitable since David knew.

She wasn't nervous about keeping Eli on as an employee. Alex needed stability, especially now that he'd begun to bond, and Eli was an excellent employee. But it was this other thing that made her anxious. This need to be close to him, to ignore his past sins. A prison record should have driven her away, but instead she felt softer toward him.

She was as bad as her sister.

"Are you going to read her email or not?" she said over his shoulder.

"It's been a wild day. I'm a little nervous my luck will run out."

"Read it, Eli."

His fingers trembled against the keyboard, breaking her heart. She hoped she'd done the right thing and had not set him up for more heartache.

She succumbed to the urge to touch him.

Hands on his shoulders, she felt the knots in his muscles. The soft feelings deepened. "She wants you to make contact."

"I don't know if I should."

"Your mother has opened the door. You have to walk through it and see what's on the other side, if not for your sake then for Alex's."

He nodded, one curt yank of his head. She stroked the hair at the nape of his neck, soothing him as she would have done Alex or Mikey.

"Her email is cautious," he said.

"Don't you think that's natural under the circumstances? Reply to her, tell her you've changed. Tell her everything."

"Okay." His chest heaved in a gusty sigh. "Okay. Later. I'll do it later after I've had time to think."

"Eli." She ran her fingers one more stroke down the back of his head. "She's your mother. She wants to reconnect."

He gave a short laugh as he closed the laptop. "Or to tell me to change my name and leave the country."

"Do you really believe that?"

He stood and thrust a hand through his shaggy hair. "I'm so hopeful I'm scared to death." He strode to the dresser, leaned into the mirror. "I need a haircut. She'd scold me for looking this unkempt."

A soft smile lifted Julia's mouth. "She might like it. I do."

He turned to face her. "You do?"

"Yes. Valery says you look sexy."

He snorted, and then said, "Val's in trouble, Julia."

Julia opened her mouth to defend her sister. Eli lifted a hand. "Go ahead and tell me it's not my business. You won't be the first, but I've been down the path she's on. She's going to hit a wall eventually."

"I don't know what to do."

"I don't, either. Nobody could help me until I decided to help myself. But I'll be there for her, if she'll let me."

"You have a good heart, Mr. Donovan. Like your son." She came up behind him, noticed the stack of old yellowed letters on the dresser. "What's this?"

"I found them in the carriage house earlier. The ink is faded, but I think we can decipher most of the words."

"Are they from the same woman? What do they say?"

He offered them to her. "Don't know yet. I wanted to read them with you."

"Then what are we waiting for?"

December, 1864

Dearest Will,

I do not know if you will ever receive this letter. Indeed, I do not know if you will hear from me again in this life. Edgar discovered our correspondence and has forbidden me to continue. Yet, I feel compelled to do so, and I pray that my disobedience is not a mortal sin. I have no way of sending this letter, but if I do not write, I will lose my mind.

He has locked me in my room under threat of sending me away without Benjamin. I spend much time in prayer, for what else have I to do but pray and write and sew?

Josie brings my meals but will not speak to me. Lizzy, it seems, has been forbidden to make contact. I have not seen her. Patience, bless her sweetness, comes to the door whenever Edgar is out of the house and whispers encouragement, but it is my precious Benjamin who keeps me going.

I am distressed that he heard the awful quarrel between

his father and me. He is terrified that I will be sent away without him. I whisper to him with great caution, afraid Josie or one of the servants will hear and tell Edgar. We both lie on the cold, drafty floor with our lips pressed close to the narrow slit beneath the door. I can smell the beeswax on wood and hear the soft words of my little boy, growing up now too quickly because of all that's happened here at Peach Orchard. He is afraid of his father now, and that breaks my heart. You were far more father to him that Edgar ever was. Even if Edgar reads these words, I will not recant them.

Today is the sixth day of my confinement. Benjamin and Tandy sit outside in the hallway playing with your beloved marbles. I hear their laughter and I smile, content for a moment. Children's laughter is the music of heaven. How can anyone despair when a child laughs? How can I complain as long as I have Ben? I can feel his love and yours, and I am sustained.

Yesterday, Edgar was in the house all day and no one came to whisper against the oak or to play marbles in the hallway. I can always tell when my husband is at home because I am totally alone. Brave Benjamin, who must pass my bedroom to reach his, rolled a marble beneath a door. I hold it in my hand now, comforted and encouraged by the childish gesture of love. He understands more deeply than a child his age should that the marble connects me to him, and both of us to you.

I glance out the window and see the dark clouds over the peach orchard, and I think of you and pray for your safety…

Julia stopped reading and raised her blue, blue eyes to his. "Did you hear that, Eli? The woman writing this had a son named Ben who played with marbles."

A chill lifted the hairs on Eli's neck. Alex had a friend named Ben. He claimed that friend gave him the antique marbles. "Impossible."

"A coincidence?"

"Has to be. Like the letters, the marbles are a part of the inn's history, not a figment of a confused boy's imagination. They're as real as you and me, and Ben is a common name."

Julia nodded, thoughtful. "That makes sense. Alex found the marbles somewhere and created a friend named Ben."

"The counselor thinks so, and I agree." Anything else was too bizarre. "It's a reasonable explanation."

"Reasonable," she said, clearly still mulling. "Do you think they were lovers? Charlotte and Will?"

"Hard to say. Look at the beginning. She's worried about committing a mortal sin by disobeying her husband. Would she cheat?"

"Apparently Edgar thought so and locked her away as punishment." She shuddered. "Horrible."

"And in those days a husband had the right to treat his wife as he saw fit."

"Remember what the Sweat twins told us?"

"About the Portland woman who took a Yankee lover?"

"Could this be her?"

"The time period is right—1864."

They both stared down at the letter, written in a tidy, flowing female hand from more than a hundred-fifty years ago.

Fascinated, Eli said, "Read the other one."

December 19, 1864
Dearest Will,
I have grown bold here in my room, knowing that no one will read these secret, hidden letters, though I wish you could. Someday, I am determined to mail them. Someday you will know. In view of all that has occurred, I will

no longer deny my feelings for you, dearest, finest Will. I love you. Putting the words to paper fills me with a feeling of strength and hope for the future, no matter how dark the days may seem. You do that for me. You have from the moment we met.

Your corporal came today, though the wind was cold and the skies gray with winter. I did not see him, but Benjamin whispered beneath the door that Edgar was angry and sent the man away. Only three Union men remain now: Johnny, Brinks, and Logan. I did not ask my son about a letter for I know Edgar will not permit the exchange. Nor did I tell Ben of how I long to hear from you. He bears too heavy a burden of subterfuge already.

As I write, he plays with your beloved marbles outside the locked door. If Edgar knows, he has said nothing. I do not know what his plans are for me, but I will not allow him to take my son away. I have made the decision to run away if necessary, but I will not lose my son. It startles me to write such a thing. A woman's place is to obey and please her husband, but I know now, regardless of my pious, perhaps hypocritical efforts, that I am incapable of either…

"The letter ends there, unfinished." Eli carefully refolded the delicate paper.

"Or perhaps the rest has been lost."

"The information is sketchy but the rumors appear true. The house was occupied by the Union Army and now we know Charlotte fell in love with Will, a Union officer, and was locked away by her husband for writing to him."

"Poor Charlotte." Julia's gaze held his. "I wonder what happened to her? Do you think Edgar ever released her? Did she run away? What happened to her son?"

"A lot of questions we'll likely never answer."

"Maybe." She rubbed a spot over one eyebrow. "Or maybe the house… There could be more letters."

"If there are, I'll find them. I'm looking."

"I wonder which room was hers?"

"What difference does it make?"

"Oh, I don't know. Just curious. The original rooms…" She gave a short, embarrassed laugh. "Nothing."

"Some of the rooms have a feeling. Is that what you were going to say?"

"Have you felt it, too?"

"Old houses have a presence. I respect that."

"Do you think a place holds memories? I've visited the battlefield at Shiloh. I don't know how to describe it, but there's an eerie sadness, a terrible kind of energy there."

"Maybe it's only imagination because you know the history."

"Maybe. Probably." She chewed at her lip. He could see she wanted to say more.

"There's nothing sad about the inn," he said.

"No, not sad. But the first time Valery brought me here and dragged me through the neglected rooms, I felt something… welcoming. A benevolent strength. As if the house has stood the test of time and trouble and continues to shelter and protect." She turned toward the window that overlooked the orchard. "I wasn't always this crazy."

He touched the back of her hair, let his hand stroke the silk as he fought the insane need to slip his arms around her waist and place his lips against her soft neck.

"You're sensitive, not crazy," he murmured. Even if she was nutty as a pecan pie, he'd adore her. "You've made this house strong again."

You've made me strong again. But he didn't say that.

"This room has always felt special to me. Probably because

blue was Mikey's favorite color, and I think of him being here and how much he would love looking out this window at the orchard and beyond to the river and hills." She turned to face him, bringing her body inches from his. Eli saw the white spokes in her blue irises, felt the rise and fall of her breathing. He should step back. She was beautiful in so many ways, and tonight he was filled with gratitude for the way she'd accepted him in spite of his prison record.

He lifted a hand to her cheek, though he hadn't intended to. Her flow of words stilled.

"*You* make this house special," he said, loving the softness of her face against his rough fingertips. "I owe you…everything."

"No." She shook her head as if to deny her value, so he threw caution to the wind and silenced her with a kiss. The soft heat of her mouth warmed a heart that had slowly thawed until it now throbbed with the love he wanted to shield her from. Julia was everything he wanted in a woman.

He deepened the kiss, letting his arms and hands caress her as he'd longed to do. She moved against him, stroking the back of his hair with such exquisite tenderness Eli thought he would die of the pleasure.

When the kiss ended, Julia remained close, touching him, making him want more, though he held himself in check. Any more than this was too much to ask.

"If that's the way you repay your debts," she said, smiling slightly, her mouth pink and moist. "I think you owe me a lot more." And she pulled his face down and kissed him again.

Much later, Julia left his bedroom. Reluctantly, Eli thought. He was certainly reluctant to let her go, but it was Alex's bedtime.

He glanced at the letters still lying on the dresser and considered the woman who'd written them. Had Charlotte felt the same deep longing for Will? Had Will loved her in return?

"Daddy?" Alex, in Spidey pajamas, cradled a picture book against his chest.

Daddy. The word made Eli's heart squeeze. He'd never tire of hearing it, of being grateful for that one, special word. "I guess you want a story before bedtime?"

Alex nodded and put the book on the bedside table before holding out his arms. "Throw me."

Throw him? Eli had a brief flashback of him and his own father roughhousing at bedtime. With Alex, he'd proceeded with extra caution, worried about upsetting the kid. The wildest they'd played was when Eli pushed him around in the wheelbarrow atop a pile of carriage house trash.

"Throw you, huh? You sure? On the bed?"

Alex's eyes sparkled as he nodded eagerly.

"All right, you asked for it, buddy." With a growl, Eli swooped down like a vulture, picked his son up high and tossed him onto the bed, then tumbled down next to him for a short round of wrestling. The resulting giggle, the flash of tiny white teeth in a face as tanned as his own, filled Eli's chest with wonder.

Something extraordinary had happened today. He wasn't sure how or why, but Alex had decided to accept him.

Man, it felt good. So many things felt good today that he was a little scared. If this bubble burst, he wasn't sure he could survive.

Alex leaned across his chest for the book then plopped his elbow on Eli's shoulder and listened to *The Giving Tree*, a book that had belonged to Mikey. When the bittersweet story ended, Eli tucked in his son and kissed his forehead.

"Good night, son."

Alex rested his hands on top of the blue coverlet. "'Night, Daddy."

Did Eli dare say, *I love you?*

He swallowed, uncertain, before deciding not to press his luck. Let their day end on a positive.

Alex flipped onto his side and dragged the coverlet to his ears. Eli remained propped on his elbow watching until the small body rose and fell in a deep rhythmic sleep. Then he went to the open window and wished he'd asked Julia to meet him on the porch. Talking into the darkness had begun to free him on the inside the way leaving the prison had freed him physically.

He leaned out, looked and listened for her, but all he heard was the pulsing song of katydids. He supposed he should close the window and preserve the air-conditioning, but he'd never quite gotten past the desperate need for fresh air and an escape hatch. If that was neurotic, he supposed he'd earned it.

He filled his lungs with the heavy, humid night and caught the hint of honeysuckle.

His life here in Honey Ridge was going better than he'd ever dreamed possible. Alex. Julia. He'd even made a friend or two, and now that his past was in the present, perhaps he could dream of a future.

He turned away from the window and saw the laptop open on the desk. Could his future possibly include his mother?

He pulled out the chair, took the computer into his lap and reread her email.

Slowly, cautiously, he placed his fingers on the keyboard.

There was only one way to find out.

31

After a hearty country breakfast, Julia dispensed advice, cookies and sunscreen to her guests and waved them off to tour the Civil War sites in Chattanooga. Valery had already begun cleaning rooms and the washing machine was full of towels.

She'd hardly slept last night. Yesterday had been eventful, to say the least, and the events rotated in her head like a tornado.

Something lovely had bloomed between her and Eli. Life hadn't been this promising in years, and though her mother would have a fit when she discovered Eli's prison record, Mom would just have to deal with it.

At breakfast, Julia had been too busy for much of a conversation with anyone, including Eli, but by midmorning, the bread maker smelled of raisin bread for afternoon refreshments, the peach tea was brewed and Julia was ready for a break. Eli should be, too, so she headed to the carriage house.

She found him and Alex upstairs sorting through a dusty pile of items next to an old trunk. Eli looked up with a smile. "Hi."

He came toward her, and her pulse jumped. She returned his smile and then tiptoed up and kissed him, light and quick.

His smile widened. "I thought nothing was better in the mornings than your coffee, but I stand corrected."

He bent for another kiss, lingering a moment.

This was nice, good, amazing. Way better than French-press coffee. Then she became aware of Alex watching them with wide, curious eyes and pulled back.

Eli stuck his hands into his back pockets as if to keep them off her. "What brings you out to the *spiderweb*?"

"I thought you hardworking men might need a break. I have a fresh pitcher of tea in the fridge."

"Sounds amazing. Right, Alex?"

"Can I have a Popsicle? Please?" The six-year-old's face was already dirty.

"Some people just don't appreciate my peach tea." She shot the boy a smile. "Popsicle, it is, but I'd like to dig around some first. I can't stop thinking about those letters your daddy found."

"If you came to look for more, I beat you to it. Look at this. Same trunk the others were in." Eli put his hand inside a nondescript wooden box and patted. The wood emitted a hollow sound. "There's an extra compartment in the bottom. I didn't notice it until I took all the old clothes out."

"You found more letters?"

He hitched his chin toward the windowsill. "I was going to bring them to you at lunch."

"I can't believe this." She crossed the room and picked up the packet tied with a dirty blue ribbon. "Do you think they've been there all these years?"

"The trunk doesn't look that old. More likely someone else found them first and stored them here for safekeeping."

"Then forgot about them." She ran her fingers over the fragile paper, recognizing the fine penmanship of Charlotte

Portland. "I can't wait to read them, but I guess I'll have to. I have a favor to ask."

"Anything."

"A party of eight called and requested an early check-in. I can be ready for their arrival, but I need some things from town. I was planning to go myself, but—"

"No problem. I'll go. I wanted to pick up some plastic storage bins, anyway. Some of these old things need to be better protected."

"Perfect. Now, let's get this boy to the house for that Popsicle."

With the letters in hand, she led the way down the narrow staircase with Alex safely sandwiched between her and Eli. As they crossed the backyard, Alex and Bingo scampered ahead of them. An interesting contentment seeped in. A boy and a dog were a marvelous combination.

Eli quietly said, "I emailed my mother."

Julia stopped in her tracks. A burst of happiness pulsed through her. "Has she replied?"

He shook his head. "I checked this morning. Nothing yet."

"Maybe by now. Come on!" She took off in a sprint.

"Hey!" he cried, and then sped after her.

Laughing, they raced toward the house. Alex looked at them as if they were lunatics and then disappeared into the mudroom.

Nearing the back door, Julia put out one palm, careful to protect the letters in the other, and slammed into the wall. Eli tumbled against her and spun her around. They were grinning like two teenagers.

"Don't smash the letters." Julia put a hand to her chest. "My heart is pounding."

Eli smirked. "Must be my nearness."

Julia went soft inside. "Must be."

For a few seconds, their gazes held and the tumblers fell into place like Las Vegas slots. Julia's throat tightened. Falling in love again was scary. Scary wonderful.

Eli kissed her on the nose, reached around her and opened the back door. "Better get inside before you're seen fraternizing with the hired help."

"I'm the boss. I can fraternize all I want." But she went inside, anyway. "Go check your email while I get Alex a Popsicle and pour the tea."

"Got any leftover cookies?" he asked hopefully.

"If the late sleepers didn't carry them off." With a song in her heart, Julia watched him disappear and listened for his steps on the staircase. She placed the letters on a shelf, then poured tea and set out the few remaining cookies.

"You're looking all smiley," Valery said as she came into the breakfast room.

"You're not."

Her sister put a hand to her forehead. "Got a migraine."

"Go lie down. I'll bring you some pain tablets."

Valery shook her head, then grimaced and stopped. "I called Doc Havens. He's phoning in a script."

"Eli's going to town in a while. He can pick it up for you."

"Thanks for the offer, but I want to stop by the muffler shop and talk to Jed about something." She ruffled Alex's hair and winked. "I won't be long. The upstairs is cleaned and I'll work on the downstairs when I get back."

With an over-the-shoulder wave, she left the house. Julia refused to worry about her sister today, though she was fairly certain Valery's "migraine" was a hangover.

"Miss Julia." The plaintive voice drew her attention to Alex. His face had crumpled. He looked as if he was about to cry.

"What's wrong, honey?"

"I dropped it."

The green Popsicle lay in a melting heap on the floor.

Julia knelt beside Alex's chair. "We have more."

"I made a mess." A big fat tear dripped onto each cheek. "Daddy says not to make messes for you to clean up."

"Oh, Alex, I'm not angry. Your daddy won't be, either. Accidents happen. Okay?"

With a long sniff, he nodded. Then he threw his arms around her neck and clung tight.

Julia thought her chest might explode. The sensations of holding a small boy against her body engulfed her. Both pain and pleasure swarmed in. She breathed him in, his lime-Popsicle and heat scent unlike Mikey but still very much a precious little boy. A boy in need of nurture, in need of a mother.

She held him awhile, amazed that she could, and then together they cleaned up the melted ice pop. They were still on the floor, Julia instructing the proper method of cleaning up sticky, when Eli came into the dining room.

Julia glanced up and knew at once something had happened.

"Eli?" She rose, a wet rag in hand. "Your mother?"

He nodded, his face paler than she'd thought possible. "She wants to see me."

32

Dear Will,

The most terrible, heinous thing has happened. I scarce can write for the shaking in my hands and the grief in my heart.

Shortly after dawn, I heard a woman scream. Terrible, heartrending screams that caused me to rattle the door-knob of my locked room and call out. No one came for a long time. I paced and prayed, waiting for Benjamin to take his place in the hallway, but he never came. My heart nearly failed, dear Will, for fear that something terrible had happened to my son.

At midmorning, rain began to fall from a dark gray sky, an omen that something was wrong. I felt it in my very marrow. Then I heard footsteps in the hallway and rushed to the door, expecting my son. But the footsteps were heavy. A man's footsteps. The doorknob jiggled. The key rattled in the lock.

It was not mealtime.

Heart in my throat, I waited. Rain tapped against the window behind me.

A smiling Edgar entered the room. In that, I found relief. If harm had come to Benjamin, Edgar would not be smiling.

"Well, my dear, you're looking well," he said.

I didn't know what to say. He seemed so jolly and pleased, and after my long confinement, I did not understand his mood.

"Have you no greeting for your husband?" He crossed to me. Excitement glittered in his eyes.

I dipped my head. "Good morning, Edgar. I trust you're well."

His smile widened. My unease grew greater.

"I am very well. Delighted, in fact. My morning has begun exactly as I'd hoped."

"Has there been good news?"

"Oh, indeed. Good news for you especially, Charlotte. You can rejoin the family today. I've decided to let you remain at Peach Orchard Farm. Isn't that generous of me to forgive my wayward, faithless wife?"

"Yes. Very generous," I said softly, submissively. His strange mood unsettled me. I rested my hands in the folds of my skirt to still their trembling. "Thank you."

"You are so cool this morning. I liked you better when you fell at my feet begging." His nostrils flared. "Perhaps you won't be so indifferent after you speak with Lizzy."

With a chuckle that chilled me, he left the room, leaving my door wide open.

And now, Lizzy weeps until she is sick and I weep with her. My freedom has cost her the greatest price. Edgar sold Tandy. Sold Lizzy's only child out of spite because she did my bidding and carried my letters to you. The cruelty of my husband is unthinkable. My punishment, it seems, is this residing guilt. Edgar said as much. If not for me, if not for my love for you, Lizzy and Tandy would not have been separated.

We do not know where he has gone. Edgar laughs when I beg to know. He is happy now in a way I've never seen. Happy to see me brought low. Happy to see Lizzy broken. It is all I can do not to hate him. That I am capable of such emotion shakes me. I am a Christian woman. How can I burn inside this way?

I have tried to make my husband love me, but no more. No more! I regret that I have failed as his wife, but I will never regret knowing you. For in you, I discovered a depth of love that I should never have otherwise known.

Benjamin's eyes were wide with disbelief and sorrow when he learned of the terrible deed. "Why did Papa sell him, Mama? Why? Did Tandy do something wrong?"

Guilt pierced me. "No, darling. Tandy did nothing at all. He was a fine boy."

"Then why? I want him to come back."

"So do I, darling," I said, for what else could I say? He is far too young to understand the circumstances that led to Tandy's sale.

"Someday when I am a man I will find him." My son's face was ferocious. "I will find Tandy and I will buy him back."

I stroked his reddened, tearstained cheek and gently said, "I hope you can."

"I will," he declared, fists tight at his sides. "He will be mine and no one can ever sell him again."

Having no answer, I pulled him to me and held him tightly, full of anger and sorrow and remorse that Lizzy might never again hold her child as I held mine.

33

Honey Ridge
Present Day

Eli's belly was a swarm of butterflies all morning as he drove into town to run Julia's errands. She'd tried to rescind the request, but he was desperate to stay busy. Even driving in the car gave him too much time to think, and he was grateful for Alex's occasional backseat comments.

His mother wanted to see him. After more than seven years without a word, she was willing to meet him face-to-face. What if she threw him out? What if she rejected him again?

"But what if she doesn't?" Julia, in her sweet wisdom, had asked.

Redemption seemed too much to hope for.

With Alex along, he picked up some nails and storage tubs at the hardware store, had a friendly conversation with the clerk and then stopped at Kroger to fill Julia's grocery list. Eight guests could eat a lot of bacon and eggs.

With the cargo space of the SUV full and Alex munching

on a banana, he headed to the nearest gas station to fill up. One of Trey Riley's sisters was there doing the same. For the life of him, he couldn't remember her name, but he asked about Trey and she asked about Julia, and then she drove away with a cheery wave.

Honey Ridge was beginning to feel like home.

He'd no more than had the thought when a new-model pickup truck pulled to the vacated pump and Valery's boyfriend stepped out. When he saw Eli, a sleazy grin slid up his face.

"Well, hello there, Donovan." Jed adjusted his blue jeans.

Eli gave a curt nod, hoping to avoid conversation. "Fletcher."

The other man reached for the gas nozzle and flipped the lever. "Heard a rumor about you."

Eli stilled, one hand on the gasoline hose. So, Valery had told her boyfriend. Great. He glanced through the backseat window at his son. How long before Alex heard, too?

"Don't you want to know what it was?" Jed laughed an ugly laugh.

"Leave him alone, Jed."

To Eli's dismay, Valery came around from the opposite side of Jed's pickup truck. She must have been inside and Eli had been so focused on the man, he hadn't noticed.

"Aw, just joking around, honey."

"That's not funny."

"It is to me. You and your sister are harboring a criminal. I think that's freakin' hilarious. Where's your sense of humor?"

Valery shot Eli an apologetic look. "I'm sorry, Eli. He's in a mood this morning."

"Shut up, and get back in the truck." Jed gave her a shove.

"Hey!" Eli released the gas trigger. "Keep your hands off her."

"Or what, jailbird? You'll hit me?" Jed tapped his jaw. "Go

ahead. Assault and battery will put you right back in the pen where you belong."

Any infraction could send him back to that stinking rat hole. But he was less than a man if he stood by while a woman was mistreated. Yet, his son was present. Was this the kind of thing he wanted Alex to witness?

Eli flexed his fists, uncertain. He'd like nothing better than to plunge his fist into Fletcher's face, but he wasn't going back to prison, either.

Jed smirked. "I guess you're not so tough now, are you?"

Valery grabbed Jed's hand. "I'm getting in the truck. Come on, baby. Let's go eat lunch. I have to get back to the inn."

The pump clicked off. Jed glared at Eli as he replaced the nozzle and screwed on the gas cap.

"Don't want to fight anymore? Letting a woman save your behind?" When Eli didn't respond, Jed shrugged and laughed. "That's what I figured. You're not such a hotshot now. Jailbird."

Fletcher opened the truck door and got inside. Eli stepped around the gas pumps and grabbed the door. He leaned in, smelled grease and pine air freshener. Jed's pupils expanded in fear.

"I'll say this only once, Fletcher." He kept his voice low and controlled and deadly. "Prison doesn't scare me. You don't scare me. But my son is with me and this is not the time or the place. Keep your hands off Valery or answer to me."

Then Eli slammed the door hard enough to draw looks from other customers before he strode to the SUV and drove away, insides shaking.

He'd been lying through his teeth. Prison scared him to death, but manhood came with a price, and he wasn't losing his again.

Alex leaned forward, banana on his breath. "Who was that man with Miss Valery?"

"Nobody important, son. Nobody at all."

34

February, 1865

We hear of fighting all around us and wonder how much more Tennessee can stand before she breaks. Rumors abound, and our news is scattered and conflicting so that we hardly know what is true. Uncertainty whispers on the streets of Honey Ridge.

I have taken over the cooking with help from Patience, who can scarce boil water. Cook has left us. She disappeared in the night along with one of Jacob Browning's slaves in Honey Ridge. Lizzy says they were lovers, but beyond that she pretends to know nothing.

Everything is changing.

Benjamin asked again today when Tandy was coming home. He knows the answer and yet he is single-minded in his resolve that Tandy will return. My heart twists in my chest. Benjamin is a strong and good boy, and if pride were not a sin, I'd boast of him. Someday Peach Orchard Farm will be his and he has begun to learn the ways of the farmer. Johnny and Brinks are much help in this. Twice of late, he accompanied Edgar to the gristmill. I wish you could have seen Ben's delight at his father's attention. He spoke of nothing else for days afterward. I wish Edgar would take him again. But I wish many things of my husband.

Edgar and I have reached a truce of sorts. Though I am uneasy in his presence, I make every effort to please him. No one else needs to suffer because of his anger toward me. So I will do my duty and be the wife I vowed to be, in deed if not in love. Even this feels disloyal to my feelings for you.

Lizzy has not forgiven me. She says nothing, of course. Indeed, she says little at all. I wish to comfort her, but there is no comfort in the loss of a child. I urge her to pray, to commend Tandy into the hands of God, for that is all I know to do. Sometimes hope is all we have in this world. If we give in to the darkness, we are lost...

35

Knoxville
Present Day

The road to Knoxville had never seemed so short.

He would see his mother today. She'd offered to speak by telephone, but he'd been afraid she'd reject him through the cold, impersonal lines, and he wouldn't get to see her. He had to see her face, at least this once. So, he was making the three-hour trip to Knoxville on a day that had nothing to do with counseling. At least not Alex's.

Julia sat in the passenger seat, calmly talking about everything except the most important thing. Alex rode in the back. He'd brought them along for moral support after Julia mentioned mall shopping while he met with his mother. She and Alex had made big plans that included the Disney store and Build-a-Bear.

He knew what she was doing and loved her for it. If the meeting went sour, Julia and Alex would be there to put him back together.

Off Kingston Pike, he pulled into the enormous lot at the covered mall to let her and Alex out.

"You sure about this?" he asked, anxious.

"You have Val's cell phone. We can call you if we run into a snag." She had Alex by the hand. "But I can promise you, I know how to shop and I know how to entertain a little boy. We'll have a blast."

He had no doubt about that, though he knew she was nervous about taking Alex into a mall.

"Thanks, Julia." He swallowed hard. "You have no idea what this means—"

She leaned through the window and hugged him, effectively cutting off his words. "I know. You'll be fine."

"I couldn't do this without you."

"Yes, you could, but you don't have to." She squeezed his arm. "Now go. See your mama and show her what a good man you've become."

That was the problem. He had little to brag about. He could only hope that a clean start and good intentions counted for something.

"Bye, Dad." Alex was already tugging on Julia, eager to get moving.

With an amused shrug, Julia waved before turning toward the mall entrance with his son.

Eli drove away, his palms sweating though the car's air conditioner blew ice cold.

Nervous, his mind jumped from topic to topic, so he let it. The impending meeting, the inn, the carriage house, Alex, the letters and Valery.

Julia's sister had said little about the confrontation with Jed. A look, a shrug, and a privately murmured, "Don't mind Jed. He's all talk."

For her sake, Eli hoped she was right. It was pretty clear

Valery didn't want her sister to learn of the incident. Neither did Eli.

Ten minutes later, he reached the neighborhood, and as he drove beneath the archway and down the tree-lined streets, his pulse pounded in his ears. A family of joggers loped by on the sidewalk. Skateboarders whizzed along the edges of the streets.

From deep memory, he made the turns, drove past the park and the elementary school and traveled onward, deep into the neighborhood before pulling into his parents' long driveway.

He wiped his hands down his pant leg, a new pair of slacks and shirt bought for the occasion. Then, he checked the mirror. He'd gotten a haircut just to be sure. Finally, when he could delay no longer, he exited the SUV and started up the walk.

The front door opened. His heart beat with such intensity, he felt faint.

His mother stood in the doorway. Refined and tailored to perfection, she'd aged some, but her hair was still as black as his and she looked perfect to him.

He could barely breathe.

"Eli." Her left hand fiddled with a single strand of pearls. Mother always wore pearls.

He stopped at the bottom of the step and somehow found his voice. "Mother."

She pushed the door open. "Won't you come in?"

The formal courtesy she'd give a stranger stung, but he had no right to expect more.

"Thank you," he said, and followed her inside the cool, dim house.

They'd redecorated at some point, and he was sorry that the familiar furniture and colors were gone—like his youth.

He stood awkwardly in the formal living room, unsure of how to proceed. As much as he'd imagined this scene, he'd never decided exactly what to say. How did a man begin to make up for the nightmare he'd caused, for years of worse than nothing?

She seemed as nervous as he was. "Would you care for refreshments? Tea? Coffee?"

He waved a hand and started to say *I'm good*, then thought better of his manners. "No, ma'am. Thank you."

They stood little more than a yard apart, but Eli felt a world away from his affluent upbringing. He'd been places, seen and done things completely out of her realm of comprehension. Why did he ever think he could come home again?

"I probably shouldn't have come." Awkward and uncomfortable, he didn't know what to do with his hands.

A pained expression crossed his mother's face. "Why is that?"

"After all that's happened…" He swallowed, though his mouth was dry as dust. "I'm sorry, Mother. Sorry for everything I ever did that broke your heart. If I could go back and change things, I would."

She blinked at him, searching, he could tell, for signs of veracity from the son who'd lied more often than he'd spoken the truth.

"Are you clean now?"

The question cut him even though she had good reason to ask.

"Yes, ma'am. Since the day I went to prison."

She flinched. Shame filled him. Prison had no place in a Donovan conversation.

"I hurt you and Dad."

"Yes."

"And you'd had…too much pain." His words stumbled. "Jessica."

She twisted the pearls in a loop, face stricken at the mention of her long-dead daughter.

"I should have swum with her that day. She asked me to. It was my fault."

His mother drew back. "That isn't true. Did you think that, Eli? Did you believe you'd somehow caused Jessica's accident?"

"Of course I did," he said, his voice rough with guilt. "You did, too."

"No, no, never." Her eyes were wide and stunned. "We never blamed you. If there is a fault, it was mine."

"But she asked me, Mom. She begged me." He squeezed his fists tight, holding in the emotion.

"Oh, Eli. Oh, my son." Her face twisted. "To think all this time, you thought we blamed you for Jessica's death? Losing both of our children nearly killed us. You every bit as much as her. Seeing you again looking well is like—" her voice broke "—a miracle."

"Mother—" At a loss, he took a step toward her. And in the next instant, he was wrapped in his mother's embrace.

She wept against his shoulder. "Eli. Oh, my son."

Eli closed his eyes, too full of emotion to speak.

The moment was better than any he'd imagined.

Eli had been gone about an hour when Julia's cell phone rang. A glance at caller ID revealed Valery's photo. Julia's stomach clutched, nervous for Eli. If his family rejected him again, he'd be shattered.

"It's your daddy, Alex."

Alex glanced up and right back down, more interested in the stuffed monkey he was busy dressing in blue overalls and a yellow shirt. The mall was fairly quiet today with only a handful of bear-building enthusiasts and the echo of shoppers in the long corridors. She'd watched every one of them with suspicion and hovered over the boy until he probably felt smothered.

Mikey had disappeared in a school yard. How much more dangerous was a mall full of strangers?

"Stay right here, Alex." Julia tapped the cellular screen, one eye on the busy six-year-old. "Hello."

"I'm coming to pick you up now." Eli's voice sounded strange.

"Are you okay? How did it go?"

There was a long pause and then, "She wants to meet Alex."

Joy bubbled up in Julia's throat. She laughed. "I told you everything would work out."

"Yes, it's pretty amazing."

"A mother's love doesn't go away, Eli, no matter what."

"That's what she said."

"What about your father? Was he there?"

"She hasn't talked to him yet."

Julia heard the tension in his voice. "He doesn't know about the meeting?"

"No."

There was more here than he was saying, but Julia decided not to press. He'd tell her when he was ready. "Where are you?"

"About five minutes away. Can you meet in the same place out front?"

Alex grinned at her over the bear. "We're almost finished. Give us ten minutes max."

By the time she and Alex exited the building, Eli waited outside. She tossed a handful of shopping bags into the cargo hold while Eli buckled Alex into his seat and listened to him chatter about Brutus, his Build-a-Bear monkey.

To the casual observer, they appeared to be a family. Julia's chest squeezed. As she got into the passenger seat, she glanced at Alex, content in the backseat, and at Eli, at his intelligent face and then at his dark competent hands that could rebuild a wall, soothe a frightened child and hold a woman with such tenderness.

A family. Was she ready to be responsible for a child again? Would she ever be?

Julia offered to remain at the park or in the SUV, but Eli wouldn't hear of it. For one thing, he wouldn't insult her that way. For another, if he'd admit it, he still jittered with a mix of excitement and anxiety, expecting the bottom to fall out any minute.

"You grew up here?" Julia asked when she saw the estate.

"It seems strange to me, too—I mean, look at this place— but as a kid I didn't even notice."

"Kids don't," she said, letting him off the hook. "Growing up, I didn't know if we were rich or poor and didn't much care."

"I suppose that's true." He opened the car door. Julia stepped out, looked again at the house and then down at her tan slacks and simple white blouse. "I'm not dressed for this."

"You look perfect. Gorgeous." He didn't know if he'd ever paid her such a compliment, but he told the truth. She was classy and pretty all the time, even at the orchard in shorts and tennis shoes. Walking next to her made him proud.

As they approached the house, he saw his mother waiting in the doorway. His stomach lifted, thrilled and nervous. He was desperate to please her and hoped she believed the change in him. Mom's perfectly composed face softened when she saw Alex clutching the stuffed monkey to his chest.

She'd cried when he'd told her about Alex. Cried for a motherless boy. Cried that she hadn't known about him. Cried for lost time. But she'd cried, too, she said, because she'd thought her dream of grandchildren was impossible.

The latter grabbed at the center of his chest. It hurt knowing he'd caused her such pain and lost dreams. Though he could never make up for the wasted years, he could share his son.

Inside the house, Eli introduced the women, watched the quiet, subtle way his mother assessed and then approved of Julia.

"And this must be Alex," Mother said. "He looks like you, Eli. So much. Look at that chin."

Eli dropped a hand to Alex's shoulder. The boy gazed up, his expression mildly curious.

"Mother, this is my son, Alex. Alex, I want you to meet my mother, Gloria Webber Donovan. She's your—" Eli's voice failed him. He swallowed.

"Grandmother," she said softly. "I'm your grandma, Alex, and I'm delighted to meet you. I've never had a grandson before."

The grabbing pain came again. So much guilt, so much remorse, and there wasn't a thing he could do to change it.

Alex clung to his leg, his brown eyes wide.

Eli bent low to whisper, then looked on with pride when his son offered a hand to his new grandmother.

"My pleasure, ma'am," he said shyly. "This is my monkey."

His mother's face crinkled into a smile. She touched the toy, touching Eli's heart with her effort. "What is this fine monkey's name?"

"Brutus."

"Eli told me wonderful things about you, but he neglected to mention your handsome monkey."

"He's new. Miss Julia let me make him."

"That was very kind of her."

"Miss Julia's nice. She has boy toys."

"Boy toys?" Mrs. Donovan tilted her head. "So you have a son, too?"

Eli felt Julia tense at his side. He reached for her hand and squeezed gently to reassure her. She looked at him with a plea.

He understood and marveled at this silent communication that had sprung up so naturally between them.

He could say the words. She couldn't.

"Julia has a son," he told his mother. "His name is Michael. He was abducted years ago and never found."

"Yet…" Julia's determined murmur tugged at him.

"Oh, my dear girl."

His mother's face filled with compassion and something few people could give to Julia, the connection no two women should ever have to share—the loss of a child. He realized then, the commonalities between the two women went deeper than Southern manners and good taste.

He thought, too, of Lizzy, the slave woman in Charlotte's letters, and was struck by the irony. She, too, had lost a child.

"It still hurts you to talk about him," his mother said.

Julia gave a single nod. "Most people are uncomfortable. They don't know what to say."

"I understand."

"Yes," Julia said, "you do."

"I'm sure you have beautiful memories as I do of our Jessica."

"But today isn't about me," Julia said graciously. "Today is for you and Eli and Alex. You have a lot of catching up to do."

"We do, indeed. The three of you please make yourselves comfortable while I bring in some refreshments."

"Could you use some help?"

"Miss Julia brings us 'freshments all the time," Alex said. "She's a good cooker."

Mrs. Donovan smiled. "An extra hand is always appreciated. Do you mind, Eli, if I confiscate Julia for a few moments?"

Before he could answer, the two women disappeared down the hall toward the kitchen.

Gloria Donovan removed a silver tray from a glass-fronted cabinet and set it on the black marble countertop. "I hope you won't think less of me for asking," she said. "But how is he really doing? He looks healthy and he appears to be doing well, but—"

Julia arranged four glasses on the tray, careful to say the right thing. "You don't want your heart broken again."

"I'm sorry. That sounds selfish, but I have to be sure before I tell his father."

"Mrs. Donovan…" Julia turned her back to the counter and as earnestly as she could, said, "Eli is one of the finest men I've ever known. In the months since he came to work at Peach Orchard Inn, he's proven himself over and over again. He works more than he has to, he's a friend I've come to depend on, and he's trying so hard to be a terrific father. He could have shirked responsibility of Alex. He chose not to though the journey hasn't been an easy one."

Gloria's face was a contrast of caution and longing. "He truly has changed?"

"I didn't know him before, but the Eli Donovan I know now desperately wants to redeem himself, especially with you and his father. I hope you'll give him that chance."

Gloria studied the pitcher of iced tea.

"I'm willing," she said in a small voice. "I only hope his father feels the same."

Eli could hear the soft chatter of the women's voices and wondered. Eavesdropping was out of the question, but his mother had wanted to speak with Julia alone. The subtle signs were there. Was she grilling Julia for information about him? His heart beat in his throat to think of all that was at stake today. His mother had welcomed him, seemed happy to see him again, but the black sheep was a long way from redemption.

Bored with the adults and the strange environment, Alex pulled his marble bag from his pocket and began teaching the game to Brutus. Eli went to the fireplace, where a single photo stood on the mantel. Jessica with his mother and father. He'd been eradicated from the photos exactly as he'd been ostracized from the family. He'd known, but it hurt just the same.

"Do you still like your tea as sweet as syrup?"

His mother's voice turned him around.

"You remember that?"

"Oh, son," she said. "A mother never forgets."

He took the tall glass of amber tea, thoughtful. She remembered.

Emotion ran high in the room. He felt it in the tight muscles of his neck and the way the potpourri air vibrated with hope and fear and love thwarted a million ways. His fault. His problem. Not his mother's or his dad's. He was the one who had to make the repairs.

The three of them sat down and sipped at icy sweet tea, though he wasn't the least bit thirsty.

There was much to be said, but Eli tiptoed around the past seven years. His mother wouldn't want to hear about that.

When conversation lagged, Julia seemed to know exactly what to say. She talked about him and Alex, about the inn and the orchard. She made him sound like a saintly genius. He saw what she was doing and loved her for it.

"He's brilliant about business," Julia said when his mother inquired politely about the mentioned peach orchard harvest. "Did he tell you he completed his business degree?"

"Julia," Eli said. Though he was proud of the degree, he feared it would bring back painful memories to his mother. His parents had sent him to the university and he'd wasted their money.

Julia waved him off. "Your mother wants to know these things."

"That's marvelous news, Eli." Gloria leaned forward. "Your father and I had always hoped—"

Eli's fingers flexed against his tea glass. They'd hoped he'd apprentice with Dad. They'd hoped he'd be as successful as his father. They'd hoped he'd take over the family business. "I know."

"Well," Julia said brightly. "He has that degree now, and there is no reason he can't use it." She laughed softly. "He already is."

He looked at her, amazed. She was as much a dynamo as Valery when she got her teeth into something.

With a long-suffering sigh, Alex put his marbles away and curled up in the floor.

"Someone is getting tired," his mother said with affection. "He could lie down in your old bedroom, Eli."

He wasn't ready for that. Surely, in the intervening years, his bedroom had undergone drastic change.

"Thank you, but we should go. It's a long drive." He rose. "And we'll have to drive it again on Wednesday."

"Wednesday?" His mother's face expressed hope.

"Alex and I come to Knoxville every week for counseling." He shifted a glance at his son.

Gloria's eyebrows came together. "Can't you do that closer to Honey Ridge?"

Eli felt the blush of humiliation creep up his neck. How did he tell his wealthy mother that he was too broke to provide for his son?

Julia came to his rescue. "The Knoxville center is free."

His mother was smart, a businesswoman who ran the family's foundation. She understood immediately. "And excellent from what I've heard."

"It is," he agreed. "They've really helped Alex." Him, too. They both had a distance to go, but at least they'd begun.

"Tell her about your idea, Eli," Julia urged.

"I don't want to bore her with that."

"I won't be bored. Tell me."

So he explained his concept of free mobile grief centers. "Especially for kids and their families. My situation with Alex has made me realize how much we need them, especially in rural areas like Honey Ridge."

"Not everyone can afford professional counsel or travel long distances to get help," Julia added.

"That *is* brilliant," his mother said thoughtfully. "I've often wondered if we'd taken Eli to counseling after Jessica's death, perhaps things would have turned out differently." Her fingertips rubbed at the pearls. "All of us were lost for a while, but he was a child. I should have realized—"

"Mom." Eli took both his mother's hands. "Don't."

All the fault was his. Not hers. Never hers or Dad's. He'd been the bad seed, the spoiled rich kid who refused to appreciate what he had. Even if Jessica's death had sent him over the edge, he should have grown out of it eventually.

Eventually had been a long time in coming.

36

February, 1865

My darling Will,
Many days have passed since I last lifted pen to paper. I was too weak and the news too agonizing to bear. Please write to me now and refute what I have read with my own eyes. You cannot be gone. A heart as brave and true as yours cannot have ceased beating.

My mind is screaming. Just as Lizzy screamed that fateful day that Tandy disappeared from us, I am screaming, though my cries are silent and unending. I scream and scream and scream.

Death is too final, too hopeless. Since the day you rode away, I have clung to hope. Clung to the shameless hope that you would return. Now, all hope is gone forever. I will never see your dear and handsome face again this side of eternity.

Lizzy brought the news and for the first time since Tandy left us, she called me by my given name. She held my hand and with tears in her eyes said, "Charlotte, I have bad news."

"What's happened?" I knew something was wrong the moment she entered the kitchen where I peeled turnips for dinner.

Her grip grew tighter. "It's Captain Will."

That was all she had to say. I knew.

All the blood drained from my head. My ears roared with a frightful rushing sound. I collapsed, wilted like boiled turnip greens.

Edgar knows, I'm certain, but he's said nothing. At dinner he watched me closely as if expecting something. I don't know what. There is a gleam in his eyes that torments me. So I forced a few turnips down my throat and tried to pretend I was not shattered. I think he wanted me to speak of you, so that he could gloat, but I will not. I cannot. Not to him.

Instead, I will write letters you will never read. I will give you my heart in these pages and I will remember a noble and worthy man. And I will mourn.

Tonight, Benjamin curled at the foot of my bed, wan and subdued. He gripped the bag of marbles in one hand as if they were proof you live and asked if the news was true. I had not intended for him to know but Josie told him. Her deed was needlessly cruel but I think she did so to hurt me, not Benjamin. She loves her nephew, but she blames the cold British interloper—her words—for Edgar's dark moods and sharp words.

I miss you, Will. I shall never forget you or what you meant to me in those short months. I shall never forget our long conversations by the fireplace, and your merry laughter when Benjamin hung upside down from the banister pretending to be a monkey. And I shall always treasure your letters.

Yours eternally,

Charlotte

37

Julia propped both feet on the front porch railing and listened to Eli's rumbling baritone as they discussed the events of the day yet again.

Night blackened the lawn and hid the orchard, but lightning bugs poked holes in the immediate darkness around the porch. Katydids whirred and crickets chirped, the natural music of a sultry Tennessee night.

She'd gone with him to tuck Alex into bed, a first and something she'd needed to do. She couldn't exactly explain why, but those moments in the Blueberry Room filled an empty spot inside her just as Eli did.

She loved him. Loved them both. The emotion was so new and precious she wanted to savor it for a while.

"You're happy," she said with a soft smile, glad for him.

Eli leaned his backside against the rail, one knee raised to prop a foot behind him. The always-on light from the entryway dappled him in shades of amber and gray. "I never thought I would be again, but yeah, I am. She's already emailed me."

"Since this afternoon?"

"Yes." His laugh was short and self-effacing. "So I called her."

"That's good, Eli. Wonderful. I'm glad for both of you."

He went serious. "She's telling Dad tonight."

Julia touched the hand he'd fisted against his thigh. "It will work out. You'll see."

"I hope you're right. I miss them." He picked up her fingers one at a time and let them go again to fall back against the chair arm. "Alex needs a grandma and grandpa."

"They need him, too."

"Yes. I think they do."

"I've read some of Charlotte's letters." She lifted the packet from her lap. "Did you?"

"A few."

"Captain Will died in battle. That makes me sad for Charlotte and for little Ben. He loved the captain, maybe more than he'd been able to love his father. It's such a tragic story."

"But there's something else, too," he said. "Strength and honor. Doing the right thing even though it hurt them both."

Julia nodded, pleased that he saw it, too. "Charlotte was a pious woman who fell in love, but she and her soldier were both too honorable for an affair. Sad, isn't it, that two people could be so right for each other and yet not be together? Would choose not to be together."

"Sometimes being right for each other isn't enough," Eli said, his voice as soft as the night wind. "People make choices and those are mixed with the Fates or God or whatever makes the universe move. They made a difficult choice during a terrible time. The Civil War separated a lot of people."

"Not just the war. Cruelty." Julia tapped the envelopes in her lap. "Edgar sold Tandy out of spite."

"I wonder what became of him?" A question with no answer.

"Do you think he was Edgar's son?"

Eli dipped his head to one side. "What makes you say that?"

She shrugged. "He was light skinned. Edgar had a mistress in the quarters. Charlotte never knew who Tandy's father was and Lizzy wouldn't tell her."

"You think Lizzy was protecting Charlotte from the truth?"

"Don't you think it's possible?"

"Now that you mention it, yes. Possible." He went silent, a warmth in the darkness lit only by the shadowy light. "The letters make me wonder."

"About what?"

"This house. The marbles. Alex and his invisible Ben. Can marbles appear from the past? Is that possible?" He huffed. "I feel stupid asking such a thing."

The hot night air seemed to shimmer with the question, pulsing on the wings of night birds. The house pressed in, hovering like a mother hen with wings spread over her chicks, as if waiting for the answer.

"I don't know," she said. "I've heard of pennies from heaven that are supposed to be a sign of comfort from loved ones passed. But that's wishful thinking. Isn't it?"

"But Charlotte and Will aren't people you know. Why would they be comforting you or any of us?"

"Coincidence, then."

"Must be."

But Julia wondered.

A week passed and then two. Eli spoke to his mother daily and took Alex to see her twice. He was careful to ask for nothing and to expect less. Though the new grandmother wanted to shower Alex with gifts, he'd refused to let her. In the future perhaps, but not yet. Not until he'd proved himself to be more than an ex-con looking for a handout from his affluent family.

He'd spoken to his father once by telephone, a tentative, cautious conversation. There would be no quick reconciliation with James Elliot Donovan. But they'd begun the long road to healing. Today he took the next step.

Heart beating in his throat, he straightened his tie for the dozenth time as he waited for the polished elevator to take him to his father's third-floor office. Money for a suit seemed like an extravagance, but when meeting with his father for the first time in over seven years, he needed the confidence booster.

At the ping, the elevator swooshed open and Eli walked the familiar distance to the receptionist's desk. Ruth, the administrative assistant from his childhood, was gone, replaced by a sleek brunette who looked at him with subtle curiosity before announcing his presence by intercom.

"Go on back, Mr. Donovan," she said with a professional smile. "The office is the first one on your right."

The same as always. If his father was anything, he was stable. Unlike his son.

Eli pecked softly at the door marked President and CEO and then stepped inside. The room smelled subtly of leather and expensive male cologne. Prepared for the rush of emotion, Eli held himself in check as his father rose, one hand smoothing his tie. He had aged. His temples and sideburns were completely gray now and he looked tired.

"Eli."

"Thank you for seeing me."

No smile, no welcome. Not that Eli had expected one.

"I didn't intend to."

The blunt response jolted. Eli drew a tortured breath. "I know."

"You were dead to me."

Eli flinched. Not the beginning he'd hoped for, but the one he deserved. "Yes, sir. Rightly so, and that's why I'm doubly grateful for this appointment."

"All right, then." James indicated a chair. "Sit. Your mother thinks I should give you another chance. I want you to convince me she's right."

The only chance he wanted was to be a son again.

For nearly an hour his father listened to him, grilled him, asked astute questions and made blunt references to his misdeeds. Eli felt on trial all over again. His palms sweated and his stomach burned. James Donovan was a tough businessman but a fair one. It was family, though, not the business that interested Eli, but by his father's actions, they were one and the same.

Finally, his father sat back in his leather chair and fell silent. Eli was sure he could hear his own blood pulsing through his veins.

Seconds ticked by as his father weighed him in the balance, much as he'd been weighed that awful day in court.

James flipped open a manila folder on his desk. "You'll understand if I've had you investigated."

Eli swallowed the sting. "Yes, sir."

"Everything you've told me lines up with the reports." He tapped his fingers on the papers, mouth pursed as if he still couldn't believe the wayward son had changed.

"I'm not the same punk who went to prison. I know you don't trust me. Understandable. I've said the words a thousand times to get out of a hot spot, but prison changes a man, Dad. It makes or breaks him." Eli felt the damp moisture under his collar. The tie was choking him. "I'm going to give my son a dad he can be proud of. A dad like I had."

His father pulled a hand down his mouth, a gesture Eli recognized as his own only he'd not known until this moment that he'd learned it from his father. "We always wondered where we'd gone wrong."

The hurt, the anguish, the questions he'd caused good parents who'd done nothing but love him. "You didn't. I did."

"No, there was something." His father gazed down at the manila folder, thoughtful. "The Donovan Foundation is your mother's baby."

Eli blinked, confused at the shift. "Excuse me?"

"Gloria told me about your concept for a mobile grief center."

Eli leaned forward, nervous for a whole new reason. "She did?"

"She was cautiously enthusiastic about considering it for a foundation project."

"I didn't come here for that, Dad."

"Understood, but is it something you'd like us to consider?"

"It could be a worthwhile project."

"Tell me about it." His dad sat back, fingers steepled over his lips.

Anxious and unprepared, Eli shared Alex's story and some of the situations he'd heard about in counseling, discussing the need and finances, the benefits. He shared about brokenhearted kids who didn't know how to express their sorrow, about the little girl who'd gone mute, fearing her last words to her sibling had caused her death. When he finished speaking, his heart pounded like drums. He hadn't been ready. He hadn't seen this coming.

"I can see you're passionate about this."

"Yes, sir."

Dad tapped his fingers together, the mind of an extremely successful businessman weighing information as he would for anyone. The air conditioner hummed and a waft of much needed coolness swept over Eli.

"Your mother thinks if we'd gotten professional advice, if we'd realized how Jessica's death pulled us apart, perhaps things would have been different. We thought we were strong enough to weather it alone."

Eli once would have grabbed on to Jessica's death as the reason for his wild, undisciplined life. He was a different man now and knew better. "I am passionate about this project, Dad, but I won't use Jessica as an excuse for my past."

"No? Well—" His father's mouth softened. "Then indulge me and your mother. Retrospect has its value. We see the mistakes we made. Omissions, blind spots. In our pain, we drifted away from each other and you. I never saw it until your mother forced the issue after your first meeting."

Eli didn't know what to say. Jessica's death so long ago was a blur of anger and silent suffering. At thirteen, he'd never considered his parents. He hadn't even considered them when he was twenty-eight. Life had been about him, his wants, his needs.

"I'm sorry, Dad," he said, wiping the moisture from his forehead. "I never realized—"

His dad held up a hand. "Neither did we, which is why we're interested in your idea. We'd like you to develop a proposal to present to the board."

Eli's heart leaped. "You would?"

"Your mother would, and I agree after speaking with you. Can you do it?"

"Absolutely." He understood now why he'd been allowed this audience. Mother ran the foundation, but Dad wanted to vet him.

"No promises, but an opportunity to put your idea before the board. And frankly, I'd like to see if you'll follow through."

"I will. Right away." He'd already been doodling thoughts in a notebook.

A small smile lifted his dad's mouth. "If the board likes your concept, they'll want someone to head it up. Someone with the passion and understanding to make it happen. The right leader is essential to the success of any venture. We'll want your input on that, too."

"Yes, sir, certainly, but I'm sure Mother will find someone. She's a genius at putting the right person with the right position."

"She thinks she *has* found someone." Cool gray eyes assessed him. "You."

A shock, like electricity, ran down Eli's arms. Fear and disbelief mixed with ferocious longing. "Me? But—I don't… Why?"

"Because you're our son. I thought you'd used up all your chances with me, but time changes a man's perspective."

"I can vouch for that," Eli murmured softly.

"I've watched your mother suffer privately while she made the world a better place for everyone else. The past few weeks, with you back in her life, she's been a happier woman."

"I wish I could take all of it back—"

"But you can't." The tough businessman had returned. "No promises, Eli. This is a large foundation with a reputation for excellence. Should you be hired, your every move would be scrutinized. You would be an employee only, not the boss's son, and treated accordingly."

Not the boss's son. He wondered if he'd ever be granted that privilege again.

Eli realized then that he'd foolishly dreamed of a biblical-type reconciliation. That his father would kill the fatted calf and throw a party to welcome him back into the fold.

This chance to be an employee, not a son, would have to be enough.

"I understand."

"I'm not sure you do." His father rose and came around the

desk. Eli rose too, holding his tie close to a jittery stomach. "I won't have your mother hurt again. Do you understand that?"

"You have my word." Then Eli realized how ridiculous he sounded. "I know that means nothing now."

The CEO stuck out his hand for a handshake. "You have your chance. Don't blow it."

38

April, 1865

Dearest Will,
The Confederacy is broken. Peace will come now, though
at far too great a price. Why could the war not have ended
before the battle that took you away?

Three of your men remain here. With them, I can
speak of you and remember. Their bodies will never be
whole again, but they talk of going home soon. I confess
I will miss their company. They do not seem elated by
the Confederate surrender. They are, I think, too much
victims of this war, to feel like conquerors.

Ragged, skeleton men, once proudly marching Confederates, stop at Peach Orchard to rest as they straggle
home to Honey Ridge and beyond. They are a sad and
desolate lot, defeated both in fact and in spirit. I feed them
and feel sorry for them, though I am not sorry the war is
ending. Indeed, had the fighting ended sooner, you would
still be in this world, breathing the air that I breathe. Is it

foolish of me to think such things? That somehow I might take a draught of the air that once graced your lungs? I like to think of it, and now that spring has returned to Honey Ridge and the peach blossoms perfume the air, I breathe deep and remember you.

We took the carriage into Honey Ridge for church. One of the women, Rosie Satterfield, sniffed loudly and flounced away when I approached her, but Mrs. Jacobs and her daughter, Jenny, invited me, Josie and Patience to a ladies meeting to rally around the widows. I shall attend and do my part to bring comfort where I can. For isn't that why the Creator put us here? To ease the way for others?

The Negroes are slowly leaving us. Since Mr. Lincoln's Emancipation Proclamation they are no longer slaves and no longer required by law to remain. Edgar had counted on loyalty, but if I were a slave, would I be loyal to those who had kept me in bondage? One by one, they disappear so that we are left to shoulder more and more of the farmwork.

Spring is here, the time to plant and plow, so all of us pitch in to do the work once done by slaves. It is hard, exhausting labor from dawn to dark. Four of our servants remain, besides Lizzy. I wonder when they, too, will disappear over the horizon.

An interesting thing occurred. A freed slave I did not know appeared at the back door and nervously asked for help. His wife lay near childbirth in the peach orchard. The memory of my own dead babies threatened to paralyze me with fear, but I took Lizzy and went to her. She was very young but stalwart, and late in the afternoon we delivered her of a fine baby girl. The mother named her Peachy because of the blossoms that fell around her as she labored. I wonder what will become of Peachy, this child born into freedom with nowhere to go?

We bedded the new family down in the barn for the night. Edgar would not allow them in the house or the cabins, though two stand empty now. I thought he might offer them shelter and work, but he did not.

Later, Lizzy asked, "Where they gonna go? Where any of us going to go now?"

"I don't know." Truly, I do not.

"I'm free now," Lizzy fretted in her wise manner. "Free to leave. Free to stay. But freedom don't feel the way I expected."

I knew then that liberty requires more than an official proclamation to take root in the soul of man. Freedom, it appears, is as much a condition of the mind as of the body.

39

Present Day

Surrounded by the scent of bleach and fabric softener, Julia folded the never-ending load of fluffy white towels. The inn was full today due to a Civil War reenactment in nearby Tullahoma. Eli and Alex had moved into the tiny room in the carriage house. Because of the renovation expense, the extra income from the Blueberry Room was needed, but she missed having Eli and Alex underfoot all the time.

Eli was a different man now that he'd reconnected with his family. Different in many ways. Animated, excited about the project proposal he'd submitted last week, encouraged about his future.

So was she, though she wondered where she might fit in. If she did at all.

His moving into the carriage house felt as if he was moving away from her. Distancing himself.

Her mother wandered in from the kitchen with two glasses of peach tea and handed her one. "Where's your sister?"

Condensation dampened Julia's fingers. "Meeting Jed for lunch."

Connie frowned. "She's not holding up her part of the inn lately."

"She owns a third, Mama. The rest is my responsibility." But she still worried about her sister. Three times this week, Val had come to breakfast with red eyes, daring Julia to say a word. Of course, Julia hadn't. It didn't do any good. Valery made her own choices.

"I'm proud of you." Her mom folded a towel into a perfect square. "You've come a long way."

Pleased, touched, Julia turned with a smile. "Thanks, Mama."

"When Mikey disappeared I was afraid I'd lose you, too."

"Oh, Mama." But she didn't stop the flow of words. Mama never talked about her missing grandson. "I still miss him so much."

"I know. That's why I'm proud of my girl. You didn't cave in even when the going seemed impossible. You and your sister have turned this old Civil War mansion into a profitable inn." Connie lifted her eyebrows. "Any more visits from the marble fairy?"

Julia shook her head. The marbles had become a point of conversation as well as a lighthearted joke, though she and Eli still wondered. "Not lately. Things are going too well. They only show up in the bad times."

"Interesting. That's what makes this place such a great bed-and-breakfast. Well, along with your excellent proprietorship." Connie sipped at her tea and then set it on the dryer. "What about those letters Eli found? I thought you were going to frame them to hang in the parlor?"

"They're so personal that I'm having second thoughts." Sometimes she imagined the letters were meant for her, not for sharing. She felt a kinship with Charlotte though she had yet to understand why. Perhaps the fact that they both had sons they adored and husbands who had betrayed them.

Julia's cell phone vibrated against her side. Laying aside the final towel, she glanced at the unfamiliar caller ID before saying, "Hello. Peach Orchard Inn. Julia speaking."

"Julia, it's Eli."

She smiled. "I know." Didn't he realize she'd recognize his voice out of a million others?

"I need to ask a favor."

"Sure." She balanced the phone between her neck and ear and reached for the stack of clean towels. "What's up?"

"Will you look after Alex for a while?"

Something in his voice sounded off. She left the towels where they lay. "Of course. What's going on? Something with the project? Did they approve it?"

"Yeah." He sighed heavily into the receiver, not at all the triumphant sound she'd expected. Worry wiggled in.

"I thought you'd be ecstatic. Is something wrong?"

A pause, a deep breath during which Julia visualized him running a hand through the top of his hair. "I've been arrested."

40

Peach Orchard Farm
May 2, 1865

Today is my birthday. I am twenty-eight years old. Lizzy laughed when I looked in the mirror for gray hairs. Sweet Benjamin wove a daisy chain for me and Patience endeavored to bake a cake. Josie embroidered a lovely lace handkerchief with tiny blue violets that pleased me no end. Even Edgar smiled at Ben's exuberance and the cake tasted quite delicious even though it was as lopsided as could be. The household was jolly beyond anything I can remember since the war began. Renewal is in the air.

I am writing this with such a joyful heart. I am quite determined to find joy in the days ahead. You, my noble captain, would have expected no less. I will live and laugh and find the good even in those who dislike me, for anyone can find good in the lovely. I will love my son and my friends, and I will honor my husband and in so doing, perhaps he will find peace with God…and with me. Hope is a tenacious thing.

Edgar and Benjamin have gone to fetch the horses up from the barn. I can scarce believe my husband today. The war's end and the beginning of summer has had an interesting effect on him. He is taking Benjamin for his first ride into Honey Ridge, something too dangerous before.

The scent of peaches wafts through my open window. Such a happy smell. The promise of a good harvest is much needed.

I hear voices below. Ben's excited one, punctuated with laughter, makes me smile.

I will put the pen away for now and hurry down to watch them ride away. My little boy on his very first ride into town.

Charlotte lifted the hem of her skirt as she trotted down the stairs and out onto the veranda. A warm sun glowed over the green grass. The heavy, sweet smell of rhododendron perfumed the air. A pair of geese, as white as the clouds above, pecked at the grass. It was a perfect day. A day for new beginnings.

"Mama, look at me."

She shaded her eyes with one hand and smiled at Benjamin's childish exuberance, delighted to see him this way. Perhaps he was coming out of the winter's strange melancholy. Astride Penny, the red-roan mare, he looked small and brave and happy.

"Ride carefully and mind your papa."

"I will." He nodded eagerly. "I will bring you a present, too. Papa said I could."

The sentiment surprised her. She let her gaze drift to her husband. Edgar, who'd grown thicker while the rest of them grew thin, rode the stallion close to the porch railing.

Charlotte rested her hands on the rail, still uneasy in his

presence. Weeks alone, locked in the blue bedroom buzzed in her memory like an unwanted horsefly, ready to draw blood again if given half the chance. She tried swatting it away, but trust destroyed took time to rebuild. Perhaps he felt the same.

Edgar looked down at her from atop the big stallion and she met his gaze with an outward calm.

"Patience and Josie asked for yard goods," he said. "Is there anything you want from town?"

The simple question, though spoken gruffly, pleased her and quelled the buzzing horsefly for a moment. Honey Ridge, like many Southern towns, had little to offer, though supplies were slowly trickling in now that the war was over and trains were moving for other than military purposes. Edgar rarely offered gifts. Today was a good day, indeed.

"Benjamin has outgrown his Sunday clothes. I would be happy for yard goods, too, if you're so inclined."

The words were hardly spoken when one of the geese flapped his wings and ran toward the horses with a loud honk.

Penny spooked and skittered sideways. Benjamin cried out. "Papa!"

Edgar twisted in the saddle. "Hold fast, boy."

The gander, for whatever reason, saw the horses as trespassers and charged with full steam. This, in turn, upset the other goose and she followed, wings aflap and voice loud.

The startled mare danced and hitched her shoulders, launching Benjamin forward onto her neck. He screamed.

"Ben!" Charlotte rushed toward the steps.

Edgar yanked the stallion around and leaned toward his son, reaching for the mare's reins.

As if loosed from hell itself, the geese honked louder and flapped wildly at the stallion's legs. Both horses spooked.

Hob, the arthritic old slave, rushed into the melee. Voices rose in fright. A horse screamed and began to buck.

As Charlotte reached the steps, her skirt caught on something, and she pitched forward into the grass. The breath slammed from her lungs. She battled to her knees. "Ben!"

In the noise and movement of horses and people, she couldn't make heads or tails of what was happening. Movement, noise, screaming animals, and then the stallion galloped away, riderless.

Edgar lay on the ground, his head bent in an unnatural angle.

An earsplitting scream shattered the perfect afternoon.

Charlotte's trembling legs wouldn't lift her. She crawled to her husband, breathless. "Edgar, are you all right?"

But she knew he wasn't. After all the commotion, Edgar remained still, his florid face now pale. His lips worked. His eyelids fluttered.

"Hob, get help. Hurry!"

"Ben," Edgar managed. Saliva pooled in one corner of his lips. His breath came in short gasps. "Is Ben...safe?"

"I'm right here, Papa." The little boy, face white as bleached muslin, fell onto his knees at his father's side. His small hand caressed Edgar's cheek.

Charlotte's heart twisted.

"Your boy is fine." She touched her husband's other cheek, a liberty. "You kept him safe."

Lizzy came flying out of the house and across the grass, screaming. She fell to her knees at Edgar's side. "Where is Tandy? Tell me, Edgar. Where is he?"

Edgar's eyes widened. His mouth worked as if he wanted to speak. "He's...Robert..."

Lizzy leaned close to his lips, straining to hear, but a shudder passed through the dying man. One long breath wheezed from his lips and his pale eyes glazed over.

"No, no. Don't you die," Lizzy said in a terrible voice. "Tell me where my boy is." Lizzy grabbed Edgar's collar. "Tell me! Who is this Robert? Who is he?"

But Edgar's hold on life loosened before he could answer.

"Edgar." Charlotte leaned in, pressed her ear to his chest. Her mouth had gone dry as the dust.

"Papa. Papa!" Through the deathly stillness came the heart-wrenching sound of Benjamin patting his father's face. "Wake up, Papa. We're going riding. Wake up, Papa."

Charlotte tugged her son into her arms and held him, rocking and rocking there in the trodden grass.

"He tried to tell me," Lizzy whispered. "Oh, Jesus, he tried to tell me."

Former slaves and the Yankees he hated surrounded her husband's inert form.

"He's gone, Miss Charlotte," Hob said, closing Edgar's eyelids for the final time.

She nodded. She'd known.

She heard her sisters-in-law sobbing, felt her son trembling and her own terrible regret. In death, Edgar Portland had become a better man than he'd ever been in life.

May 9, 1865
My dearest Will,
A week has passed since I became a widow. The gift of yard goods Edgar had kindly offered to buy for my birthday was purchased in black. The house and all within it suffer a strange malaise since the accident. Benjamin, who'd only recently put your death and the sale of Tandy behind him, has now withdrawn to his marbles and hiding places. No one knows of this mysterious Robert mentioned by Edgar in his final moments. Oh, if only we did. Perhaps the return of Tandy would help cheer us all.

Josie wanted the stallion shot and was enraged when I

sold him instead. I am, perhaps, too practical for her liking, but I have mouths to feed, a farm to run, no husband, no slaves and little money.

Whenever at a crossroads, I ask myself, "What would Will say? What would Will advise?" You were always wise and sensible, and your memory, like Edgar's final brave act, helps me carry on.

Edgar would have been pleased by the numbers at his funeral, a well-attended affair of Honey Ridge residents and local farmers who use the gristmill to grind their corn and wheat. He would have been surprised that the leftover Yankees paid him homage. They stood guard over his body as it lay in the parlor and helped dig his grave. Their kindness to me has been unparalleled. I could not get along without them, and when they came into the study as I labored over the ledgers Edgar had kept from me, this damaged trio I've come to admire offered to stay on the farm until Benjamin reached majority and took his rightful place as owner of Peach Orchard. I, who am not much given to emotional displays, cried with relief. Brinks and Johnny know about farming and Logan is good with figures. Edgar would shudder to hear me admit how very much I trust the Yankee soldiers you left behind.

Gentle, loyal Hob will never leave until heaven calls him, for which I am thankful as I dearly love his wizened black face. I have offered room and board and a small share of profits, should there be any, to the three other freed slaves. We are all in desperate straits since the war's end and even more so since Edgar's death. I know little about running a farm or a mill.

This morning, I donned my widow's weeds and walked through the fields and crossed the creek to the gristmill. Though I offered a pony and trap for his use, Mr. Logan accompanied me on crutches he carved himself. The infection that took his limbs has healed and, though he is thin to the point of breaking, I daresay his spirit heals a bit more each day. Teaching me of financial matters has given him purpose, I think, a blessing for us both. I have much to learn, but learn it I shall, and I shall teach my son.

Tonight I am exhausted, and rumors will doubtless abound about the crazy Widow Portland who insisted on working beside the servants and feeding corn onto the grinding stone. How else can I learn unless I do the work?

The farmers and residents of Honey Ridge need the mill to survive, and I am determined that Peach Orchard Farm and Mill will prosper. By God's good grace and our own perseverance, we shall survive.

41

"I don't believe this. It's crazy." Julia pressed a hand to each side of her head to keep it from blowing apart. "I have to go after Alex."

"Julia, calm down and tell me what's going on."

"Eli's been arrested. The police found drugs in his car."

"Oh, my God." Connie's hand flew to her mouth.

"It's not true. It can't be."

"But David said he was in prison for dealing drugs."

Julia whirled on her mother. "He had Alex in the car with him! He wouldn't. He couldn't."

Connie retreated a step, shocked by Julia's vehemence. A beat passed, then two, before she shifted into mother mode. "Whatever happened, we have to get to that poor child."

"Will you call Valery and look after the inn while I go?" To the police station. To the jail. Julia could hardly stand to think the words.

"Yes. Now go. Get Alex. The rest will work itself out."

Julia could see that her mother struggled to trust in Eli's innocence. She struggled herself, but the man she knew would not jeopardize his son.

Shaking inside, her mind raced to understand the incomprehensible as she drove to the police station, a low modern building on the north edge of Honey Ridge.

Alex, his little legs dangling from a too-big chair, was with Trey Riley inside an office cubicle. When the boy saw Julia, he rushed into her arms. His body trembled.

"The policeman took my daddy," he said in a voice choked with tears. "I want my daddy."

"I know, baby. I know, but don't worry. We'll get this straightened out." Over the child's head, she spoke to the officer. "What's going on, Trey?"

Trey leaned his forearms on the scarred brown desk, his face grim. "I'm having a hard time with this, too, Julia. Eli's a friend."

"He didn't do this."

"I don't want to believe it, either, but the evidence was in his car. Enough to charge him with intent to distribute." He dragged a hand across the back of his neck. "With his record, it doesn't look good."

Something in Trey's voice made her ask, "You knew, didn't you? About his record?"

The officer lifted a shoulder. "I'm paid to be suspicious. First day we met, I ran him through the database. He was clean, only a few months out of the pen, and I figured to give the guy a chance."

"Is that why you befriended him? So you could keep an eye on him?"

"At first." Trey blew out a frustrated breath. "I like the man,

Julia. I want to believe he's innocent, but I can't explain away hard evidence."

"In the times you've spent with Eli, did you ever suspect anything?"

"Nothing." Trey squeezed the bridge of his nose with a thumb and finger. "They found cash, too."

Julia would have laughed if the statement wasn't so sad. "Eli has no cash."

"He did. Four thousand dollars."

Julia sat down hard. "There has to be an explanation. He had Alex with him. Even if he had fallen back into drugs, he wouldn't involve his son."

"People do."

"Not Eli, and not now. He's just getting his life back together. Things are going well, he's back in touch with his family—" Horror raised the hair on the back of her neck. His family. This could undo all the good Eli had accomplished. It could ruin the opportunity for the mobile centers, for the job he wanted so badly. Indeed, it could ruin his life all over again. Julia set her jaw. "I want to talk to him."

Eli sat on the sickeningly familiar jail bunk, his head in his hands. Hopelessness was a concrete cell with four gray walls and a toilet.

The place echoed with footsteps and voices, curses and metallic clangs. All prisons did. His head echoed, too, with the words of his father. *You have your chance. Don't blow it.*

A loser, an unfit father. Eli's gut tightened as he thought of that hideous moment with cops around him and cars sailing past when he'd knelt to reassure his son, and Alex had clung to his neck, crying "Daddy! Daddy!"

In a choked voice, he'd said the only thing he could. "I love you, Alex. I love you, son." But because his hands were cuffed behind him, he couldn't even hold his frightened boy.

Losers screw up even when they don't want to.

"Donovan." A jailer appeared at the bars. "Company."

He didn't bother getting his hopes up. With Alex's cries echoing in his head, Eli followed the jailer to a small, bare room where Julia paced the concrete floor. He observed her for a moment before she saw him. Her blond ponytail was disheveled and the scarf crooked, but she was beautiful. Too good and beautiful for him. He didn't want her to see him here like this.

"Take Alex and go home. He's scared and confused."

"So am I." She spun in his direction. "We have to talk first. Sit down. Please."

With the jailer standing a discreet distance but close enough to watch, Eli went to the bare table and sat out of courtesy. The sooner she was gone, the better. He knew all about the inner workings of the correction system, but she didn't, and he didn't want her exposed.

"Take care of my son. That's all I need from you." He hardened his face and tone, hiding the well of pleasure at seeing her. "I don't want you here, Julia. Go away."

Jailhouse orange came with a price a good woman like her knew nothing about. He'd been handcuffed, interrogated, strip-searched, a humiliation he'd hoped never to endure again. But the greatest humiliation was having her see him like this.

Eli noted the anxiety in her pretty blue eyes and hated that he'd put it there. He wanted to touch her, to hold her but kept himself aloof. He'd been so hopeful, so confident that he had turned a corner and would soon be a man with something to offer an incredible woman like her. Some cosmic joke had decided against him.

He dropped his head, ashamed.

"Are you guilty?"

His head jerked up. The question hurt, but she had a right to ask. "No."

"How did the drugs get into your car?"

"I don't know." He gripped the edges of the table, frustrated. "I've been asking myself that question since the arrest."

"Could they have been in the car when you bought it?"

"I guess it's possible, but who's going to believe that?"

"They'll get this straightened out. They have to."

For Alex's sake, he prayed she was right. He wasn't much, but his son needed him.

"I'm an ex-con on parole for drug dealing. No one will believe I'm innocent."

"I do."

Eli closed his eyes and let those two precious words seep into him, warm as a fur coat in winter. But the fact remained. This was his world, not hers. "You don't belong here."

"Neither do you."

He sighed. So stubborn. "Look after Alex, okay? He's been through so much, and now this."

"I know." She touched him. He shivered from the sheer glory of it. "Is there anything you need? I could talk to David."

The lawyer ex. David would probably get him put away forever.

Eli slid his hand from beneath hers.

"Go home, Julia." With a loud scraping of wood against concrete, he pushed out of the chair. "Go now, and don't come back."

Julia returned to Trey Riley's office, frustrated at Eli's attitude and worried about what she'd tell Alex. He'd want his daddy. He wouldn't understand that Daddy couldn't come home, and his father's absence could deepen Alex's emotional wounds.

Eli was innocent. She'd seen through his bluster, knew he was protecting her, and loved him for the effort. He was worried sick about Alex. So was she. There had to be a way to discover the truth and set Eli free.

As she turned down the hallway, Alex, accompanied by a strange woman in a green dress, came out of Trey's office.

"Miss Julia!" Alex jerked away from the woman and ran to Julia. She caught him against her, instantly suspicious of the woman.

"Where is Officer Riley? What are you doing with Alex?"

The woman offered a professional smile. "I'm with social services. I have an order to pick him up."

"That won't be necessary. He lives with me."

The brunette frowned at a sheet of paper in her hand. "Are you a relative?"

"No, but—"

"I'm sorry, but I have no choice." She offered the document as proof. "Alex's father was charged with child endangerment and you aren't a relative, so he is now a ward of the state."

The social worker took Alex's hand and led him out of the building into the hot sunshine. Julia followed her to a silver Nissan, pleading and peppering her with questions. Tears ran down Alex's face as he was loaded into the backseat. The sight was a razor slash to Julia's heart.

"Miss Julia! I want my daddy. I want my daddy!"

This could not be happening.

Julia reached a hand into the backseat to soothe him.

"I'm sorry, ma'am. We have to go."

"But—"

"I'm really sorry."

The social worker handed her a card and then closed the door and drove away. Julia's world, the one she'd rebuilt moment by moment over the past six years, shattered around her like hundred-year-old glass on concrete.

Eli arrested. Alex taken away.

She'd lost them. She'd lost her loves again.

Julia's body went limp, her stomach sick. Helpless despair crept in, a familiar enemy that had taken her down before. She should have known it would be back, and this time it would steal her sanity for good.

Julia lay on her bed in the darkened bedroom and longed to escape into sleep, though the sun remained high and night far away. She didn't care about the inn or the guests or the fact that Valery and her mother ran the business without her. Her head pounded, and she was as dry and empty as the locust shell Alex had found attached to a magnolia trunk and carefully preserved in a glass jelly jar.

Alex. Mikey. They ran together inside her head. Two precious little boys she loved, and she hadn't been able to help either one when he needed her most.

Had Mikey called out "Mama, Mama!" the way Alex had cried for his daddy? The reality that he surely had circled inside her brain, a buzzard eager to peck away her sanity.

Around her on the bed were the remnants of her son's life. *Things.* A baby blanket, his baseball glove, photos, drawings of radiant suns smiling above stick figures.

How long had he cried for her? How long had he waited for her to find him until he'd given up? Did he wait still?

Her fingers grazed each keepsake, touching, remembering, until they came upon the stack of Charlotte's letters. She couldn't say why she'd taken them from the dresser and added them to the collection of comforting keepsakes.

How had Charlotte remained strong and loving amidst all the heartache?

She sat up then, heart pounding along with her head, and clicked on the lamp at her bedside. Something from one of the letters niggled along the edges of thought, just out of reach.

One by one, she opened the fragile pages and began to read:

July 3, 1865

Tears of happiness mist my eyes. Imagine my great surprise when your gift arrived all the way from Ohio! At first, my wayward heart leapt within me, convinced for that brief, shining moment that you were still alive in this world. But then I read the letter accompanying the package of vibrant blue marbles sent to Benjamin and, sadly, to Tandy. Tandy, of course, will never know you thought so kindly of him. He will never play with the bag of gleaming blue marbles, but Ben is ecstatic. Finally something has pulled him from his sorrow and solitude. He has talked of nothing else except the gift that came from you through your parents. Oh, how I wish you were here so I could thank you properly for such a thoughtful gesture.

Even in your last terrible days of battle and despair, you thought of us. How this thrills me, fills me, comforts me.

I wish you could have seen Benjamin's excitement.

"Captain Will sent these," he proudly proclaimed at supper.

Patience, ever kind, leaned in and touched them with wonder. "They're beautiful, Ben. Captain Will was wonderful."

Josie held rigid and said nothing, but now that Edgar is gone, I refuse to pretend that you did not matter.

"Yes," I said, "Captain Will was a fine man who cared deeply for us."

"I want to see him again," Ben said. "I wish he and Papa…"

His precious face twitched so that I knew he battled tears. I squeezed the top of his hand. "Will you help me compose a letter of thanks to the captain's family? I'm sure they will be comforted to know you cherish the marbles."

After that, Benjamin regained his composure, though he clung to the bag of marbles all through dinner. He has become a different child this year, but then, we have all become different people.

Indeed, the marbles are a comfort. In idle moments, which are few, I find myself sitting in the parlor, thinking of you, watching Ben play and wondering if your hands touched those small orbs. I shouldn't, I know, when my husband is barely in the ground. But you know, as I do, that Edgar never loved me. It hurts to admit such a thing. I had wondered why he married me until Josie blurted out her ugly version of the truth. No suitable girl in Honey Ridge would have a lame man. Thinking I was pretty enough, he married me to flaunt my looks in the face of Honey Ridge society. How sad that I never knew, and I never completely fit in with the people he longed to impress. I daresay, not a single girl in Honey Ridge was ever one whit jealous of Edgar's British bride.

Your mother writes a lovely hand and generously shared a page from the letter you wrote to her. When my heart aches for you so that I think I cannot bear it, I reread her words and think about your dear mother. This I know— losing a child is the worst thing that can happen to a woman, and yet during her deepest night of the soul, your mother offered solace to another woman's son…

Julia stopped reading and put the page aside to go the window. She opened the blinds and stared out, seeing Charlotte's world below her as the century-old words swirled through her head.

"The worst thing that can happen to a woman," she murmured. Charlotte, like Will's mother, understood loss and suffering. She mourned her babies, and yet she'd not become bitter. She hadn't hidden away in a dark room in despair. She'd clung to this wonderful house, determined to make it thrive for the benefit of others, and she'd kept on believing in the good.

Julia took the letter up again and reread the last lines.

"In the deepest night of her soul," she whispered, "Will's mother had comforted another woman's son."

Charlotte had done the same, offering kindness to the wounded soldiers, to the slaves and even to the husband who had misused and abused her. Other women's children, every one.

Tears pushed at the back of Julia's eyelids as the message settled over her.

Alex and Eli needed her now. Other women's sons.

42

"I cannot get involved with this again."

Julia heard the heartache in Gloria Donovan's voice and wondered at her decision to make a phone call in lieu of driving to Knoxville. Face-to-face, she might have had a better chance to convince Gloria of what she believed. But a phone call was faster and Gloria's son and grandson required attention now.

"Eli didn't do this, Mrs. Donovan." Julia's voice quivered as she paced her living quarters, the reclaimed wood floor reminding her anew of Charlotte Portland.

"He's always proclaimed his innocence even when it was a lie." The other woman's breath hitched as if she fought tears. "I had such hope for my son this time. I truly thought he'd transformed. Every moment we spent together, the phone calls, even the foundation proposal, was the man I always dreamed my son could be. But now, this. Again. It's too hard. I don't think I can bear another loss."

"Then don't let it happen. Believe in the man you know today, not the Eli of the past. He's paid his debt and worked hard at making a new start. He's worried sick about Alex. Do you actually think he'd commit a felony with him in the car?"

"Oh, my—" Gloria's gasp registered horror and disbelief. "Alex was with him?"

"Yes, and Eli would never do that. You have to know that. You've seen them together. Eli would take on a den of lions for Alex."

"He does adore the boy."

"Nor would Eli destroy the chance you've given him to be part of your family again. He loves you, and deeply regrets the heartache he caused." Julia had to make her understand. Alex's future, as well as Eli's, was at stake. "He was thrilled over the foundation's acceptance of his proposal and excited about the offer to head the new project. Good things were happening in his life. He believed he could make a difference."

"I believed it, too."

Julia gripped the cell phone like a lifeline. Indeed, it was Eli's lifeline. Alex's, too.

"The charges don't make sense. You have to see that."

"I don't know…"

"He was ashamed, Gloria, and humiliated. Ashamed of being in jail. Ashamed of me seeing him there. He didn't want you to know. In fact, he sent me away. All he asked was that I take care of Alex."

"Thank goodness, he's with you."

Julia's shoulders slumped, remembering the terrible, tearing moment. "He isn't."

"What? Where is he?"

"That's what I've been trying to tell you. Social services picked him up at the police station, and even though I told them he lived with me, they refused to let me take him. Instead, he's going to total strangers in the foster system, and unless Eli is exonerated, that's where he'll stay." Her voice caught on a sob. "He'll be scared and worried, and who knows how much he'll regress. I'm concerned about what might happen to him emotionally. He's already lost his mother, his aunt, and now his daddy."

"I don't understand. Why did they refuse you? Being with you in the familiar makes more sense."

"I'm not a relative." Though she'd take him in a heartbeat if she could. "That's the main reason I called. You're—"

"His grandmother." Gloria's voice was quiet, thoughtful. "Darling Alex. He must feel frightened and terribly alone."

"He doesn't have to be. Please. I have the social worker's number. Call her. Come and get Alex. Give him back his family."

A long pause ensued in which Julia wondered if she'd pushed too hard and if Gloria had ended the call. Finally, the other woman spoke. "Let me have the number. And Julia?"

"Yes?"

"I know some very good attorneys."

Relief flooded through every bone in Julia's body until she felt as fragile as the old letters lying on her bed.

"You'll help Eli?" Thank God, Thank God!

"You're quite convincing."

"You won't regret this."

"I sincerely hope not."

Eli was arraigned the next day. A well-dressed attorney from Knoxville stood at his side although his parents were absent, not that he'd expected them. He'd let them down again, however unintentionally, and was still stunned that they'd retained an attorney on his behalf. He hadn't expected anything at all. In fact, he'd preferred they never knew, but that was inevitable.

They'd welcomed him back into the Donovan family, given him the job of his dreams and offered him a future with the foundation, a way to regain his self-respect and make a good life for Alex. And once again, he'd kicked them in the teeth.

If his parents didn't hate him, they should. But they cared about Alex.

Julia had returned to the jail last night with news that Alex was with his grandparents. Eli had nearly wept with gratitude. He'd never considered the legalities of child care or that being charged with a felony would rob him of his right to determine who would care for his son.

Worry about Alex burned his gut like acid.

He'd really messed up this time. Seven years ago, he'd believed himself to be the only one to suffer for his crimes. He knew better now. His family had suffered. Mindy had suffered. And this time, his son would suffer. It tore him apart. The little man must be wondering why his daddy didn't come get him.

Sweating and scared, Eli quickly gazed around the courtroom and spotted a lanky man in city blues. Trey Riley had come, a good guy who'd spent a couple of hours in his cell last night going over every detail of the case. His friend wanted to help him, but how did he account for all that crack cocaine?

The money was easy to explain and easier to prove. His mother had given him an advance on his salary with the foundation, but the cocaine was a mystery.

No one believed the drugs had been there when he'd bought the car, not even him, though Trey was tracing the vehicle back to the last owners. He and Trey had been under that car and all through it. They would have found contraband if it had existed.

Besides, according to Trey, someone had phoned in an anonymous tip, claiming Eli tried to sell the drugs to a friend. Someone knew those drugs were there and that someone was not him.

When Trey had asked about enemies, Eli had laughed a short humorless bark. A man didn't go to prison without making a lot of enemies. Even here in Honey Ridge, he'd bumped up against a few people—Valery's boyfriend and Julia's squeaky-clean, lawyer ex. He had his suspicions, which he'd shared with Trey, but suspicions weren't proof.

He'd even made a list of places he'd parked his car for any length of time, though the concept of someone slipping drugs under the fender well in front of Ace Hardware or the grocery store sounded ridiculous even to him.

Except for the shuffle of feet and papers while the accused waited to see the judge, the courtroom was respectfully quiet. When his turn came, the judge asked him to stand. His attorney, Jenkins, stood with him, fastening his coat front. Eli wished for the suit he'd bought a couple of weeks ago instead of the demeaning jailhouse orange.

As he rose, Eli made a quick survey of the courtroom, and his heart lurched, stuttered and his breath stopped.

Near the rear of the rectangular room, the Sweat twins sat as prim as Victorian schoolmarms, white straw purses on their laps and lemon-yellow dresses bright enough to rival the sun. Next to them, in a soft blue suit he'd never seen, was Julia.

He'd told her not to come. He'd not wanted to smear her good name, to taint her with his dark paintbrush. Why hadn't she stayed away?

Sweat pooled at the base of his spine.

The judge was talking, reading the charges one by one. The words came in a blur. Eli's ears roared and his heart beat so hard he thought his chest might crack open. He stared down at the polished table, at the tidy folder of paperwork on his lawyer's side. Going back to prison would hurt. Losing his son would be the end of him.

"Do you understand the charges against you, Mr. Donovan?"

"Yes, Your Honor."

"How do you plead?"

With every last vestige of dignity he could muster, Eli lifted his eyes to the judge and told the truth, wishing it would be enough and knowing it wasn't. "Not guilty."

"Mother shouldn't have called you, David."

Julia plucked a weed from the rose bed at the side of the house and listened to her ex-husband tell her what she should and should not do in the matter of Eli Donovan.

"The news is all over town, Julia. I already knew before she telephoned that you'd made Donovan's bail and brought him back here. People talk."

"I didn't pay his bond. Not that it's anyone's business." The Sweat twins had, and though no one in Honey Ridge was ever surprised at anything the ladies did, Eli had been deeply touched. A mere token, the twins had declared, for the time he'd cleared their clogged gutter. Besides, they did not believe for one moment a man who looked that much like Colonel Champ would be involved with something as inappropriate as drugs.

David, on the other hand, believed the worst.

"Your mother is worried. So am I. What were you think-ing to let an ex-con come back to your place of business?" He slipped a hand in his pants pocket, gray jacket opened wide to display a belly kept flat by hours at the country club. "You should rid yourself of this scum today before you get hurt."

"Oh, you're one to talk to me about getting hurt." She sat back on her knees and rubbed a clean part of her glove over an itchy cheek. Everything about this conversation made her itchy. No matter how smart he was at law, David had a lot of nerve showing up here again. "Shouldn't you be at the office? Or at home with your pregnant mistress? Oh, excuse me, I meant wife."

"You've become bitter. It's not an appealing attribute."

Julia's peel of laughter made him blink. "Neither is adultery."

David lifted both hands. "I just wanted to help."

"No, you didn't. You wanted to gloat. If you wanted to help, you'd have offered your services to Eli. Or you would be trying to help Trey discover who planted those drugs in Eli's car."

"Don't be foolish, Julia. The man is a convicted felon. Tigers don't change their stripes. He's guilty as sin."

"I disagree."

"All right, then, cling to your stubborn fantasy, but when he's ruined your business and broken your heart, where will you be then?"

Her handsome, smart, *furious* ex-husband strode to his Mercedes, slammed the door hard enough to send the birds fluttering from the trees, and roared down the driveway, leaving her to yank angrily at the weeds.

Valery came out on the front veranda and down the steps, white sandals making clip-clops on the wood. Her flowered skirt swirled around her trim, tanned legs. Dark hair loose and bouncing, she looked like an ad for summertime lemonade.

"What's David doing here?" she asked.

"Bet you can guess."

"Hassling you about Eli?"

"Bingo."

At his name, the dog, sleeping in the shade of the eaves, lifted his head from his paws. His back end wiggled.

Valery grinned and patted the Aussie's head. "Not you, Bingo. Go back to sleep."

"My nosy, cheating, ambulance-chasing ex thinks I should kick Eli out. He's bad for business."

A masculine voice broke into the conversation. "He's right."

Both women jerked their attention toward the shaded area beside the back porch.

"Eli." Julia stood, removing her gloves. "Eavesdropping?"

"Sorry. I was looking for you. We need to talk about this situation."

She flapped the dusty gloves against her thigh. "Innocent until proven guilty. That's the law."

"You're a stubborn woman."

"I don't believe in kicking a man when he's down." Her big talk was mostly bluster. She was scared of being wrong, of getting hurt, of being a fool. But sometimes a woman had to take a chance.

Eli shifted, posture tense. She could see he had something on his mind.

"I talked to my mother."

"Good." A lock of hair had come loose from her ponytail. She tucked it behind one ear. "Is she hiring a private investigator to figure out what happened?"

"I didn't ask." The lines of worry had deepened in the two days since his arrest. "Dad wants me out of the picture. They're talking about taking custody of Alex."

"Oh, Eli." Julia sucked in a worried breath. "They have to give you a chance."

"They've given me dozens. I think this is the straw that broke the camel's back." He raked a hand down his face. "Maybe Alex will be better off with them. He'll have a good life. Things he needs."

Julia's heart twisted into a knot. "He has that with you."

"Not if I go back to prison." He stared down at his hands, those strong, work-weathered hands she'd come to admire. "I love my son, Julia. I don't want to lose him, but if letting him go is the best thing for him…"

"Stop it!" Valery whirled on Eli with a vehemence that surprised Julia and had Eli taking a step backward. "Alex has had enough disruption to his life. He belongs with you. The courts will see that and put you on probation or something. They won't separate you from your son. They can't."

"If I was a first offender, maybe. But I'm not."

Valery's face turned as pale as the magnolia blossoms.

"That's just stupid." She stomped off toward the house like an angry child.

All the rest of the day, the occupants of Peach Orchard Inn were tense and anxious. Julia was not surprised when Eli disappeared into the carriage house right after dinner and Valery drove into town in her red car. Left alone with her thoughts, Julia did the one thing that calmed her. She cooked.

The situation looked hopeless. No one could explain away the drugs, and only a handful wanted to believe in Eli's innocence. Now, with the threat of losing Alex for good, her anxiety ratcheted up to red alert.

She assembled tomorrow's breakfast casserole and afterward called Trey Riley to discuss the situation. He was no closer to answers than she was.

The Sweat twins telephoned. Or rather, Vida Jean called and Willa Dean spoke in the background so that Julia was hard-pressed to understand them both, particularly since Binky, the parrot, added his two cents at intervals. They had, they declared, spoken to Judge Hansen on Eli's behalf. The judge's mama was a Rothberger and therefore a second cousin to the twins.

Listening to their jumbled conversation cheered her, though minimally.

When they rang off, she reread Charlotte Portland's letters, rechecked Mikey's website, stared out the window at the light in the carriage house and resisted the temptation to go to Eli.

The house felt lonely without Alex. *She* felt lonely.

The admission troubled her some. She hadn't meant to fall in love with someone else's child.

Eli was desperately worried about him and planned a trip to Knoxville tomorrow. She hoped the Donovans would allow the visit. Both father and son needed the contact.

At eleven, she crawled into bed but couldn't sleep. She tossed and turned, fluffed her pillow and listened to the comforting sounds of the house. The clock on the bedside table glowed a red midnight.

The negative voice in her head chided. What if Eli was guilty? What if, in her fragile state of mind, she'd been deluded by his handsome face and winsome ways? She didn't want to be the lonely divorcée who foolishly believed the first man who showed her any attention. But what if David was right and she'd done exactly that?

Was this the way Eli's mother felt? Did Gloria, too, want to believe in Eli but couldn't quell the doubts?

She heard a noise in the hallway, saw a light come on and tossed the duvet cover back. Opening the door a crack, she said, "Valery?"

"It's me."

Julia stepped out into the hall. "I couldn't sleep."

"Understandable."

Julia couldn't tell if her sister had been drinking and was ashamed to realize she'd opened the door for the purpose of finding out.

"Can we talk?"

Julia opened the door wider. She flipped on the overhead light and studied her younger sister. Valery's eyes were wild and shifty.

"Is something wrong? You sound funny."

"I'm not drunk, if that's what you mean." Valery's lip quivered. She paced to the easy chair but didn't sit.

"I'm sorry. I couldn't tell, and you seem upset. Did you and Jed have your weekly breakup? Is that it?"

"Eli won't go to prison, will he? I mean, his parents will do something. They have money and power. They can fix this and he'll get Alex back. Right?"

"They think he's guilty. At least his father does."

"But he didn't do anything wrong!" Tears gathered in Valery's wild eyes. "He's innocent, Julia. This is all messed up and I don't know what to do."

"There's nothing you *can* do."

"But that's not true. If I—" She whirled away, hands to her face. Her shoulders began to shake.

A chill pimpled the flesh on Julia's arms. "What are you talking about? What could you possibly do?"

"Nothing. Nothing. I just—" Valery slumped into the chair. "This is wrong. I hate this. Eli's one of the good guys and sweet Alex. I—" Fidgety, wringing her hands, she jumped up and went to the door. "I need to go bed. Good night, Julia."

The next morning, Julia rose at five-thirty, her eyes gritty from lack of sleep and worry in her chest as heavy as an eighteen wheeler. She put on the coffee and had a quiet moment on the veranda as the sun turned the skies pink and gold, expecting Eli to join her as usual. He didn't and his absence spoke volumes. He was pulling away. Leaving her. Readying himself and her for the goodbye.

He was more afraid for her than himself.

At seven, she went to wake Valery to help with breakfast. Her sister was gone.

Annoyed, and remembering the bizarre late-night conversation, she texted Valery but received no reply. So she served breakfast to the guests and got on with the work of running a bed-and-breakfast. Today she simply could not deal with Valery's problems.

From the back door she spotted Eli working outside the carriage house. He'd skipped breakfast.

Her landline rang. She dried her hands, wet from rinsing dishes, and answered. The call was for Eli. His attorney.

With a lump in her throat, afraid of more bad news, Julia hurried across the dew-wet grass with the message.

"You can use my cell," she said, holding out the device and the number.

"I wasn't expecting to hear from him." Eli frowned at the numbers on the slip of paper. "Did he say what this was about?"

"No."

He took a deep breath. Julia could see he was nervous. So was she. "Give me a minute here, okay? If it's bad news, I—"

"You don't have to say anything." She longed to hold him, touch him, assure him that everything would be all right. He hadn't touched her since this madness began, and she didn't know if it was because of him or because of her.

She walked a few feet away to a small plot of purple verbena surrounding a birdbath. Mom and Valery had planted the showy flowers, but the birdbath had been Julia's addition. Someday she'd have a big garden here.

Eli's voice rumbled behind her, but Julia couldn't make out the words.

She plucked a stem of citrus-scented verbena and held it to her nose.

The flow of conversation stopped. She turned just in time to see Eli slump down the carriage house wall.

"Eli!" She hurried to his side, flower crushed in one hand, pulse beating in her temple, knees shaky. "What is it? What's wrong?"

He sat on the shady grass, arms limp at his side, the cell phone in his lap. "They want me back at the police station right away."

Her stomach knotted. "No. Why?"

His olive skin had paled to beige. "They're dropping the charges. Jed Fletcher was arrested for planting the coke in my car. Here. At the inn. Late one night."

The flower fluttered to the grass.

"Valery knew," Julia whispered.

"Yeah," he said. "She turned in her boyfriend. For me."

43

The rest of the day was a blur of paperwork, phone calls and a long trip to Knoxville, where Eli spent his first night in more than seven years in his childhood bedroom. He was amazed that his father had allowed the liberty. His mother and Alex were the reasons, of course. The tough CEO had succumbed to being a granddad, and he'd always been a soft touch with Mom.

Theirs had been a tense meeting rife with warnings that told Eli he still had a long way to go to win his father back, but his mother was a different matter. She believed him, wanted him and was already making plans. When Gloria Donovan sank her steel-magnolia teeth into something or someone, the rest of the world got out of the way, his father included.

Tears pushed at the back of Eli's eyelids and he let them come, loving his mother, broken that he'd hurt her and swearing by all that mattered never to make her cry again.

Beside him, Alex slept, his tiny arms around Eli's neck as if he feared his daddy would disappear again. Eli lay awake for hours, filled with love and gratitude, afraid to sleep for fear he'd wake in a cell and discover his good fortune was all a dream.

For the next few weeks, he and Alex remained in Knoxville to lay the groundwork for the mobile grief centers and retie the tenuous threads of family. He took Alex everywhere, hesitant to let him out of his sight. Every moment was precious.

After so long as the black sheep, Eli was careful to tread lightly, particularly with his father. If time healed, someday his father would love him again. And if the friends and associates of James and Gloria Donovan thought it curious that the prodigal son had come home, they wisely kept the opinions to themselves. He'd squirmed through a few uncomfortable moments—nothing compared to the misery of prison.

He was so incredibly grateful to be exonerated and to have his family in his life again.

As he slipped into the skin of his former life, he felt like a male version of Cinderella. Thanks to his mother, he had a dependable car, a cell phone, a bank account and a challenging job he already loved.

He would prove himself, no matter what it took.

Each morning he woke filled with the possibilities, and if some days the old skin chafed, he would adjust. Julia was happy for him. She told him on the phone each day with enthusiasm, though she never asked when he would return just as she never said she missed him.

He was good with that in a self-punishing kind of way. He'd caused enough chaos in her world. Even exonerated, he would always be a man with a criminal record. Honey Ridge was a small town. His absence protected her and the reputation of her business.

Staying out of her life sounded lofty and noble, but it was darned hard to do.

Late into the third week in Knoxville, Alex asked when

they were going home. Home to Honey Ridge and Peach Orchard Inn.

Eli realized then that he'd been putting off the inevitable out of fear that when push came to shove, he wouldn't be able to let go.

On the other hand, he and Alex couldn't abandon Aunt Opal or forget the friends who'd stood by him. He'd have to return, collect his belongings and establish some kind of closure.

So, on a steamy afternoon when the air was thick and still, he drove his new silver SUV beneath the double row of magnolias leading to Peach Orchard Inn. He had a sudden thought, so real it could have been a memory, of horses and bloody, bedraggled men traveling this same road exactly as Charlotte's letters described.

As he rounded the final bend, Peach Orchard Inn came into sight. Majestic and welcoming, arms flung as wide as its porches and rimmed by red and yellow daisies. The history swamped him then as it had never done before. A house of trouble and tragedy, war, death and loss that somehow remained a strong sanctuary beneath the Tennessee sun.

As he parked beside two unfamiliar vehicles, probably guests, and Alex slid out of the backseat, the Australian shepherd bounded off the back porch and raced toward them, tongue lolling in a happy welcome. With a joyful cry of "Bingo!" Alex threw himself onto the ecstatic dog.

Julia came, too, smiling, her hair golden in the sunlight, her eyes bluer than ever above a bright blue blouse.

Eli's whole being strained toward her, though he held his emotions sternly in check. Alex didn't suffer the same constraints and threw himself into her arms. Julia held his son against her, rocking and murmuring about how glad she was to see him and hadn't he had a marvelous time at his grandmother's house.

When at last she stood and turned her attention to Eli, Alex bounded toward the carriage house with Bingo in search of the Frisbee. A boy and a dog that adored him.

"Valery loved the Godiva chocolates and roses," Julia said.

He shrugged, uncomfortable. He owed Valery more than he could ever repay. Jed had bragged to her, and she'd had the courage to turn him in. "The least I could do."

"Come inside out of this heat. The tea is fresh."

He shook his head. He needed to get his stuff and get moving before he did something crazy. "We'll just pack up and drive over to see Opal before we head back."

"Back to Knoxville?"

"That seems best," he said, yearning, wanting her to ask him to stay, though he was confident for her sake he was doing the right thing.

Julia's smile was bright and encouraging. She was glad he was going. He'd made the right choice.

Then why he did he feel as if he'd swallowed a bucket of lead?

"Are you—will you—" She laughed a little, though the sound was hollow. "Will you be moving to Knoxville... permanently?"

"It looks that way." She was killing him.

"That's...great," she said, head bobbing up and down with an enthusiasm he didn't want her to feel. "You deserve this opportunity to start fresh. I'm happy for you."

"It should be good." Lousy without her, but for the best.

He shifted on the crunching gravel, the heat of late summer like a laser beam on his arms and face.

"Well, I'll just—" he waved toward the carriage house "—collect my stuff."

A guest appeared at the back door and Julia left Eli. As he watched her, slim arms swinging, bright hair shining, he knew with a surety that he wanted Julia Presley in his life. In his son's life. But having him around would only drag her down, especially now that the whole town—her town—knew of his background.

He'd be coming back to Honey Ridge on a regular basis for business. He could stop in, say hello, have a glass of peach tea.

And pretend it was all he wanted.

He passed the orchard, bare now of fruit though the limbs were ready to prune. Someone else would have to take on the task. The carriage house would be someone else's responsibility, too, as would the mountain of stored items he'd been sorting. He'd miss this. All of it, though he wanted the position in Knoxville, the chance to do something good for grieving kids like him and Alex, and he wanted the chance to please his father and someday be his son again.

Freedom to choose was both a blessing and a curse, especially when the heart was involved.

"Dad, watch!" Alex's sweet voice called to him. Eli paused to watch the flight of Frisbee and the churn of short legs as his son raced after Bingo. Alex's gurgling laugh, as refreshing as a dip in Magnolia Creek, lifted on the sultry air.

Alex loved being in the country. Maybe, Eli thought, once he'd gotten established, he'd buy a place outside Knoxville, a little piece of land with an orchard and a couple of magnolias. Maybe get a dog. An Australian shepherd who chased Frisbees and unearthed old marbles.

Confused, troubled, but resolute, Eli went inside the carriage house. His rooms were exactly as he'd left them. The bed tidy, a towel folded on the bar to dry, a pair of Alex's jeans over the back of a chair. His idea pad still lay on the dresser along with some rudimentary drawings, the notes for the foundation proposal and a stack of old papers he'd found upstairs.

Julia would want to go through them in search of more information about Charlotte and the others they'd come to know through the letters. She was a fascinating subject, someone else Eli would miss.

Chest heavy, he dragged his tattered duffel bag out of the closet. A clay marble rolled along the baseboard. He reached for it, felt the warmth against his palm and smiled. He'd miss this, too, the mysterious marbles and the fascinating history.

"I don't suppose you'll follow me to Knoxville."

Thoughtful, he pocketed the small ball of clay and packed his meager belongings into the duffel bag.

He had nothing in which to put Alex's things so he trotted up the steps for the final time to grab a cardboard box.

His mind drifted back to that first day with Julia, the spiderwebs, the attraction, the desperate hope that she'd let him stay. He couldn't ask that of her now. He loved her too much.

He found a cardboard box, emptied it and was about to leave, when his gaze fell on the battered steamer trunk, a wood-and-leather case secured with brass. He flipped open the heavy lid, releasing a musty smell, and slid his hand inside the hidden compartment at the bottom, disappointed to find nothing else inside. Julia had the letters but they'd hoped to find more, to better understand the house's history and the mystery of the marbles Alex insisted came from a boy named Ben.

He was about to close the heavy lid when he noticed something poking out of one corner. Carefully, he pried the wood away to reveal a single sheet of paper, yellowed and frayed.

October, 1865
My dearest love,
As summer pushes into fall, I think of you and remember the day you rode into Peach Orchard Farm. That day, I began to fall in love with you, though I didn't know it

then. Your noble character reached out and gently wove around my heart.

In your last letter to me, which I know by memory and which is now bound with my favorite blue ribbon and tucked away in the bureau for safekeeping, you wrote in despair of the terrible consequences of war. My response was never sent. It was part of the letter Edgar discovered and ripped to shreds before my eyes as he called me such unspeakable names.

Though I have forgiven Edgar and I pray he forgave me before his death, I grieve that you had no chance to read my reply. I grieve that you went to your heavenly reward with such agony of spirit. For my own peace of mind, I recall my words of love and encouragement, and I write them to you now, though you will never read them.

I have often pondered the manner in which our paths crossed. I was broken when you came, though I did not know it then. The loss of my babies and Edgar's lack of affection, his infidelity, and the longing for my home far away in England that I shall never see again were sharp swords piercing me until you came. Until your kindness, your acceptance, your love came and healed me.

And so I have learned, dearest Will, through the trials of war and grief and loss, that love, given the chance, will always triumph.

So that is my prayer for you as I put pen to paper this evening while the house sleeps. Though war is evil and you despair of good's prevail, I promise you it shall. Choose love, dear Will, as you always have done, for it will sustain you when nothing else will. Whether in the care of your men or your generosity to the enemy, or in the throes of joy or sorrow, always, always choose love.

I choose, my darling captain, to lay aside the weights

of the past and press onward toward the prize that lies ahead. I choose to love you, to love my son, to love this country and my home and, yes, even to love the memory of my husband. I am, indeed, a blessed woman to have so much love and provision.

Forever,

Charlotte

Eli remained still and thoughtful for several long minutes after finishing Charlotte's letter. A weak ray of sunlight penetrated the filthy windows, and dust motes swirled around him like Charlotte's words.

"Julia," he murmured, his throat thick.

He saw then the parallels he'd missed before when his focus had been on Alex and Ben and the mysterious marbles.

Like Charlotte, Julia had suffered loss and grief and betrayal, but she'd bravely forged on and made others' lives better because of her love and strength.

"Eli! Where are you?" Julia called from below.

He leaned over the stairs and yelled, "Up here. Just a sec."

Carrying the fragile missive, he bounded down the steps to where she waited in the cluttered, messy, unfinished bay opposite his bedroom—his *former* bedroom, where the smell of chocolate-chip cookies fragranced the air.

Julia gave a self-conscious laugh. "What can I say? I feed people."

"Nurture them," he said, indicating the letter. "Like Charlotte did."

"You found another one?" She set the cookie plate aside and came toward him.

He handed her the page. "She was incredible, no matter the hardship. She's like you, you know. Read it."

Julia took the letter and began to read. At one point, she

glanced up, tears glistening, and said, "I could have written this to you. Listen…

I have often pondered the manner in which our paths crossed. I was broken when you came, though I did not know it then. The loss of my babies and Edgar's lack of affection, his infidelity, and the longing for my home far away in England that I shall never see again were sharp swords piercing me until you came. Until your kindness, your acceptance, your love came and healed me."

Suddenly as if a light had turned on inside him bright enough to rival the sun, Eli understood. The parallels were uncanny. In so many ways, they were both like Charlotte, wounded and yearning for something out of reach. She had lost her son and husband. He'd lost his freedom and his family and was yearning for home as Charlotte had.

Then by a bizarre quirk of fate, he'd crossed paths with Julia at Peach Orchard Inn, and love had changed him. Her love.

"Choose love," Julia whispered, quoting Charlotte as she captured Eli with her summer-blue eyes. "I want the world for you, and I'm so proud of your new job, but I don't want to lose you. I'd never meant to tell you but, after reading Charlotte's letters, I realize love matters too much to keep silent. I love you, Eli Donovan. Just as Charlotte loved Will after he left, I will go on loving you."

Wild hope surged up inside him. "But Will didn't have a prison record."

"Oh, Eli." She put the letter aside and said softly, "Do you think that matters one iota to me?"

"I don't want my past to hurt you."

"And I don't want to stand in the way of your future."

The wash of emotion nearly took him to his knees. "Are you serious? Having you in my life would make the future better."

"Really?" As if he was some kind of prize, Julia looked bedazzled.

"No wonder I'm crazy about you." He reached for her, threaded his fingers into her hair and held her beautiful face close to his. "I thought getting rid of me would be the best thing for you."

And all along, she'd thought she was in his way. He shook his head. Crazy. Just crazy.

"*You're* the best thing that's happened to me in years," she said. "Having you and Alex here brought me back to life."

"I feel the same." He'd been afraid to believe, but Julia had believed for him. "I love you, and if you think we can work this out—"

She touched his lips with one finger, silencing him. "I choose love, Eli. Choose with me."

Dumbfounded, moved, and shaking at the beauty of her love, Eli had no words left. All he could do was kiss her.

And for the rest of his life, chocolate-chip cookies would smell like love.

44

Peach Orchard Farm, 1866

On a bright June day when the corn was high and the peach trees drooped with their bounty, Charlotte ran the back of her hand over her forehead and arched her aching back. Her bonnet offered scant protection from the sun and her English skin was rosy as she plucked ripe ears of corn from the tall green stalks. In the adjacent rows, Benjamin and Lizzy worked in tandem with Johnny, whose fingers could see what his eyes could not. He had become a fine farm hand and a good friend. She hoped he someday gained the courage to return to Ohio, though no one waited for him there anymore.

"Someone's coming, Miss Charlotte," Johnny said, his head cocked to one side.

She listened and heard nothing. "How do you always know that?"

He smiled his misshapen, mysterious smile. "I feel the ground and hear the horses." He pointed. "Coming from the direction of Honey Ridge."

A visitor. More and more in the past year life had developed a steadier rhythm and visitors were plentiful. News of Charlotte's generosity and her backbreaking effort to keep the farm and mill producing had spread so that she was no longer the suspicious Brit of days past. Hunger changed a man's perspective.

Honey Ridge and all of Tennessee was different now—battered, needy and vanquished—and yet a determined hopefulness prevailed.

Last Saturday, the family had attended a barn raising followed by a dance at Thaddeus Adcock's farm. Charlotte had baked peach pies and cakes from the mill wheat but hadn't danced. Edgar's mourning period was over, but dancing was for the available, and her heart was taken, buried with Will Gadsden. Patience and Josie had spun about the barn like pretty tops, colored ribbons flying and faces flushed with laughter. Josie waited for Tommy with a growing acceptance that he, like so many others, would never come home again.

"Who's coming, Mama?" Benjamin, taller and stronger at nearly eleven, moved to her side. As man of the house, he was learning that protection would be his role someday, far sooner than his mother wanted. The Yankee men were teaching him to be a man, and she was teaching him the way of a farmer and miller.

"A carriage I don't recognize." Sweat trickled down her backbone, and her nose itched from the corn silks. She rubbed it with hands rough and callused from physical labor. She was no longer the English rose spending her days inside the house. A farm didn't come indoors.

The rattle of carriage wheels grew louder as the clip-clop of hooves brought the conveyance through the magnolias.

Charlotte left the tow sack in the row, her skirt whispering against the stalks as she moved out of the corn field. Josie stepped onto the veranda and shaded her eyes toward the coming carriage, a heart-breaking sight repeated many times over as she longed for her Tommy. Though she remained of strong opinions, Josie had softened in the year since Edgar's death. The constant rasp of suffering had dulled the sharpest edges.

Hob limped around the corner of the house and followed Charlotte as he had always done. Good and faithful and ever-protective Hob with a hoe at his side. The other men were at the mill, but Charlotte had no fear of visitors. She no longer feared anything except losing Benjamin.

The carriage slowed, raising little dust as the driver pulled to a stop in front of the porch. Charlotte's throat ached in compassion as her sister-in-law peered eagerly toward the covered carriage. A tall man sat in shadow though Charlotte could not recognize him from this distance.

Suddenly, Josie gripped the whitewashed railing and exclaimed, "Charlotte!"

Josie's face had turned as white as cotton bolls.

Hoping, praying, that Tommy had returned, Charlotte hurried to the carriage as the door sprang open and a man stepped out.

Charlotte's breath froze in her lungs. She forgot how to breathe, forgot how to speak. She stopped, feet away from the carriage. Had she suffered a sunstroke?

"Charlotte?" That voice, that dear, beloved voice.

"Will? Is it you?" She reached out a hand, afraid that any moment he would disappear in a wisp of smoke, a figment of her imagination.

"It's me." And that quickly, she was in his arms, crushed to his chest, clinging to his too-thin back with both hands. She did not care that Josie watched and the others came running from the fields.

"Will. Will." Tears streamed from her face, all composure gone. Her captain was alive. Alive! "I thought you were—"

"I know." He pressed a hand to both of her cheeks, drying her tears as his gaze hungrily swept her face, as if he, too, could scarcely believe they were together again.

"But how? I don't understand." Neither did she care. He was here and whole and alive. She touched his face and smoothed his hair, saw the darkness beneath his eyes and the hollow cheekbones. "You've been ill."

"Wounded and then ill, though I was more fortunate than many other prisoners at Andersonville. I survived."

A prisoner. She'd heard the tales of starvation and disease, of cruelties worse than death. Her mind could scarcely accept that Will, her Will, had suffered so.

"After Lee's surrender, I was sent home to Ohio, though I don't remember the trip."

"But you came all the way back to Tennessee."

"Mother showed me your letter." His dark gaze held hers. "I had to come. I left my heart here."

Charlotte placed a hand on his chest. "And you took mine with you."

He covered her hand with his. "I am welcome, then?"

She laughed, embarrassed by her exuberant greeting, though she did not regret it. "Was there ever any doubt? Come inside, rest, eat, and tell me everything."

"One moment. I have something for you." He turned back to the carriage, opened a satchel and withdrew a packet.

Charlotte recognized the contents immediately. "My letters."

"Yes. These letters and thoughts of you and our time together gave me courage to go on when the days were too dark and painful to endure. When Mother showed me the letter you wrote to her, about Edgar's death and the work you had taken on, I knew I had to come. That I had a right to see you again."

Charlotte thought of the many other letters she'd written, but there would time to share them. Today, she wanted to revel in his company, to stare at his wonderful, war-weary face and love him freely and openly as she'd not been able to do before.

"Will you stay?" War and loss made a woman bold.

If he was shocked, her captain did not show it. "Will you have me?"

The months and years since their last meeting dropped away in the dusty heat. Two hearts, torn apart by circumstance and distance, finally came together.

With a smile to rival the blazing sun, Charlotte took her captain's hand and simply said, "I will."

EPILOGUE

"We will grieve not, rather find strength
in what remains behind…"

—William Wordsworth

With fatherly pride, Eli walked beside his son down the immaculate corridor of Honey Ridge Care and Rehabilitation Center. Alex, a colorful daisy bouquet in one hand and a crayon drawing in the other, said a charmingly shy hello to the nurses as they passed. His once-broken boy was on the mend.

"Hi, Alex. Mr. Donovan," the gray-haired nurse called with a wave. "Good to see you. Opal is expecting you."

Every Sunday afternoon for the past seven months, Eli and Alex, dressed in their Sunday best, paid Opal Kimble a visit at the long-term facility. They were no longer her only visitors, because the church and Julia's family had adopted her, too.

"How's she doing?"

"About the same as last week. She's cranky about the lack of progress but gutsy and still trying."

That was Opal. Gutsy and gruff, except in the case of her great-great nephew and with him she was soft as butter.

"The orderly got her up in the wheelchair," the nurse went on. "She's hoping for a trip out into the sunshine."

"She's got it."

When they reached the room, Alex tapped and then slowly pushed the door open.

When she saw her nephew, Opal's wrinkled, drawn mouth lifted in a lopsided smile. "There's my boy."

Her speech was slow and slurred, and she hadn't regained use of her right side or the ability to walk. Though doctors didn't expect her to, Eli made sure she had the best therapists and care available. It was the least he could do in exchange for the care she'd given Mindy and Alex.

Bouquet extended, Alex rushed to the wheelchair. "I brought you flowers."

During the early days of Opal's hospitalization, Alex had been fearful of the changes in his aunt and reluctant to be close to her. But with time, his natural sweetness and compassion had overtaken his anxiety.

"Pretty." With her good hand, Opal grasped the bouquet and sniffed appreciatively. "Mmm. Smells clean and green."

"And a picture." Alex unfolded the paper and pushed it in front of her eyes.

With a chuckle, Opal tilted back from the too-close drawing. "Tell me 'bout it."

Face serious, Alex pointed out each figure. "See that house? That's my grandma's house. And that's my grandpa and my daddy and Miss Julia. She's going to marry us but I don't know when. Right, Daddy?"

Opal lifted her gaze to Eli. He knew she was pleased that Alex now had family who'd embraced him. She'd also let him know she approved of Julia, particularly after one visit when Julia had expressed a desire to keep Mindy's memory alive for Alex.

"We haven't set a date yet." Work with the family foundation and other projects had swamped him, and Julia understood his need to have everything in order before they married. But he was as eager as Alex.

"See up here in the clouds?" Alex tugged Opal's attention back to the drawing. "That's my mama. She's looking at us from heaven. That's what Miss Julia says. Mama smiles all the time because we're happy again. And she's not sick anymore either."

"Julia is right. Good woman." Opal patted his shoulder. "You have...a new suit? Handsome."

"Like Daddy's." Alex stood back to show off his gray suit and maroon tie. "He has to wear one for his job."

"He told me about it."

Eli had wanted her to know he was a better man than either of them had ever thought, and if he was honest, her approval mattered.

"I get to wear one, too, 'cause Miss Julia takes us to church now. 'Cause we have a lot to be thankful for."

"Sounds like...your mama. She'd be pleased." She pointed a bony finger at Eli. "Me, too."

"Be careful, Opal," Eli teased. "I'll start thinking you like me."

She snorted, but her eyes twinkled. "You'll do." She patted the wheel of her chair. "Be useful. Take me for a spin."

"Yes, ma'am." He took the bouquet and drawing and put them on the side table. "Still up for our date next weekend?"

She grunted, though the eyes still twinkled. "Don't try to back out now."

Making no effort to hide his grin, Eli, with Alex assisting, rolled Opal out into the spring sunshine, grateful to this lionhearted woman who had changed his future the day she'd called him to Honey Ridge and forced him to become a dad.

The dedication of Michael's Garden was a simple affair that took place the next Saturday afternoon, a day gray with clouds and the threat of rain. Julia's family came, along with a few friends and neighbors including the Sweat twins and the Rileys. Because Mindy was to be included in the memorial, Eli had made special arrangements for the rehab center to bring Opal and her nurse. And out of compassion and too happy with her life to do less, she and Eli had invited David, and he'd come with Cindy and their two little boys.

Seeing them together didn't hurt anymore.

The idea for a meditation garden had been Eli's when he'd given her an engagement ring at Christmas and she'd cried, both from joy and sorrow. Joy for the future, and sorrow for the unresolved past that was Mikey. Would he ever know Eli, the man she'd come to love with all her being? Would he ever know his gentle, thoughtful stepbrother, Alex, who loved Bingo as he had?

"I understand," Eli had said that day, green eyes serious and so full of love they'd taken her breath away. "Having the Jessica Center to honor my sister helps me and my family cope. You need something, too."

"So does Alex," she'd said, seeing the connection just as she saw the connections with Charlotte and Ben.

So, in his usual resolute way, Eli had set about to create a garden retreat in the backyard to honor the son he'd yet to meet, as well as Alex's mother. Alex had helped, a task that had bonded them even more. They were, in every way now, father and son.

She didn't know how Eli had found the time considering his trips to Knoxville and the travel for the mobile bereavement centers, but he'd created the garden himself with minimal help from a landscaper. A labor of love, he claimed.

Benches and flowers bordered a perpetual fountain and a statue of the angel Michael. Inside the fountain, dubbed Mindy's Fountain, they'd carefully formed the letter M with some of Alex's antique marbles, a fitting tribute, they all agreed.

There was nothing formal about the dedication. Guests, including those fortunate enough to be staying at Peach Orchard Inn, partook of Julia's peach tea or coffee and freshly baked cookies while ambling the now beautiful backyard and murmuring among themselves in low tones about how perfect it all was, especially the engagement of two such fine, deserving people as Julia and Eli. When the mist began to fall, releasing the scent of the blooming orchard, all but the occupants of the inn departed.

Valery stayed behind to clean up while Connie entertained the Donovans in the parlor. Alex had long grown bored, as gap-toothed seven-year-olds do, and ran off to the carriage house with Bingo.

"Perfect day," Julia said, not caring one whit if the skies opened. She clasped Eli's hand and waved away the last of the guests, promising to attend a cookout at the Rileys next Saturday. It felt good and right to be part of the world again, at least the world of Honey Ridge.

Together and wonderfully content, they strolled around the antebellum mansion, past the sweeping verandas where they'd shared many confidences and even more kisses, along the gravel walkway leading to the backyard.

The space, once sprawling and unsightly, was now mostly garden, an oasis between the house and the yet to be completed carriage house. Not that she cared about the remodel so much anymore. She loved having Eli and Alex in the carriage house.

Being a Donovan, he could live in luxury, but he'd chosen here. He'd chosen her. He'd chosen love.

"Have I said thank-you today?" she asked.

"At least a million times." His arm went around her waist. "I'm glad you like it."

She loved it. Loved him. Loved her life today in a way she'd never have thought possible.

She smoothed a hand over the cool white plaster of the angel Michael. The diamond Eli had placed on her left hand winked, a promise of the wedding to come.

"He'll come home someday."

"Love always hopes," Eli said, quoting the words engraved on the angel's base. "And we'll be here waiting for him."

She smiled then, through tears that would never completely dry. She'd never forget her son or abandon hope that he would someday be found, but while she waited for that glad reunion, Julia would model herself after Charlotte and embrace each day, thankful for her provisions, thankful for love.

Somewhere in the mist Julia heard a little boy laugh. She'd heard the sound many times before, laughter as comforting as the marbles, as comforting as her faith that someday Mikey would return.

Maybe the sound was only the wind among the peach trees or the babble of Magnolia Creek. She couldn't say for sure and she didn't really care. Fantasy or not, she chose to believe that a gentle child from long ago who'd lost his best friend and his father and the soldier he'd loved was somehow reaching across time to another boy—or perhaps to three little boys—Eli, Alex and Mikey—who'd also lost too much. If such things were not possible, Julia thought they should be.

The mist turned to rain.

"Ready?" Eli asked, his arm around her, his beloved face close to hers.

With one final glance at the beauty Eli Donovan had created for her, Julia nodded. Then she and her true love turned toward the inn, where the rain dripped off the roof and the peach leaves whispered of times past and memories kept.

And the wonderful old house that had sheltered them all seemed to smile.

★ ★ ★ ★ ★

ACKNOWLEDGMENTS

The Memory House was inspired by news reports of children who are abducted and never found, particularly by the story of Morgan Nick, whose family lives near my son, a family who still waits, with love and hope, for Morgan to come home. According to the National Center for Missing and Exploited Children, roughly 115 children are abducted each year by strangers. My question was what happens to the families left behind? My research took me to high-profile cases, books, websites, the invaluable resources of the National Center for Missing and Exploited Children, as well as the Morgan Nick Foundation. Each one provided valuable insight and information that was crucial to the accuracy of *The Memory House.*

The Dougy Center in Portland, Oregon, was the first to provide peer support for grieving children at no cost to the family. Their website and videos, along with information from other grief centers and counselors provided background to my grieving characters.

Tennessee was the site of more Civil War battles than any other state except Virginia. Middle and Southern Tennessee saw much of that combat and it is there, in the rolling hills, winding roads and thick woods, that I focused my research. Interestingly, a peach orchard figured largely in at least two major Tennessee battles, the Battle of Shiloh and the Battle of Nashville. Because much of the war took place away from major cities, a number of homes became makeshift hospitals for both the Confederate and Union armies. Along with reading many books and diaries about the Civil War in Tennessee, I was privileged to visit several antebellum homes to research their roles in the war, including Carnton Plantation in Franklin, Tennessee, which became the model, on a smaller scale, for Peach Orchard Farm. I am also grateful to the owners of Winston Place Plantation at the base of Lookout Mountain who allowed me to roam freely through their antebellum mansion, now a bed-and-breakfast, and who answered dozens of my questions.

In the 1840s a factory in Ohio began to produce marbles. I have taken literary license with this fact and given that factory of handmade marbles to the family of Captain Will Gadsden. For her excellent information on antique marbles, I am indebted to the work of Marilyn Barrett in her book *Aggies, Immies, Shooters, and Swirls*.

Turn the page for some great questions to jump-start the conversation with your book club!

THE
MEMORY
HOUSE

LINDA GOODNIGHT

Reader's Guide

QUESTIONS FOR DISCUSSION

1. Why do you think this book is titled *The Memory House*? What role do memories, both past and present, play in the novel? Discuss the memories that define Eli and Julia and cause them to be who they are at the beginning of the story.

2. Julia and Eli find antique marbles in the antebellum mansion. To whom did they originally belong? How do the marbles come to be in the present-day inn? How do the characters feel whenever they find one? What role do the marbles play in connecting the past with the present?

3. In the opening chapter, both Julia and Eli are wounded souls. Describe their characters and personalities. Do they change during the course of the story? If so, how? And what causes the changes?

4. In the opening line, Eli thinks that freedom is its own kind of prison. What does he mean? Do you agree with this statement? How can freedom be a prison?

5. Grief and loss are major themes of *The Memory House*. Describe the grief or loss that each of these characters—Julia, Eli, Charlotte, Lizzie and Ben—had to bear. What coping mechanism did each use to deal with the pain?

Were these negative or positive mechanisms, and how did the choice affect each character's life?

6. Discuss the parallels between the two story lines. How does the past affect the present? What do the characters in the present learn from the past? How does this affect their relationships and help them heal?

7. Mother-and-son relationships are integral to *The Memory House*. Discuss Julia, Charlotte, Mindy and Gloria and their relationships with their sons. How are the mothers alike? How are they different?

8. "The child is father of the man" is quoted in the opening. What does this mean? How does this apply to Eli? What past incident began his downward spiral and brought him to the opening chapter? What part does Alex play in his father's journey to healing? Would Eli have ever healed if he had refused to be Alex's father?

9. Charlotte was restricted and defined by the expectations of women during the nineteenth century. Cite examples where she bows to those expectations. Discuss the times when she did not.

10. Charlotte and Will cared deeply for each other. Why could they not express their feelings? Why was Charlotte determined to remain faithful to her husband even though he had not been faithful to her? How did she succeed? How did she fail? What incident occurred that allowed her to speak her true feelings within the context of her letters?

11. Discuss the significance of Michael's garden. What does it symbolize to Julia? What part does Eli play? Why does Alex place his beloved marbles in the fountain?